kentuckiana

# kentuckiana

*johnny payne*

TRIQUARTERLY BOOKS
NORTHWESTERN UNIVERSITY PRESS

Evanston, Illinois

TriQuarterly Books
Northwestern University Press
Evanston, Illinois 60208-4210

Portions of this novel have appeared in somewhat different form in the following publications: "Notes from Poor Stephen's Almanac: The Gagoose" in *Beloit Fiction Journal;* "My Talia" in *Southern Review;* "Domestic Animals" in *Sequoia;* "Our Lady of Comity" in *Thinker Review;* "Tall Tales" in *TriQuarterly.*

Printed in the United States of America

First paperback printing 1999

ISBN 0-8101-5090-5

**Library of Congress Cataloging-in-Publication Data**

Payne, Johnny, 1958–
        Kentuckiana / Johnny Payne.
                p. cm.
        ISBN 0-8101-5090-5 (pbk. : alk. paper)
        I. Title.
        PS3566.A9375K46 1997
        813'.54—dc21
                                                                97-23378
                                                                CIP

The paper used in this publication meets the minimum requirements of the American National Standard for Information Sciences—Permanence of Paper for Printed Library Materials, ANSI Z39.48-1984.

*For Miriam, and for John, Joy, Kathy, Mary Helen, Stephanie, Tracy*

Kentucky, the great wilderness beyond the western edge of the world, the dark and bloody ground of coming years, seemed to the colonists along the eastern North American seaboard as far away, nearly, and as difficult of approach as had the problematical world itself beyond the western ocean in the times prior to Columbus. A country there was, of this none could doubt who thought at all; but whether land or water, mountain or plain, fertility or barrenness, preponderated; whether it was inhabited by men or beasts, or both or neither, they knew not.

—"The Discovery of Kentucky"

# contents

I n the pleasant May of 1958, a group of pioneers, engineers, second-generation Americans, speculators, ne'er-do-wells, and visionaries known as the Chocinoe Management Group gathered by a bubbling spring in the middle fork of Lansill's Creek and talked about creating a settlement to be called Garden Springs. The next month they received a use permit from the Planning Commission of the City of Lexington, and began clear-cutting and bulldozing, in preparation for the excavation of sites where the cement foundations of this subdivision would be laid.

Chocinoe is an ancient Indian word meaning bloody battle-ground, an allusion to the tendency of developers to take on the name of whatever their development means to drive out—in this case mainly squirrels, high weeds, chiggers, starlings, poison ivy, stray bitches about to deliver their puppies in the underbrush, abundant insect life, and rabbits who once came to drink at the bubbling Garden Springs. Chocinoe is also a cheap literary device known as an anagram, and when transposed spells No Choice. It's designed to be deciphered by the reader, or, if not, to sub-liminally prejudice her or him against the Chocinoe Management Group, since the real author of this fictitious account has a bad attitude about developers.

I, on the other hand, must make the point that without the birth and growth of Garden Springs subdivision, there can be no habitat for the Miles family, of whom I will speak in more detail later. After a succession of brief sojourns in trailer parks, apartments, and houses, whose leases were broken due to Constance's health problems and Jean's trouble keeping a job, they remained in the house in Garden Springs for eight years, the one house that the children—Judy, Elaine, Stephen, Talia, and Lynnette—without exception speak of in retrospect as their home.

Garden Springs is a middle- and lower middle-class subdivision conspicuously lacking in gothic qualities. Many of its inhabitants work for IBM, Trane, Dixie Cup, or as employees of clothing stores, fast-food chains, and the minimum security federal penitentiary, with a scattering of doctors, lawyers, teachers, career officers, Indian chiefs. It doesn't possess the dark, historical heaviness of Yoknapatawpha County, the cosmic quaintness of Grover's Corners, or even the wistful lyric Biblicism of Knoxville: Summer, 1915. The horse farms a few miles away, populated with world-famous thoroughbreds, seem as remote as a desert oasis. They hold yearling sales that attract sheiks of Araby and members of the international playboisie, who scatter the town with hundred-dollar gratuities.

The proximity of such subdivisions to the garish commercial zones found with little variation in thousands of American towns and cities produces an anxiety in writers born in those subdivisions that causes them to write sarcastic remarks like the foregoing one about the playboisie. The white writer is caught between a secret desire to belong to an enclave, a Southern renascence, an Afro-American ethnicity, a Latin boom, and a gravitation toward lethal irony, narrative distance, and a profusion of brand names on the page—of Kentucky Fried Chickens and Mrs. Smith's frozen pies, of going Krogering and having it your way at Burger King, the literary disposable feast of a late-night novelist with the munchies who withdraws verbal currency at the ATM at the twenty-four-hour Shopper's Choice and heads for the delicatessen of Americana, and for a stomachache curable only by Alka-Seltzer. The writer dreads the homogeneity of America, its shopping centers, fire stations, junior highs, its courts, lanes, boulevards, streets, ways, drives, Park Places,

Marvin Gardens, Kentucky Avenues, the massive grids of the master blueprint it was built on, and begins to develop a bad attitude toward the Chocinoe Management Group.

This rash attitude, in my studied opinion as a planning consultant and omniscient narrator of considerable experience, is ill-advised and serves no purpose. To deny Garden Springs, with its pointed if grossly inappropriate allusion to the Garden of Eden, is to deny the origin—the bubbling wellsprings, if you will—of its inhabitants' existence. Given this ontological state of affairs, the Chocinoe Management Group had *no choice* but to proceed with cement trucks to pave the streets, with telephone wire to be strung and power lines to be laid, hod carriers, electricians, carpenters, painters, poets. I might add that most of the subcontracting was to local businesses, and our contribution to Lexington's housing boom at that time did a great deal to stimulate its economy. Jean's brother-in-law even worked on one of the construction crews.

Before long, strips of seed-grass were being rolled out onto the barren dirt of future front lawns, the lampposts that Stephen and his friends would shinny up so as to hang out over the street and shout at passing cars were in place, the blacktop driveways whose tar would turn soft as fresh oatmeal cookies in the summer sun were graded, the manhole covers with the comforting legend Sanitary Sewer were fitted snugly into place, trees were planted as abundant, if not as varied, as the names of the streets they lined: Oleander, Palms, Juniper, Winterberry, Tamarack, Balsam, Cypress, Larkspur, Azalea, Violet, Lily. The crosswalks were painted where safety patrol guards would soon stand, wearing orange fluorescent vests and white sashes emblazoned with a metal badge, to guide schoolchildren across the street to Garden Springs Elementary and Beaumont Junior High, both located within convenient walking distance of all the streets in the subdivision.

Since most of the homes were single-family constructions, in strict accordance with zoning ordinance FJ60511-8C, and since only limited portions of the subdivision were approved for mixed-use development, the population density was destined to remain low in the foreseeable future. Likewise the crime rate, being mostly confined to an occasional housebreaking, instance of spouse abuse, or defacement of public or private property by drunken juveniles. Indeed, the very homogeneity of the contiguous subdivisions, about which our author is apt to complain, provided a generous buffer zone that protected Garden Springs from the kind of urban and semiurban problems—assault, rape, auto theft, murder—commonly associated with mixed-use and high-density areas. Surely his tragical pretensions will not take him so far as to retrospectively wish on himself, his relations, and his neighbors the kind of actual socioeconomic, infrastructural trauma that produces the intensity of anger so often attributed to, for example, Afro-American or Chicano writing. That wish is more hyperbolic than actual. The fact is, the author, like the other inhabitants of Garden Springs, enjoyed the feeling of security derived from living in his subdivision. Its dwellings, if on the whole visually unprepossessing, were adequate to the needs of their respective occupants. Whatever personal problems the author, his parents, and siblings may have had to deal with had little to do with any deficiency in the subdivision as such, unless one begins to degenerate into far-fetched Marxist analyses of urbanization. Our author secretly thinks of his subdivision with fondness, and will no doubt raise his family, if he has one, in a general physical environment not terribly different from the one in which he spent those years.

My vested financial interest, as a planning consultant, in the development of Garden Springs doesn't negate the validity of my characterization of it. This report is an unclassified public document, which will be on file at the county courthouse so that it can be inspected at any time during regular business hours. Its accuracy can be verified by a simple visit to Garden Springs, taking into account, of course, that the subdivision might have undergone certain appreciable changes since the time when the author grew up there. As for my reliability as a narrator, that will have to be judged in the context of the rest of the novel, or in any other context in which the reader chooses to put it. Omniscience doesn't relieve me of prejudices, it simply supplies me with the godlike capability of knowing everything. I'm not an advocate of insane, uncontrolled growth, but neither am I crazy about overly restrictive planning commissions who are stingy with my bread and butter, and whose aesthetic, horse-farm, and National Historic Register mentality fails to take into account the needs of a swelling population. My first allegiance is to growth, even when it leads to the kind of frantic demographic explosion that Lexington experienced.

The building of this subdivision was part of the all-important process of Lexington's becoming The Greater Lexington Area, and I take special pride in noting that this general shift away from its tobacco-town heritage was bemoaned by scarcely anyone. Lexington's AM disc jockeys, arguably as lightweight and energetic as any of the real jockeys out at Keeneland Racetrack, best described this metropolitan urge to merge the dwellers of city and county into a single new geographic and conceptual space when they began to refer to the listening area within reach of their mammoth broadcast towers (often built on plots of land leased from small farms on outlying rural routes) as Kentuckiana. Kentuckiana was on its way, well before the inception of Garden Springs, to becoming the kind of omnibus in which there is a welcoming space for everyone and everything.

The Miles family rented a house cheaply from an absentee landlord with the verbal agreement that the monthly rent would not be upped so long as they didn't bother the owner for maintenance. For eight years, it remained at $150. This arrangement suited Jean just fine, since for him it was no big deal to replace a spigot, a broken hinge, a window screen damaged when his children unhooked it to sneak out at night in the summer for a swim in motel pools, nor to repair the holes he punched in the wall during some of the most agonizing moments of his drinking.

Jean and Constance Miles were people not well educated but intelligent, who had carefully chosen this particular house because of its location in a neighborhood more middle class than itself, and in a superb public school district that included the mildly experimental model school, Garden Springs Elementary. In other words, the family could have some of the advantages of a more or less bourgeois existence without paying extra for it. And Constance, a coupon-clipper and all-around smart shopper with a lot of experience handling inadequate sums of money, was always on the lookout for a bargain, and she recognized one in the house on Palms Drive. Jean was in "one of his good periods," to use Constance's phrase, and was determined at that moment to escape his greatest fear, which was that he and his family would irrevocably slide into what he called, with a mixture of contempt, self-mockery, and sadness, "a redneck life." Like many people of their temperament and position, Constance and Jean wanted their children to have a better life and a good education, and were as methodical as anyone, in certain respects, in going about obtaining it.

Constance was worried in particular about Stephen, due to enter third grade, who had since infancy demonstrated flourishes of extraordinary intelligence (such as reading the exit signs and billboards on New Circle Road at age two) and who had on account of frequent changes of address bounced from school to school—this would be his fifth so far. He'd spent much of his time in the past few months indoors and alone, reading entirely too many comic books. When she'd tried to take him outside to teach him to throw a baseball, he got scared and ducked. The baseball knocked him upside the head and he started to cry. Then, when she'd taken him for a visit to a child psychologist, which wasn't cheap, the woman had the nerve to tell her that the problem wasn't Stephen's fear of baseballs, but her insistence on teaching him to play catch.

All Constance knew was that he didn't have any friends; that although he professed to like school and did brilliantly in certain subjects, if a project didn't interest him he would simply leave the homework undone; that he came home from school with headaches, and she with her migraines could certainly appreciate a headache. She knew that the headaches had a lot to do with

Stephen's home life, and she didn't need to pay a child psychologist thirty dollars an hour to tell her that. Some of Stephen's teachers and his principal wanted to skip him a grade or two, because they said he wasn't challenged enough in his normal grade, but she wasn't going to allow that because it would deprive him of the emotional stability of his peer group. And besides, he was already the smallest boy in his class; it would only make him feel more like a runt to be chucked in with even bigger boys. She'd rather have children his age refer to him as "Miles and Miles of Brains" than have older boys bullying him around for the next five or six years. In this model elementary school they had a program where they could send him up to grades five and six for certain subjects, like math and language arts, but keep him in third for P.E. and other classes.

Constance worried that all the children, not only Stephen, wouldn't make any friends if they had to start in yet another new neighborhood and school. Judy and Elaine had penetrated certain cliques where they lived now, and she didn't want to put them through that again. She couldn't have foreseen that the Miles children would in fact become among the most popular in their new surroundings (despite friends' private criticisms of their unorthodox behavior), and that the Miles household, once a mere anonymous subdivision house with a fresh coat of unattractive beige paint, would exert a gravitational pull for miles around.

But all of that has yet to occur in my chronology, since the Mileses didn't move to Garden Springs until 1966. In the meantime, I'll provide a more detailed description of some of the neighbors in the immediate vicinity of this legendary house. Directly across the street live the Tadarinos. Their only daughter is a baton-twirling sensation in spangles who practices tosses in the middle of the street, as high as the lamppost, several hours a day (yielding only to passing cars). The Miles children will make prank phone calls resulting in numerous unrequested taxis and pizzas being delivered to the Tadarinos. Their two cocky elder sons will predictably become all-state wrestling champi-

ons; the youngest will have his tennis shoe and three toes mutilated in an escalator, and the Tadarino family will sue the department store. In his spare time Mr. Tadarino makes and engraves
sports trophies in the basement. Some he sells at flea markets
on the weekend; others he adds to the already sizable collection
his sons have won legitimately over the years, because he
believes the boys are glorious and deserve even more trophies.

The Lajhres live next door to the Mileses. They're considered
the foreign family on the street because the father is a merchant
with darkling skin and salient eyes, and expostulates with a heavy
accent, and the mother, although she hails from Idaho, once had
reconstructive surgery for severe burns, giving her skin a glassy
appearance. This trait, coupled with an irresistible voice and the
finest white hair, makes her seem to have arrived from someplace
else altogether. Some say they're Lebanese and some South
American, much of this speculation based on a spicy dish called
"kibby" which the mother makes once a week. One of her sons
started at an early age filming home movies that usually involved
stalking a cat through mazes of cardboard boxes. The other son
will loosely pattern his life after Ernest Hemingway's, and, as a
foreign correspondent for the BBC, will be captured by Israelis,
who, like his neighbors, will think he's Lebanese. They'll threat-
en to kill him, and only with great difficulty will he convince
them otherwise.

The Hantrells down the way find themselves always in the
midst of another room addition. In perpetual violation of city
ordinances, they harbor not merely cats and dogs but a horse
that chews the wooden fence, turkeys and chickens too numerous to count, and a sizable smokehouse. On the other side of
where the Mileses will live, the Wharton father, Nick, calls his
children home for supper every evening by whistling between
his fingers, a piercing signal known as "Nick's Trick," which he
perfected in the Marines. And wherever those children may be,
they listen up and come running, while their playmates imagine
the awful consequences that would befall them should they ever
fail to hear or heed the signal, but they never have.

At the end of the street Jimbo Shaver lives with three people: his mother, a divorced sometime waitress who likes to shack up with policemen only; his grandmother, the oldest private nursing assistant in Lexington, who dyes her hair a black as fierce and forbidding as her personality; and his grandfather. The latter, stertorously fat, spends most of his time in an easy chair filling and refilling a spittoon, or in the backyard tending his small but beautiful orchard and making jug wine that Jimbo and Stephen will sample generously at a later date.

The Somebodys, as the two elderly ladies and gentleman at the curve in the road are known, since they never interact with any of their neighbors, find great satisfaction in watching everyone's goings-on from their front porch, especially the antics-to-come of the teenage Miles girls and their excitable boyfriends. A few children tried to convince themselves that the three were German immigrants, maybe ex-Nazis even, but the Somebodys lack that certain Something that gives the Lajhres their foreignness.

Every day of the year without exception, the neighborhood bachelor, Tim Spinks, polishes the car-show Corvette in his driveway with a soft rag, until the day he inexplicably takes it out to do donuts on the ice of the mall parking lot and totals it. The Carlas, whose last name sounds like a girl group from the fifties, appropriately have all daughters. The Pritchards' last name is almost as full of possibility, in the best novelistic tradition, since the father, Gus, mason/contractor extraordinaire (he, too, helped build the subdivision), was once a preacher, or a "pritcher," as he likes to tell people. The name has its troubling connotations too, since at the time he preached he had pretensions as a singer and made a race-baiting underground '45 (as loaded as the .45 he keeps in his gun case), sponsored by an anonymous member of his congregation, entitled "Nigger Hatin' Me," containing the lyrics: "Jigaboo, jigaboo, where are you / I's in the woodpile watching you. / Jigaboo, jigaboo, come on out / I's 'fraid of de white man way down South." One of his sons, Larry, is fond of playing this record when he and his friends sleep out in the backyard camper.

This brief, random sampling of the neighbors isn't exhaustive, nor can it be. I could go on and on, but the Mileses are, after all, at the center of this fiction, and the neighbors are only important insofar as they, like the subdivision, provide a milieu for the arbitrarily emphasized (from my point of view) family in question. Were I to continue any longer or more in depth with this overview of the Tadarinos, Lajhres, et alia, I'd quickly begin to feel narrative strictures closing in around me, sinking me and my report about the subdivison in a narrative quagmire as deep, thick, and sticky as a batch of Gus Pritchard's mortar.

At the same time I can't help feeling, as a planning consultant and omniscient narrator of considerable experience, that all the neighbors listed thus far have as much potential for dominating the novel as do the Mileses, even based on this superficial and partial catalogue of their quirks, if only the author weren't so obsessed with the exploration into the psyche of his own family, or what he mistakes for his family. The Tolstoian sweep is my natural tendency, even if it's only a sweep of Palms Drive. But alas, I'm reduced to the status of a necromancer doing parlor tricks for the Somebodys, in the winter when they must remain indoors with the storm windows up and can't sit out on the porch to speculate about the neighbors on their own.

I must make a partial retraction if I implied earlier that Garden Springs was created chiefly as an occasion for the Mileses to move in. Such a notion is fiscally irresponsible, in addition to cramping my fully omniscient style. The inhabitants of a subdivision must be fruitful and multiply, like the twelve tribes of Israel, if there are to be more subdivisions. Otherwise, such a factual sentence as "Many years would pass before Jean, relieved for an instant of the burden of identity when he sat in a circle of anonymous listeners and said, 'My name is Jean Miles and I'm an alcoholic,' would begin truly to conceive of himself as a person, one of many, and give up the hubris of self-excoriation in the comforting knowledge that at that instant not only he, but hundreds, more likely thousands of others were coming to the identical realization of blank refreshment, in identical meetings all around the state of Kentucky, the nation, and maybe even in other parts of the world"—such a sentence, I say, without new subdivisions of inhabitants, becomes as impossible as its syntax.

But, to return to the Miles family. Jean's fear of becoming a terminal redneck had catalyzed him into a productive period that led him into insurance sales, which broke local office records for Mutual of Omaha for November and December of 1965, and February, April, May, June, and July of 1966. This nearly uninterrupted stretch as sales kingpin allowed him to win in monthly contests a vacuum cleaner, a waterproof watch with a sweep hand, two bonus checks, a croquet set, a pup tent, and an AM-FM/hi-fi/TV console in a walnut cabinet. He also made a hell of a lot in commissions. With Jean—to borrow a phrase he sometimes employed with friends who shared his sense of the precarious—it was either feast or famine. Stunned by this sudden influx of money, the family not only moved to Garden Springs in July of '66, but without fully unpacking, they bought a late-model car, a Galaxy 500, and headed off for eighteen days on an impromptu trip to Florida.

They were so wildly ecstatic that Jean drove single-handed and nonstop (except for bathroom and food breaks) from Lexington to Saint Augustine, Florida, where they arrived just as the Ripley's Believe It or Not Museum opened for the day, and all seven of them went inside to comb the building, less incredulous at the exhibits than at the fact that they themselves were standing in Saint Augustine looking at them. Afterward, at a restaurant with a bamboo roof, they chowed down on French toast, pepper sausage, bacon, biscuits, fresh-squeezed OJ, hash browns, and eggs over every which way. After checking in at a hotel, they took a dip in the pool with a slide, Elaine putting her waterproof watch to the test, the season passes from Lexington's Castlewood Pool still sewn to their bathing suits. The hotel room had carpet on the walls, and the air conditioning deliciously froze their still-wet skin. After long steamy showers by infrared light (they had to keep turning the timer back on), they slept all afternoon in two giant beds and three rollaways. The wake-up call came in a

Deep Southern accent as friendly and encouraging as the voice of the id itself, and they lay in the dark talking about where they'd go for supper, finally deciding on the Fisherman's Wharf. The warmth of the night air allowed for sandals, shorts, and culottes, and off they went to the buffet, all you could eat for one price, and they ate, and it was good—shrimp Creole, fried clams, corn on the cob, okra in tomato sauce, flounder stuffed with deviled crab, twice-baked potatoes, peach cobbler, pecan pie, and to top it off, Neapolitan ice cream. An amusement park lit up the main drag along the oceanside, and after a walk in the sand to digest supper and wet their feet in the surf (so they could technically claim to have been in the ocean on the first day of the trip), the Mileses boarded the bumper cars, the ponies and red benches of the merry-go-round, and (with the exception of Constance, who wouldn't ride that thing even if you made her president of the United States of America) the tilt-a-whirl.

The first evening ended with a slow drive down the strip and further out along the coast, with all four windows open. Salt air in their noses and saltwater taffy in their mouths, the Mileses began to think about the unpacked boxes in their new home, which seemed to them as appealing as a villa somewhere, or one of the beach cottages on the outskirts of Saint Augustine that locals had the foresight to own before the real estate prices went through the roof. I could rehearse the next seventeen days of the trip, but let me say it was simply more of the same, down one coast and up the other, with occasional car sickness, sunburns, and mixups about room reservations. Florida was a developer's nightmare even in the sixties, one that makes me queasy when I contemplate it, since its planners never made the slightest attempt to exercise any control over its growth. The fifty-mile roadside stretches of one commercial enterprise after another, and the aggressive condo salesmen who accost visitors on the beach like land sharks, with promises of Epcot tickets and dinners for four, are today nothing more than the predictable result of the absolute lack of a plan, as shameful as the ramblings of an omniscient narrator who abdicates responsibility and simply lets the story sprawl. Tolstoy's narrators, after all, didn't say everything; it only *seemed* as if they did. Sunny Florida leaves me cold, and now that it has served to afford the Mileses their small epiphany, I'd just as soon turn the odometer over and set them back in Garden Springs.

In very little time, their newness on the block had disappeared, mostly thanks to the summer ubiquity of neighborhood children outdoors, where they serve as ambassadors of their respective parents, from the first brief instant of morning cool through the scorch of afternoon to the final glimmer of a twilight postponed by daylight savings time. As all adult subdivision dwellers can attest, it is through their children that they come to know one another, so a husband and wife with five offspring have a distinct advantage in the process of integrating themselves. Within the first week Marilee Lajhre had come next door to borrow a cup of sugar from Constance, just as Sheila Tadarino had borrowed sugar from Marilee when she moved in—a proverbial system of barter still extant in the sixties, with symbolic value for breaking down barriers between houses, sometimes known as the Domino effect.

All was not sweetness, though. Darryl, the elder of the Pritchard boys, in the midst of a group of boys checking out newcomer Stephen with casual questions about the size of the dolphins in Marineland, accused Stephen of having farted. Stephen tried to ignore the remark and the involuntary laughter it provoked in the others, but Darryl Pritchard persisted. Wanting to avoid a fight, due to his intense fear of Darryl's superior strength and size, but conscious that at this crucial juncture inaction would lower him in the eyes of his new companions, Stephen decided on a middle course, and with the clinical impartiality of one who asks the witnesses to examine the evidence for themselves, he replied, "Smeller's the feller."

Darryl cuffed him upside the head hard enough to knock him to the ground. Though Stephen was of a mind to simply suffer the succeeding blows in the hope that passive resistance would make Darryl lose interest, the pain of the next blow made him decide that he'd better get a few in himself while he still could. Though his valor may render him a more can-do and sympathetic character, and though he managed to land one hard crack on Darryl's face, the neighborhood bully soon delivered the TKO, and the young bystanders, satisfied once the rite had been accomplished, separated the two combatants. In their minds they secretly railed against Darryl, having been subjected to similar humilations at his hands.

The mini-saga does not end there, though, because when Stephen returned home, his mother, aghast that her worst fears of her son's rejection had come to pass so quickly, and not realizing that he had in fact been initiated into several friendships that morning at a relatively low cost to himself, demanded satisfaction. Nobody was going to treat her kids that way, they were as good as anybody, and she didn't give a dang if it was the Prince of Denmark (an extreme instance of hyperbole if meant as a reference to Darryl Pritchard). If Jean didn't go down to the Pritchards' and tell off Darryl's father, Constance would do it herself. Jean, though relieved and even proud that his diminutive son had stuck up for himself (he wouldn't have placed a wager on it beforehand), was extremely eager to avoid starting his new life on Palms Drive by becoming embroiled in a redneck quarrel.

The time would come, a decade later, when he'd be arrested for smashing out the car windows of the participants in an imitation Charles Manson cult that Judy became involved with, and threatening the life of its leader, who had given her syphillis. But for now, what he really wanted was to get along with the neighbors, to live and let live. He was inclined to let the incident slide, and cheer Stephen up by making chili dogs, Kool-Aid, and popcorn, and taking it all with them to the Circle 25 drive-in, where *Barbarella* and *The Russians Are Coming* were showing as a double feature.

He also recognized his plan as a fantasy not to be achieved that day, for he knew Constance wouldn't rest until the family honor had either been restored or further compromised (more likely the latter). Marching up the street like a lady from the Unwelcome Wagon, Constance punched the doorbell of the Pritchards' house with a forefinger, and when the younger son, Larry, answered, she demanded to speak to Gus, whom she supposed had encouraged his offspring in their unfair martial practices. Gus, not one to fight directly with women except as a last resort, sent his wife out as a delegate. Gay Pritchard, a tough broad in her own right, wasn't apt to be intimidated by someone like Constance. Gay possessed a tongue just as sharp as Constance's own, and a hefty body that had withstood years of assaults inflicted by a dangerous husband. It's a pity the two women, united as they were in the abstract as abused women (albeit in different degrees), couldn't find a common ground of mutual empathy. But if I get onto a purely sociological bent, I'll never get off it, and my narrative will begin to suffer from preachiness, a disease known to be fatal to twentieth-century fiction. Dickens's or George Eliot's narrator could get away with it; I can't. Besides, the two women couldn't stand each other in real life.

"Your son beat up my son," said Constance, getting right down to business.

"Tough titty," answered Gay, not mincing words either.

You can reconstruct the ever-increasing intensity of the verbal exchanges for yourself. These led to shoving, to Gay's pushing Constance off the front porch, and, in a move unexpected considering her fearless Viking nature, running inside the house. Constance picked herself up, and as she wavered between pursuing Gay inside or remaining satisfied with the knowledge she'd made her opponent turn tail and run, Gay reappeared on the porch brandishing her husband's Colt .45. (As Chekhov cautions us, a loaded gun must never be mentioned unless it is destined to reappear with a purpose later in the play. I have here abided by Chekhov's rule, and refer you to the initial description of Gus Pritchard for confirmation.) The situation might have turned tragic, and brusquely undercut the overriding comic tone of my account, had Jean not decided after a few minutes to follow his wife up the street and see what trouble she'd gotten herself into.

By then, Gus was in the front yard trying to convince his wife to give him the gun. It wasn't registered, and he was afraid the police would discover this omission if they appeared on the scene. Several onlookers had gathered in the street at a distance. Though Constance was in too much of a state to allow Jean to touch her, she let herself be calmed just below the point of hysteria by his talk, as she was not in a mood to die by gunfire that day. The two men stiffly shook hands, more with an expedient eye toward diminishing a hostility that would require an enormous amount of energy to maintain than out of genuine goodwill. They agreed to give their respective sons a "talking to," and parted on the note of strained cordiality that would characterize relations between the two families henceforth. This upshot may seem remarkable, given the volatile situation the women had suddenly found themselves in, and given that Gus would just as soon blow somebody's head off as look at him. But it's no casual coincidence that at the moment Gay pointed the pistol at Constance's head, the safety was on. Gus always kept the safety on, and after this historical incident he took the extra precaution of keeping the bullets in a separate room from the gun.

To explain his behavior, I must again toot the horn of us planners and developers of the Garden Springs subdivision. I won't even attempt to deny that domestic violence, including murder, can and does occur there; the names and addresses of its inhabitants have been known to appear in the police blotter of the *Lexington Herald-Leader*. And I'm the first to say that safety catches can be flipped off in a heated moment with very little trouble. But the fact that the safety catch was even on attests to a certain sense of orderliness ingrained in the semipolite inhabitants of a subdivision by the very structure of their surroundings. If Jean had lived in Irishtown, or Little Georgetown, or down around DeWees Street, or out by the viaduct, the safety would have been off, and Constance probably would have died or been severely wounded. Police statistics bear me out on this point. Garden Springs is a place of safety catches and safety valves, where the only real pressures are those for coexistence and a peaceful resolution of conflict.

Misunderstandings there may turn tragic in our modern sense of the word, but not with the sense of inevitability that characterizes a Shakespearean tragedy. It's difficult to imagine the bystanders taking the place of the opening Chorus in *The Tragedy of Romeo and Juliet*, who recount the feud between the Capulets and the Montagues:

> Two households, both alike in dignity,
> In Garden Springs, where streets are fair and clean,
> From Stephen's wind-break into shootin' sprees
> Ungay and constant (seconds: Gus and Jean).

Kentuckians may be famous for their blood feuds, but the Kentuckians in this subdivision prefer to avoid them, or at least keep them to a manageable level.

I must now move on and treat the succeeding years in somewhat more summary fashion, after having succumbed to the temptation to linger over my pet landscape. Lynnette stayed at home; Elaine, Stephen, and Talia attended Garden Springs Elementary; Judy went to Beaumont Junior High, where the rest would follow, often via the same teachers, like the successive waves that finally wear a rock to nothing. Later, most of them would attend Lafayette High.

All right—maybe that's *too* fast. I'll try again. Elaine Miles and Fanny Tadarino (the baton twirler) entered fifth grade together and soon became fast friends. Both were indifferent students, despite Elaine's intelligence, which would later manifest itself as a keen head for business. Fanny's lack of enthusiasm for the academic demands of fifth grade made it easy for Elaine to adopt the same attitude, although, try as she might, she couldn't efface her elegant penmanship to match Fanny's sloppy hand. For both of them, elementary school was chiefly an opportunity to interact with a lot of boys. Judy may have been the first and quickest of the Miles girls to develop breasts and start her period, but slender Elaine outpaced all her sisters in precocious boy-craziness.

Given the lack of reciprocal interest from the fifth-grade boys, who had yet to demonstrate any appreciation of the lure of femininity except for vague stirrings of consciousness that big knockers were desirable, Elaine and Fanny had to resort to acting out lurid orgies with naked Kens and Barbies in Fanny's basement among the unengraved sports trophies. In their excitement they would occasionally give one another the famous "pretend kiss," encircling the mock-lover's head with an arm so that the hand can be placed over her mouth and frantically pressing one's lips against one's own fingers. Once in a while they became so feverish and daring that they *really* kissed each other, and the thrill was almost unbearable.

Elaine's seeming lack of panache, weirdness, brilliance, etc., vis-à-vis some of her siblings masked an eventful private life. This private life, unlike that of her sister Lynnette, was not occult and self-contained, but rather shared with a select circle of friends. Elaine founded a club called the Hi-Jinx, making herself the president and Fanny the vice-president, positions they faithfully alternated during the six months that the club lasted. The main purpose of the Hi-Jinx was to have slumber parties, make four-way fortune-tellers out of paper during class, and hold lengthy debates about who was the cutest boy in school, which sometimes ended in a filibuster.

Elaine was frustrated by the lack of responsiveness in boys her age. She was horny, very very horny, she complained to Fanny, using a word she'd recently learned, which, from what she could make out about it, seemed perfectly to describe her current situation. Fanny decided she herself must be horny too, though she had her doubts after a recent encounter in which she'd talked Elaine's little brother into the Mileses' shed, locked her jaws onto his, and received a thump in the chest in return.

Things began to look up when the two decided to accompany Judy, now an "A-team" cheerleader, to a night basketball game at Beaumont. Here was a whole new world of boys—practically men!—to choose from. Sitting in the bleachers of the musky junior-high gym, Elaine divided her attention between the males in blue-and-white or green-and-yellow sleeveless jerseys, with tight little muscles, crowding under the baskets, and those who lounged in the bleachers or slouched against the wall, drinking suicide Cokes and crunching the ice. Elaine had heard that crunching ice was a sign of sexual frustration. Maybe Judy would introduce her to some of the basketball players after the game, if she didn't forget. Judy wasn't mean-spirited about that sort of thing, but her memory needed a lot of prompting since she'd started junior high.

After the second quarter, Judy had disappeared into the off-limits girls' locker room, so Elaine and Fanny went to the concession stand. The dumb line would take forever, if they didn't die of thirst before their turn came. But these dire predictions had no chance to come true, for a boy—a guy, that is—approached the two girls, bearing three suicide Cokes, and asked them politely, with only a very discreet snort of laughter at his own joke, if they would like to commit mass suicide with him. Fanny and Elaine followed him outside. His name was Rusty DeChevraux, a ninth grader—so tall!—he must have been at least five-seven!—with cowlicked hair parted on the side so that his bangs sort of covered one eye, and a red-and-black checkered CPO like lumberjacks wore. He told them he was from the school of the visiting team, Tates Creek Junior High, and poured some Rebel Yell into the three Cokes. When Rusty asked them how they liked it, Elaine told him, between sips, it was the smoothest she'd ever had. She tried not to crunch her ice so as not to call attention to the fact that she was a horny person.

Rusty may seem like a bit of a jerk from my description of him, but let me give him the benefit of the doubt in your eyes by confessing that my sense of territoriality has grown ever stronger since I began this report, and the fact that Rusty comes from outside the magic circle of Garden Springs makes me harbor secret and unarticulated prejudices against him, and makes me want to make him the heavy. Were I a male, fourteen years old and present at this Tates Creek–Beaumont game, I'd no doubt sit on the metaphorical Beaumont side (there's only one set of bleachers), vociferate obnoxiously, throw crushed paper cups when the other team made a basket, and probably get into a fight with Rusty on the way home, especially if we lost.

But Rusty has no interest in fighting me, only in wooing Elaine, and is contemplating how to get rid of Fanny. His next move is the kind of shrewd, savvy one that Elaine, with her nascent eleven-year-old business head, can appreciate. He decides not to exclude Fanny at all, but instead to make a proposal so daring that only Elaine, his intuition tells him, will accept. His parents will soon be asleep, and he can get one of his friends to drop them at Rusty's house, where he will proceed to swipe the spare key to his Dad's Cutlass Supreme from the nail in the laundry room. Then they can go for a nighttime joyride. Fanny, though far from lacking in adventurous spirit, knows that her own parents, with their eagle eyes, stricter rules, and close supervision (she was lucky to get to go to this game!), will quickly swoop down on her if she arrives so much as half an hour after the prescribed time, and that she'll get grounded even if they don't find out exactly what she did. Realizing that she's about to miss out on all the fun, she shoots her friend a pained look. But out of the generosity of her Italian heart, she offers to call Elaine's parents if Elaine doesn't tap on her window by ten o'clock, and fabricate a story that entails Elaine spending the night at the Tadarinos'. Both girls know the risks involved, lest Constance says no or wants to speak to her daughter, or in the less likely event that Judy comes looking for them after the game, but the pact is made, and Fanny returns to the game alone and a little dejected, though not mad. "Are you mad?" Elaine repeatedly asked her, and she just as repeatedly denied that she was. Due to the high turnover of friendships in elementary (much higher than the divorce rate in America at the time), it was extremely important to be sensitive to where a friend's emotions might rest, at any given moment, along the scale of "really mad," "mad," "peed off," "just in a bad mood," etc.

In the friend's car on the way over, Elaine could smell her favorite men's scent, English Leather, on Rusty, and everybody passed around a bottle of something frothy and bitter called "ale." The friend's girlfriend in the front seat had giant boobs, some of the biggest Elaine had ever seen, but Rusty didn't seem particularly interested in them, and paid a lot of attention to Elaine, telling the friend, "Doesn't she look like a junior-high girl? I could have sworn she was a junior-high girl." By the time they reached Rusty's house she had let him give her a couple of dry kisses on the mouth. Once they were left alone in the driveway, though, their interests became strategic, as they had to figure out how to get the car away from the house without making any noise. Putting the Cutlass in neutral, Rusty let it roll back into the street, and Elaine, pretty strong for an eleven-year-old, pushed from behind.

Once they'd coasted for about a block, he started the engine and they drove out of the Tates Creek subdivision until they reached New Circle Road. As they cruised along in the dark, she told him how her little brother used to read these road signs aloud when he was just a baby, not even two years old. Rusty, handling the car with assurance, didn't seem that impressed, but he nodded affably. Approaching the exit that would take them to I-64, he asked her if she wanted to go to Louisville. She knew that Louisville was seventy miles away, and that her assent to such a long trip meant there was no turning back about staying out all night, and might be taken as an implicit first step to "going all the way." She let her silence signify agreement.

Along the way, Rusty popped into the tape player a tape of the Moody Blues—not the music he normally listened to, but the group's name suggested the tape might serve as mood music. Besides, his mother often referred to him as "moody," and he secretly enjoyed the term's suggestion of roguery, independence, and unpredictability. The interstate seemed very quiet. The weigh stations were closed, and there were no cars parked at the rest stop where they pulled over so Elaine could get rid of some of the Coke and ale she'd drunk. The women's rest room, through a Providence that wished to warn her back from foolish actions, was out of order and locked, so she had to use the men's. Going in and seeing two urinals attached to the wall at different levels gave her a creepy feeling. She wondered which one Rusty would use. On another wall, a machine for dispensing something called "ribbed condoms" had scratched-up pictures of the bare shoulders and tilted-back heads of women with open mouths.

Elaine, with her euphemistic turn of mind, put two and two together and concluded ribbed condoms must be dirty pictures of naked women. This discovery surprised her, and she wondered whether all men's public rest rooms contained them, and what this fact intimated about the proclivities of men in general. The stall partition had a crude drawing of a giant penis and a lot of unimaginative graffiti, most of it about cocks, pussies, and the like, and Elaine decided (in so many words) that this entire bathroom experience was erotically overdetermined in a somber fashion she didn't approve of. It reminded her of a novel, *The Scarlet Letter*, that one of the progressive teachers was reading aloud to them every day after lunch, and in which symbols abounded, like red letters on people's chests. Everything in the men's rest room was highly symbolic and foreboding, and she decided she didn't like Hawthorne very much.

In the car, she deliberately let Rusty put his arms around her, while they shared another bottle of warm ale. He asked her how she felt about "parking," and she thought it sounded like a good idea, reasoning with herself that since she had a small bladder, it made sense to stay parked close to a rest room if she was going to drink beer, even a rest room as gross as this one. On KRZY, girls and guys were calling in requests dedicated to their boyfriends and girlfriends, and she used the change in her purse to make a long-distance call to Lexington from the rest stop's pay phone and request "The Rain, the Park, and Other Things," for Rusty, since it had the word *park* in the title, and that word seemed to have a special, sensual weight for him, the way *horny* did for her.

When she returned again and accommodated herself on the seat, he began kissing her madly all over her face, and inside her mouth with his tongue. This was what she'd been waiting for! After those immature boys who talked about cooties and squirted chocolate milk at each other through straws, she needed a real man, one who would take her in his arms and never let her go. He started to suck on her neck. She knew about hickeys, because Judy had come home with some and gotten in trouble, and told her they were a sign of uncontrollable passion. "Not on my neck," Elaine said to Rusty, "my parents will see it there," and she opened her shirt so he could suck on her chest, stomach, or wherever he thought best. Her skin became hot, and she felt the pleasant tingle between her legs that riding her bicycle had begun to give her in recent weeks. Rusty's caresses were pure heaven, and all she wanted was to remain exactly like this, rubbing for hours against the hard spot his penis made beneath his pants, letting him kiss the tender skin of her shoulders while a warm glow suffused her body and remained there forever and ever.

But Rusty seemed to have other ideas, because he was taking off her pants and working his own down below his knees. His thing was purple and pretty big, and she had an idea, based on sketchy secondhand information, that he meant to put it inside her. "What are you doing?" she asked, and he answered, with a cryptic smile, "What do you think I'm doing?" and pulled her legs toward him so he could lie on top of her better. She didn't like this turn of events one bit, and their song wouldn't be played on the radio for at least another half-hour. But since his passion was uncontrollable, as evidenced by the hickeys he'd given her, what choice did she have but "to have Him and hold Him, for better and for worse," as she'd sworn in the boyfriend subclause of the Pledge of Allegiance to the Hi-Jinx. All the same, the intense pain when he started to force his way in gave her a sensory reminder of a concept that had stood her in good stead during the yearly achievement tests at school, namely, that a larger object doesn't go into a smaller container. "It won't fit," she told Rusty in a matter-of-fact tone, trying not to succumb to a rising panic that had an all-too-scientific basis. He didn't seem to hear her, though, or respond to her attempts to push his panting, quivering body away. In a rapid review of her mental catalogue of last resorts, the desperate thought occurred to her that maybe a packet of the dirty pictures in the rest room dispenser would satisfy his lust, and scratching him, wrenching her mouth away from his, she shouted, "Stop it! Stop it! Let me go to the men's room and buy you some ribbed condoms!"

"Ribbed condoms?" he repeated, lifting his chest off her with a start. "How the shit do you know about ribbed condoms?" She felt his penis begin to go soft. "How old are you? Eleven-year-olds don't know about that stuff. They can't get pregnant."

"It isn't that," she said. "I just thought you would enjoy yourself more, and it would be better for me, too, if you had some ribbed condoms instead of doing it like this with me. I went in the men's room a little while ago, and they're only a quarter."

Rusty pulled his pants back on, and Elaine took advantage of the opportunity to do the same. "You little slut," he said. "I'd like to know how many guys you've slept with. Why didn't you just bring some of your own condoms along in your purse, for convenience? What's your favorite kind, French Tickler or Roman Fingers?"

Elaine didn't know quite how to interpret these last remarks; whether he thought she possessed nude photos of herself, or photo packets she'd bought, or whether he referred to something else altogether. But her intuitive sense for taking care of business told her that he wasn't in a very good mood. And that she had best play it cool and pretend she knew exactly what he meant. "I had a lot of condoms," she said brazenly, "but I belong to a club, and I passed them out to everybody at our last meeting."

"Christ!" he said in a voice of disgust, peeling out in the Cutlass and racing down the exit ramp of the rest stop onto the interstate.

Now she was really scared. Maybe he meant to take her to a secluded spot and force her to strip so he could photograph her naked body, or would try to force his penis inside her again, or worse. Surely her mother would have the FBI, the CIA, the Fayette County Police Department, and Efram Zimbalist Jr. out looking for her, as she'd recently taken to threatening Judy she'd do if Judy showed up so much as five minutes after the appointed hour from some pizza party, sock hop, or evening cheerleading practice. Surely she'd show the same mistrust in Elaine, thus saving her daughter's life. Some roadblock ahead with flashing lights would keep them from traveling any further in the direction of Louisville, or Rusty's fast driving would alert all patrol cars to a Cutlass Supreme westbound on I-64, the one they'd been looking for. But Rusty for the third time that night cut short her predictions when he plowed across the grassy median so fast she thought it would rip the chassis off, and headed back toward Lexington.

He punched in the dashboard cigarette lighter, and when it popped out and he touched it to a cigarette, it occurred to Elaine that the glowing coil would make a good symbol, a scarlet letter, and that Rusty (his name was red too, like a devil's!) probably wouldn't mind using it to burn an A in her breast, except that he was too busy being sulky. Yes, he'd love to brand her an *adulteress*. She had no clear idea of the word's meaning, but once again she came close enough to its import to suit her purposes.

When Rusty let her off in her subdivision—and she would say that much for his niceness, even though he made her feel yucky enough to lie to him about which street she lived on—she walked to her house through streets quiet except for barking dogs, and climbed through her and Judy's unlocked window. She hoped Mignon would bark as loud as other dogs in the neighborhood so everybody'd wake up, because she wanted to be caught red-handed, red like sin, red like Judy's menstrual blood, and have her mother scold her and then embrace her and say, "You shouldn't scare me like that." Not only did Mignon fail her, but so did Judy, who wasn't in bed and had no doubt caught their mother in a lenient mood and been given permission to sleep over at another cheerleader's house. Elaine undressed and lay in the double bed by herself, trying to cry because she felt really down—really, really down, so down it went off the scale of downness—but all the relief she could get was a couple of sobs. She comforted herself that in the morning she'd be found out, when her mother discovered her asleep in her own bed.

But she didn't sleep. When the walls of Elaine's bedroom turned white and she could make out the perfume bottles on her side of the dresser, she padded into the kitchen, the taste of ale still in her mouth, to make herself a bowl of rice puffs and milk. A little later her mother came out of the bedroom rubbing her face. "I thought I heard somebody in here," she said. "What are you doing back from Fanny's so early? I figured you'd stay over there and watch cartoons this morning."

Elaine shrugged. "I just felt like coming back."

"Oh. Well, did you have a good time?"

"It was okay. We stayed up late."

"Yes, you look tired. I went to bed at nine myself, because I had a terrible migraine. I barely remember Fanny calling, or Judy either. Judy stayed over at Gayle's, I think she said. Well, if you don't mind, I'm going back to bed for a while. I still don't feel so hot."

"See you later," said Elaine. When she finished her rice puffs, she went into the living room, and with the sound kept low, so as not to disturb her mother, she watched cartoons until she fell asleep.

I hope this tale of Elaine serves to "flesh her out," if that figure of speech doesn't sound erotically overdetermined after what has just gone before. My zeal in giving her a "well-rounded figure" will perhaps compensate for her mother Constance's anxiety about acknowledging her young daughter, who so resembles herself, as a sexual being. The same could be said about her conveniently going to bed early with a migraine headache (how often have we heard that one!) on the very night her daughter undergoes a rite of passage into adult sexuality, a coincidence that allows Constance to remain forever unaware of this significant experience in her daughter's life. The failure of any of the other first-person narrators in the Miles family to "flesh her out" as fully as I have, in later chapters of this novel that they themselves narrate, can be chalked up to the natural hesitancy that a limited narrator might be expected to feel. I, on the other hand, as an omniscient narrator of considerable experience, am enjoined by my nature to know all, see all, to stare unflinching into the personal affairs of my progeny, without passing judgment. The nakedness of your offspring isn't always comfortable, once they get past a certain age, but one gets used to it in time. I flatter myself that I can maintain my dignity without being prudish about it.

Jean would be the first to admit he didn't know what the hell his kids were about, especially Judy. At the end of the sixties, her cheerleading days gave way to hippiedom. Being a hippie in her neighborhood usually had little to do with a marked political and social agenda. During Judy's adolescence, hippiedom mostly took place in the bedrooms of apartments, the family rooms of split-levels with shag carpet, the esplanades and parking lot of the mall, in basements, isolated fields, and the municipal park after hours. Judy experienced hippiedom as a matter of personal style, but one she never connected in any conscious way with a national movement.

She and Cynthia Gosse and Angie Lamas, all residents of Garden Springs, had traded in their Aigner purses and pleated skirts for halter tops, embroidered jeans, sandals, tooled-leather ponytail holders, and Guatemalan bags. Lying in the grass in halter tops passing around a doobie (cleverly rolled in a hand-held rolling machine to look like a real cigarette) with teenage dudes, watching, for free, Kiwanis fireworks explode in the distant sky, made them feel like sexy chicks. One of the dudes was learning to play the twelve-string guitar, and could do the neatest versions of "The House of the Rising Sun" and "Black Dog," which sounded like they came right off the album. In the winter, Cynthia's downstairs room, with its innumerable Tibetan and South American furry rugs to lie on, was the perfect place to throw the tarot deck by the light of scented candles, and to be felt up by obliging teenage boys.

Angie's parents' residence, in the almost palatial splendor of its circular drive, remote-control three-car garage, a doorbell that played music, and, most importantly, its screened-in veranda and separate guest cottage, was the site the three teenagers reserved for more daring exploits. Angie's parents, a psychologist and a forensic medical specialist, who were into trusting their children, allowed Angie and her friends to spend the night in sleeping bags on the veranda, or in the guest cottage when it was unoccupied.

It was in the cottage that Judy, Cynthia, and Angie experienced their first hit of four-way windowpane acid (as in bridge, they had to find a fourth partner on that occasion), and that Judy, in a fog as dense and chocolaty as the hash brownies she'd consumed, first learned the intricacies of the erotic maneuver known as sixty-nine, to the overpowering background music of Iron Butterfly's "In-A-Gadda-Da-Vida," with its infamous six-minute drum solo. *In-A-Gadda-Da-Vida* may sound like a phrase from one of Lynnette's invented langauges, but its translation is "In the Garden of Eden," a name which you may recall I mentioned at the outset of this report as standing in close relation to the name Garden Springs. Judy thought herself in an earthly Paradise that night, and she was, in more ways than she realized. Though she tried to escape Paradise several times during her adolescence by running away to other towns and states, her father always brought her back within forty-eight hours.

If you asked Judy to reconstruct a detailed chronology of events in the years between 1969 and 1973, she would have difficulty putting them in a definite order, since she experienced much of that time as a repetitive flux, as though the endless days of summer had bled into the school year, holidays into ordinary days, as if the landmarks of an orderly progress toward adulthood had been rearranged into random, if often exciting, combinations. In this respect she shared a certain sense of time with her father, who had a hard time piecing together some of the days and weeks in his life, and who sometimes, especially during the seventies, had to fight the overwhelming feeling that he had accumulated a worthless jumble of ideas and experiences. Judy, outwardly robust, healthy and aglow, smoked pot and consumed 'ludes, PCP, reds, windowpane, blotter, crystal speed, and eventually angel dust and heroin, with the incessant promiscuity of a vitamin freak, and for a long time with seemingly similar results, since the fresh elasticity of her face and skin, and the firm proportions of her body, didn't diminish or alter in the least.

This youthful resilience of the soul's temple will come to an abrupt (but only temporary) halt at age nineteen, when Judy contracts serum hepatitis from shooting up heroin, is hospitalized with a jaundice so yellow it stains the sheets, then drops to seventy-one pounds (a fearful sight to her brother and sisters, who must wear gowns and masks to visit her), is almost sure to die (but doesn't), and is forbidden to take drugs or drink alcohol for the rest of her life at the risk of destroying her already unutterably distressed liver. Though she refrains for several months, while her poor body replenishes itself and regathers its flesh, within a year she resumes both drugs and alcohol, in more moderation but once again as a regular thing.

Years later, she continued to do "just a teeny-weeny hit of acid," as she put it, some "itty-bitty psilocybin mushrooms" now and then, and had her glass of wine when she felt like it, all on a recreational basis. During this same time she became an aerobics instructor, as fit as her younger bodybuilder sister Talia, as revved up as in the first blush of hippiedom, and in constant demand on the workout circuit where she lived. Friends who knew her history of substance abuse and the probable condition of her innards marveled that she might drop dead at any moment but didn't, as through the Plexiglas wall of a sometime racquetball court they watched her inflict a low-impact/high-sweat, congenial hour-long punishment that made flabpots and hardbodies alike reach their target heart rates.

Many narrators might be tempted to make Judy's teenage years into a morality play about drugs, a kind of modern-day *Pilgrim's Progress* or *Everywoman*, falsifying the curve by cutting the story off in one of the months just after her bout of hepatitis, when she has sworn off her vices altogether. I've felt the same temptation myself, as an omniscient narrator always on the lookout to broaden my considerable experience. Unfortunately, Judy's case history up to the present won't allow it. Those gentle readers who crave a moral comeuppance will have to satisfy themselves with the psychic torments that Judy suffers throughout much of her childhood and adult life.

For it's true that Judy was in a great deal of distress. As the oldest child, she liked to think of herself as the one helping to raise the rest of the kids, to cover for her mother, who spent the entire day working as a secretary in an automotive body shop, and for her father, whose various types of sales work (she wasn't even sure what his job was at any given time) were punctuated by sabbaticals in his friends' houseboats and shanties on the Kentucky River and other points unknown. But the truth is, Judy had enough trouble taking care of herself. Half the time she didn't know where her sisters and brother were, and much of her mental energy was focused on keeping tabs on herself.

One night her little brother showed up at an outdoor party in Cynthia Gosse's backyard when Judy had taken too much speed. He was only twelve or thirteen, and with his shoulder-length hair, pretty-girl face, slender chest covered by a skintight body shirt with a glittery spiderweb on it, bare feet, a can of beer in hand, he seemed vulnerable and in need of advice. She knew he and his friends were just getting into smoking pot, and his red eyes showed he was stoned right then. But his presence and the anxiety she felt about him only served to make her have thoughts of her parents and heighten a latent paranoia that they, or Cynthia's parents, or the neighbors, or the police, would show up to bust everybody at the party. It had happened before, somewhere else when everybody was dropping acid, and she'd barely escaped out a window. It could happen again tonight, and she wouldn't have the same luck twice. If Stephen got busted too, it would be her fault, and they'd kick him out of school and the Latin Club, and he had all the brains in the family, but having a record would ruin him anyway. Soon she was crying and shaking her brother by the shoulders, sloshing beer on his spiderweb shirt and everybody looking around at the commotion.

Next thing she knew Stephen had taken her into Cynthia's downstairs bathroom, she sat on the toilet and he talked to her in a voice that had just started changing and broke in all the wrong places, she couldn't tell if he was upset too or just having trouble with his vocal cords, it almost could have been funny if she hadn't been so freaked out, and people with bladders full of beer kept knocking on the bathroom door, and Stephen would have to break off in the middle of an earnest sentence to call out *SomeBOdy's IN here right NOW,* the two of them in that ittybitty cubicle and he probably had to pee as well, but he held it, she could have gotten off the seat to let him go at least, even if none of those people knocking could come in, but Stephen would never go with somebody else in the bathroom, she and Elaine could parade around the house naked all they wanted and leave the door open but he was modest, she liked that about him, he was a good brother and she was glad he'd let his hair grow long and turned into something besides an egghead, or at least a different kind of egghead, a cool one, minus the third-grade burr haircut, she only hoped he wasn't doing anything besides smoking pot, especially not speed because it really fucked up your mind and that was one thing for her since she was a little older and had made up her mind that if she finished high school that was about enough for her but Stephen could go on to become a scientist, God knows he brought home those parts of a sheep when somebody came to his elementary to dissect a sheep and he left the parts floating in jars of alcohol until their mother made him throw them out, it seemed weird but he just had a curious mind and liked to experiment, she could appreciate that, and she especially liked acid because once you dropped it you were committed to it for four or five hours, she remembered how she and some friends did hits before they drove to the Humble Pie concert in Cincinnati so it would take effect right about the time they arrived and along the way a car had passed them going about a hundred twenty miles an hour and *What the hell is going on?* they wondered when another car zoomed by going about a hundred twenty miles an hour, maybe a cop chasing a speeder or chasing a getaway car so they looked at their own speedometer to get a frame of reference to clock the speed and they were only going five miles an hour, on the interstate, God it was so damn funny they had to pull onto the shoulder to get their shit together, five miles an hour on the interstate, once you committed to acid you couldn't come down even if you wanted to until it wore off, but she wished she could come off this speed, it was a bad drug for her because she was so hyper to start with, a more mellow drug suited her personality type, psychedelics, mushrooms, hash oil, because she was an expressive person and creative, good with people, because she had other talents besides doing drugs and hanging out and getting laid

and she wondered whether Stephen had heard bad rumors about her that would make him not respect her and not look up to her as a role model, however much they fought sometimes and however different they were by nature she couldn't stand that, for him to be thinking of her as some kind of tramp or deadhead when in reality she was his oldest sister and that was a big responsibility for anybody, especially when you found in a dresser drawer underneath a lot of canceled checks the certificate of your illegitimate birth by one parent and the papers of your adoption by the other at a later date, which might not seem like a very big deal but it had made her realize that you couldn't necessarily trust in your parents' firm resolve to take care of you or even claim you, they too had their moment of doubt, not so bad in itself but the fact that they'd never told her made her wonder what else they were hiding and whether they hadn't maybe come this close to giving her away, but just hadn't had the courage to go through with it, that possibility put her in a position, as the oldest, of needing to keep an eye on the others who needed her protection, which sometimes made her feel even more pressure to want to get away from a family where every other day was like a soap opera, or seemed like it, but the five of them, the kids and her, had always stuck together for that very reason, and they all knew how to cook and clean and feel very close when they weren't actively fighting, and it was only in recent months that they'd all begun to go in different directions, to the point that it could surprise her to find Stephen at the same party as herself, even though they weren't ten blocks from home, and although her little brother was crouching here beside her at the commode, talking her down in a patient voice punctuated with occasional squeaks, he no doubt had friends of his own waiting for him out in the backyard and wondering where he'd got to and one of them who'd witnessed the little scene she'd made earlier would say *Some chick was flipping out and he had to take her into the house,* it made her feel ashamed that it shouldn't be the other way around, not that she wished on Stephen the legs that vibrated while she rolled the balls of her feet or the holes on the inside of her cheek or the fast breath that didn't want to slow down even when she made a conscious effort to take deep ones

but she wished he was the one with a tangible need, so she could cradle him in her arms to keep him from going nuts like he did when he was three or four in Tennessee and kept screaming bloody murder every five minutes and holding his head and would get very quiet in between and then start screaming bloody murder again and it turned out a lightning bug had flown in his ear and would beat its wings for a while trying to get out and be still for a little then beat its wings again and the doctor afterward said the only thing that had saved Stephen from going deaf was all the earwax built up in his ear which had smothered the lightning bug, he probably didn't even remember that or how she'd taught him to read a book, not that she wanted any credit for doing the things any good sister would do without giving it a second thought, but just to know that she herself having learned how to read had a purpose, that learning how to write and think and speak and supposedly getting smarter as you grew older had a purpose, because some of the people who'd dropped out took a shortcut later and got their GEDs but the next week you'd see them back at the same party, like that guy with the unbelievable nickname Wiener who Angie was seeing now, who could play the guitar really well and was ugly but had the most beautiful hair to his waist and got a discount on cases of beer from working at the liquor store but he must be up in his twenties at least and looked like he ought to be hanging out with an older crowd instead of with a teenybopper like Angie, he got the diploma to satisfy her, but the next week he was back at one of the parties like everybody else is, unless they hitch to the Keys or Atlanta or Dayton, that's where she and Cynthia had gone the first time she ran away, but of course her dad had found her, like he always did, just as they were sitting down to birthday cake because it was somebody's birthday and there was champagne and special fat doobies of some Jamaican somebody had copped, which had to be thrown down the toilet, a perfect waste, while her dad was coming through the front door, acting perfectly calm, and he always brought Stephen, as if to teach his son a little lesson, or maybe just for company on the road, but if he was so calm and such a family man, why did he beat the hell out of her when they got home

not that he did it every time, but enough, he'd given her plenty of bruises to nurse, he was a real bastard, and if he was such a great father, why didn't he take Stephen to baseball games or science fairs or wherever it was that fathers took their sons, but instead Stephen's entertainment and consolation prize was to stay up half the night riding to Dayton, and she could tell anybody the return trip would have been boring as hell too if she hadn't been scared half out of her mind by her dad's quiet manner, since it probably meant she'd get slapped around when they arrived home, and then, as now, only Stephen's being there made her feel a little better, she could feel herself starting to come down and she wanted a drink of water, luckily they had Dixie cups right by the sink in a dispenser, like a normal household, her mouth was so dry almost as if she'd been talking the whole time, and maybe she had talked some, but her little brother had done most of the talking and she wished she'd been listening better because she knew he had a lot to say, she knew he was smart even if he hadn't lived as much as her, he was a good brother and they needed to do more things together, maybe tomorrow she'd take him to the mall and buy him a shirt that fit a little better, because she'd made forty dollars selling speed this past week, or maybe she'd take him out to lunch at the oyster bar, but then again tomorrow she'd have to help Cynthia clean up the mess from the party and she'd probably feel so burned out from tonight she'd sleep half the afternoon away, but maybe she and Stephen could do something the day after tomorrow.

Reaching the end of the foregoing, hopped-up passage leaves me as breathless as Judy (and possibly as breathless as you yourself), despite my own penchant for convoluted sentences. As I wrote the sentence, it occurred to me that perhaps streams of consciousness are not only technically but also technologically obsolete, since the word processor on which I composed this particular stream refused to allow me to make it into a single, uninterrupted paragraph. Instead, it periodically flashed onto the screen a window reading, "This operation will create a paragraph that's too large," forcing me to hit the return bar if I wished to continue to write. Being who I am, and I need not repeat my credentials yet another time, I'm always sensitive to criticisms of excess and exhortations toward moderation, even when they come from a machine, and perhaps that is why I abandoned the stream of Judy's consciousness after only a few pages. But I must defend my rhetorical intent in undertaking it in the first place. My own narrative style, as expansive and flexible as it may be, tends to sound a little staid, and ultimately orderly, and I feared I might orient Judy's disorientation too much, filter her through the homogenizing veil of her emotion recollected in my tranquillity, if I insisted on my own natural cadences. While some might have applauded me for giving a sense of direction to a bewildered youth, they would doubtless also have read the reformed version of Judy's manic monologue with less interest.

But now I must retake the initiative, assume the more parental guise I have just shunned, and make a few remarks concerning Judy's father. It's conceivable that he has, to put it in Judy's slang, "been getting a bad rap." As the working-class alcoholic in this novel, he has a hard row to hoe, and particularly when one considers his literary predecessors, a host of them, including brutish colliers embittered by thankless labor, brooding for an excuse to wallop their wives, and pitiable papas beating time on little boys' heads with palms caked hard by dirt. The misgivings that Constance and Judy will express toward him in their accounts are understandable, since no one likes to be knocked around, no matter how infrequently and no matter how legitimate the psychosocial and economic determinants of this behavior may be. It's even understandable that in later years, when Jean "mellows out," becomes almost an entirely different person, and tries to make up for three decades of false starts and highly mixed successes, Constance will find herself bearing a grudge she can't get rid of entirely no matter what Jean does, since a resentment thirty years in the making can take as long or longer to unmake. Readers who have not felt so directly the effects of Jean's bad days may have allowed their harsh judgments of him to be assuaged by some intimations I've already made, namely that he is destined to become a reformed alcoholic and stay sober. I may provide further solace by mentioning that Judy will grow to love this recovered father in her late twenties and will make long-distance collect calls to him from the Southwest at all hours of the night when she feels depressed.

But we mustn't let this vision of a sweetly maudlin, aerobic Judy and her clean-shaven, clean-living father lull us into a false forgivingness that none of the parties involved desires of us. Neither should it provide us with an alibi for indefinitely postponing taking a stand on the present situation, waiting until all the facts are in before we decide how we feel about Jean. For all the facts are never in. Jean knows this only too well, and is deliberate in never referring to himself as "a former alcoholic" but always as "an alcoholic." Although he may feel confident and steadfast in his resolve not to drink, he is not omniscient and thus cannot see, as I can, that he will remain sober for the rest of his life. Thus, Jean is not mouthing a facile cliché when he says (and he is fond of saying it, with a frequency almost irritating) that he is "taking it one day at a time." He is fully aware how possible it is to begin to drink again at any moment, and that one does not deal with alcoholism by transcending it. His son Stephen is known to become angry when intellectual companions congratulate him on having overcome his background, since in Stephen's mind a background by definition is not something to be overcome. Just so, it is futile for us (and I make deliberate use of the sophistical royal "we" to suit the pedagogical humor I find myself in) to develop certain feelings for Jean in spite of his alcoholism, or to make allowances for it and try to look around it, for to do so would be to negate the larger part of Jean's being. That attempt is what the real bad rap consists of.

If Jean were to write the entirety of this novel himself, it is likely that he, too, would cast himself as the Alcoholic, recognizing it as his archetype despite the shenanigans of most of his more immediate literary predecessors. To find an appropriate model he would probably go back even further, to the Middle Ages, where allegorical figures abounded, Lust and Sloth and Avarice, ones who had no shame about naming themselves after the predominant quality that possessed them and defined them, unlike the humanoid alcoholics in twentieth-century literature who try to have two sides to their character at all costs, and duck the issue altogether. I hope and expect that Jean will have more to say himself about his alcoholism in a later chapter.

Let me simply point out, though, that the contentiousness that characterized relations between Jean and Judy did not extend to all of his children, and least of all to Lynnette. Judy shows a marked resemblance to her mother in her need to either resolve a conflict immediately or raise it to a higher degree of tension. It's almost impossible for her simply to let an argument cool out or blow over. If she senses that someone is the slightest bit upset with her, she will always demand, "What's wrong? What did I do? What's bugging you?" without understanding that with some people (her father being one of these) it's best simply to let them simmer for a while if the situation is to be set aright. The thrashings Jean administered were always spontaneous, and their genesis, unbeknownst to his conscious mind, was usually in the protests and just recriminations Judy uttered from the backseat of the car during the long drive home, for silence is one thing she cannot stand. Judy will have her say no matter what the consequences. She is fearless in the sense that she will persist even when she foresees the heavy price she must pay for exercising her rights. This attitude, when applied toward her second husband, a war veteran given to smashing furniture and other things and trying to set certain people afire, will almost cost Judy her life on more than one occasion. Her highest priority is to make herself understood immediately, if not sooner.

Lynnette, on the other hand, has no particular desire to be understood. For Jean, who by his own admission can't get a good grasp on his children in the seventies, Lynnette's personality, and her entry into adolescence, not with a bang or a whimper but with a simple aside spoken upstage where it can't be heard anyway, comes as something of a relief. She possesses the infinitely attractive quality of not questioning his every motive, or any of them for that matter. The two of them have an unspoken mutual nonaggression pact, so that whatever opinions she may have about his performance as a family man (and he knows she must have them), she keeps to herself. In return, he makes few demands of her, listens to what she has to say about her own activities, but without ever probing, and is glad to spend time with her when they happen to find themselves together, always with the implicit understanding that these meetings cannot infringe on the free comings and goings of either.

At the time of this accord, circa 1974, Constance's job at the automotive body shop has her out of the house early every morning, and she does bookkeeping weekend mornings for a prosthetist in town. The mania for staying overnight at friends' houses reaches its peak that summer, so Stephen and Talia are often absent, and Elaine is married and living half a block behind the restaurant she assistant-manages. Judy, too, lives "independently and on her own," having rented the upstairs of someone's house over in Chevy Chase, so Jean seldom sees her except when she drops in at the steak house he's managing, to ask for carry-out sandwiches and frozen T-bone steaks for herself and her friends, since she's working at a card shop at minimum wage and has little money to spare for food.

This head count leaves only Lynnette and Jean at home most mornings. In the evenings Jean is pulling off the exacting combination—usually credited only to high-level executives in American middle-class lore—of drinking heavily and working long, hard hours at a demanding job. He has been hired some months before to manage one of the older steak houses in town (before the large-scale renovation of downtown Lexington is fully under way), and the neighborhoood where it's located is in a state of decay. The steak house had become a haven for go-go girls in hot pants, riffraff on their way to or from the bus station, drunkards who needed a booth to sleep where they wouldn't be bothered, and ruffians on high-carbohydrate diets who needed quick infusions of protein for their upcoming brawls. The former manager kept a pistol behind the bar, but Jean's philosophy is that you shouldn't have a pistol around unless you're really willing to use it.

The new owner of the steak house, a shrewd businessman, hired Jean to make it into a place where families could come to eat without fearing for their lives. He knew that Jean possessed certain qualities above and beyond his good business sense, willingness to work like a dog for decent pay and experience in high-pressure job situations—commendable traits all, but ones he could find in any number of prospective managers. Jean, though, had also lived on the seamier side and had more than a passing familiarity with the ruffians and go-go girls in question, or ones just like them. He was capable of making conversation with a chopper thug or the head of the chamber of commerce, with equal ease, and had an extensive network of acquaintances at all social levels in Lexington and its outlying towns. The new owner's hunch was that Jean could effectively use persuasion rather than force to clean up the steak house, and his hunch proved correct.

Jean immediately befriended the restaurant's badasses, giving them a round of beers on the house while he sat at the table with them and called them sonuvabitches and sissy-bar machos. When fights broke out, he stepped in, armed only with a dirty joke, or maybe a true story he'd heard up in eastern Kentucky about one son in a mountain family who had shot the other one at the dinner table when he tried to take the last baked potato. The brawlers would shake their heads in disbelief and admiration at such a tale of barbarity, wishing they'd been present at the table in person to watch it happen. Soon they'd be sitting down at a table in the steak house to eat, trying to outdo each other with stories of adventures they'd seen or, they insisted, participated in themselves.

Jean's idea, of course, was to phase out this clientele altogether, and as soon as he could maintain the chronic tension at the steak house at an acceptable level, he began to invite his friends on the police force in for complimentary drinks or dinners, to try the place out, have a look-see, and pretty soon it became the hangout for the Metro police, and they picked up their own tabs, or each other's. Before long it wasn't as fun a place to pass the time for the most extreme of the former regulars, and they found somewhere else to gather, leaving only their more moderate cronies behind. Only then did Jean renovate the interior, and begin appearing himself in a blitz of radio and TV ads (sales, after all, was his forte), talking up the nightly special and suggesting the steak house, with its superb central location, as the spot to come after basketball games. After a good deal of bartering, he procured genuine Wildcat paraphernalia—posters signed by present and past teams and by the legendary Adolph Rupp, game basketballs, even a trophy on loan, which he displayed behind glass. Since he, like many an American male, kept up with the stats from moment to moment, with the concentration and seriousness of an air-traffic controller, it was no trouble for him to move from table to table making analyses and predictions, and to coach from a stool the tiny figures running across the new TV screen mounted in the corner above the bar. He had always fancied himself a bit of an amateur bookie, so he organized and administered a betting pool for those who frequented Jean's place (as the new regulars insisted on calling it), and although he couldn't participate in the pool himself, he made silent bets of his own, for his luck seemed good just then.

Part of his success with the employees was that he never asked them to do anything he wouldn't do himself. He cooked, prepped salads, cut up sides of beef, washed pans caked with petrified grease at the end of the night, seated patrons, waited tables in a pinch, carrying up to three plates on one arm (a trick even Nick might be proud of), ran the register, tended bar, fixed the damn jukebox, swabbed the decks, righted the jib sail, toted the barge, lifted the bale, opened the place when it opened and closed it when it closed at 2 A.M., and stayed on afterward to count up the receipts, make sure everybody got to their cars, and drop the profits in the night deposit on his way home. He was a popular boss, beloved by his crew, who would have done anything for him except take his place.

It gives me great pleasure to write about Jean's stint as manager and metamorphoser of the steak house. I admire entrepeneurial skill, the kind that makes for a bustling and prosperous Lexington. The Chocinoe Management Group would do well to look to someone like Jean, although they probably wouldn't at present, since although they count former rascals and scalawags among their number, they have solidified into a stodgy and respectable enclave, fond only of insured risks. But leaving them aside (as much as one can), my enjoyment of Jean's success isn't diminished in the least by my knowledge that he will eventually be fired when his boozing becomes too frequent and the pressure of the job therefore becomes too great, and that he will later contemplate with sadness and some bitterness the proliferation of the steak house into not one, but three locations in Lexington, another slated for Louisville, and the ubiquitousness of their billboards around town will become a sore reminder of inhumanly long shifts that had once seemed happy. I prefer to enjoy the present moment with Jean, adopting his philosophy of one day at a time, a philosophy that he, in his ambitions circa 1974, is as yet unaware of.

The steak house opens at 5 P.M. and he doesn't arrive home until around 4 A.M. most mornings, so he allows himself to sleep until ten or eleven, a fan propped in the open window against the swelter of late morning, lying in bed face down in his jockey shorts, with the sheets off, relishing a well-deserved rest after spending hours on his throbbing feet in the restaurant and its hellishly hot kitchen. Lynnette, too, likes sleeping, almost as a hobby, and in particular sleeping late. Therefore, the two of them could be found during much of that summer at midday, looking somewhat rumpled and eating bowls of Rice Krispies together at the kitchen table, while the cries and lawnmowers of the more active population resounded outside. Father and daughter fell into the habit of watching daytime TV, no conscious discrimination guiding their choice of channels, except that they both liked *Jeopardy*. These hours from Jean's rising until some afternoon errand called him away from the house came to be his favorite time of day, and though he never would have dreamed of insisting on Lynnette's presence, he could almost count on her to be there when he awoke, acting slightly grumpy in her pajamas and not saying very much.

If Jean was the embodiment of ambition in those days, Lynnette was its antithesis. Some afternoons she accompanied the Carla sisters to the pool, as she had a natural talent for diving and could impress onlookers with her flips, jackknifes, half-gainers, and backdives. But she made no special effort to cultivate these gifts and was just as fond of the more pedestrian pleasures of the pool, such as chicken-fights, Marco Polo, and see-how-long-you-can-hold-your-breath-underwater-without-com-ing-up. She had little desire for a summer job, although she could with a small effort be prevailed upon to work the conces-sion stand once in a while, and babysit the children and animals at the Hantrells down the street, or the youngest Wharton girl next door. She needed hardly any money for her own purposes, and it was not within her purview to provide for the general fam-ily fund, which went not only for rent, food, and clothing, but also for things like Talia's abortion, which her father had paid for at Talia's request without her mother's knowledge (and Talia had then tried to economize to have some money left over and nearly gotten herself butchered), or to cover Judy's rent checks when they were returned from the bank for insufficient funds.

Watching Stephen sell lids of marijuana to try to supplement his paychecks from Kentucky Fried Chicken, so he could go on a yearlong exchange program to some country she'd never heard of—a task made all the more difficult because Talia was picking the lock to his strongbox and stealing both marijuana and money from him—Lynnette wondered why he went to all the trouble, since as soon as he had almost enough money together, their mother began to make Stephen feel guilty about how his father had always wanted a boat, and that they wouldn't be a family much longer, and there was an old cabin cruiser his father had his eye on to buy and fix up, and how much it would mean to him if they went in on it together, as a father-son project, and Stephen acceded to her wishes, putting his savings into the cabin cruiser, so that he could spend his afternoons not in a foreign country, but in the driveway stripping the old fiberglass off the hull and in the process getting the fibers down his shirt, where they burned like the devil. It was clear to Lynnette that Stephen must know how their mother's enthusiasm about the boat was only a ploy to keep him from going abroad, because she couldn't stand the thought of her son being gone for a whole year, and he surely had figured out that Talia was the culprit in the strong-box thefts, but in both cases Stephen surrendered his prerogatives because he was eaten up by some guilt that Lynnette couldn't fathom.

He seemed to hold himself responsible for the family's success, as if his monetary contribution could really make any crucial difference, especially in a time when everybody already seemed to be making money. Lynnette had complete confidence in her parents' abilities to provide for the bare necessities of her own and her siblings' lives, and she had no illusions that her own minute contribution could have more than a symbolic value, and she wasn't quite sure what the symbol was even supposed to mean. Money had always been a topic of discussion for as long as she could remember, and now that everybody seemed to have some, it seemed like they should be able to stop thinking so much about it, treat themselves to a vacation from that particular obsession. It puzzled and pained her to watch Stephen go through the contortions of an unformulated penance, and sometimes she'd look at him and simply say, "Poor Stephen," because she didn't know what else to say to him about actions that he already seemed to be fully aware of.

As for her father, she didn't doubt that he had wanted the boat to begin with, but it was like so many of the objects in his idealistic and ever-changing attention span—herself and her siblings, for instance—cherished but not destined to be dwelt upon, and, besides, he was tired from work, dead tired, so when he moseyed over to the window during the commercial breaks in the early afternoon and peered out the window at Stephen stripping the fiberglass off the boat in the heat as if it were an ark that had to be prepared, another symbol for a family fond of symbols, and looked to be on the verge of going outside to join him, it didn't surprise her when he turned from the window and walked back to the couch for the second half of *The Price Is Right*. Let Stephen work on the boat, she wanted to tell him, it's in him to strip the fiberglass and he can't help it. You rest, she wanted to tell him, but she knew that it was also in her father to go to the window and that he couldn't help it either. Anyway, her silence was what he cherished, and she felt lucky to have been given that role, rather than Stephen's, or Talia's, or Judy's, or Elaine's. Especially Elaine's. Elaine, weary of fulfilling the role of second mother, rock, dependable one, proxy, den mother, overseer, assistant manager, second in command, had abdicated not too long ago. She'd married just to get out of the house and away from the feeling that she was responsible for raising Stephen, Talia, and Lynnette herself. Now Elaine worked a shift almost as long as their father's, plus keeping a spotless home of her own with hot cooked meals, in the perfectionist manner she'd been growing into, and still she was always calling or dropping by with a pineapple-upside down cake or a giant bottle of Coke to see how the rest of the kids were getting along, when half the time she found no one at home except Lynnette. Lynnette appreciated why her sister felt she had to marry, but it was too bad she had to leave home to do it, since she now had all the extra work of driving across town every time she came back, which was almost every day.

Then there was her mother. If a contest were ever held to see who had contracted the most illnesses before age forty, she felt sure that her mother would win. Her kidney stones could be found in test tubes in various drawers around the house (for some reason she liked to keep them, as a kind of memento), and Lynnette sometimes ran across them when she was looking for a scratch pad or a deck of cards, along with outdated pill bottles of various descriptions, probably some of the same pills her mother gave them when they were small and had throat infections and she couldn't afford a doctor's visit or even a phone prescription to buy whole new bottles at the pharmacy. She wondered if her mother had come down with so many things by getting in the habit of saving a few pills at the end, just in case the need might arise for them later. There had been pneumonia, and a hysterectomy, and migraine headaches, and something having to do with Eastern State Hospital when Lynnette was very small, and she and Talia had gone to live with their Grandmother Mamie and Granddad Edward for a few months while Stephen went to their uncle's and Elaine and Judy to Birmingham. Everybody had conspired to keep that one from her, even her brother, and she never had found out the reason. Now her mother suffered from high blood pressure, the doctor had certified it, putting her on medication and advising her not to work so much. Right after that her mother had taken the bookkeeping job on weekends, insisting that they needed the money when she knew very well that their father had a steady income now, almost as much as when they took that trip to Florida, and not even commissions but a regular paycheck, the same amount every week plus bonuses and all the free steaks they could eat (the freezer was so full of them that one fell out every time she opened the door for a popsicle).

But she knew her mother would rather die, literally die, than admit that everything was okay, that they were going to make it, that no crisis had to be headed off except for all the predictable ones, that they could all be as happy as her father was when he came out of the bedroom in his underwear and saw that his bowl of Rice Krispies had been poured, since she might as well do it since she had the box out anyway, and only the milk needed to be added. It was such a stupid simple thing, not even an act of tender devotion, because Lynnette refused to get caught up in anything that could be construed as her marking out a position in the ever-shifting web of allegiances, whose intricacies took too much energy to keep sorted out. She knew very well the subterfuges both her parents had resorted to at different times in the ongoing struggle for their children's affections, and she didn't want anything to do with that. Each parent had a version of the events of the past and present to tell, always with sizable omissions when told to her. Right now she preferred her father's version, but only because it was silent, a series of gaps she could fill any way she pleased, and even if it resulted from his simply being too tired to speak, she admired him for it just as much, maybe more. But she wished that her mother and father could come to the uncomplicated realization that there was enough love for both of them, for everybody in the family, no matter how selfish they'd acted or who they'd locked out of the house or had an affair with in a moment of frailty or cheated or threatened with suicide or compared to someone else they could have married, no matter when they'd come home or failed to, there was enough love for everybody, there was forgiveness, unconditional forgiveness, and she wasn't about to parcel it out as a reward or a special favor.

It made her happy to float on an air mattress in the swimming pool because there was no effort involved. Diving gave her the same pleasure, she simply did it the way it felt. Mrs. Carla had watched her one day at the municipal pool and talked to her about joining the Aquatic Club, where they did competitive swimming. It cost twenty dollars a month, and Mrs. Carla thought she could get her a discount since she worked as a deputy coach or swimming mother or something like that. The sauna and the tanning lamps held some appeal for Lynnette, and she knew her father would give her the money if she simply asked him for it—he was that way when he had it to give—but she didn't want to enter contests or think about finals and regionals and personal bests, not this summer at least. Mrs. Carla had mentioned it to her father, she felt pretty sure, but Lynnette could count on him not to bring it up unless she let drop that she was interested, and she didn't plan to.

In the evening, after adult swim ended and almost everybody had gone home, she liked to do a few laps just before dark and the final whistle, with the water still warm from the day's heat like it had been in Destin on the Panhandle that time they all went down to Florida. Her dad and some guy he'd met at the ice machine rented a sailboat, neither of them knew anything about sailing, but they put on like he-men and how hard can it be there's not even a motor, and they took Stephen with them— men only, ladies to their umbrellas—then it took them seven hours to bring the boat back in, all three of them burned red as lobsters. It was a big family joke, and her dad wasn't so hot on sailing after that. They couldn't even see a sailboat on TV now without a wisecrack from her mother. Lynnette saw it less as a jab at her father than a kind of comment on water itself, for her mother had never learned to swim and water made her deathly afraid. You could see it from the tense way she thrashed around in the shallows and got short of breath when the waves came up to her chest. That same vacation her father had tried to teach her mother to swim. They had acted very lovey-dovey the whole trip, quite remarkable with five kids in tow, and thinking back on it Lynnette believed that their sex life must have been pretty good about that time, even though the seven of them always shared a single motel room.

The only real moments of friction were during those swimming lessons. Her mother would put her head down into the water, flap her arms a few times, and come up with water streaming from her bangs, gasping like a drowned person. And her father, very patient at first, like when he'd taught Judy to drive a standard shift, finally about the third day began to say, "You're not *going* anywhere. You start to panic before you're even in motion."

"I'm *trying*," her mother answered. "What makes me nervous is you forcing me when I'm not ready."

Her father had rolled his eyes then, that had been his big mistake. Her mother smacked him on the mouth, like she used to do them when they got her really riled, only harder, in that awkward way she had because she wasn't used to hitting. He didn't do anything, only licked his lips to taste the saltwater on them and looked embarrassed. That evening they went to the early-bird special without her, and Lynnette realized how upset her mother was because she'd gone instead to the lounge to drink a daiquiri at happy hour, two for one, and she was such a lightweight that two daiquiris for her was almost the same as getting drunk for anybody else. From the booth Lynnette could see her mother in the lounge, wearing sunglasses, and wanted to go over to talk to her, but her father made everybody stay at the table and he read them the menu out loud. Later her mother took a walk with Lynnette on the beach, barefoot, holding her clogs in her hand, and even though it was after dark, she let Lynnette splash through the runnels of tide sliding up the sand, keeping an eye on her from a few feet away.

Lynnette had offered to teach her mother to swim this summer, one afternoon when they were laying out on chaise lounges in the backyard, both getting tan except for her mother's stretch marks, and she'd said she'd think about it, but now with her high blood pressure Lynnette knew it would never happen. It was a shame, because she'd been practicing up her coaching on the Whartons' little girl, not even eighteen months old yet, out in the three-foot-deep plastic pool in the Whartons' backyard when she babysat. All you had to do was count three and the baby knew on three you'd go under and held her breath, both arms around your neck. Now when Lynnette let her go and backed away a few feet, Kimmie could swim to her, not a very accomplished stroke of course, but the dog paddle anyway, or as Lynnette had renamed it in Kimmie's honor, the baby crawl. She supposed you had to get them while they were still really young like that, before water meant anything to them besides something they drank and peed.

But if you couldn't, maybe it was better just to leave them alone, because once people got raised up to a certain point, they weren't going to do things or not do things unless they decided to themselves, at least among her relations that was true. Her father smoked two packs of Pall Malls a day, and the new warnings on the side of the pack from the surgeon general hadn't made any difference to him. Even the name Pall Malls sounded like the name of a funeral home, so he couldn't have any illusions about the contents of the package, but he liked to joke that if he quit smoking he still might not live to be a hundred, but after a few weeks he'd *feel* like he'd lived to be a hundred. And the same way with his drinking. She couldn't understand why her mother insisted on harping on it in the little time they spent together most days, asking him if he'd tended bar the night before and trying to get him to join some kind of anonymous group for drinkers.

Her mother's criticisms had no visible effect on her father's alcohol consumption, not even the opposite effect of making him drink more. Lynnette was grateful that her father, even in times when he'd had harsh things to say about her mother, never uttered any of the clichés like "Your mother's driving me to drink." The actual act of drinking was his affair, one that mostly took place away from the house, and not one he tried to involve any of them in or felt obligated to render any account of, with one exception. In recent weeks, since Lynnette and he had fallen into their little routine, he had taken to keeping a few beers in the refrigerator, and having one at some point during the course of the day. It was almost touching to her the way that he would ask her permission to drink a beer before he went to the refrigerator to retrieve it, as if a child's say-so might be necessary for him to take one of his own beers out of his own refrigerator. Maybe he did need her say-so, but surely he couldn't imagine she would ever say anything but yes. It wasn't a matter of her approval, because she didn't approve nor did she disapprove, and she felt he must also know that. At the same time, watching him drink the beer did give her a certain vicarious pleasure that she couldn't quite explain. The fact that he brought home different brands, no doubt just grabbing the nearest six-pack out of the restaurant cooler on his way out, made her think that as a rule he probably wasn't aware what brand or type of liquor he was drinking, or perhaps even that he *was* drinking during the busy times from some glass or two or three perched on ledges behind the bar and in the kitchen and the waitress station.

Yet when he drank his single beer in her presence, he nursed it like she'd nursed the last few sips in her canteen when she'd gone camping with the Whartons, and read the label as if it were a good book he didn't want to finish. Some days he wouldn't go for the beer until later in the afternoon, and while he sat on the couch watching television, she could fairly see the gears creaking in his head as he thought about the allotted beer in the refrigerator, waiting for him anytime he should decide to walk into the kitchen and open the door, delaying that moment as long as he possibly could. It seemed to her that if he could enjoy all his drinks as much as he did that one, he wouldn't have a "drinking problem," as her mother referred to it.

The game was his, though, and she was satisfied to merely

play her small part in it, a smile and shrug of the shoulders, the kind of gesture her father understood very well but which more than once had infuriated Judy, who insisted on a more patently theatrical response to her demands for approval. Though Judy depended on subsidies from her parents and a job that paid peanuts to meet her expenses, and thus had little cash to spare for entertainment, she had used inventiveness when she made it her project in the early spring on her days off to pick up Lynnette, in a Rambler that was falling apart and leaked exhaust fumes into the car, and take her on outings that didn't cost very much money. Judy had apparently come to the conclusion that Lynnette was neglected, always had been, and set out to remedy the situation by escorting her to the Waveland Museum, filled mostly with Civil War memorabilia, way out on a country road and only charging fifty cents on Tuesdays; to the cemetery, where they walked past simple gravestones and elaborate monuments under the shade of weeping-willow trees, admiring the dogwood in bloom and the swans gliding on the artificial lake; to Jacobsen Park, its extensive empty fields perfect for flying a paper kite they'd bought in the Kmart; downtown to a luncheonette for a patty melt; or on a drive out Parker's Mill Road, where they could look at horses, sometimes with riders on them practicing hurdle jumps, and Judy would turn the Rambler around at the airport, always with an eye on the gas gauge, which remained perpetually under the quarter-tank mark.

The activities themselves were very much to Lynnette's liking, but she cared a good deal less for the conversations they inspired. Judy had in her mind a notion she wouldn't give up, namely that Lynnette was deep, that her quiet concealed profound sufferings aching to be revealed by the right approach, and that Lynnette possessed a wisdom, far beyond that of any normal twelve-year-old, which had simply escaped the notice of others. The older sister was also eager for mutual commiseration with the younger, since they had shared the same general tribulations, and she confided to Lynnette some of her own secrets and opinions in an attempt to draw her out, even going so far as to disclose to her youngest sister information the family had done its best to keep from her, like her mother's suicide attempt last year, and Judy's own visits to a therapist at Comprehensive Care. Lynnette did not especially like Judy's taking for granted that they shared the same opinions, as when she complained that Elaine was acting like a selfish newlywed who threw a fit if any of her sisters dropped by unannounced at dinnertime for a visit, but Lynnette preferred to keep her peace rather than try to set up a counterexample or define her own relationship to Elaine for Judy's benefit. The tensions between Elaine and Judy, like those between Talia and Lynnette, had their own peculiar nature and had to run their own cyclical course, and she didn't feel that talking about her own relationship to Elaine would be instructive or have much bearing on Judy's case.

Judy was persistent, though. She would spoil a perfectly breezy walk in cotton-sweater weather by turning to Lynnette and asking in a significant voice, "How is Everything going?" When Lynnette in answer smiled and shrugged, a habitual bodily gesture she really had no control over, it proved an irritant to Judy, who would begin to feel paranoid and snubbed, as if Lynnette had utterly rejected her sister's being and the shrug were intended to imply that Judy didn't belong in the Miles family on account of her technical illegitimacy, a matter which Judy hadn't yet apprised Lynnette of, as she was saving it for the final trump card. "I guess I'm probing into off-limits stuff," she said, jingling the ever-present car keys in her hand. "You're probably not having a very good time." And before Lynnette could stop herself, she had smiled and shrugged again, simply to indicate that, yes, she had so far and would continue to if they would just drop the subject, but the gesture sent Judy off on a galloping rage, and required Lynnette to redirect the conversation down avenues that would remind Judy of all the nice things she'd done for her littlest sister over the years, giving her clothes that no longer fit, letting her stay up late to watch *Hush, Hush, Sweet Charlotte* when their parents were out, a movie that scared the hell out of her and made her wet the bed, but Judy washed the sheets and mattress pad herself without making a big deal out of it, and always putting the special metal cup, the one Lynnette liked and called the "cold glass," in the freezer on the nights she cooked for the rest of them, and pretty soon Judy felt better and stopped jingling her keys, and then they could enjoy the rest of their walk and finish off the rest of the afternoon with a dip of ice cream on a sugar cone. Judy could afford one dip each, which was exactly enough to satisfy Lynnette.

Lynnette wouldn't have minded these strenuous therapy sessions in the least if her sister hadn't insisted on group therapy. Judy had always been prone to large gestures, and at present her demands for Lynnette's affection took the form of frequent hugs, whether at stoplights, in the women's rest room, or at a salad bar while they were holding full plates topped with blue-cheese dressing. Certainly there had never been a lack of physical affection in their family—they had Italian ancestry, or so they were told every time their mother made spaghetti or poured a glass of Lambrusco—and touching had been a part of their upbringing. But Judy was overdoing it. When you greeted somebody you hugged them and maybe again when you left, or a little more on special occasions or just when it felt right. Not every twenty minutes though, and not the kind of long, soulful embraces Judy favored, as if the two of them had been orphans separated for years by cruel circumstance. Lynnette understood Judy needed lots of affirmation right now on account of passing through a period of distress more intense than usual, but Lynnette herself, for reasons she couldn't explain very well, wasn't into touchy-feely just then, it really bugged her for people to be putting their hands all over her. It was different with Chichi, who would lick you all over the face and leave white scratch marks on your arms, but you could set him down on the floor and tell him to stay, or her father, who might lean over and pat you on the leg and that was it.

Otherwise she felt suffocated, like how going in the water against her will—or even when she tried to want to go in—must make her mother feel, that's the best way she could explain it if she'd wanted to, which she didn't. Because you really couldn't explain anything to Judy or even ask her a direct question, as much as she might solicit your opinion or offer information about herself. It's true that Lynnette would have liked to pose a question or two, for instance, how come every time Judy had run away she deliberately left a clue behind as if by accident, a telephone number given to one of her less prominent friends, one who wouldn't come readily to mind, or her Guatemalan bag stuffed underneath the passenger seat of their father's car, containing the names of two or three different cities scrawled on a piece of paper, small and difficult clues, but ones their father made the most of. The easy explanation was to call them cries for help, or attention-getters, but really Judy had never had very much trouble getting their father's attention. He had always been only too ready to respond on two hours' sleep to any commotion she caused, even if only a local one. If she had truly wanted to run away and disappear for a while, as Lynnette thought she indeed had, why didn't she just do it? Everything would have been waiting for her unchanged when she returned. She might have at least experienced some adventures to compensate for all the time spent on the road. But Judy preferred to let herself be caught, at a moment inconvenient both to herself and to their father, and then afterward tell and retell the story of those frustrated trips, with a bitterness toward her father that never seemed to lessen.

If Judy felt such enmity toward their father, then instead of continually explaining how he had screwed her up for life, how if she never got it together he'd know the reason why, it might be better to adopt Talia's attitude toward him, essentially one of indifference, or at least almost total disregard. They were the two official rebellious daughters, and everyone knew it, so Judy ought to make use of a tactic that had worked so well for Talia. Talia had made clear early on that she didn't really give a damn what her father thought, that he was of so little importance in her life that he would be flattering himself if he thought he could have any significant influence, positive or negative, on her emotional development. If he'd ever tried to hit her, she would do her damndest to hit him right back, and since he was bigger she would just have to use a chair or a brick or wait until he was asleep, because he had to sleep sometime. And though she'd asked him to pay for her abortion, she made no bones about the fact that the solicitation put her under no obligation to him, and that if he didn't give her the money she'd find it somewhere else.

At this point I'll attempt to wrest the narrative away from Lynnette's control, as I find I've allowed the measured flow of her perceptions to continue for longer than I had intended. I'm tempted to agree with Judy's conviction that Lynnette's capacity for sophisticated self-expression surpasses that of the average twelve-year-old, this belief being a luxury I can afford since I, by definition and unlike Judy, have no need to make Lynnette speak in order to understand her. Indeed, I stand to lose something, namely the distinctive sound of my own voice, which will blend inextricably with hers if she speaks at too great length. This report would slowly become yet another example of the dreaded and ubiquitous "third person limited," a nomenclature which has always had for me the ring of a sinister and not quite successful grafting of two whole humans into a third being, partial and unspeakable in appearance.

I do confess that I find my stylized version of Lynnette's "voice" seductive, but you may have also noted that she's worked her way through all the other family members, leaving Talia for last. I, likewise, by a fortunate coincidence, have thus far featured all the Mileses except Talia in some kind of solo spot, and since we are drawing toward the finale of my report, I might as well do the honors myself. You needn't look for any personal bias behind my own postponement of Talia, since I, as a planning, omniscient, etc., am generally able to remain less passionate about the personages at hand. My motivation for this ploy doubtless lies rather in my desire for symmetry and balance (my sacred gods!).

There is a great deal of truth in the brief remarks about Talia that Lynnette managed to get by me before I cut her off. Her disregard for others is beginning to quicken. At the end of 1974 and beginning of 1975, the final year of the Mileses' residence on Palms Drive, Talia had physically, though not psychically, recuperated from her abortion the year before, and was gearing up for an even more momentous event that would occur around April of '75, right about the time the Mileses moved from Palms Drive to Louisville en route to their eventual destination, the townhouse over on the north side of Lexington. I will tell you straight out about this momentous event, since to withhold it would only heighten its veneer of melodrama, and I wish to avoid at all costs, in the interests of durable literature and responsible reportage, giving my portion of the novel the feel of a potboiler. Talia will attempt suicide by swallowing an entire bottle of adult aspirin, will be rushed to the hospital to have her stomach pumped out, and will subsequently be interned in a psychiatric hospital in Louisville for a period of approximately six months. There you have it, a simple three-act trauma.

It perhaps seems curious that Constance, in the account she will give of Talia's teenage years, omits this crucial event, considering she is almost alarmingly frank about most of the other gory details of her daughter's life. I may throw some light on the mother's selective reticence by revealing the nature of the occurrence having to do with Eastern State Hospital that was never made clear to Lynnette (and which you may have already guessed). Constance, after bearing five children in a row, at the height of that period of poverty and trailer parks in the early sixties, herself tried to commit suicide with an overdose of sleeping pills (the first of several tries) and spent several months in a local psychiatric hospital, one much less plush than her daughter's. Her stay was not unpleasant, as she managed to rest and relax to a degree otherwise unattainable, and the nursing assistants taught her a lot of card games that she would continue, back on the outside, to play for many years. Nonetheless, the stigma of having spent time in a state psychiatric hospital was great, even in her impoverished circles, and she never refers to that time, even among her husband and children. Although she remembers it all extremely clearly, for her it's a blank space, and she carries this attitude over to Talia's own sojourn.

Jean's sudden change in relations with Talia, signaled by their protracted struggle in her junior year, did not simply arise out of the blue. His campaign of rules and regulations dates precisely to the moment when Talia returned home from the psychiatric hospital and began to manipulate her parents by threatening a rerun of her suicide attempt. Her swallowing the half-bottle of orange aspirin was merely a kiddie-flavored version of the bottle she'd swallowed the first time. Jean felt that they had treated Talia with kid gloves long enough, running themselves thousands of dollars more into debt only to end up right back where they started, after all the doctors telling the parents to do this and not do that, letting them visit their daughter only at certain times and only with Talia's consent. He didn't begrudge her the money, and didn't have anything against all that psychiatric stuff, but he hoped to hell the point of it all wasn't to train them to be obedient parents, because Constance had already trained him into that policy and they'd tried it with Talia even before the suicide thing and it hadn't worked. No, they'd come to a pass where somebody had to lay down the law that if she wanted to live in their house it would be by their rules, and if she couldn't accept that, fine, she was a big girl with lots of life experience and plenty of friends whose families would probably take her in if she couldn't afford her own apartment, especially if she explained to them how unreasonable her parents had acted, or she could move in with Judy, who she wouldn't even have to explain that to since Judy already knew what a son of a bitch her father was.

Jean's own life at the time of Talia's hospital stay wasn't going so well. He'd been offered a very decent position in Louisville, half insurance sales and half administrative, the first good job that had come along since the restaurant fiasco. He'd only half-persauded his family to accompany him, since Constance had kept her job in Lexington, commuting there during the week, where she stayed Monday through Thursday nights at the house of the prosthetist and his wife, and Stephen, not wanting to change high schools in his senior year, had chosen to remain in Lexington with a minister. That left only Jean, Talia, and Lynnette full time in the gigantic house that Jean had rented with an option to buy in a brand-new housing development not even completed yet. Their old furniture wasn't even enough to go in all the rooms, but he had big plans, and if everybody would only give him moral support this venture could turn out to be something stupendous. Then all the business with Talia began, he'd cut his own throat by giving in before when she'd demanded the money for the abortion, now he'd found her lying in her new room with the aspirin bottle on the carpet, and Constance blamed him because it was his fault she had to commute to Lexington and so had been far away from her baby when she needed her mother most. Then the hospital payments started, which he hadn't planned for when he rented such a huge house, the house he and Constance had talked about and dreamed about for many years but didn't exactly need now for just him and Lynnette and Constance on the weekends. Then the problems with work started: they wanted to take him out of what he did best, sales, and put him in administration, which paid more, and they meant it as a promotion for his good performance, and he accepted because he really did need the money, but he recognized it as the beginning of the end, the cycle so familiar he could almost predict it down to the exact minute he'd be fired after the pressures became too great and his drinking started to get in the way. The devastating effects of this failure would be bad enough by themselves without his having in addition to admit to Constance that he had been wrong to take the job in Louisville and disrupt their life in Lexington, not to mention her unspoken but clear accusation that Talia might not have ended up in the hospital if they'd stayed in Lexington, and all he would have to be grateful for is her not knowing he'd given Talia the money for the abortion, a piece of knowledge that would allow her to grind his failure in completely.

But, as I say, Talia was merely gearing up for these events

around the end of 1974. Her indifference toward her father was nothing personal when you got right down to it, since she had more or less the same response to everyone. She would be the first to admit it, as she didn't want to go to the trouble of fostering any illusions about herself. It seemed like her life was just one fucking thing after another. One bad thing happened, and instead of clearing up her karma or whatver the hell they called it, it just led to worse luck, and after that worse luck still. She didn't care to complain about the badness, because people would feel sorry for her, they always had, and she was too burned out to even respond to their sympathy with a polite nod. They might as well pour cold water on cold ashes.

First the thing with the baby. She could understand Billy's upset. Part of his charm was that sweet, wonderful sensitivity of his, a trait she'd sometimes loved in him and sometimes couldn't stand. It made him turn misty-eyed about the miracle of life, and bring over those gauzy photos in the Time-Life books about the different stages of the fetus in the womb, floating in the amniotic sphere like the brilliant and beautiful organisms from slime mold she'd viewed swimming in solution on microscopic slides in biology class. But she couldn't understand her mother's disappointment, or imagine how a woman could get sentimental about the miracle of birth after five times around in nine years, since her contractions had probably been a lot more painful than the half-hour of scraping Talia had to undergo, if you didn't count the bleeding afterward, and contractions were only the beginning. Mrs. Pritchard, who was fond of crude jokes, had once told her that giving birth was like shitting a refrigerator with the door open, or taking your upper lip and trying to pull it back over your head, and she didn't doubt Mrs. Pritchard's word. Even if it came out easy on a fluke, Talia didn't want at thirteen to have to go through the hell she'd put her own mother through. It had taken her so long to make up her mind because all her friends and her mother and Billy had oohed and ahed about the baby, but in the end you were the main one stuck with it, and it stuck with you for keeps and everybody else could go back to their business, just like when she'd gone to that supposed pregnancy consultation center for advice about her options, and they'd given her advice all right, soft music that slowly changed so that it sounded like heavy-metal backmasking while she watched a film, first gauzy images similar to the Time-Life photos, that pretty soon turned into a sick horror show about murdering babies, and when she became agitated they wanted to help, but of course she knew very well that once she'd had the baby those people had no intention of taking care of it themselves, they had children of their own to keep them busy and more pregnancy consultations to attend to. Well, they'd helped her make up her mind. People could have all the babies they wanted as long as they stayed out of her shit.

For a few weeks she felt as empty as she was, cried all the time for no reason, and experienced what she supposed must be motherly feelings of loss. It passed, though, pretty much, and she started to handle it because she figured she must be over the worst, that nothing else could happen to match that. She might as well not have knocked on wood, for all the good it did her. Judy scolded her that she had a habit of bringing bad luck on herself by inviting it, a funny thing for Judy of all people to say. Talia admittedly had been careless in leaving the midnight movie downtown at the Kentucky Theater early, against the advice of friends who wanted her to stay for the second feature, but she would never give those friends or Judy the satisfaction of finding out what a mistake she'd made. A huge mistake, one that time and again tricked her into believing it had left for good and then returned through the back door in the form of a single recurrent nightmare, one strong enough to drive out every single one of the other nightmares she'd accumulated over the years and have the whole place to itself.

He'd wanted to fuck her and then probably kill her, but those were two wishes that didn't come true after he forced her to get on her knees in the parking lot for the blow job with the knife blade flat against the side of her head to hold her steady, exactly the scenario she'd always imagined, because she supposed all women must carry some scenario in the back of their minds—if they walked around alone as much as she did—one against which she'd been warned a hundred times by people who told her she was careless. Well, they'd told her so, if that gave them any satisfaction. He didn't really want her to suck on it or do anything sexual, he was more interested in jamming it down her throat if he could, making her gag, as if the very nature of the experience weren't itself enough to make her gag. Even now she couldn't take too much food into her mouth, she had to take small bites, otherwise her gorge would rise involuntarily. Once or twice he'd tapped the knife blade against her hair with impatience, wanting to hurry up and get this part over with so they could move on to the rest.

But there hadn't been any rest. He hadn't fucked her and he wasn't going to fuck anybody else, not for a long time, if he was even still alive. The way he didn't say a word, as if it were all a standard routine he'd gone through many times before, made her believe he meant to stab her to death afterward, and she wasn't in much of a position to trust in his goodwill to spare her life. So she figured she had nothing to lose and bit him as hard as she could, and felt the sickening crunch of gristle against her teeth. What had happened to him after that she couldn't say, because she ran as fast as she could. She wanted to find out whether he'd live or die, so with the blood still in her mouth, she'd called the police from the pay phone of a twenty-four-hour gas station on Limestone while Rob was on his way to pick her up, refusing to give her name but saying that she'd been raped by a man in the parking lot behind the Kentucky Theater and that he'd been hurt so she thought he might still be there.

The next night she saw the report on the news. They said a trail of blood indicated that the suspect had fled, perhaps to seek medical attention for what appeared to be a severe wound to the groin area. But a check with area hospitals yielded no results, as there had been no admissions for such an injury. Nor had the police found a body anywhere in the surrounding streets or buildings. She wanted to just forget about it, but thanks to two or three news updates that revealed no further information, it became the topic of conversation all over town for more than a week, even among the students at Lafayette. People were fascinated by a rape in which both the rapist and the victim had disappeared into anonymity without any trace except a trail of blood. It pissed her off to hear how quickly the story mutated into something else altogether. A few days after it had happened, she actually heard some old guy in blue coveralls eating lunch in the Pizza Hut telling his co-workers how he knew somebody down at the police station who'd been on duty the night of the attack, and that the girl had come into the police station in the middle of the night, laid a severed penis on the counter, and said, "This man tried to rape me, but I fixed his wagon." The police just hadn't released that piece of information to the public in order to protect the girl.

Why did people have to make up stories like that? What was wrong with them that they couldn't accept a straightforward account of something that was already grotesque enough by itself, that they insisted on making it even more grotesque and sensational? I walked through the parking lot. He pulled a knife on me. I got on my knees. He tried to force his penis down my throat. I bit it hard. He went away bleeding. That's all there was to tell about the matter. But your life couldn't be just a simple shitty bitch, because people had to make a fucking myth out of it.

Everybody wanted to mind your business. Rob was the only one who knew she had been the victim of the attack, and he knew damn well he'd better not tell anybody else. He was so afraid the incident was going to affect their sex life that he kept urging her to go to the Rape Crisis Center for counseling. But she'd had it with counseling after that crap with the abortion thing. Nobody else was going to mess with her head. Of *course* it was going to affect their sex life for a while, what the hell did he expect? She'd been through a fucking sex ordeal, for Christ's sake. If he wanted her to just lie there like a dead animal while he got his rocks off, he had another think coming. Well, she didn't need to work on her relationship with him anyway, because they'd broken up and now she was just dating different guys, not the kind she'd want to marry or anything, but ones who would take her to a concert or a horse show without trying to get heavy.

She wasn't too stupid to realize that certain things about her had changed as a result of the rape. With Elaine married, she and Lynnette finally had their own separate rooms, but now she wished that they had continued to share the same one. Some nights she felt an intense desire to wake up Lynnette and ask her to come in and sleep with her in the double bed that Elaine had left behind, but she knew that after all the grief she'd put Lynnette through over the years—not letting her put up those little animal posters or use her record player, stuff like that— she couldn't really ask that kind of favor. All the windows had catches on them, and she made sure all the doors were locked before going to bed, though they'd always kept them unlocked except when they went on vacation, and still she couldn't make herself feel secure enough to fall asleep very well, and if she did, the slightest creak of wind on the window would wake her. Stupid habits she had abandoned long ago returned, like when she was little and had seen a scary movie. She'd look under the bed and in the closets, or would leave the door open a crack so that light would come in from the hall, and if her mother happened to get up in the middle of the night to go to the bathroom and would turn out the hall light because she didn't want them wasting electricity, if they only knew how high the electric bills were, Talia was afraid to get out of bed long enough to turn on the overhead light.

During the day she kept up a constant companionship with one friend or another, but in the evenings she didn't like to go out unless somebody specifically came to the house to pick her up. What made it worse is that sometimes everybody in the family except her would have someplace to be in the evenings, which left her alone in the house, with lights on in every room and the TV going. Once she'd called over to the grocery where Stephen worked as a sacker and made up a lie, asking him if he could come home because she'd heard a burglar or something snooping around in the backyard and she thought he might still be back there. He told her to call the police, but she replied that, well, she thought the burglar had gone away but it still made her nervous. "We're incredibly busy right now, Talia," said Stephen. "I'll be off in an hour or so, if you can wait until then." She couldn't wait an hour, she really really needed him to please, please come home right that very second. He did, still wearing his name tag and frayed blue tie. They sat at the kitchen table playing rummy, her eyes brimming with tears she was so glad to see him, knowing he was a little irked at her, but it didn't matter, because she knew he would sit and play rummy with her for as long as she needed.

Pretty soon, though, she would put this behind her, like the abortion, except for wanting to know for sure if that bastard had bled to death. Well, it didn't matter. She *had* fixed his wagon, like the guy in the coveralls said. There were other things to think about. It could have been worse if he'd made it as far as the intercourse and she'd gotten pregnant again; at least she hadn't ended up like a hillbilly, with one kid already and another one on the way at age fifteen. She was free. Her whole life was ahead of her, which ought to provide her with some consolation, but only made her depressed to think about. Maybe she should marry somebody. The guys she was dating now were all very nice, for some reason she attracted all the best ones and no matter how good she treated them or bad she treated them they kept being nice to her, and even the macho jerks respected her wishes. When she'd broken up with Rob some kind of bulletin must have gone around, because as soon as they finalized it every other eligible male in the high school started buddying up to her and asking her out. Although in a way it was a blessing, since the dates seemed to take it for granted among themselves that she would naturally take her time and play the field before she made her choice, a circumstance allowing her to keep them all at a distance, in another way it made her tired to even have to think about who she might care for more than the others, and it almost seemed simpler to choose one of the older ones, maybe a senior with a pleasant disposition, laid back enough not to make too many demands on her, and who might be ready for marriage soon after he graduated.

Something had to happen, because she was getting tired of school, of men, of her family, of her own erratic temper, of things you had to struggle against, even of horses, which she used to draw on a sketch pad when she rode her bike out to those farms off Versailles Road, like the farm with the peacock feathers strewn all around the yard of the main house, and sat in the grass outside a white fence the horses would come up to, to see what she was doing. Smoking pot wasn't very interesting anymore. A few tokes before she went to bed used to put her right out, and all it accomplished now was making her more paranoid than she already was. Maybe she could go to art school or something, but that couldn't happen for another two and a half years at least, and in the meantime she'd have to pass all her courses at Lafayette. It was too bad you had to take English and math and civics when all you wanted to do was draw. They ought to make it so you only had to send a sample of your drawings, and if they thought you had a talent for it they'd let you in. But why should she keep it up if the best she could hope for was that somebody might include her drawings in a display of the tenth grade at the mall, where people would stop to take a quick look on their way from the department store to the record store?

She knew she was taking a cynical attitude. What did that mean, though? People coined a term, cynical, and fit you into that personality type, and if you made a negative comment they thought of you as cynical and that was the end of it. If people she knew at school found out she'd done the damage to that guy, they might be a little shocked at first, but not for long. Pretty soon they'd be saying with ultracool respect, "That Talia, man, she can be a pretty mean bitch when she wants to." Instead of thinking of it as something she had to do to save her own life, it would become just one more item in her reputation, like the two or three fights she'd recently gotten into, with a black girl and a couple of white girls and almost been suspended for. The first one had been her fault. It was the first fight like that in her life, and after it ended she meant for it to be her last. But once you got a reputation, other girls thought of you as somebody who fought and would pick an argument with you just to see how you'd react, especially if you were built small and they thought they could take you. She didn't want a reputation. She didn't want to be tough. All she wanted now was to be left alone, but nobody would stay out of her shit, and she'd be damned if she'd stand back while somebody harassed her.

In a way she almost wished Billy would take her back. She knew he would if she simply called him, because the couple of times she'd run into him, once at the drive-in and once at the roller rink, he'd nodded at her and smiled that very sweet, timid smile of his, and too embarassed to talk to her, he'd crunched away across the gravel toward the concession stand, or glided off backward on his skates, because he was a pretty good skater. She realized, though, that she'd only be using him, as someone understanding and tender, someone who loved her so much that he still, after almost two years, sent her in every season unsigned Valentine's cards that she never responded to, someone who believed in all the corny clichés like to have and to hold, for richer or poorer, for better or worse, because she was definitely worse, so what was wrong with being involved with somebody like Billy, who could give her exactly what she yearned for right then, who already knew most of her idiosyncrasies and was willing to put up with them, and, best of all, who belonged to a period before any of the worst stuff had happened? But there was something about him she couldn't love, the very gushy naïveté she craved right now but which sooner or later would begin to bother her and make her say cruel things to him to make him wise up, to make him as callous as herself. She might be a mean bitch, as mean as her reputation, but she wasn't yet so mean as to once again build up Billy's false illusions of their life together as two lovebirds, with love and marriage and a baby carriage. Even putting it that way was another injustice to Billy, who might have grown up just as much as she had in these last two years in his own way—he'd certainly grown taller, and his face was now old enough that she could imagine him as a man. But there would be so much stuff to work through, it made her tired to think about it, and if it didn't work out he would suffer even more than the last time, because he felt everything very deeply, and the way her luck had been running he might try to kill himself.

Having begun my report with such gusto and cheer, I am as reluctant to let it end in Talia's grim state of mind as I am to have the Mileses move from my subdivision, and almost chastise myself for being foolishly led to this impasse by my preoccupation with symmetry. At the same time, Talia's frustration with her claustrophobic self-confinement in the Miles house makes me aware of her impatience to move beyond the strictures that this report and this subdivision have imposed. And her profound sense of deadness reminds me of the symbolic death gesture that will shortly be required of me, namely, my silence. The pains of writing a report, like those of human suffering, sometimes give way to relief when it becomes clear that they are finite and about to end. On the other hand, I must confess that the preceding sentence is more than anything the kind of histrionic utterance and stalling for time that most speeches lapse into when the speaker begins to realize that the jig is up. For the writing of this report has in truth probably been the easiest act of my life as a planning consultant and omniscient narrator of considerable experience. If the subdvision had been an imaginary space, it might have taxed my powers of invention, but its prior creation by the Chocinoe Management Group (in consultation with myself) has allowed the facts to rush forward profusely, all by themselves, leaving me the mere modest task of interpreting them. It would be excessive on my part to wish to continue indefinitely, since I could do so without great difficulty, especially given my omniscience. And, as many authors, and their jerked-around narrators, will attest, good writing is supposed to be difficult.

But as long as I'm stalling for time, let me relate a final anecdote, one with an appropriate sense of closure. On the day the Mileses moved to Louisville, many of the younger inhabitants of Palms Drive found themselves at home, because spring break was under way. The weather had turned unseasonably warm for late winter, a phenomenon that makes sense when one considers that by the calendar winter had in fact passed on two days before. So, along with the Somebodys, a number of people had manned their porches to watch the Mileses load up their furniture. Jean, in accordance with his belief that you never have to pay full price for anything if you're willing to bargain, had secured a moving van the day before at a portion of its stated rental value by playing three rental companies against each other and agreeing to accept, for the fixed bargain price, whatever van became available, which turned out to have low mileage but to be a much larger one than he actually needed. The impressive size of the van, in addition to foreshadowing the oversized new house that he will inhabit the following day, also motivated some of the onlooking neighbors to mosey over and lend their services, including Nick Wharton, who had stayed home too sick with the flu to show up at IBM, but not too sick to work up a sweat lofting armchairs and boxes of books over his head. The older Lajhre boy was there, and his mother Marilee helped to wrap last-minute dishes and odds and ends. Constance, over Marilee's protests, gave her a Wedgwood plate, which had withstood the assaults of five children, but which Constance said would probably get broken en route so she wanted Marilee to have it. The Tadarino brothers, who'd been conditioning for an upcoming all-state wrestling meet, decided it wouldn't hurt to do a little heavy work that day, so they too put in an appearance. The Carla girls didn't offer much practical help, but they had a lot of fun going through Lynnette's old school papers, toys, animal postcards, and outgrown clothes with her.

I'd like nothing better than to leave this collection of neighbors in the company of the Mileses, enjoying the spring day and one another, but the family at hand has miles to go before they sleep (seventy-three and four-tenths, to be exact), and besides, I did promise an anecdote and therefore an incident must occur to make it complete. When Nick's cough began to grow more persistent, Jean tried to persuade him to go home or at least to sit in a lawn chair that hadn't yet been packed, and rest up while he and the Tadarino boys loaded up the washer and dryer. Nick, of course, would hear nothing of it. He'd been a Marine, albeit many years before, and had had to carry a ninety-pound pack on a forced march fifty miles in the rain, and the least he could do was help finish the job for a man who'd been his neighbor for eight years. This might be his last chance to do his good buddy Jean a turn, because you never knew in this life when you might see each other again, and they could have gotten together a lot more than they had, hell, their backyards ran right together without any fence, the kids had always taken advantage of that to play superheroes and have a longer football field, and Lynnette had always known she and the others were free to use the rinky-dink pool, so he was glad she'd treated it like her own, and they as adults could have had cookouts or put their heads together and built a playhouse for both sets of kids to use, they'd even talked about that when Jean came over that one day to help him lay new blacktop on the driveway, did he remember, hell it must have been a hundred degrees that day. And so he'd damn well better not tell Nick Wharton to sit by in a lawn chair while he and the Tadarinos busted their butts hauling the washer and dryer up the ramp, because two grown men could handle the job just fine.

In short, Jean reluctantly agreed to allow Nick to push from the bottom while he guided and pulled the hand truck from the upper end. The washer was strapped securely to the hand truck and the two men started out of the house and up the ramp. A washer is always heavier than you remember, and the more so since Nick, for all his mental preparedness, wasn't able to push as hard as he needed to. Still, with some moaning and groaning and a few cusswords, they made it nearly to the top and would have continued into the bed of the truck if Nick's stamina hadn't given out at the crucial moment, causing his foot to slip and his hands to let go of the underside of the washer. In his soul of souls, Jean would have liked to keep hold of the hand truck, but he had moved a lot of furniture and other heavy things in his day, and his involuntary memory reminded him that he had back problems, and that if he didn't let go he'd probably throw his back out and spend the next two months recuperating in a hospital, a luxury he couldn't afford just then.

Even so, the washer would probably have survived if it had simply plowed over Nick on its way back down the ramp. But anyone who has moved a few washers will know that the washer always goes where you don't want it to. It toppled over the side of the ramp and fell with a crash to the pavement, caving in its side and busting its innards. Nick, of course, when his life had finished passing before him, felt absolutely awful and like a total jerk. He knew that it would take years for him to recover from this embarrassment, and he began the process by offering to run out and buy Jean a brand-new washer that very second, because he knew his neighbor needed to get on the road before it got too late, and to also buy a new dryer to go with it so the Mileses wouldn't have to break up a matched set. Jean told him not to be ridiculous, that washer was on its last legs, the drum would barely spin, and if they used it much longer they'd have to stand inside the drum and stomp on the clothes to get them clean. Finally, he prevailed on Nick to let the matter drop (as he had the washer). Nick accepted Jean's generosity in part because he knew the incident had already been inscribed in the neighborhood lore and would never be erased anyway, and in part because although he would never in a million years have gone back on his word, the prospect of having to shell out several hundred bucks for somebody else's major appliance made him feel even sicker than he already was.

At last the preparations to move were complete, and after hauling the washer over to the curbside to be picked up by the junk men, the family drove off, Jean leading the way in the van, Constance and Lynnette following in the Pontiac, and Stephen (who had agreed to stay with them over spring break and help unpack) bringing up the rear in Jean's '59 Ford pickup truck, a standard shift Stephen had practiced on to obtain his freshly minted driver's license. All the neighbors on their porches waved them off, and before long nothing tangible remained behind as a reminder of the Miles family except the mangled washer sitting by the curb, where it might remain for a long time, since the junk men, in accordance with municipal restrictions on garbage collection, have no intention of picking up something as large as a washer.

It won't remain, though. Jean, waking up with his usual indigestion in the new house in Louisville in the middle of the night, in a bedroom empty except for the bed he and Constance slept in, began to have second thoughts about the washer. With all the moving-out and moving-in expenses, they couldn't really afford to buy a new one just then, and he could probably fix the old one if he tinkered with it. So he got up, dressed, and driving back to Lexington in the '59 pickup, went straight to Garden Springs and the house on Palms Drive. As Constance is fond of saying, he's lucky nobody called the police on him, for he arrived in the wee hours of morning, but he managed to load up the washer and make off with it long before the junk men had a chance to beat him to it.

The ideal of a common language is hampered by the existence of families. I mean family in the sense of a clan, though it's no accident that people also speak of a family of languages, since both supposedly descend from a single ancestor. Family is the symbol of world unity that my fellow members of the Esperanto and Worldbeat Society like to invoke. Our society shouldn't be confused with the Esperanto Society, which we splintered from a few months ago because of differences of opinion, mainly having to do with our passion for meeting in a club featuring worldbeat music, which the Esperanto Society members accuse of being a mishmash and not the kind of music they can dance to. Leaving that rift aside, I've tried to convince my remaining fellow members that the further a family descends from a single ancestor, the more it develops its own peculiarities and becomes attached to a private language, resisting a return to that pristine state. But when I try to convince them of that fact, I might as well be talking to myself.

My own family is a perfect illustration of my theory. One day a long while ago, when all seven of us were riding along the interstate in a VW Bug—and I can remember it was about the time the bales of hay in the fields turned cylindrical instead of square—Lynnette, looking out the window at some cows, pointed at one and named it a *gagoose*. Adam and Eve, or so we're told, took care of descriptive taxonomy long before Lynnette came into the picture. But for our family, a cow is indisputably a gagoose. Even today, in the midst of a soporific trip in the dog days of summer, if two or more of us happen to be passengers in the same car, any of its other dozing occupants run the risk of being startled out of the sweltering drool of a day-nightmare by the bewildering cry, in unison, of *gagoose!* The weekend my father and I drove to New York to collect Judy (who had run off with a boy who changed his mind along the way and turned left toward California), she and I occupied the backseat together during the trip home in the middle of the night. While my father chain-smoked in absentminded silence, like a professional driver hired for our diversion, Judy and I passed the time peering past the glare of fingerprint smudges on the glass into the dark fields of Pennsylvania and Ohio. We thought we might catch a glimpse of a stray gagoose still up at that hour, or better yet on its side, as they were sometimes rumored to sleep. But you might have imagined from our lack of success that they were mythical beasts we'd made out of thin air, instead of a creature already in existence that Lynnette had simply named. That's how creation works for us descendants—a deformation of the real that makes it live for us.

I've looked into the etymology of the word *gagoose* to determine what Lynnette might have had in mind at the time. If the term is simply an ellision of *gag* and *goose*, then *gag* of course derives from Middle English *gaggen*, i.e., *strangle.* This violent first step in the preparation of a goose for the table suggests the next step, a phrase with a similar feel, *my goose is cooked.* It's well known that children at an early stage of language acquisition often group animals according to their own peculiar logic, as when they go around calling everything in animal form *doggie*, or in this case *goose.* Lynnette has always shown an extraordinary sensitivity toward animals, as when our poodle (one of an ill-fated succession) developed a mange and had to be put to sleep. My family's policy was usually to leave Lynnette in the dark about any situation of crisis, whether it concerned alcohol, money (the perennial top two), a lost job, a suicide attempt, an unexpected move to new lodgings, or having the dog put to sleep.

Neighborhood lore has it that dogs always sense when they're about to be taken somewhere unpleasant, no matter how well the family tries to disguise the sinister truth with beckoning baby talk and bug-eyed exaggerations of good cheer. But Gemini, our poodle, wasn't especially bright to begin with, and though cynical by nature, he'd grown too morose with mange to speculate in much detail about what the immediate future might hold for him.

Lynnette had her premonition, though. Our family, myself included, no doubt kept facts from her out of an unconscious wish to maintain her innocence, to make her the repository of alternative endings, to turn her as the youngest into our family's oral historian, one whose unwitting unreliability would, at some always unspecified future date, reconstruct a more attractive version of events for listeners in the next generation. And these earlier self-censorings of ours probably account in large part for Lynnette's developing an extensive private language, one different in emphasis from what we had intended for her to develop. She was in full possession of the sixth sense that Gemini lacked. Even though I participated, in the beginning at least, in these familial fictions, Lynnette invariably came to me with her uncomfortable questions because she knew that while my slippery code of ethics at that time permitted me to neglect passing on information to her, it wouldn't allow me to evade a direct question. So when, in the midst of helping me address a batch of envelopes to various cereal makers who had tempted me with valuable prizes in exchange for proof-of-purchase seals, she strategically asked, "Is Gemini about to be dead?" I had to answer that he was.

Groping among the dustballs under the couch and finding Gemini there, she took him into the bathroom and placed him in warm water, where he trembled with one paw poised in the air. With an acrid medicated shampoo the vet had recommended, she gave Gemini a slow bath, devoting to him attentions akin in spirit to the elaborate funeral preparations for a pharaoh. And of course she spoke to him in the esoteric dialect she'd developed for this particular poodle, and which had spread not only among us siblings, but also to selected friends, and its currency among us nearly drove my parents insane. I think they almost would have preferred to see us all afflicted with Gemini's mange rather than with this peculiar way of talking. It was known among us as Fyyewz language (that was the poodle's secret name) and was nearly incomprehensible to the adult ear, spoken through a tongue either rolled or pressed against the roof of the mouth. On someone who didn't know its provenance (i.e., a passerby in the supermarket), it made the impression that the speaker was retarded.

"Ana baey syew bod, ya Fyyewz," Lynnette crooned, lathering a naked red patch of skin on the poodle's haunch. It would be difficult to write a grammar of Fyyewz language, since it fell into disuse so soon after its inception, and besides, none of us was truly fluent in it except Lynnette. But having been an initiate, I can give a rough translation of her utterance as "Everything's going to turn out, Gemini." My translation is inadequate in failing to communicate that the statement isn't based on deception or false hope, but is intended as an understated declaration of solidarity and, if anything, an unflinching preparation for what must come to pass.

Lynnette needs only the barest outward vibration to pick up on. In my room I kept an aquarium and a fishbowl, and it became her habit to daily feed my neon tetras and the lone Siamese fighting fish. As I sat at my desk reading a book, not even conscious I was brooding over the prospect of yet another sudden change of schools (which didn't occur), or merely troubled by what psychologists now like to call "free-floating anxiety," she'd watch the flakes of fish food drift down the water like the snow in her paperweight (her simile, because she was intrigued by how it would feel and sound to walk on the ocean floor, or in a snowfall that took place underwater), and in a voice full of pity she'd murmur, "Poor Stephen. Poor Stephen." More than once, especially during adolescence, but even now, in times when I'm inclined to feel sorry for myself, that nomenclature causes me a mixture of pleasure and embarrassment. I suspect at such moments that I've been grouped in Lynnette's taxonomy with the poodles and the cows, the *gagoose*s and the Fyyewzes, a member of their species, genus, or family. I begin to wonder, even if I'm far away from her, whether she has some vague premonition about me, and whether or not my goose is cooked.

Another possibility for *gagoose*, dating back to an expression that officially entered the English language in the seventeenth century, is that she had picked *gadzooks* out of the dictionary of her unconscious. It's a mild oath bastardized from the exclamation *God's hooks!*—a reference to the nails in the crucifix. Lynnette has never worked up much interest in religion, but perhaps she saw in the cow's face a stoical look, an admission that for as long as it had no choice but to stand behind barbed wire on Interstate 75 breathing in the carbon monoxide of hundreds of thousands of automobiles, day in, day out, it would have to develop an attitude that might help it weather its given environment. *Gadzooks* is archaic to be sure, and not likely to have been heard among our acquaintances, but it's the kind of pithy saying that would have come in very handy among my sisters and me, in situations where words failed us.

In a mobile home of two rooms scarcely large enough to go around its two beds, one of which was shared by the five of us, and on whose collapsible springs we pitched back and forth during windstorms like wretched waifs in the steerage of a seventeenth-century brigantine—when our parents' nightly discussions about finances turned them on each other in spite of themselves and reached the inevitable pitch of recriminations, not a syllable of which it was in our power to escape—wouldn't it have been a relief if Lynnette, squashed and suffocating as she was in the middle of the sinking mattress, sweating even more on account of the covers pulled tight over her head, had suddenly thrown them off, sat up, and shouted, "Gadzooks! When will the five of us get a decent night's rest?"

She never would have shouted it, though. Lynnette, unlike the rest of us, doesn't believe in shouting. It isn't so much that she wants to recede from conflict. Although that would be her natural tendency, she's nonetheless probably the least passive among us, in her way. Lynnette doesn't shout because for her language is a private tic by its nature, and for all her flair in engineering word systems, the Esperanto and Worldbeat Society would no doubt interest her very little. Her predilection instead would be to name a pet salamander Gadzooks, as if it could almost have once been used in the making of a Japanese horror movie, a gargantuan fiend that had run amok in its day, striking terror into the hearts of defenseless citizens, but which was now quite content to wallow and burrow with weak limbs in Lynnette's windowbox to keep its smooth skin moist and eat the snail or housefly she punctually brought.

I'm often referred to as the linguist in the family, but perhaps Lynnette's talent has been overlooked, not because her contributions to our family's adaptation of the English language have been ephemeral, but rather because they've permeated our speech habits so completely. Usage panels, in recommending which neologisms are to be made official by their inclusion in a dictionary, tend to be conservative, in the older sense of that word, waiting to see which ones will survive in the vox populi. There's little chance of Lynnette's contributions making it into any of the known dictionaries. A new dictionary will have to be made to accommodate her neologisms, if I can ever get around to writing it—not out of whole cloth, which goes without saying, because every dictionary has its etymology. But in this case the etymology itself might have to be invented, since Lynnette, when asked what a *gagoose* has to do with a cow, always shrugs and answers, "It doesn't have anything to do with a cow. It *is* a cow."

There was this insane person, well not really insane but kind of a crazy aspirin-eating bitch who kept saying *Not tonight Rob I have a headache Not tonight Rob I have a headache* and every time she said *Not tonight Rob I have a headache* she'd take another aspirin and Rob would run for a glass of water until pretty soon she ended up in a psych hospital, not the kind with chains screwed to the wall, but the most spacious cloister she could ever hope to freak out in, with forsythia, hyacinths, and rose gardens visible from every room, blooming all over the grounds, with botanists instead of lobotomists, the kind of place where the nurses are so devoted and quietly sure about knowing their shit that she suspects they're medieval nuns, although they all seem to have bachelor's degrees and master's degrees, and the saintly pilgrimages they take in their time off are to spots like Saint-Tropez where they can snorkel, or jetting off like the Flying Nun to Santa Barbara for continuing education seminars in Psychosocial Complications of the Post-Suicidal Patient.

Or this hospital is like a hotel, a big Cuban casino hotel with tapestries and curved wood banisters and stained-glass Tiffany lamps, an overdecorated Catholic kind of place so swinging with therapeutic social activities that any minute you expect Ricky Ricardo to bust in with marimbas and rhumbas and ka-choom-bom-bays, shouting *Loooo-sie! Loooo-sie!* like the nickname of his favorite prostitute, the one who always puts out with a big smile and never has a headache. When the crazy bitch comes to her senses in this place, her head is pounding like the timbales in the percussion section of Ricky's orchestra, she has a bigger headache than the one she took the aspirin to get rid of. And when she asks the intern, one just out of med school and still a little freaked about what the hell he's supposed to be doing to manufacture wellness, when she says *Oh Doctor, how can I get rid of this splitting headache?* he doesn't mind playing the vaudevillian, he knows how to do at least that for the length of his five-minute gigs, to help get to the punch line of the joke she started, even though it's a bad one, as much of a groaner as her life so far, so he glances at her chart upside down on his way out the door and says *Take two aspirin and call me in the morning.*

Oh, oh, an attack of humor, ill humor at that, I have a stitch in my side, I hope it's a surgeon knocking at the door. But no, it's Suzanne, my main day nurse, who also doubles as an activities coordinator here, who's very sweet and considerate, always knocking before she enters, always teaching us new stuff you can do with your hands like play some xylophone thing called a kalimba or make God's eyes. I want to please her so she won't look disappointed after yesterday successfully teaching sex education with rubbers and anatomical dolls to severely retarded adolescents and now failing to motivate such a simple case as me to join in a little macrame. But right now I'm not in the mood to function, not even for her. She explains to me that *comity,* that word I've been wondering about since I arrived, means a friendly social atmosphere, social harmony, sort of a community of mutual understanding, it's what they work for here instead of having us lie in our beds like teenage zombies, and frivolous routines can be a good thing, especially, she says, in a concentration camp like this place. The emphasis on the words *concentration camp* is her way of downplaying her basic irrepressible optimism about life in general and the fact that she loves her job and this place and all of us. She knows that a little cynicism goes a long way toward reaching me.

But not today. My brother Stephen hithchiked up from Lexington to visit me on Thursday and in his melancholy cautious way he was trying to ask me why I hate him so much, but I still don't really know why, so I couldn't give him an answer or even let him ask the question. I could tell by the way he kept loitering on making chitchat that he sensed how bummed out I was that particular afternoon and he was afraid to leave because he thought I was going to try to kill myself again. Stupid Stephen! I was only down, I didn't feel then like I do now, if I had I really could have given you something to feel anxious about. His lack of confidence in me made me so angry I forced him to leave. His visit upset me enough that I told the psychiatrist, with Suzanne backing me, not to let Mom or Dad or the rest of them see me this coming Mother's Day weekend, the great prefabricated family holiday, even though they want to take me along for the Sunday dinner, allowable on account of my recent stability. Then Rob was here to find out if I'd be released anytime soon, he's thought of me a lot since we split and did I need anything, an extra blanket or a reconciliation, before he moved off to Yellowstone to work for the forest service. He smuggled me in a nickel bag, which I smoked some of about an hour ago. Suzanne has a hunch I'm high off something besides my legal institutional buzz, but she's smart enough to let the matter slide and have this be one of my days for bonus erratic behavior, a luxury she allows me from time to time as one of the unwritten items in the contract between us. She's a good negotiator, and got me to agree the very first week of my internment—or is it my interment? I always get those two words mixed up—anyway, she got me to agree during my first week here not to try suicide again without consulting her first. I've kept to that bargain and others I've made because she cuts me slack when I need it most, but doesn't when I don't, and she can almost always judge the situation correctly.

At the moment I don't even feel like standing up, and the only comity I plan to create between now and bedtime is to lie here and wait for frivolous thoughts to occur, a kind of lie-down comity routine. Two weeks ago I thought I was making progress, I was off all medications and the only sickness I felt was a little homesickness, the one sickness I probably need to cultivate. Even that big split-level house with no furniture in it and with a muddy yard surrounded by split-level skeletons and vacant lots was starting to seem homier than this place, and I could imagine returning to it and having the den full of all my family and old friends and boyfriends, all of us getting along in a group marriage, listening to acid rock on Lynnette's old Close-n-Play with the penny taped to the record arm, a suburban hippie commune. But this morning I just want to tell everybody I've ever known to fuck off, I don't want to be part of any communities or friendly atmospheres, and if for some reason I end by not living up to the one big promise in my contract with Suzanne, it won't matter because she won't be able to punish me with that involuntary look of disappointment, her biggest secret weapon, the one that's so effective because she doesn't even know about it, but what good is a contract that can't be enforced by anything except my supposed conscience. Suzanne's one weakness is that she operates on the principle that everybody has a conscience.

The best argument in Stephen's favor as far as I'm concerned is that right now he's playing the part of a singing, tap-dancing Dracula in Lafayette's spring musical, *Dracula Baby.*

iiiit's good to be bad
it's right to be wrong
be callous and cruel
a regular ghoul
and you'll get along

it's good to be bad
that's wisdom because
the bigger your crime
the higher you'll climb
in public applause

That's my theme song, that's the kind of role I was born to play, and I envy Stephen for landing it. But his problem is that he's not enough of a real bastard for a role like that, I mean a real goddamned fucking bastard. Oh sure, he has a hot temper sometimes, just as bad as mine, and can make cutting remarks worthy of me in my most vicious mood, but almost always in service of trying to do The Right Thing. He believes, in a minor-chord sort of way, that our family can rehabilitate itself. He gets depressed after fights and wants to make up rather than nurse a grudge to absolute sharpness, he co-features you in poetry he writes, and as your fair percentage gives you a copy of those touching and soul-searching verses about all his glaring faults and yours too. To figure out Life he listens to "Funeral for a Friend":

> I wonder if those changes have left a scar on you
> And all those burning hoops of fire
> that you and I passed through

He plays it a hundred and eighty-seven times in the room next to yours, until you've memorized the lyrics in spite of yourself and are so sick of it that you wish you were his friend just so it could be your funeral. He's into coffins because they're geometrical and maudlin, but he's too full of goodfuckingwill toward men to make an indecent evil Count. At the end of *Dracula Baby*, so he tells me, a reformed Dracula comes out for the final chorus-number extravaganza wearing rose-colored glasses that let him see in daylight without shriveling up, and he marries the nurse that takes care of Lucy in the sanatorium, so maybe the role is right for Stephen after all. I could imagine him marrying Suzanne, then they could spend the rest of their lives at Our Lady of Comity nursing me back from despair, and Stephen would only occasionally suck my blood when he felt the call of the old vampire ways too strongly, also because I would beg him from time to time to sink his fangs into my neck, just to preserve the seductive loving enmity between us, the irresistible sickness that lies somewhere between death and the damnation of life everlasting.

LUCY (wearing a gown as diaphanous as angel wings, and the

desperately sweet face of a chorister on angel dust): Oh Dracula, I mean Oh Doctor, isn't it time for another dose of my antidepressant? Those long needles the nurse uses put me in a panic, and I'd feel so much more comforted if you'd give me the injection with your teeth instead. I'm used to them.

SUZANNE (in fresh, crisp, professional, white A-line skirt offset by Adidas and a feminine, pink, peasant-style blouse—no Victorian bustle or starched cap): Lucy, the Doctor's teeth aren't sterile. In any case, he and I in our last collaborative practice consultation determined that since you've stopped singing "Fly with Me Over Night's Black Sea," all your medications can be eliminated. Besides, to be completely up front with you, you have a dependent personality, and if you keep taking these antidepressants you'll turn into a drug fiend, a medicated monster. Nursing's expanded role today allows me to offer you patient education and alternate forms of therapy. Let's try some relaxation techniques.

LUCY (cannily sulking): Drug fiend! Dependent personality! You're the ones who encouraged my dependence, wouldn't rest until I put my trust in you, and now you ask me to take responsibility for my actions cold turkey.

DR. DRACULA BABY (still attached to his cape and certain traces of nineteenth-century melancholia; removing his rose-colored glasses with a flamboyant bedside manner): My darling Nurse Suzanne, let's not let our clearsighted modern diagnostic techniques discount the night vision that sees into the black depth of Lucy's brooding humors. (Flourishing his cape and tapdancing around the bed.) Perhaps we should revampire—I mean, revamp 'er treatment to include the tried-and-true bleeding method of my Transylvanian ancestors. She may feel dead afterward, but she'll live on for all eternity.

SUZANNE (seductively, draping her arms around his neck and looking into his hypnotic eyes): Yes, sweetheart, yes, just like us. (Sings, pianissimo)

Fly with me over night's black sea where no mortal man can go
High we'll be with our two souls free of the dull, dull earth below
While common men lie tossing in their beds
With common dreams inside their common heads
We'll travel where the stars are all afire
Up where the wind sings of desire.

Now that we're alone, I can tell you in confidence, Dracula Baby, that I fear these visits from old boyfriends of hers may push her despondence too far and take her precious life from us. I've always been an outspoken advocate of patient rights, but the presence of these boys is reawakening all of her sexual anxieties and guilt—you know, the rape, the abortion, and the horrible way she treated her former lovers. (Removing her arms from his neck, suddenly aware again of Lucy's presence.) Oh, I'm sorry, Lucy. I hope my little tête-à-tête with the Doctor doesn't constitute unprofessional behavior.

ROB and BILLY and THE ATTACKER (all doing a mad rhumba through the sanatorium, shaking their shoulders and impersonating Ricky Ricardo): Loooosie! Loooosie! Loooosie!

LUCY: Please, Doctor, sink your fangs into me. Give me a lobotomy. Give me a libidomy. I repent of all my trespasses against my former fiancés, whom I now renounce for a life in the sanatorium. Just don't bring around any more men!

ALL (Final chorus number; LUCY in her diaphanous gown doing a buck-and-angel-wing):

You say libido
And I say loboto
Let's call the whole thing ooooooofff!!

Yes, a life of devotion would suit me. That's my preferred role: a novice, a saint, a holy terror. I'd adopt the sweet name of a fifteen-year-old with a sordid past, but with a Vegas ring to it: Lolita Falana. I'd hold the microphone too close to my lips to get that fuzzy sound, and draw out the ends of certain words to jazz the song up.

I gotta be meee-ah

Unfortunateleee-ah
What else can I beee-ah but what I am

But I never could sing worth a crap, I'm naturally hoarse, or maybe from all the pot and menthol cigarettes. No, it would have to be a stand-up act, I'd come out in a frumpy blue nun's habit and baggy pantyhose. My stage name? Our Lady of Comity herself.

How's everybody feeling tonight? In a good mood? I don't mind saying I'm a little suicidal myself, as can sometimes happen to a woman with a habit. But you know, girls, as my mother, who worked in cosmetics, used to say, even when you're in a perpetual state of suffering and anguish, that's no reason you have to look like hell. I was thinking about her advice the other day as I was walking through the chapel searching for the chaplain, chewing on the ends of my fingers, an absolute wreck, and suddenly I saw Jesus hanging there on the cross. I got an inspiration. I said, "Jesus, who does your nails? Can you give me a referral?"

Mom, oh Mom, why did you teach us to stay fresh and feminine even at our most fucked-up hour? I take twenty-minute showers and always sprinkle cornstarch over my breasts. I put on Chanel and shave my legs even when I wear jeans with holes in the knees and my Black Sabbath shirt with the bleach stains on it. Right before I swallowed the bottle of aspirin, I packed a travel kit with mascara, eyeliner, and unscented deodorant. I don't know where I thought I was going. Judy's the same as me, she stays clean and delectable, but for who? You don't know that Judy just got the clap from a guy who doesn't wash his hair and probably doesn't change his underwear very often, if he even wears any. She's only one of several women he smears himself over. How that knowledge would make you cringe, and this: I want to look like shit, like a nervous wreck, a madwoman in a madhouse, a self-neglecting saint with bags under my eyes and rat's nests in my hair, a Saint Stinking Rose, wrapped in a stinking soiled garment, a nasty habit, so I can offer some visible proof of what I am and how I feel, so I can be here, where you put me, with a vengeance, so men will find me repulsive and stop falling on their knees before me or making me fall on my knees before them, so that if they found me sleeping on the street downtown they would step over me or go around me to avoid the smell, and I could lie there serene, undisturbed, rotting in my moist rags.

All of them tell me how attractive they find me, even the psychiatrist can't restrain his little ongoing flirtation with me, I always smell so nice, and he probably fantasizes, within the limits of professional behavior of course, that my apricot douche is all for his sake. And what about you? Did you have an asylum romance to pass the time at Eastern State while you were begging Dad every day to have you released, but he couldn't oblige, not after the first time he signed you out and you repaid his trust by wandering off while he was at work, nobody could find you until you surfaced that night in a service-station washroom over in Idle Hour wearing a nightgown and holding a pair of scissors? Was the place itself horrendous, with electrodes and concrete and padlocked doors, or just your knowledge that you belonged there? You never talk about it, so I can only imagine Eastern State, like everybody else—including the patients here—as the Frankenstein's Castle you go to if nobody has the money to put you here in the elite facility. But in three months, the same amount of time I've been interned, you came out of there better and stronger than you went in, didn't you, well enough to take over running a family of the five kids who put you there in the first place, you treated your time there as vocational training and made crisis management into a career. Maybe it wasn't so bad, then, or am I just a more messed up and weaker specimen of womanhood? Maybe I need someplace less progressive, where they chain you to the wall and give you shock therapy more frequently than showers and there's no middle ground between getting well and going Screaming Yellow Zonkers.

Suzanne has worked at Eastern State and doesn't go into the kinds of specifics I want to know, because of what she calls confidentiality, meaning none of my damn business. She says it's a decent hospital, underfunded and understaffed, but with a capable, caring workforce and a healthy atmosphere. I might believe her if she weren't such an optimist about everything, if she talked less about wellness and more about sickness. There must be some differences. Here, it's not so hard for me to get out, but instead it's hard for people to come see me, because I have the luxury of deciding who gets visiting privileges. You and Dad are paying out the ass to put me up in this resort, this last resort, but you can't even take me out to help you celebrate Mother's Day unless I give the word. Maybe I shouldn't punish you and myself on your special day, I should let you come visit me alone and we can have some girl talk, compare notes as one asylum veteran to another, as Our Lady of Comity to her mother superior.

OLC: Welcome to *Girl Talk*, the live, unedited, unexpurgated talk show where you get to hear actual girls talk about their actual problems and neuroses. Today's guest is My Mom, who— if you don't mind my saying so, Mom—we're *very* lucky to have with us, since she's tried to waste herself on more than one occasion.

MM: I don't mind at all, honey. You know, dear, my internment was so much more difficult than yours, because your father and I were poor at the time, and I couldn't afford a private room, so I was in a ward with, oh, around sixty or seventy people who were wailing and gnashing their teeth, impersonating werewolves and drooling on me, and whenever I made the least complaint, one of the attendants would come around and force my head under water for long periods of time. The whole experience was very similar to the conditions under which I gave birth to you. Yes, I think yours was my most difficult delivery. It was Eastern State all over again. But me and your father—me, especially— have worked very hard to overcome our limitations so that when it came your time to choose an asylum, you could have all the little luxuries and advantages that I never did. We wanted a better life for you.

OLC: I'm glad you mentioned that, Mom, because I've been wanting to tell you and our studio audience how incredibly guilty I feel about the sacrifices you and Dad are making for me right now, which I in no way deserve. Our listeners may be interested to know that the staggering expense of keeping an airhead like me aloft, more costly than the Goofy float in the Macy's Day Parade, is driving you two once again back into debt and exacerbating Dad's alcohol problems. And, according to Jeanne Dixon's latest predictions in the *Star*, the two of you, along with Lee Majors and Farrah Fawcett, and Mr. and Mrs. Robert Redford, are headed for splitsville in the coming year, mostly on my account.

MM: It's sweet of you to notice. But we've really learned to take everything in stride, because this latest stunt of yours is nothing more than an encore performance of the exciting showmanship and dramatic flair we've come to expect from our little problem child. You just wouldn't be you if you weren't stirring up a ruckus and—as Stephen made a point of reminding me in one of our recent shouting matches—causing us, in our constant spectatorly dumbfoundment at you, to neglect Lynnette's needs.

OLC: Still, I'd like to insist on my little modicum of guilt, as a special treat in honor of your consenting to be with me and no one else on this beautiful springtime Mother's Day. It's a chance for you to witness something more dazzling than an ego the size of a parade float: I mean a rare display of self-reproach, from someone you once so eloquently accused of being biologically incapable of feeling any emotion except rage toward other people. Here's a bouquet of forsythia, which I illegally picked for you on the premises, the charming gesture of your favorite incorrigible ragamuffin, and even if I'd bought this bouquet it would have been with your money anyway, since I have none. And now, as an added special treat, let's bring on our surprise mystery guest, the neglected, rejected, but never dejected youngest member of our family, my little-known sister of charity, Lynnette!

But she doesn't appear on command. Or if she does, she doesn't say anything, and dead air follows, the nightmare of every performer whose livelihood depends on keeping the words coming. Lynnette's silence at this moment is as terrifying to me as if we two were onstage together in a play, not a musical but a simple melodrama, all about me naturally, and she began to drop her lines and could only give me a pleading look. The longer she's unable, or unwilling, to say what's required of her, the more she rattles me, and I lose my temper because I think she's doing it on purpose. I supply dialogue for her, anything to keep things moving, and this is what she says:

What would happen if you died? It's not a question I would ever ask you, or anyone, and I've tried to keep from even thinking about it myself, because I don't really understand exactly why you did what you did, or how anybody could. But what if? It would be nice for you if we all went crazy with grief and hung ourselves the next day, which would probably be your last request, but if we said that would happen we'd be pulling your leg, the one that tends to go to sleep as if it had premature rigor mortis. Don't you remember when Dad's father had a stroke—we never called him granddaddy or anything, just Bart, because he never looked at us when we went to visit; he mumbled and stank of tobacco and sat in front of the TV watching the golf tournament and eating bourbon balls and Red Man. We thought he was really old, like ninety or something, because of the way he acted, but Judy said he was only in his sixties. When we had to go to Berea for the funeral, and afterward everybody was sitting around Mamaw's living room drinking coffee, they gave you and me dollars and let us walk up to the movie house. On the way I asked you if a stroke had anything to do with golf, if he'd died from watching too many golf tournaments, and you told me the joke about the golf gun making a hole in Juan, and we were laughing pretty hard. Then we were singing the Name Game, using Bart's name, *Bart Bart mo Mart banana fana fo Fart*, and we could never get past Fart, we were giggling way too much, so we kept starting over and saying it again, then one of us actually farted by accident, and that put us over the edge completely. Because of that song, I can never think of him as anything but

Bart the Fart, the match-up didn't even seem like a coincidence because he was kind of an old fart. That's sad to say, to realize that nothing is left of him for me but that smelly name and a joke about a golf gun, but even though I really wanted to like Bart and think of him as my grandfather, he was just this person who didn't seem to give much of a hoot about anybody else.

Try to die around a holiday, like Mom's brother Byron did, so that you can ruin the season for your siblings the way he did for them. That way you'll make sure we don't start to forget you as the years go by, talking about you less and less and feeling nothing so much as a vague, subconscious sense of relief that the source of torment is gone, the ingrown toenail that used to bring constant tears to my eyes, but which I'm cured of and so don't give a thought to anymore. Mother's Day would be a good choice, so we could get all choked up on our roast beef and mashed potatoes each year remembering how hard we'd tried to per-suade you to come with us to celebrate that day, and how even as we were wolfing down strawberry shortcake, you were lying on the floor of your hospital room almost unconscious, crying feebly for help because you'd poignantly changed your mind at the last moment, you wanted to live but it was too late and we, like the nurses, remained fatally out of earshot. Dad would be especially eaten up with remorse because he'd found you the first time and so could visualize in detail the probable position of your body, the feel of its weight when he'd picked you up off the floor, and despite the fact that he'd saved your life on that occa-sion by calling the ambulance, all his paternal mistakes and inat-tentions would return to him for a second time with a vengeance just as vivid, increased rather than diminished by the fact that he'd been responsible for prolonging your miserable life a few extra months.

Stop me, Lynnette. Why do you keep silent? Why do you let me put this poison in your mouth? In order to feel it corroding your stomach wall, the place of gut feelings, so you'll begin to intuit why I did what I did, how anybody could? If denying you understanding means sparing you the experience of how you use up those last hyperheaded thoughts in the minutes while you're waiting for the stuff to take effect, let me leave you ignorant, and call that cowardice my one small kindness to you, a kindness I can cling to in case I go to be with Fulton, 'cause Fulton had a steamboat, steamboat had a bell, steamboat went to heaven, Fulton went to helllll-o operator, give me a volunteer from the audience, one who will talk back to me, keep up the banter, because if I'm condemned to spend eternity shovelin' coal and passin' the hot potato, I'd like to keep my mind off my situation, and besides, I need someone suitably keyed up to assist me in the DEATH-DEFYING feat of trying to ESCAPE from the ETERNAL FLAMES of the BURNING LAKE OF FIRE, the place so diabolically dangerous that not even Evel Knievel has tried this stunt. I will be using no aids or devices of any kind except this child's toy, this simplest of aerodynamic contraptions, which was damaged when two little angels, all dressed in white, tried to get to heaven on the end of a kite, but the kite got broken and down they both fell, instead of going to heaven, they all went to—one little angel will be my sister Judy, who, like me, has been high as a kite so often that both of us feel rigorously conditioned for this challenge. Judy, how are you feeling about today's impending flight?

JUDY: Just super, Angel Two. I've been in training a long time for this one. Though I am a little concerned about the means of transportation. I had the impression, considering where we are, that we were two little devils, all dressed in red, who tried to get to heaven on the end of a thread.

ANGEL TWO: Yes, there's been some exegetical dispute among our friends and family members about that verse, and certainly the way in which the Creator of All Things understands its meaning has a direct bearing on our likelihood of escaping the fiery lake. But I personally feel the thread metaphor to be a reference to our former fleshly existence, in which we were always hanging to life, sanity, and so on by a thread. Your own journey here, for instance, came as the dramatic upshot of a severe case of serum hepatitis—contracted from shooting up heroin—in which you lay for many days, deliriously yellow and emaciated, your life suspended by a mere thread. The situation looked hopeless, but it was quite possible that you could have, like a crack air force ace over enemy lines, survived that Yellow Peril and lived to fight again.

JUDY: Roger, Angel Two. I unfortunately didn't. The only important question now is whether a couple of atheists like us—

ANGEL TWO: Agnostics.

JUDY (rolling her eyes): Oh, right. As if that made a difference. The question now is whether a couple of atheist-slash-agnostics like us—alike as two peas in a kamikaze cockpit in our utter disregard of the value of life, which we casually cast aside like a dirty needle to be picked up again when we need it—can fly to our salvation on the end of a kite.

ANGEL TWO: I *never* in my entire life said I was an atheist, Judy. I don't deny the existence of God, I just don't think it's knowable, or at least I don't *think* I think it's knowable.

JUDY: Whatever. This academic angst of yours is about as exciting as trying to decide how many angels can dance on the head of a pin. But I suppose the fact that you'd now like to consider yourself one of those angels gives the theological debate an importance it never had until your little moment of truth.

ANGEL TWO: It isn't fucking academic. I'm *dying*.

JUDY: Dead.

ANGEL TWO: Dying, and I'm scared as shitless as you were when I was wearing that hospital gown and mask, standing over your bed holding a hand so yellow it looked like resin was coming out your pores, and you said, "Sweetie, whenever I close my eyes I want you to shake me. I know I look weak, but I'm a teenager and my bones are still soft." You can call me other names besides Sweetie now if you want, but you can't deny me the right to be scared about what happens to me in the afterlife.

JUDY: Fine, I'd grant that in a second, except that the truth is you're not dying and you're not dead. You're lying in a comfortable adjustable bed, remembering your first half-assed attempt to end it all, and trying to decide, in the most premeditated way, whether you have the nerve to come close enough again to work the crisis to your advantage afterward. That's the thing about you; you plan all your turmoil out in advance like a goddamned mercenary. Either go for the gusto, babe, or stop bitching about your dilemma.

ANGEL TWO: You go to hell. Your real objection is that my anguish doesn't measure up to yours. Was choosing aspirin too mundane to suit your sense of appropriateness? Next time I'll borrow one of your dirty syringes for that little extra flair. How many eons do I have to burn in hell before I get a sympathetic word from you?

JUDY: Don't panic, babe. Maybe you will get to heaven on the end of a kite. I forgot to tell you that when Billy heard you'd been rushed to the emergency room, he started singing: Earth Angel, can you hear me? Earth Angel, can you see me? Are you somewhere up above? And am I still your own true love? Doowah doo-wah.

ANGEL TWO: God, you piss me off. Don't drag Billy into this argument. You always save him for when you've really got me worked up. I see now why you've been goading me. Billy ran to my big sis for advice whenever he and I had problems, so you have this sisterly erotic thing about him, and you blame me for fucking him over. Why don't the two of you have a baby together, so you can make up for all my hardnesses to him?

JUDY: Make up for all your hardnesses? I think I'd rather attempt something easier, like trying to get to heaven on the end of a thread.

Please don't say that, Judy. Please don't, because I brought you here for comfort, since I, like you, couldn't stand the quiet. You said your bones were soft and for me to shake you when you closed your eyes, and I did, very gently, and talked to you about mud flying up behind the horses' hooves at the trotting track when we won the Exacta on a three-dollar ticket, and Robert Plant's voice, the voice we said we'd most like to fuck. I kept talking until the nurses made me leave so you could get some rest. Now I'm asking you to return the favor. I'm not even saying I deserve it. Or what about you, Billy? I've avoided calling you to me, but you came of your own free will, or Judy brought you up, not me, so maybe it's all right for me to ask you to finish the song about angels and devils, with the funny cornball ending in which everything turns out so hunky-dory that you wonder what all the fuss was about. Just sing:

> But the thread got broken and down they all fell
> Instead of going to heaven, they all went to—
> Don't get excited, don't lose your head,
> Instead of going to heaven, they all went to bed!

It was a pleasure to skip school and lie in the bottom bunk together with the lava lamp on and smell your strawberry body oil. Sometimes we hung a sheet from the top bunk to feel like we were in a canopy bed. You could never get over the fact that you were actually with me, you just ran your hand down my silky side and said Talia, Talia, over and over again, and I want you to repeat my name as many times as it pleases you, if you're foolish enough and reckless enough to attach some worth to that name and believe it a privilege to be permitted to come close to me, then I want to grant you that privilege wholeheartedly, without imposing any preconditions or holding back the least part of my being, I want you to take all of me, because you alone allow me the indulgence of wallowing for a little while in selfish and unconstructive self-pity. You offer me the further luxury of sentimentality, and you of all people understand what a vital and nourishing emotion that can be, and what an effort it takes for me to feel it.

With you, I can start as many sentences as I like with that beautiful interjection *Oh!* I can throw up my hands in total despair and say, with as close to utter sincerity as I'm capable of coming, Oh Billy why am I such a fucked-up human being? Oh how I wanted to love you, and want to love you still. Oh what a wonderful father you would have made, singing funny songs with happy endings to our kid, like the one where Bill Grogan's goat eats three red shirts off the line and gets tied to the railroad track, but at the last second coughs up the shirts and flags the train. We could live in a trailer; people could snub us for it if they wanted, but we'd have equity and domestic peace, the three of us. You'd work hard at Procter & Gamble sweeping the factory floor and loading boxes, but with your industrious ways you'd eventually be a warehouse foreman, and you'd bring home lots of free product samples, solvents, furniture polish and drain cleaners with warnings printed on the side, KEEP OUT OF THE REACH OF CHILDREN, and we would keep all chemicals scrupulously out of reach, we'd obey each warning to the letter, and make our home a safe and happy haven. After your hard day at the warehouse we could smoke a joint or two or drop a little acid before dinner, kind of a hippie cocktail hour, the relaxation of responsible adults, though never enough to set a bad example.

Maybe I'd have a job too, but I'd always keep the home fires burning, both a working woman and a successful housewife, just like Elaine. She and I have always gotten along pretty well because we don't have anything in common and hardly ever see each other, our lives have remained mostly separate since the age when we played Red Rover, and Elaine's favorite game, Mother May I. If there is any possibility of rehabilitating me as an outpatient, I could go to live back in Lexington at Elaine's house, on the understanding that I was bound to follow her instructions exactly, never thinking for myself or making any decisions that might get me into trouble. She could teach me to be a productive worker and a good wife to Billy, offer me cooking lessons, threatening to terminate my instruction and send me back to Our Lady of Comity if I gave her any lip.

ELAINE: Hello everybody, it's time for another edition of *Elaine May I*, the friendly morning show where everybody gets a lot done because nobody gives me any backtalk. Today we'll be preparing a specialty that comes out of my quasi-Appalachian Kentucky heritage, a recipe that has been handed down by my ancestors for thousands of years, possibly since the beginning of time, and so it's particularly important that it be prepared exactly according to instructions without the minutest departure from tradition. I'm talking about Cooked Possum. I'm really a city girl myself, but I've made a special extra effort to cultivate the kinds of family delicacies that any woman worth her dash of salt should know in order to be considered even minimally competent. My assistant today is someone not related to me in any way, despite what may appear to be physical resemblances. I'm prohibited from mentioning her real name, since she's a local psychiatric oupatient, volatile, fragile, and subject to having a nervous breakdown at the drop of a pan, so let's just call her Betty Crocker. Betty, how are you doing this morning? Are you keeping your head together?

BETTY: Yes, I think so. Well, I'm trying to, anyway. Elaine May I go bring in the possum?

ELAINE: Yes you may, Betty. (Exit Betty.) The possum, of course, must first be caught in the piney woods and brought home, a step which I've had the foresight to complete in advance, due to the intense pressure of having to prepare my dish in twenty minutes before a live audience. You don't want the possum to be too big, just medium-sized. Then you skin him, wash that feller out good and clean, then hang him outside and let him freeze all night. Once again, I've already taken care of these details, or rather allowed Betty to perform these less-refined butchering tasks, in an attempt to develop trust with her by allowing her access to sharp objects. (Enter Betty, holding frozen-stiff possum with skin still on.) Betty, what on earth have you done? I instructed you to *first* skin and clean the possum, *then* hang him outside to freeze. Can't you follow a simple command? Now I can't even skin him myself at my amazing lightning speed, because the fur is frozen to the flesh.

BETTY: I'm sorry. I'm really, really sorry. Elaine May I hold the possum under scalding water?

ELAINE: No, you may not. You'll spoil the meat. I'm afraid you'll just have to try to skin it right here on the spot while I go ahead and walk my viewers through the rest of the preparations. (Betty goes to work on the stiff possum with a penknife that wouldn't cut country butter in a summer drought, the only knife Elaine felt it prudent to allow her.) You put the possum in a big pot, about the size of Betty's mistake, and parboil him until the meat is almost ready to fall off the bone, take him out, put him in a bread pan, pack all around with sweet potatoes, cover with strips of bacon, and stick spicewood sticks all through it.

BETTY: Elaine May I stop for a minute? My fingers are hurting from the cold.

ELAINE: No, you may not. By the way, this dish goes marvelously with a fresh green poke salad, a vinaigrette dressing, and that famous apple pie my Mamaw makes that is famous for a hundred country miles in every direction from her house.

BETTY (hyperventilating): I'm not going to finish this in time, Elaine. My hands are starting to shake.

ELAINE: For Pete's sake, Talia—I mean Betty—you're not going to crack up again, are you? I let you come live here as a special favor to Mom, because she said you wouldn't go live at their house, and I'm trying to help you get straightened out, but I'm harried enough working fifty hours a week at my job plus running a household without you giving me this kind of grief. Everybody else can be enslaved to your shenanigans if they want to, but I don't have the patience for it. I moved away from home in the first place so I wouldn't have to be surrounded by this kind of weirdness all the time. Mike and I have a stable marriage, and we plan to keep it that way.

BETTY: Please don't send me back to the asylum, Elaine. I want to be a good cook. I don't want to fail this time. (She turns the knife on herself.)

ELAINE: Would you please cut out the wrist-slashing histrionics? I gave you a penknife that came out of a gumball machine because I knew you'd try something like this.

BETTY (with a look as wild as the wolves in the Hainted Holler): Hey, I know what happened to the possum. I must have had like a temporary childhood regression, which my psychiatrist says is to be expected sometimes in the normal course of my recovery. I was playing freeze tag with it, my favorite game, one I like better than Mother May I, and I must have really frozen the possum when I touched it. Remember freeze tag, Elaine, how fun it was? (Starts chasing Elaine around the kitchen island.) You're it! You're it!

ELAINE (panting and dabbing her face with an apron): Stop it, Betty. There were some very nice things about childhood, but certainly not enough to justify a return to it. That's the problem with our family; we get too nostalgic about recovering things that weren't that hot to begin with. You're going on sixteen years old, and if you and I are going to come to any kind of understanding, we must learn to relate to one another as adults. I'm not doing either of us any favors if I pretend we're still frisking around in the side yard on Palms Drive.

BETTY: Elaine May I have one more chance? I'm okay. See, my palsy has stopped. I'm acting normal.

ELAINE (taking off her apron and throwing it into a hamper): Not today. I've got to get to work. The whole evening crew will be in total chaos if I'm not there on time to oversee them. I'm going to give you a recipe simple enough for you to follow. Are you writing this down? Because I don't have time to repeat it. Cut open a possum any way you like, without bothering to see first whether he's really dead or just playing dead. Stuff him full of his own droppings and cook in a pot. You can add water or not depending on whether in your lucid moments you happen to get around to remembering. When it's good and done, go drop it in a hole and cover it up with dirt. If you botch those instructions, it really doesn't make a whole lot of difference.

It does make a difference, though. If not to me, then to Dad, because Mamaw really did make possum when he was little, he said it was pretty greasy but tasted good, and he hasn't had much appetite since he and Lynnette and I moved to Louisville and the situation with me got worse, except when he snacks late at night in front of the TV, on crackers and the snappy beer cheese he buys down at Hall's Restaurant on the Kentucky River. For him it isn't just a plastic container of beer cheese, it means something, like when we went to Florida and brought back sand in a jar. Some of the nights he didn't come home I think he must have driven down to sleep on the houseboat of one of his river-rat friends, because coming to a house where Lynnette was already asleep and he knew he'd have to watch reruns and listen to the heavy metal blasting from my closed bedroom door upstairs was just too depressing. Lynnette is right, Dad, you did save my life; still, I must have wanted to punish you most of all, since I knew you'd probably be the one to find my body, whether before or after the fact. Everyone can call my act theatrics if they want, a cry for help, an attempt not really that dangerous because the bottle of aspirin was taken shortly before your normal arrival. All that may be true, I can never really decide myself, but you know and I know that I took a big chance, because that night could easily have been one of the many nights you went to the river or wherever it is that you needed to go, and in that case I would have been shit out of luck.

I can assure everyone this time around that if I do make an attempt tonight or this weekend, it will be premeditated, deliberate, not for show, because I know the rounds and movements of Suzanne and the rest of the staff very well, and I've calculated that there are at least three adequate opportunities in the course of twenty-four hours, so I won't disappoint anyone, including myself, by failing. All decisions are final. I've forgiven you enough, Dad, for whatever it is I think you've done to me, to make sure you won't be the one to find me this time; there are trained professionals for that kind of dirty work. But I'd like to request the honor of having you take me to The Other Side on a houseboat, which you may have to borrow for the occasion.

Rob and I drove down to the river ourselves a few times after the rape, trying, I suppose, to capture that craving for the river that you seem to have—he and I were desperate for any kind of fondness that might prevent or at least delay our breakup and my crackup, but I can never associate the river with anything besides gasoline fumes from outboard motors and that hissing sound right before going under whenever my ears are just at the level of the water, or accidentally running over still-hot charcoal that somebody had dumped on the beach, or walking with a crunch over the shells of seven-year locusts that littered the riverbanks. But maybe if we could spend a little time together in your element, the place you escape to, the outcome might be different between us. Even if the arrangement didn't work out, you could take me on across and drop me, do me that last little favor, and we could both part with a clean conscience, that thing Suzanne keeps trying to make me believe I have.

*The houseboat is pitching in a gale-force wind, while the river rises rapidly, covering one after another the watermarks on the Clay's Ferry Bridge. Countless locusts chirr madly in the trees along the bank, like the objective correlative of a person in severe distress, many of them dropping like flies from the branches.*

FERRYMAN: Old Man River roils with unbidden ferocity this morrow.

TALIA (shouting to make herself heard): I must have brought the weather with me. I don't like this, Dad. Why are you wearing blackface and talking that way?

FERRYMAN: Lo! I am come from out the charnel house and gates of gloom, where Hades dwells apart from gods. I wot thou taks't me, as thou always hast, for an untutor'd fool. E'en so, I betook me within my poor powers to blend Charon and Old Man River into one sole personage, knowing how thou aspirest to a death of vaudeville kind, yet crowned with tragic overtones.

TALIA (clinging to the rail while waves buffet lawn chairs to and fro about the deck): You've got me all wrong. What I was really hoping for at this particular moment was a relaxing, indolent cruise down the rolling river. Sort of a homegrown, fresh water version of the Cunard Line, with horseshoe pitching and a climate-controlled swimmin' hole on deck.

FERRYMAN: What words, or cries, or lamentations can I utter, for the sorrows of my closing years? My child is no more. Which way am I to go, or this or that? I softshoed to her grave, and tipped my hat. Where is any god or power divine to succor me? My child, come forth; come forth, thou daughter of sorrows.

TALIA: No, Dad! It's hard to be at close quarters together, but maybe this is the only way to break our lifelong stalemate. Why are you in that ridiculous disguise of humility? Do you have a conscience as bad as mine?

*FERRYMAN washes off his face in one of the frothy waves and stumps up and down the deck, scowling and wringing his hands, while the houseboat careens upon the fumy deeps at the whim of the gods, catfish leaping a good ten feet into the air alongside, as in the watercolor mural* Fishin' for a Compliment *in the dining room of Hall's Restaurant.*

FERRYMAN: Ah, Saint Christopher and Honorable Happy Chandler! How sharper than a sea-serpent's tooth, and how difficult to carry over the water! Must I justify as well as provide? Every bad child deserves favor, but not the right to stow away on the beggarly forty-six borrowed feet her father claims for the night as his sole refuge now and again. Whatsoe'er ye may believe, Talia, I've not been put on this earth only to parent! I had a life before ye were spawned, missy, and so will I when ye've gone.

TALIA: Stow away? But you agreed to take me aboard.

FERRYMAN: Aye, long enough to act as your ferryman and bear ye to the opposite shore, just as requested. But I'll not have ye turn my retreat into a Hateful River any longer than I must, nor bear this vessel down with your excess emotional baggage.

TALIA (a pathetically fallacious rain weeping copiously on her head): No, no, the river isn't hateful, I promise. This weather is just the tornado season. I'm having a swell current time with you.

*YARLETT THE HARLOT emerges from the cabin, dressed in short shorts, flip-flops, a bathing suit top over her doodads, and over her Rit-red hair, a sailor's hat emblazoned I'M THE CREW. She is bearing refreshments and dancing as lasciviously as the Whore of Lebanon, Ky.*

YARLETT: Would you lak some Ale Eight-One and a snappy beer cheese samewich? You prob'ly thaink yore diddy's been down here a-drainking and carousing, but my snacks is nonalcoholic. Ale Eight-One is made ritecheer nearby in Winchester, Ky., and is pure as the Winchester Cathedral.

TALIA (sadly): Dad, I didn't expect to find you here with Loosie.

Why did you have to choose somebody so scuzzy? It makes you seem like just another one of the rednecks who hang out around the marina, selling crawdaddys for a living and throwing Hudepohl 14-K cans in the water. Is this where you were that night when I prayed you'd arrive in time?

FERRYMAN: Are ye astounded, then? I thought it might please ye to discover I matched your lowest expectation of me, and I was sure ye'd die happy with the knowledge that my seamy and seamanish necessities occasioned your death. Like yourself, I have just enough residue of footwashing Baptist conscience to regret my ways, if not to change them, so between fornications I'll be hounding myself with remorse about your end to the very last moment of my own life. Aye, we've both our bit of measly conscience, worse luck. And now, if ye've no objection, I'll ferry on across, and save my regrets for the return trip.

But you can't, Dad, not yet, not until I make up my mind, I still have the luxury of postponing my decision a little bit longer. That's the bitch of the matter for both of us, that accidents like suicide have to happen accidentally on purpose, even though lately I've been wishing it would happen on its own, the way some women wish they'd get knocked up without having to decide one way or another how they feel about the matter, and figure they'll get used to the idea afterward. Anyway, for the moment I have company to make other demands of me. Suzanne has returned with another dose of antidepressant before her evening shift ends, and is giving me her involuntary look of disappointment, since she'd rather see me make do with one of her deliciously relaxing backrubs, but she knows I'm too far gone right now to do without my medication. I take it, but ask her if she has enough time left to give me a backrub too, which she really doesn't, but she makes time, has me turn on my stomach and pulls up my shirt, not knowing how much her attentions mean to me right now, or maybe she does know but is too smart to let on, instead giving a cynical sigh of resignation about the hopelessness of lavishing extra effort on patients like me who will probably end up in the morgue pretty soon, as she squirts lotion onto her hands and starts in on my shoulders.

I say one of my agnostic prayers, praying that she's given me a placebo without telling me and has maybe been giving me placebos all along, because how wonderful it would be to believe that I could get through tonight without any medication whatsoever, that all this time without chemicals I've been keeping my shit together, at least together enough to make it each time to the next dosage of placebo. Suzanne knows exactly where the trigger points are in my muscles, her fingers have gone right to one and relieved the tension in that area. I try to think of a way to repay her devotion, and all I come up with is the dubious gift of keeping to the terms of our contract, which I suppose I can't technically even consider a gift, since it's a behavior she's already bargained for.

Or I could reconsider spending Mother's Day with my parents and sisters and brother. Even though Suzanne backed me in my decision not to see them this weekend, I know it would make her happy if I did. With all the messed-up domestic cases she deals with here every day, she still puts her faith in the next of kin, wants them to visit as often as possible, and probably believes that deep down all of them are the way she describes hers as being—loving and supportive people who she can talk to about almost anything that's getting her down. I have a hard time imagining Suzanne feeling down, but I guess it's selfish of me not to credit her with the capacity for that emotion, when she's been generous enough to credit me with a conscience and a lot of other things. It's kind of funny to think of offering my family as a gift to Suzanne or to anyone, but the truth is I don't have much else to offer, and I guess the idea wouldn't seem as odd to her as it does to me. So maybe I'll invite my entire family, in all its upsetting weirdness, as a present to palm off not only on her but on myself this weekend, and with some practice I might get used to the idea of them as a gift, a kind of gag gift, a white elephant, the kind whose footprints you find in the jelly jar in the refrigerator, because if I possess nothing else I possess a sense of humor. Or I should say my sense of humor possesses me, the way some people are possessed by demons.

*The next of kin are flattened against the various walls, trying to stay out of the way of a bed that is moving erratically about the room. On it lies* OUR LADY OF COMITY, *dressed in her favorite knee-less jeans, glittery Black Sabbath shirt, and a devotee's headdress, austere except for the plastic fruit—she's decked out like the camp-iest nun who ever took orders from a Satanic Blue Oyster Cult. Her tongue is flickering like Alice Cooper's, and as she jerks about, her eyes rock 'n' roll back in her head.* SUZANNE, *a devout believer of the Patient, Heal Thyself! school of thought, is acting only as a kind of attending exorcist, as Our Lady's aide-de-camp, her sec-ond-to-nun.*

SUZANNE (waving head-shop incense about the writhing body): *In nomine pater, mater, soror, frater*—why do their visits always have such an effect on you? I don't mind playing your straight man, but my shift ended twenty minutes ago, and my head nurse will have a conniption fit as severe as yours if she finds me still in here. I swear, sometimes I think you clown around this way just to get me laughing.

*OUR LADY OF COMITY, foaming at the mouth, leaps to her feet on the mattress and starts playing on an air guitar.*

OLC:

My heart is black and my lips are cold
Cities on flame with rock and roll
Three thousand guitars, they seem to cry
My ears will melt, and then my eyes.

SUZANNE (making OLC lie back down on her stomach): Does everybody in your family have this extravagant sense of humor? It must be genetic—I'll bet you guys are a scream around the dinner table.

OLC (her head rotating 180 degrees to face SUZANNE): Did I tell you I won a Black Sabbath album off the radio yesterday by being the 666th caller?

SUZANNE (anointing Our Lady's shoulders with oil and massaging): Talia, Talia. You must be feeling a little better or you wouldn't be tormenting me with your bad jokes. I can see it's time we started thinking about getting you out of this place, what do you say? And if you want me to rub you down, you're going to have to stop thrashing around so much.

OLC: I can't help it. I need the exorcise.

*OUR LADY rises into the air above the bed and hovers there. Hands on hips, her legs kicking about, she dances to the Satanic calypso accompaniment of Ricky Ricardo's band, which has materialized among a backdrop of potted palms for the grand finale. She sings:*

Limbo, limbo, I'm doin' the limbo,
My soul's in limbo, my arms akimbo

In this darkest hour, when I hover above you all in my spangled shirt like a hotel chandelier, in this tropical room where all the plants are in alignment and the tattoo of the congas plays to beat the band, where Ricky croons to Lucy with mystic oil shining in his hair, where there's nothing left to do but dig that crazy beat, I call to my side the people I've cared for enough to have constant waking nightmares about them—Suzanne, Mom, Rob, Elaine, Stephen, Lynnette, Billy, Judy, Dad. Worship with me the great Antidepressant, Comity. My jokes can be long-winded, I know, and this one has been more complicated, self-indulgent, cruel, difficult to follow, trying, and theatrical than usual, and the punch line's not usually worth waiting for, but here it is: I've made a decision, so you don't have keep hanging on in suspense anymore, and—neither do I! (She drops from the air to the floor with a thud.)

CONSTANCE (rushing forward with everyone else and bending over her daughter): Nurse, what's happening? Is she dispossessed?

SUZANNE: No, thank God. I think she's faking it.

There are words a mother should never think, and to speak them aloud to a stranger, an entrepeneur like you with a professional eye on my daughter, makes me feel I'm pronouncing a curse on her. Sometimes, though, I wish I hadn't been the one responsible for bringing Talia into this world. My other children don't believe me capable of such a statement. They think they've got me figured out. But those years when they were being born, from the time I was fifteen to whenever it stopped, were one long uninterrupted pregnancy, and all my children are to me like a single child. If any of them had a special claim on my affections it should be my firstborn, Judy, whom I carried to full term through the streets like a life-size birth announcement on a sandwich board (which is about how far I stuck out), then brought her to the hardware store where I cashiered and made her bed in a wheelbarrow I kept by the counter, before Jean ever came back from where he was stationed in Texas to speak for her.

Judy won first prize for her blue eyes and curly red hair in a baby contest, I've got the clippings from her head and from the paper to prove it, the only illegitimate one in the contest, and I said since people are going to gawk anyway they might as well contribute to the grocery money. None of my children have to go around apologizing for their looks. If Judy's wild now, that's no mystery, with a father who used to entertain her by opening beer bottles with his teeth. Or I should be partial to Stephen, who in first grade finished in one week a whole trimester's language arts plus all the fuschia and magenta SRA lessons. His teacher didn't know what else to do with him, and Stephen could have made as much money as you have by now if he hadn't been more interested in computer poetry, or building his own synthesizer, or whatever he does now, which is fine with me, but I never can remember what it is. Or I could have made a favorite of Lynnette or Elaine, either one, but of course it's none of them that interests you; it's Talia.

When she first started to lift weights, and right from the start three and four hours a day, I'll tell you I didn't approve. I was afraid she'd turn into a troglodyte with the kind of skin you see on a potato, like one or two of those girls she introduced me to, and I believe a woman can do a lot in this world and still not lose her feminine look. Just like when she went through that phase where she wouldn't shave her legs or armpits, when of course now the shoe's on the other foot and she has to shave even her little love triangle to compete in those tangas and bikinis—you in the promotion business know all about that stuff. There's no escaping that we are a family of hairy women, all of us have little black mustaches by age twenty, and when I worked as the cosmetician for a drugstore I brought home to my girls every free sample of cream, wax, tweezers, gel, whatever I could lay my hands on.

But Talia's going to do what she will. She's as hardheaded as the rest of my children and more so, exactly the way I raised them all. Only sometimes I wish she wouldn't take my example to such extremes. When Talia started to drink, before long she was a drunk, and when she started to pump barbells this last year, well, that became her whole life. I'll admit now it's the best thing to ever happen to her, because a girl as full of her temperament as she is needs to wear herself out on a daily basis. So far, that bird-boned, smooth-skinned, soft body of a little girl, and a face that's a promise to stay youthful and always need your protection—it's just like Jean's face—all those things that draw men to her, have only become greater attractions than before.

The only time she turns hunky is when she's on the crash diet right before the competition, and all the body fat disappears, and she cuts up, isn't that the phrase? When they grease her down every muscle stands out, and she struts the more onstage because those muscles have been there all along and she didn't show them until she was ready to, until the time suited her. In that first competition the judges only gave her third place, but anybody could tell who the crowd elected by voice vote—even Jean's mother, all hunkered down in her seat for shame at the wild catcalls her granddaughter caused, had to admit as much.

After that contest, though, Talia had a hard time gaining any weight back; she looked so pitiful and got an awful case of bronchitis, which is because I never nursed her. She wouldn't sit still to take the breast, so I put her on Morgan's Milk; that was the big sensation at the time. Morgan's feeds the best even better than the breast; Morgan's gives you rest. The Lord knows I needed a rest at that time with Elaine and Stephen still in rubber pants, Judy peeing the bed for attention, and the way Talia choked and squirmed you'd think I meant to suffocate her, so I gave up on it. Now she compensates by drinking milkshakes made with—what do they call it?—yes, double-helix amino powder, which she made her relations buy packets of at Thanksgiving. One of her sidelines.

Whether she'll take to you any more than she did me those first few years I can't say. When Talia decides she's finished with you, or doesn't intend to start in the first place, that's that. If she won't sign a five-year contract, maybe it's just as well. A hundred thousand dollars is a lot of money to groom my daughter with, no matter what the chance of returns after she becomes the next Miss Infinity. Not that I don't believe you've seen gyms full of women competing across the country and none of them "possesses the bas-relief definition, the innate sense of gesture and choreography in poses that appear forced in others." This mock-up of your new magazine leaves no doubt that you're announcing your cover girl, your find, to the world for future reference.

I'd make a good talent scout because I'm a watcher like you.

When I first started at the bank, as a teller, and someone wanted me to cash a check, I never asked for ID, because I knew right off whether that check would bounce or lay where it's supposed to, and all the credit cards and driver's licenses in the world won't change the outcome. Right from the word go I have a feeling about a person, including you. The way you listen without any hurry speaks more to me than anything you might say, because whoever intends to handle Talia can't rush, no matter if she does.

As soon as she started to cut teeth she wanted to suckle, where she never had before, and of course I'd started in my youngest by then. She made me smart; bit me on purpose. Made me so raw I couldn't stand to nurse Lynnette, and I had to put that one on a formula. Whenever Jean tried to take Talia in his arms, she made herself go stiff. And he'd never diapered the babies in the middle of the night, not even Judy, but the note Talia pitched her cry on, like a cricket loose in the house to find and put outside, had him up and down whenever she decided.

Sometimes I regret I ever said to her that motherhood should be a choice. Would she have learned how when there's nowhere to escape the cry, whether you love it or not you respond, and learn to make room even when your body is an airless trailer like the one I lived in when she was born? Even though she was only thirteen when her turn came, it might have been best for her, if not for the child, had she brought it up.

I don't say she'd have needed to marry the father. Billy wore strawberry body oil he must have bought at a head shop for a dollar a quart. I could smell it whenever he'd been around. From the cosmetics counter I'd see him in the mall esplanade in the afternoon, carrying a lava lamp or a black-light poster that would end up on Talia's bedside table or wall. One day I came home from work early, caught a whiff of imitation strawberry, and when I went into her room found nobody, but I noticed part of the ceiling was covered in aluminum foil, and blobs of protoplasm were erupting in slow motion inside the lava lamp. Only then did I realize they'd been skipping school and that I'd been too lax. I could have forbid her to see him, but by then she was already knocked up.

Not for a moment did Billy try to deny his part. No such luck. He asked for Talia's hand, his very words, promised to go for his GED soon as he could, said he'd wear a hair net—I think that was the biggest sacrifice in his mind—if I could get him on as dishwasher at the drugstore luncheonette. I'll say in his favor that young as he was, he acted more like an expectant father than Jean ever did for years. Not only did he not disappear, but he lurked about and pestered us with brochures from the health department. A damiana smoker who could barely read became an expert overnight on rubella and prenatal nutrition, and he tried his best to keep Talia away from the hamburger line at the cafeteria.

Now, Talia never said two actual words either way about her plans for the baby. More than ever she craved salty french fries that made her retain water, and smoked as many menthol cigarettes as always. But as the weeks progressed, and she began to show, and everyone at her junior high discovered the obvious, we all let ourselves suppose she meant to keep it. You might think teenyboppers would snub her, little adults as they pretend to be even though most have as much identity at that stage as the gold-plated ID rings on their pinkies. None needed to knock to enter my house—it always seemed other people's kids would rather spend time there than at home, even though the paint on our shutters had flaked and we had bagworms in our one tree; a good thing there wasn't a neighborhood association to condemn the dandelions all over the yard and the boat with the stripped fiberglass bottom in the driveway for years before Jean finally traded it for more junk. Jean has laid down in three inches of water in a hailstorm to fix a friend's bilge pump but never got around to his own boat. After school Talia's girlfriends would lounge about our living room while they felt her stomach for the umpteenth time and flipped through sewing magazines for infant patterns like a bunch of married women. I believe they considered the baby a kind of pet or a future mascot for the school, and thought up names for it like Ashley and Monique.

One afternoon near the end of her second trimester, when the rain had brought earthworms out onto the sidewalk, Talia came home in a calf-length winter coat and walked straight back to her room, as pale and wrapped up in herself as a cocoon. One of the reasons Billy hung around so much is because he wanted that baby more than any of us, and must have been afraid to let its mother out of his sight. With those dishwasher's latex gloves always in his back pocket, you'd think he planned to handle the delivery himself, but if he did, he never had the chance to use them. I put a towel between her legs, and when I couldn't stanch the blood called the hospital. They said from the look of it she'd gone to a real cut-rate surgeon—it was legal only in New York and a few other places. I had an idea she'd done it herself, in that abandoned tower over in the vacant field, but never could make myself climb the tower to look for stains.

When Billy heard, he showed up at the hospital in the middle of his shift and stood there crying with his hair net on like a widow at a funeral. He asked her how could she do that to their child, and she answered that anything in her body was her property, including his sperm. If she meant that answer to repulse him, she didn't get her wish. He said he wanted her to be his bride anyway. But she never would see or speak to him after that, and he started to blame himself for the breakup, even though he couldn't figure out the reason for it. Now and again he calls me still, and last year sent a God's eye he made himself.

Afterward, when she had to return to the other facts of life like schoolmates who avoid you because you're no longer pregnant—as mine avoided me because I was—she had me in a dither about what she might try next. But however Talia may dispose of the lives of others, she clings to her own. She molts and begins again. Each of her three weddings was virginal, with a white lace dress like a fresh skin, the full set of bridesmaids and groomsmen, jokes on the car about her maidenhead, in shaving cream like a new snowfall. Most of the relations showed up and brought gifts, even though it was tougher on each occasion to supply one Talia still needed in the way of housewarming.

When she moved back in with us, the presents that remained in her possession had to be put into storage, some still unopened. We had barely enough room in the townhouse for Jean, me, and our youngest, Lynnette, who was nearly grown. There comes a point when you've cared for the children ever since you can remember, and however much you love them you'd like to do so on selected occasions. It was the first time we'd ever been out of debt. More than half a year passed without any envelopes stamped FINAL NOTICE in red block letters, or wake-up threats from collection agencies. We'd started to fix up our place, even though we didn't own it. Jean dug postholes for a stockade fence and bought so much insulation for the attic that he ended up doing some of the neighbors' attics too. Lynnette gave us a lava-rock grill, and the three of us barbecued every kind of flesh Adam ever named.

But I suppose a woman's never through with her kids. One of Jean's river cronies called to let us know he'd found Talia living in this rusted-out barge Jean had bartered for when he had the big idea of making it into a storefront, a place to sell snacks and nightcrawlers. Months would go by without a word from Talia, so her latest bout of silence hadn't surprised us—as a rule we had to hope for the best and try not to imagine too much beyond that. I don't know what she'd eaten for however long she'd holed up in the barge, but it might have been nightcrawlers from the way she looked.

No sooner had she moved home than Lynnette was relegated to the hide-a-bed in the living room, and the hall closet for her clothes. I know Lynnette had waited patiently all her life to have her own bedroom, since the days when Talia allowed her only a certain number of square feet on the wall for posters of dogs and ducks, who had to share an uneasy proximity with a transvestite rock star and his pet python. If you say I shouldn't have allowed it, I'll agree, I know it was wrong, and more so because Lynnette would always rather give way than raise her voice or listen to any fights. Because it takes so much effort to resist

Talia. Unless you get in the habit early on it's all too easy to let her have her will. One of Stephen's vegetarian friends told us one time, when they dropped in right after we'd taken steaks off the grill, did we know a cow had to eat sixteen pounds of grain to put one pound of meat on our table? We had a good laugh, said we've eaten plenty of grain over the years and not for philosophy either; but when I think about what he said it puts me in mind of Talia.

When the trouble with Lynnette started, it wasn't trouble, by which I mean I didn't notice. I'd read this book called *What Makes Teens Stop Ticking*, and was alert to Talia's every move. Jean calls it slop psychology, but he'll never know the times a three-dollar paperpack was the only thing between me and crazy. I'm no expert, I don't have any Ph.D.'s, but when you get right down to it, what kind of help is there besides self-help? Answer me that. And people can afford it. Talia displayed the classic symptoms of the suicidal personality type. She gave away the two or three wedding presents she'd kept with her at the townhouse, like a lacquered end table made from the cross section of an oak tree, and one day asked me how I thought a bird feels when it's sucked into a jet engine and atomized.

Lynnette, on the other hand, is the type you feel will pull through, right from the start. Very quiet, like you, but not the kind of quiet that makes you run into the other room in case she's about to stick a bobby pin in the outlet or put a drop of cold water on a hot lightbulb to see what will happen. I almost wish she had. She should have shouted at me, accused me of neglect, instead of practicing that sweet, unselfish acceptance. Even now that she's working overtime at a family steak house to cover the bad checks of her day manager, who she lives with, she still comes over once a week, although he doesn't approve, to watch our mutual favorite evening soap with me. She never complains. For now, she's as untouchable by me as Talia always was. I tell myself she'll come through it all intact. For however long she's set on martyrdom though, I'd almost prefer for her to have . . . I don't know, a religious conversion.

I've let the children grope their own way though, in religion as well as everything else. When Stephen was nine he got religion on account of a Sunday-school teacher who took him to watch the Cincinnati Reds play baseball and always mistook me for Stephen's sister. Now that was a handsome devil, and he'd just taught my son to dive into the public pool with a noseplug, and Stephen was fascinated by the pastor's rubber fisherman's boots, so baptism in the tank behind the choir loft was a big adventure for him. But then Stephen sneaked into Talia's top bunk and kept her up half the night reading, by the light of a luminous green Wiffle ball, some comic book the pastor had given him about how when you die God makes you watch a documentary movie of your whole life with special emphasis on the sins you thought nobody else had noticed. Talia has a vivid imagination, so it didn't require much persuasion for him to coax her to a prayer meeting, where she dedicated her life to Christ. When I found out, I was furious and grounded Stephen for a month, Sunday school included.

That's one of the stories that gets told at Christmas, even though it happened in the summer. Since they're grown, it's about the only time I can get them all together. Usually Stephen is the quickest to laugh, because he loves to tell stories on himself, but his junior year when he came back from college, he snapped Talia's head off when she brought it up. That particular Christmas was a little strange all around. It had been a hard year for him, and he was in a therapy called co-counseling, where you and your friends go into a room together and laugh and cry a lot. Also, he was in the middle of rehearsals for a play in French or Spanish, or was it Portugese, and while I basted the turkey with an eyedropper, I could hear him in the bedroom above me by himself, shouting out these speeches in a foreign language, like somebody speaking in tongues. Elaine was the only one who had her act together enough to help me cook, make the dumplings and oysters and so forth. Judy had flown back from the Southwest on a midnight cargo flight, and she stayed at the attic Talia was renting because as it turned out they were both into black men and discotheques that year—well, Talia was at least, and Judy curious, on the rebound after her divorce.

Scorcher dresses, black hose with seams, bangles and bracelets, hump-me pumps, peek-a-boo blouses, that's what they wore to the Christmas Eve dinner. Talia loaned Judy one of her outfits. All the in-laws and grandparents and nieces and family friends, twenty five or thirty of us, crowded downstairs in the tiny townhouse, had to wait dinner on those two, which I never ever do because when I say six I mean six, and when I say seven I mean seven. In they rolled, and Talia had brought with her a black man they'd met, a real hunk who was touring with a male revue, and the performance had held them up, as she informed us while she plucked a Swedish meatball out of the Crock-Pot with her thumb and forefinger. I don't know where she'd told this dancer they were going, but he was as quiet as if Talia had just showed up late to one of her weddings and revealed him as the surprise groom. You had to feel bad for him. I doubt he meant for her to announce his profession, not for an audience that included my sister-in-law, as sweet as the Marshmallow Heaven she brings every year, who once said she didn't have anything against black persons, she just wouldn't want to touch one.

But I'll say in her favor that Babs fixed Jocque a plate, even if she didn't hand it to him herself. She was as determined to ignore the uncomfortable nature of the situation as were Jocque and the rest of us. Talia, though, wouldn't let it lie. She insisted on sharing a plate with Jocque, and feeding him grapes from the fruit salad. When he tried to protest softly that he wasn't very hungry, she said eating was the best part of Christmas, the main reason families got together, and that she would die if a year went by that Mom didn't make her famous fruit salad.

Stephen was ready to knock the shitake out of her, but the strange thing, and I don't think anybody else saw it this way, is that she really meant what she said. When she lived in the barge, she probably thought of the famous fruit salad often. Every year she asks me for the recipe, and writes it down faithfully, although I don't think she's ever made it.

After dinner, she read Jocque's palm, and traced the veins up his arm to his bicep, making up stories as she went along. "I see a lot of paths," she said, "leading from the doors of a lot of beautiful babes. Hmm, that must be your wicked past. But they all converge in this one spot—whoa, what an incredible muscle, and he hasn't even made it hard yet. Judy, you should feel this. The convergence of the veins must mean your roaming days are over and you'll soon end up in a single place—a nice, warm, fitting, family place. Hey, why don't you do a little bit of your routine for everybody? No, I'm serious, it's a beautiful art form. You don't have to do anything lascivious or embarrassing, just a few innocent steps. You're such an incredible dancer, I want my family to appreciate you."

Then Stephen said, "Talia, why don't you leave the poor bastard alone?"

"Hey, Stephen," she said, as with another sudden inspiration, "do you think this day will be included in the eternal documentary? You know, Jocque, Stephen and I used to be real conspirators, and sleep together in my bunk as often as we could manage, even though we weren't allowed to. Once he let me hold his fluorescent ball, and we read this Baptist comic book together that terrified us of our wicked childish sins. It all seems very Freudian now."

"You shut your sluttish little mouth," Stephen shouted then. "Why the hell did you have to pick somebody up on Christmas Eve, of all nights, and bring him here? Why do you do these things to the rest of us?"

Talia, of course, didn't lose a second in answering him. "Do you have something against blacks, like Aunt Babs? I don't know what your perverted, prejudiced mind is imagining, but Jocque and I have done nothing indecent, with Judy as our witness. He didn't have anywhere to go on the most special night of the year, and I wanted him to spend it with our family, in a traditional way. Is there something different about him that won't allow it?"

"Yes," said Stephen, "there is something different—he should thank God he's a one-night stand who has somewhere else to be tomorrow, unlike your former boyfriends and ex-husband. Otherwise he'd end up like everybody else, whimpering after you for years on end."

She started to cry. I don't know why, but I lashed out at Stephen, said why did he have to bully her? I was supposed to take him back to school after the break, but he left that very night and hitchhiked. It took him something like seventeen hours. But when one of my kids decides to hitchhike on state roads covered with ice in the middle of the night, you might as well not make any objection.

Jean, of course, went after him sometime before dawn, after waking up with indigestion, and drove all the way out of state in second gear without finding him on the road. Although Jean lays back on the day-to-day stuff, he peps right up for emergencies, especially if it involves driving all over the country in the middle of the night. I knew it wouldn't do any good even if he had found Stephen, because when Stephen gets really heated up, it takes a certain number of hours before he'll listen to reason, after which he's usually fine, and you might as well not try to make him get in the car because he won't and never has nor will until he's ready. He's particular in that way, and different from Talia, who carries everything that ever happened to her with her, and doesn't let it go completely no matter how much time passes. But I kept quiet and let Jean go. Each of us has our ideas about parenthood, and if we didn't give each other some leeway we wouldn't have made it to the silver anniversary.

Thirty-one years straight together, if you don't count the three-month separation and the six days after Jean's and my divorce went through before we remarried each other. Even though he and Talia had never quite hit it off, when he moved into an efficiency—carpeted only so you wouldn't notice the waves in the floor as much, and with a vista of the Dumpsters behind the shopping center—she decided to go with him. Back when the kids were still kids, whenever he showed up as plastered as the holes he'd punch in the sheetrock and then mend the next day, Talia was the only one not too frozen in the hall to beat on our bedroom door when Jean started in on me. She'd call him an SOB and a mother you-know-what, I mean she could match his vocabulary word for shining word, and she knew the police station number by heart and had called so often in the middle of the night that Jean's policemen friends down there would sometimes ask how little Talia was doing when they ran into him at the drive-in restaurant where they all drink coffee and eat jelly donuts instead of enforcing the law. Once when he sold stocks and bonds up and down the rural routes, he came home late, and sober, and crept into her bedroom to show her a twenty-thousand-dollar check before he turned it in at the office the next morning. He found her asleep in a flannel gown with a steak knife clasped to her breast. He put the knife back in the silverware drawer, and after that detoxified for a while.

When he was good, he'd do things like surprise the children with fifty pounds of oranges, or a cotton-candy machine he'd traded a set of retread tires for. The kids were more than eager to forgive him, just grateful for a temporary letup in suspense, all except Talia, who wouldn't eat any of the oranges, or the cotton candy Jean made on Fourth of July for every Tom, Dick, and Horatio for twenty blocks around. He'd try to make her mind, and she'd shout, "You're not my real father. My real father had red hair." You see, one summer the sun had turned her hair almost the color of Judy's baby curls, and it surprised her so much that for a joke I winked and said her real father's hair had been red. Jean knew she only repeated it to gall him, but every time it got his goat as if it had been true. But he never laid a finger on Talia.

Their standoff ran up through high school, when out of the blue he started a campaign of rules and regulations. Bedtime by ten o'clock, in the summer, if you can believe that. She had to report in by phone three times a day, to the fire and casualty, and the office secretary notified him in the field on the mobile two-way. Once or twice he swung by the address Talia gave to spot-check her story. At first she threatened to kill herself if he didn't give her more freedom, and he told her to go right ahead, as long as they brought her body home from the morgue by ten o'clock. And she did make one halfhearted attempt, with half a bottle of orange baby aspirin, but all it gave her was a horrible stomachache.

She went along with the restrictions, for a while, and actually seemed to settle down. Sometimes when she reported in they would decide to meet for lunch—I don't know where, or what they discussed, since I wasn't invited. Jean and I didn't have much to say to one another just before we separated, so the subject of Talia didn't come up between us very often. But when Jean's in one of his good periods he can be a regular salesman, and you can be sure he didn't waste the opportunity to give her his version of our marriage. The same way if he were sitting here with you and me this second, he'd contradict ninety-nine and forty-four one-hundreths of what I've told you so far. Anyway, he'd picked up weight, and he was determined to get back in shape, on the spur, in his usual overdone fashion, which was to run like a maniac around the neighborhood at night in regular street clothes and boating sneakers—it's a wonder nobody called the police—and make himself so sore he could barely engage the automobile clutch in the morning. Talia joined him on some of the runs, since she had to be at home anyway, and afterward they'd walk down the street for a diet root beer.

Then a rock concert she was dying to attend came to the coliseum, and Jean wouldn't budge because the headliner didn't start until nine-thirty. So she came to me on the sly. She'd behaved very well for weeks—don't you think?—and it wasn't going to kill any of us to stretch the curfew an hour or two just once, if for nothing else as a reward. I ask you because you're outside the family, and sometimes when I think back on these events, I feel we need an objective opinion from somebody who's not one of us. Jean didn't usually come in until after eight, so I loaned Talia and her date my car the night of the concert, and bought them a bottle of Chianti to put in their bota. See, there's another difference in Jean's philosophy and mine. I'm not the one in this family with an alcohol problem, and yet I believe you should recognize that teenagers are going to drink no matter what you do, so I prefer to buy them a limited amount myself and impress on them the responsibility for bringing back both the car and themselves at a reasonable hour and in a reasonable condition. When it comes right down to it, you have to trust your kids, not police them. But when Jean is off the booze and living clean, he's so afraid he's going to do something wrong himself that he projects that fear onto everybody else's actions. I've read about all of this stuff and the description fits him like the yellow monogrammed sweater he was wearing that night, which the kids had bought him for Father's Day.

When Jean got home around quarter after nine, he asked where Talia was, and I simply said *Out*. Right away I could tell he was uneasy, but he did nothing except fix himself some braunschweiger and saltines and sit down with the radio to listen to the end of some ball game or other, because ten o'clock was the agreed-upon hour, and so she had until ten. One of his ears was trained on the front door though, and when ten o'clock came he shut off the radio before the final score—the game was in overtime—and took his jacket, still wet from the rain, back out of the closet. I asked him where he was going and he simply said *Out*. He never had laid a finger on her, but I jumped up from my easy chair and said, "Jean, please don't do anything to her. I gave her permission to go to the concert, and I paid for the tickets and let them drive my car. If anybody has to be punished over this, it should be me." When I tried to restrain him he pushed me away, and I fell back on the carpet.

I had to borrow our next-door neighbor's pickup truck to follow him. There was nowhere to park around the coliseum; I don't know where Jean found a spot, but he always manages one right next to the mall even at the height of Christmas shopping. I drove up and down side streets in the rain with barely enough room for the truck to squeak through, the windows steamed up, and I couldn't figure out how to make the windshield wipers work either, and finally pulled two wheels up on the curb right in front of the coliseum entrance, because our neighbor's pickup has one of those yellow flashing lights on top. I suppose Jean paid the twelve dollars or whatever for a ticket, but I told the security guard it was an emergency and he waved me through.

Inside, the giant steel rafters were nearly hidden in smoke, and Jean not easy to spot in a size crowd I'd only seen at basketball playoffs there. Boys and girls alike wore sequined shirts, embroidered jeans, mascara, tie-dye vests—the gypsy getup Talia loved. On the stage, in blue light, the singer was holding a silver bust of a woman—I mean literally a bust. He spit on those breasts, let the saliva run down between them, and caught it in his mouth. Then he lifted his python out of a basket, and wrapping it around his neck, French-kissed its tongue. As horrible as it was, I found myself watching. A boy with no shirt and a muscular chest, on the end of the aisle, handed me a joint. I took a puff, in part because I thought it might calm my nerves, but also because I wanted to see what it was like.

With the explosions of fuzz, from speakers bigger than some of the trailers we've lived in, it's a wonder I spied the ruckus at one end of the floor. Now you might ask how Jean found my daughter among twenty or thirty thousand people, I know I couldn't in a leap year, but he has a traveling man's sixth sense of direction. I ran toward the commotion, but the singer must have thought he'd worked the audience to a frenzy, because he started throwing rolled posters into the crowd. By the time I could push through to Talia, you'd never seen so many security guards, and they had Jean on the floor. He'd knocked down two or three boys, one of them holding a bandana to his face, and struck Talia once, which with Jean's strength is more than enough. You've probably noticed a crooked scar under her chin that turns real white before competitions when she's spent a lot of time in the tanning booth, the same way my stretch marks do when I lay out in the sun.

That night and the next Jean spent in the city jail, and I can assure you I didn't post bail. His friends down there released him after forty-eight hours, and he went on one of the biggest drunks of his life. When the next weekend rolled around, so did he, with a man I'd never laid eyes on, at three in the morning, and they were trying to put up a basketball hoop for Stephen in the driveway. I asked for a separation and threatened to take out a peace bond on him. He didn't try to argue, just took a few clothes and his shaving kit, like he does for a short trip, moved into a furnished efficiency, and Talia went with him.

I'd have promised most anything for her to stay with me. I even said to her I'd take Jean back, if that's what troubled her, but she couldn't say what she wanted, except to leave. She had no money of her own, and I suppose she didn't want to go back to the barge. I told Jean I hoped he was happy. But he didn't seem any happier than Talia, to tell you the truth. Whenever I drove by their place, his old Mustang was in the parking lot, so I checked up and found he was working as a clerk in a glass booth at one of those all-night gas stations that only takes exact change. Talia hadn't attended school in over three weeks, and her counselor said it looked like she might have to repeat the year. Sometimes on my lunch hour or before work, I sat in the Plexiglas bus shelter across the street from their apartment. When Jean returned dead tired from the graveyard shift, he could hardly have slept since Talia played the stereo almost non-stop. And I don't think she wanted him to sleep. No, she wasn't any abused woman following her abuser around, like you're always hearing about. Whether she knew it or not, she knew Jean wouldn't lay another finger on her.

Some young hoodlum with an army jacket and a burr haircut, like maybe he'd just discharged from the service and couldn't think of anywhere else to go, hung around a lot, and nuzzled her sometimes on the stairs. One morning, after Jean had gone in, and those two showed up a little later, I crossed the street. The curtains were drawn, but when I put my ear to the door I heard sounds—well, sounds you can't mistake for any other, unless I was mistaken, which I very well could have been and hope I was. I don't know how Jean stood it, right there in the same room! He always threw a fit if the girls even ran around the house in their panties. Most of his life, he himself felt naked if he didn't wear an undershirt beneath his dress shirt. So I knew he didn't much care or understand where he was or why, and I prayed for his sake he was passed out cold. But I filed the papers anyhow, and mailed them to him to sign, which he did and sent back without any comment. It seemed to me we'd spent most of our life in a way station between marriage and divorce, and I decided I had to go through the motion and see how it felt to be in one definite place.

All those weeks, I didn't see him up close until he appeared at the proceedings. He put me in mind of my pharmacist—you know how tall they look behind a counter—who one year had something with his bones, and I didn't notice how stooped he'd become until I ran into him outdoors. Jean wasn't stooped, but it shocked me how puffy and red as brick his face had turned, and I could tell he'd been forgetting to eat and change his clothes. No matter how badly Jean treated himself over the years, he kept those Little Boy Blue looks. When first we met he was so fresh out of the oven I wanted to gobble him up still hot, and he hasn't changed too much since. But when he walked into the chambers that day, I broke the vow I'd made to leave him and Talia to each other's company. Not that they wouldn't have deserved it. Still, I brought Talia into this world—my other children have said she's made in my image—and I feel responsible for her. Which also means I can't be easy about letting loose such a holy terror on anybody, not even Jean who helped make her.

I understand why you shake your head. Because even terrors can be holy, and if the term hadn't already been coined, I would have invented it specially for Talia. You hardly recognize the girl, the woman I've been speaking of? Have I neglected that other side of her? In the telling, I mean. When you live in a perpetual upheaval, after a certain time you feel like the only language you know how to speak anymore is Hotline.

Well, if you want to bid so high on what's in the kitty, I guess you will. I've got a hunch from watching you fidget that you want to sign Talia on even more than you did when you came here to see me. She needs a handler, I'll agree with you there. None of us has managed her so far, but there's no reason why you shouldn't try. I hope to high heaven she signs that contract, because a contract is a lot more of a binding document than a birth certificate, and I want her to stay with this body-building stuff and not just drop it on a whim and take up God only knows what next. If she didn't have such a way with people, she might be better off. At least the rest of us would. I know a mother probably shouldn't say this, but I worry more about her than I do about the rest. I always have. She needs twice as much love and affection as a normal person. That's not any personal preference speaking; it's just a plain fact, plain as the stamp of a personality on a baby's squinched-up face as soon as it comes out after hard labor, and you know there's trouble ahead. But she was so sweet, with clear, tender skin, a head full of hair from day one, and a baby gaze staring you down until it nearly made you cross-eyed. Yes, the only way to avoid having Talia get under your skin for a lifetime is not to look on her in the first place. Once you do, I believe you're just about lost.

**M**e and another girl and Jimmy were sitting on the couch in front of the fireplace. In the middle of the afternoon, listening to the wood pop. The couch had a high back and a pattern of roses, the old-fashioned drawing-room kind like the one Mamie used to have in her place, but this couch had turned the color of soot from smoke always backing up out of the chimney. So the pattern was hard to make out. The room had high ceilings, but it was still pretty warm. The other girl was in just her panties, cross-legged, eating cottage cheese out of the container. The cat stayed on the couch arm watching her eat. Her fork was scraping the bottom. The cat didn't really belong to anybody, but some of us would feed it sometimes. An album cover, Steppenwolf's *Monster* I think, lay on Jimmy's lap with pot gathered in the spine where he'd been rolling himself a doobie. He had on his jeans. His hair was wet, and the wetness made it look black and oily. He was smoking the doobie by himself, and crushing between his fingernails the seeds he'd separated out, as if they were ticks or fleas he'd groomed from the cat's fur. I had on a tie-dye top and these beautiful glazed-shell earrings. I still have one of those earrings in my jewelry box. The firewood we used was branches and stumps gathered from around the grounds by whoever was living at the Mansion in a given week and happened to go outside to collect some. A lot of the wood was mossy and covered with resin, like the resin in the chamber of a pipe when you clean it out, so it manufactured a lot of smoke when it burned. She didn't offer the cat any cottage cheese, and at last it jumped down and started rubbing against his leg. I guess it thought he had something to eat as well. He told me to take the album cover off his lap so he could move around better. When I did, he caught the cat by the nape of its neck, and tossed it sidearm into the fireplace, with a forward twist of his hand and his shoulder blade thrust forward, the same way he always threw a Frisbee. She and I both started crying, the way you suddenly do in the middle of a sentence just when you think everything's fine and you've got yourself under control. My sense of smell has never been very good, because I have a deviated septum and sinus problems, but right away I could smell the singed fur. The cat was trying to get away from the fire by scrambling up the chimney, but the bricks were very hot too, and so it kept falling back into the fire.

I'd go out to meet Eddie and he'd open the trunk of his car, which would be full of all sizes and thicknesses of scratch pads, also different colors, pale pink, blue, newsprint, yellow. I was extravagant with them. I'd take one big, beautiful, fat one and draw a tiny cartoon sequence on the very edge, leaving the rest of each sheet blank, so that when you flipped all the edges with your thumb it made an animation of a stick woman in a bathing cap diving off a board into the water. The woman would disappear and then all you could see was a splash coming up from below the edge of the page and subsiding. Even if he was going to use the hand mower, or take me down to the pool and sit in a chair at the concrete poolside, he always wore a pressed white shirt, a tie, and an undershirt. His work as a printer involved a lot of sweating and lifting, setting linotype, fooling with ink, and it would have made more sense to wear work clothes. Still, he managed to keep his shirts clean. Mamie used a lot of starch in them so they would stay fresh longer. She used to call him Prince Edward, but he pretended not to understand what she meant by that. He didn't want to be any trouble to anybody. When they visited on the weekends, he positioned himself at the back corner of the dinner table at mealtimes, so he couldn't wait on himself, and then said to me or to Mamie, as politely as could be, "Oh, little sweets, could you give me another splash of tea? I can't seem to get out. Just enough to cover the ice." His glass rattling. It was one of his rituals. "Just enough to cover the ice." One time he forgot to say it, and I ran outside and hid under the car. Nobody, including him, could figure out what was wrong with me. He got on his hands and knees to peer underneath the car and coax me out. In his white shirt, trying to avoid the oil spots on the asphalt. At Six Flags he rode the runaway mine car with me, wearing a tie of course, as if we were sitting in a church pew, and at the top, right about the time I could see down the other side, he'd give my leg a hard squeeze and shout, "You're my main squeeze!" Then his tie would start flapping. I never let on that my screams were real, and tried hard not to throw up, because I didn't want to give up that moment at the top. My mother never liked it that I called him Eddie. She said that all the grandchildren called him Granddad, and I should call him Granddad too. She said that nobody called him Eddie, not even his closest friends. His name was Edward. She said he couldn't stand it when gas-station mechanics assumed an instant familiarity and called him Eddie. I said I'm not a mechanic.

When I married Guy he looked in the face like he was about thirteen years old, and he had a ponytail as long and black as a Cherokee's. Even though his chest was big from doing bench presses in his basement, he didn't have any hair on it, or anywhere else to speak of except around his dick. Now that I'm a little bit older I like hairy men just fine, but back then they seemed gross to me. Hairy men are definitely as much of an acquired taste as beer. My Uncle Micky, Eddie's son, who wore tinted glasses and a gold initial ring as thick as brass knuckles, offered me a free trip to Europe if I wouldn't marry this guy. He laid the hundred-dollar bills right down in front of me, so I wouldn't think he was bluffing. Uncle Micky isn't that much older than me, and we grew up together for a while, when I was very small and staying at Mamie's. I considered him then more a brother than an uncle. We collected coins and dead bugs and nails that we found lying around. Watched each other pee. Took baths together.

Micky and his wife did flea markets and coin shows, and got free lodgings by working as live-in motel clerks. She had a degree in home economics. The desk buzzer could sound off at any hour, day or night, so it was like being on call. But most of their money came from the all-night poker games Micky ran in their teeny motel efficiency, since he was always getting waked up anyway. They had to put a cloth over their parakeet's cage so it could get some rest, and Micky's wife wore a sleep mask and wax earplugs so she could get some rest too. The parakeet would go nuts when they let it out to fly around the efficiency and get some exercise. Sometimes it banged into the walls and off the windows, since the apartment was so small. Another way Micky made money was by fencing antique guns, jewelry, tapestries. He wouldn't fence just anything. He was kind of a connoisseur. Later on he got into the antique business. The import business. He bought a discotheque, and the bouncers made extra money by collecting debts for him, and loading into trucks the contents of the containers he shipped over from England. That's where he wanted me to go. He said women a long time ago used to be sent over there to put the finishing touches on their charm and education. He said he and I were both hicks, and we needed to smarten up by traveling. He said there was a lot more culture over there, and a lot more interesting stuff to buy at auctions. Grandfather clocks, leather. Back when he married, Micky let me hang out like a punk kid at his bachelor party, where he and his friends drank straight bourbon whiskey and played albums by a group called Doug Clark and the Hot Nuts. He made me promise then to remain a bachelorette.

But when he offered me the trip to Europe, I told him I didn't like to fly on planes, and married Guy. Guy's Cherokee ponytail really stood out against his white tuxedo. We didn't have any money for a regular honeymoon, so we rented a hotel room at the Ramada over on Waller Avenue. We also rented an 8mm projector and a stag film, but we were too drunk on champagne to get it threaded right. So we decided to forget about it. We took off our clothes and mainlined some heroin. He was really into mainlining, and that was the special present he'd been saving for our wedding night, turning me on to heroin. When we were good and doped up, we started massaging each other in slow motion with edible body oil, almond flavored, that somebody had given us as a wedding gift. It didn't really taste like almonds but it was pretty good. Since he didn't have any hair on him, I could really spread the oil over his skin. It went on for miles. His skin was almost squeaky, very soft and slick, and his muscles were nice and hard. My hand just kept sliding in one long wave right over the surface. Then we started licking each other, the way newborn kittens do when they're piled up together, our eyes half-closed, absentminded. We licked and we licked. We must have done everything else too, eventually, but all I can remember is us licking each other clean like that for hours.

My father is hiking with me up to Natural Bridge, followed by his Lhasa apso, Milky. With his bottom teeth jutting out, black doggy nose, bugged-out eyes, and long white strands of hair framing his face, Milky looks like a werewolf, so ugly he's cute. Darkly handsome, as my father says. Milky's legs are short, and he pants even when he's lying around on the living-room rug. Still, he keeps up with us on the path and doesn't complain. Dad, wearing a baseball cap that says #1 Papaw, keeps his end of the unspoken bargain by stopping for frequent cigarette breaks and carrying Milky up the places where there are ladders. Normally I won't go up ladders, and my knees are weak already, but today I want the feel of open space around me. Pine trees sweeping at sharp angles down to the river below give me the sensation of walking on the lip of a bowl, a wooden valley carved out by geology. Bluffs and passes. It doesn't seem to bother Milky to dangle from my father's arm as they ascend the ladder, even though he can see down into the depths of the gorge. Milky's used to going places, ever since my parents bought him in a pet store while they were visiting me; he took a fifteen-hundred-mile car trip on the floorboard in the first weeks of his life. He's living proof that the definition of a preposition is, as my eighth-grade English teacher used to tell me, anywhere a dog can go. My father had never been that keen on dogs, but when he saw Milky in his cage, it was love at first sight. When my mother agreed to their buying it, as long as it was a male, Dad did an expert illegal U-turn from the wrong lane of traffic, returned to the shop, and came back out holding Milky aloft.

After two packs of cigarettes a day for forty years, my father gets a little winded on the climb himself, but he makes it through the rock squeeze called Fat Man's Misery without any trouble. He likes telling me how in his forties, when he ran the steak house, he won twenty dollars apiece from two college kids eating there when they bet him he couldn't do as many push-ups as they could, and he did more than both put together. He never works out, but has always stayed in good shape by building decks and fences and docks, and working on a lot of people's cars for free, including several of my junkers.

Eddie is dead. His heart couldn't chug along anymore. All of his children and grandchildren converged on the hospital from everywhere in the country, and we spent a week listening to him sweat out the fluid in his lungs. My mother has taken off a whole week of discretionary days from the bank. This is her last chance to lavish on Eddie her daughterly attentions. She's venting her grief by managing everybody else's. She's in charge of choosing a coffin, tracking down the minister, receiving and divvying up the sympathy casseroles, making sure the kindness of the nurses is acknowledged with a box of Godiva chocolates, reminding Micky to give Mamie her sedatives at regular intervals, and so on. When the last out-of-town relative has been driven to the airport, Mom will let her agony catch up with her. For now, she holds it off by sheer will, the same way she held off a massive strep infection the weekend of her high-school reunion, only to end up with pneumonia the week after.

I'm not very good at holding mine off, but I'm doing OK, comparatively speaking. During the funeral-home visitation, when people who'd known Eddie all his life came to lament with Mamie as one old person to another, I talked Stephen and Lynnette and Elaine into going out to a restaurant for margaritas with me. We're the junior mourners, so people expect us to be a little frivolous. Lynnette's pretty good at telling jokes when everybody's stressed out, and while we were drinking our second round of double margaritas, she told one about me and Robert Redford, so we all got to laugh a little. And I had the chance to blubber without having to compete with anybody.

My aunt actually tried to throw herself in Eddie's grave after the cemetery service, and had to be restrained. And then there's Micky, who for the past several years has dragged Mamie and Eddie from state to state with him like a bad conscience, setting them up in apartment after apartment while he tried to run from legal problems and respiratory ailments. Mamie and Eddie stayed a few months with me when they were migrating west, to give Micky time to get back on his feet before they rejoined him. Mamie believes she's indispensable to his business operations, keeping books and minding stores, and Micky didn't have the heart to tell her this last time that there aren't any stores left to mind, and that he couldn't afford her upkeep and Eddie's plus his own medical expenses. I hadn't laid eyes on Micky himself in a couple of years, until I stepped off the elevator onto the coronary-care floor where Eddie was dying. Seeing Micky from the back at first, I mistook him for a convalescent old man. Living in Florida, where fungus, molds, and cocaine proliferate, was the worst possible thing for his asthma. It's gotten worse even since he moved to Arizona to do flea markets, and the corticosteroid therapy is softening his leg bones and destroying his hips. He stood outside in the funeral home parking lot, in a suit too big for him now. On aluminum crutches, sniffing and clenching his fists, ticking with asthma and sadness and osteoporosis, his eyes doubly red behind tinted glasses. Trying to keep his dignity. More full of rage and bitterness than ever. Several of us had to take turns driving the Lincoln Continental, big as a boat, he'd rented for the week, so we could be sure he didn't run a pedestrian over, either accidentally or on purpose.

In the hospital, my only real contribution was sitting with my arm around Mamie in the waiting room to try to keep her from going berserk. But even there I was pretty much a fifth wheel. She was so whacked-out that she hugged anybody and everybody, temporarily forgetting all the various grudges she's been holding against them, some for years and years.

Now I've escaped again, this time into the woods with Dad. He doesn't seem to mind being singled out for this duty. This is what he does best in times of crisis—be at one's disposal in his easygoing way, a mixture of professional escort and kindly country uncle. Adjusting his cap, squinting into the sun, he could almost be expected to hunker down, take a pouch of tobacco from his pocket, and stick a chaw in his cheek. But he's a diehard smoker. With his roguish good looks and work-broad shoulders, standing with one foot hoisted on a rock, taking a drag off his Pall Mall, he could be the approachable but silent male model in the cigarette ad, waiting for me to slip my arm in his.

Both of us are relieved to be out from underfoot. As we sit in a clearing so I can have a smoke too, on a log planed off by the park service, my father picks burrs off Milky, listening to me bitch at the universe to my heart's content. The man I've lived with for the past two years won't marry me because in the eyes of his family I'm nothing more than a hillbilly shiksa and two-time divorcée. *Divorcée* is the kind of word Eddie would have used. He had a single, unshakable marriage with Mamie for fifty-four years, and now he's gone to his death believing I'll never settle down and be happy, will never find a man who'll make me a good husband. Both of the times I married, he bought me a racy wedding garter made of lace. Hot pink the first time, scarlet the second. When I went to see him and Mamie after the second breakup, he never made any comment about it except calling me his little Wallis Warfield. His little duchess.

My father doesn't seem to take offense at me yearning after

Eddie's posthumous approval as if he were my father. Nor does he take my reference to the stability of Eddie and Mamie's marriage as an implied criticism of his. These days, as far as our relationship is concerned, there aren't supposed to be any subterfuges. Everything is straightforward. He's spent this afternoon, and the last four years, since he gave up booze, telling me in no uncertain terms that he loves me. When not in person, at least once a week long distance. He hugs me without stiffening up, and I receive his hugs without flinching, and return them. He listens to me attentively whenever I have something to say, and makes sure we spend time together, just the two of us, when I come to visit or he does. He drives me down to Natural Bridge, and I take him out for chiles rellenos at my favorite Mexican restaurant, which is in a bowling alley. He tells me he was never there for me when I was growing up, except to screw things up, and that he has a lot to atone for. I tell him it isn't so, and can almost believe myself.

Dad and Milky and I take a rickety bridge across a ravine with water rushing underneath. For the first time Milky shivers, cradled in my father's arms, looking left and right over the side. To soothe him, my father sings a song, one I used to hear him sing many years ago when he sat up alone late at night, listening to Charlie Poole records and trying to teach himself the banjo.

Me and my wife and my little brown dog
Crossed the creek on a hickory log
My foot slipped and I fell in
Busted my jug on a hickory limb
Ha ha ha hee hee hee
Little brown jug how I love thee
Ha ha ha hee hee hee
Little brown jug how I love thee

Milky approves of the song, and licks Dad all over the face and mouth. Dad lets him. I've discovered on this trip home that my father sleeps downstairs every night on the hide-a-bed, with Milky stretched out across his ankles. It's a fact he hasn't mentioned in any of our weekly phone conversations. When I ask Dad about this arrangement, he shrugs and tells me that my mother says he thrashes around too much, and that with her heart condition and high blood pressure and the heat she has enough trouble sleeping already.

"And what did you say to her after she told you that?" I persist.

"Nothing," he answers, "for the first few weeks. I hoped it was maybe just all the tension of your grandfather getting sicker. On top of the heart condition, he developed that Parkinson's shuffle, that wooden expression, and couldn't hardly feed himself. We had to take turns doing it. Mamie was scared to go in the other room, in case he might hurt himself, so we kept having to drive over there. Seems he had this disease a couple of years, but nobody had diagnosed it. He kept calling your mother different names, Mamie, or Judy, or Tinker—you know, the cat they had for such a long time. Course he's always gotten names mixed up like that, for years. But after we found out he had the disease, it upset your mother no end when he'd call her Tinker, or any other name. So I thought, well, if it helped her sleep better with me being in the other room, I'd give it a whirl. We do, you know, bicker a lot, carry on.

"But one afternoon we'd gone over, and I put some metal rungs on the bathtub, to make the whole bathing business less tricky for Edward. The whole time I was attaching those rungs, he sat on the couch with his wooden-Indian look, watching the same wrestling tape over and over on the VCR. I couldn't stand it anymore. I couldn't. Seemed like I'd been trying to prove to all of them for thirty-odd years, Mamie and Edward and your mom, that I'm not a jerk. And not getting that far. Edward didn't even know who I was anymore, didn't know whether I was Tinker or Stinker or Micky or who, and I was still trying to prove it to him. In the car on the way back, I said to your mother, 'I know your father's going downhill fast, and I'm sorry there's not any more we can do about it. But we need to think a little bit about what's going to happen to the two of us. I give you my paycheck every week, and take only coffee money for myself and a couple of bucks to play cards down at the Token Club on Saturday afternoons. I've given up booze. I clean the house. Dust. I come home every evening straight from work. I laid carpet for your parents, painted their walls, fixed their toilet and sink, so Edward doesn't have to die in a rented dump. I mean, it wasn't even their place. I drove all the way to Saint Petersburg, Florida, to load their furniture by myself with a hand truck, and sweated my ass off driving it back here with no air conditioning. What else do you want me to do, Constance? Just tell me. How long is it going to be until you admit that I've changed?'

"And do you know what your mother's answer to me was?"

Even with his #1 Papaw baseball hat on, his face is as grim and corticosteroid-bitter as Micky's. His carpenter's hand, cradling his Lhasa apso just beneath the chin, is veiny and tendony, the fingers actually muscular. It looks as if it could rip Milky's head off without meaning to. For a brief second I'm as confused as Eddie, and I have to focus very hard on exactly who I'm talking to. "No," I finally say. "What was her answer?"

"She said, 'Two things have changed about you, Jean. You don't drink and you work regular. Other than that you're the same son of a bitch you always were.' That was her answer. I've tried hard, Judy, but I don't know what more to say to her."

I believe him. This week I've watched him vacuum the carpet; run to the convenience store umpteen times; smoke outside on the deck he built, on account of my mother's heart condition, and remind everybody else to do so; wash up the dishes continually left by the relatives and other mourners as they nibble halfheartedly at the sympathy casseroles. I'll defend him to the death against anyone who dares to say a single bad word about him. After many years of struggling against him hard as I can, I don't want to hear my mother's side of the story, not even if there is one. I don't want to know anything more about beatings years ago, or absences, or days in court, or how she supported us single-handedly for years, supported five hungry beaks in the nest screaming for food. I was there. I saw it all. I nursed my bruises too. I was one of the beaks screaming for food. But now, for today at least, I'm going to act like one of those tan, spoiled Daddy's girls from Alabama, the ones who walk around the campus wearing Mexican wedding dresses, the ones with gold cards and student condos and license plates on their Porsches that say SUGR BBY. I'm going to tell my mother that my father is perfect, nearly perfect, and that she's forbidden to make any criticisms, now and forevermore. Ashes to ashes, dust to dust. Eddie is dead. Neither of us can have him anymore.

We walk out onto the broad, mostly flat expanse of rock that forms the Natural Bridge. A few people are milling around in the middle, not knowing quite what to do with themselves now that they're finally at the top. Dad and Milky and I walk over to the edge. We're protected from the drop-off by metal posts supporting a chain-link fence. A sign on the other side informs us of the obvious in big block letters. It says: DO NOT CLIMB OVER THIS FENCE. DO NOT ENGAGE IN HORSEPLAY. IF YOU SLIP AND FALL OVER THE EDGE, YOU WILL DIE.

The three of us are in no such danger. We don't plan to climb over the fence. My acrophobia has returned with a vengeance. My palms and fingers tingle with pinpricks of damp, and the Natural Bridge, massive as it is, part of the earth, seems to sway like a suspension bridge in a high wind. I feel woozier, now that I'm safe, than when I was making the climb. Maybe the crude, graphic reminder of the sign has brought this episode on. I ask myself how I'm going to hike down all the way we came up. I may have to be carried down in Daddy's arms while Milky walks. The forest service may have to bring in a helicopter to airlift me out, a damsel in distress. I make no mention of acrophobia, suppress all outward signs of it for the moment, and the three of us contemplate the view of the Red River valley, with its clayey banks and endless vistas of unspoiled forest. It's the bowl we're on the lip of. My father, now that he's unburdened himself, slips his paternal arms around me. We are father and daughter, closer than ever. I know I am safe, fence or no fence, standing at the edge of the world in his grasp. He gives me a hug, and I try not to flinch.

For seventy-five cents an hour I babysat for our next-door neighbors the Lajhres, watched their two kids and cleaned house. I was barely an adolescent myself, but I looked mature for my age. Their youngest kid was Danny, and he was for the most part a sweet little boy, always tracing cartoons and imitating cartoon voices, but he had one mean streak in him. His parents had given him a pet cat, and when he thought nobody was around he'd tape it inside a shoe box and throw it high in the air, pretending it was in a space capsule. I think its name was Space Kitty or something like that. When I found him tossing it up, I scolded him and told his parents, but even when they punished him, he'd slip right off and do it again. Finally they had to take the cat to the Humane Society to be put to sleep, because its mind was so fucked up. They were going to give it away, but it had become too unpredictable, started slashing people. Other than that one small cruelty, Danny was a happy kid and no trouble at all to watch.

Not that he didn't make mischief. One time when I was there, I didn't have much housework to do, so I went in his parents' bedroom and was trying on some new bikinis I'd bought for the summer. I was standing naked in front of their full-length mirror, checking out how much my tan line had faded over the winter, and plucking a couple of black hairs from my nipples with tweezers, when I noticed somebody stretched out at floor level watching me through the air vent. At first it startled me, because I thought a stranger had slipped into the house. Then I heard Danny laughing. I threw my clothes on and stomped into the other room. I was steamed, ready to spank him even if he wasn't my kid. I started giving him hell, said, "Why were you looking at me through that vent?" He looked cornered, lowered his eyes, and I expected some lame-brained excuse, the kind little boys give even when they know you know they're lying through their teeth. But what he said, in the timidest peep I'd ever heard out of him, was "Don't be mad, Judy. I just wanted to look at your inky-jinks." Then it was my turn to laugh. Inky-jinks! For a minute I didn't know what he was talking about. I thought he meant my bikinis or something. Or the birthmark on my hip, which I'm self-conscious about because it's wine-colored, sort of inky looking. It took me a minute to figure out he meant my breasts. I have to admit I thought his answer was kind of cute. I know I'm supposed to make some kind of connection between him tossing that cat up in the air and his peeking through the vent, conclude that he was a junior pervert. But there's a big difference between a kid who plays Space Kitty and wants to see my inky-jinks, and some goddamned bastard who gets his kicks by throwing a cat in a fireplace. I mean, my brother Stephen is like the most normal guy in the world, and even he and his little friends used to tear the legs off grasshoppers and tie the grasshoppers to their Hot Wheels with thread, so they could have races with them. It's just something boys have to get out of their system. And most of them do, don't they? If I hadn't been so flustered, I probably should have just taken off my blouse and said to Danny, "You want to look at my inky-jinks? Go ahead and take a good long look. There they are. Look as long as you want, and get it out of your system."

His name isn't really Guy. That's what I call some of the men I've been involved with when I think about the crap they laid on me. You come home off your shift and get all dolled up, after-bath splash, baby powder on your ass, all sexy sweet, and then they come home off their shift. You say, "Hi, honey." They say, "Whap! Whap!" Then next day at work you're walking around with two black eyes and five tons of makeup on, foundation, eyeliner, mascara, a quaalude for breakfast. Everybody's asking, "Is everything OK?" or mostly just trying to be cool about it, and you try to be normal too, saying, "Oh, didn't you guys know it's National Raccoon Day? Everybody's supposed to be made up like a raccoon." Then you finally split with the fucker, and he gets born again, calls your mom up a year later, all concerned about getting you right with the Lord. "Mrs. Miles, this is Guy. I was wondering if it were possible to localize Judy. I've been doing a lot of praying about her lately, and I'd like to talk to her awfully." Of course, my mom's great in situations like that. She'll say stuff like, "You had your chance to talk to her awfully when you were married, and from what I hear, you made good use of it." Once it's over, I'm not into "Let's be friends" and hearing about all their new hobbies and orgasms and personal revelations. If they're doing fine, that's great. But if I happen to run into one of them at a restaurant and somebody asks me who that was, I say that was Guy. That was just this Guy.

When we came home to the duplex we were renting, we found our panties stuck to the wall with Vaseline, the crotches cut out. Of course we knew who'd done it. We hadn't told anybody we were leaving, our new address, anything, but Jimmy found us anyway. Why do all the depraved ones end up having names like Jimmy and Bobby and Skipper? She and I would have moved out of the Mansion a lot sooner except that we were afraid to. I used to brush his hair out every night, otherwise he'd just let it tangle up. He definitely got his rocks off with us sweet young things. If I described him physically—wiry muscles, almost scrawny, hair to his waist, not that great of a complexion, kind of a Cat Stevens beard, only scragglier, big dark eyes but sunken—you wouldn't find anything special. Darkly handsome at best. But all of us were crazy about him. We were practically fighting each other to see who would get to sleep in his bed, on his mattress I should say, and he, of course, let us fight it out. The peacock and his flock of pea-brains. What kills me is that at that very time I was actually reading *Helter Skelter*, it was on the bestseller list, and I remember wondering how Ouija and Squeaky could let themselves be drawn into all that insanity. Well, not so much Squeaky, who looked pretty hard-bitten from the start, a grim reaper with freckles, but Ouija, who'd been the prom queen, the deb. But I kept that paperback right by the bedside, I was his preferred woman at that time, his *wohw*-man, and I can remember him with his face in the pillow, griping at me to turn off the light and stop reading. I couldn't put the book down. The other thing that kills me is if I was going to get mesmerized by a diabolical type, I should have at least gone for the real McCoy, instead of a cheap homegrown imitation. Sometimes I wonder if maybe he'd read *Helter Skelter* himself, because he was such a B-grade version of Charles Manson. He'd do stuff like make us help him steal a riding mower out of the garage of somebody's parents we knew. Didn't know how to hot-wire a car, I guess. Or locking me, on acid, in that cruddy, infested basement all night, with those big water roaches and God knows what else. Throwing the cat was part of building his image. And the crotchless panties and Vaseline. Something you'd expect an eight-year-old to do. His equivalent of painting words on the walls in blood. Only instead of Helter Skelter he would've written Inky Jinky. I have to admit that the thing with the panties really did scare me, though. My dad came over and put storm windows in, a dead-bolt, changed the locks, and my girlfriend and I started sleeping together with the phone by the bed. Because he really might have murdered us or forced us to have sex with him. He'd already given me the clap. We were young and small and scared of him, and he knew it. Our murders probably wouldn't have made more than the local news, but we would have been just as dead as Sharon Tate. Not as glamorously dead, but as dead. His sex kittens.

They had to shave his whole body. When the surgeon makes an incision from the top of your breastbone to your navel, there's a big chance of infection. It must have looked like a barbershop floor around there when they finished prepping him. And he reminded me of a shaved chinchilla when I went to his hospital room afterward. I'd never seen him without even his mustache. It was pretty shocking. He'd always been self-conscious about his excessive body hairiness. One time when the family got together at Boonesboro Beach, they couldn't get him to bring swimming trunks, but they finally talked him into taking his shirt off to lie on the chaise lounge and get a little sun on something besides his pate. All of the family are smartasses, everybody likes to joke around, and one of his kids, as he was lying there, called him Edwere-wolf. Not even a good joke, just clumsy. I mean nobody hardly even heard it with all the patter going on, but he put his shirt right back on, and didn't show his chest any more in public after that. But after that first heart operation, I could tell the absolute nakedness bothered him more than the discomfort of nasogastral tubes or his sawed breastbone. I think he couldn't wait for it to grow back. He had a hard recovery. There were complications, a secondary infection, and I sat up in his room a couple of nights to force Mamie to go home and get some rest. I'm the only one she trusted to turn the watch over to, because she knew I'd always babied him as much as she had. Those first couple of days he couldn't say much, or hardly even smile, his breathing was so labored, but once in a while he'd squeeze my fingertips and mumble, "A gentleman and a scholar, little sweets. A gentleman and a scholar."

That was my nickname for him. He'd taught himself to read Spanish, and corresponded with a pen pal in Cuba, a fellow stamp collector, for more than forty years. It's funny how he was always considered, and treated, as such a royal patriarch. Lionized. For reasons that were never clear, on the cardiac unit he was treated like a VIP, like someone of obvious public consequence, even though he never complained or asked for any special attentions. At first I thought maybe he'd been mistaken for some government official or other kind of big cheese. All of us in the family, especially the women, worshipped him. He hardly even seemed aware of it. He just worked at the printery, collected stamps, read about a dozen different newspapers. Made biscuits from scratch on Sunday mornings. Quiet stuff like that. He wasn't keen on socializing with anyone outside the family, although he wrote lots of postcards to his pen pals. When I was about to visit him, he'd send me a postcard too, with some little saying on it like: As the monkey said when he backed up to the fan, it won't be long now!

His two great indulgences were wrestling shows and crime magazines of the *True Detective* type. The gorier the better. He loved those ones with the pictures of mutilated bodies being carted off to the morgue, of motel rooms scored with chalk lines and spattered with blood. He'd sit there in his armchair chuckling as he turned the pages, as if he were reading some little private comedy that only he understood. Mamie would say, "Really, Edward. I can't imagine what you could find humorous about those magazines. They're downright offensive." But she never failed to buy him the latest issue when she went to the grocery store. And he watched *Championship Wrestling* on television every Saturday night, come hell or high water. Big fat guys in gladiator costumes and Apache costumes throwing each other for loops and banging each other's heads on the mat. Eddie would sit by himself in the living room shouting encouragement, carrying on, smoking a drugstore panatela, sometimes jumping up out of his armchair to protest a call. Nobody could tell him the wrestlers were faking it. That was the only time I ever saw him get upset. He never, ever raised his voice to Mamie, or his kids, or had an unfriendly word to say about anybody. He was a very tender person. But when somebody made fun of those programs and insisted to Eddie that the matches were hokey and prearranged, it really steamed him. And even then he didn't seem so much angry at the skeptic as flabbergasted. "This stuff isn't preplanned!" he'd insist, his voice full of righteous indignation, while the tag teams and referees and assorted ringside spectators illegally duked it out in the ring. "This is a free for all!" he'd say, jabbing his finger at the screen's irrefutable evidence. "Harum-scarum! Helter-skelter! Rockum-sockum! That fellow's really bleeding! He's really hurt!"

Elaine, Lynnette, and I all died and went to heaven. At least we thought it was heaven at first, because we were standing on a kind of cloudbank, shrouded in mist, and pretty soon a curtain of fog rolled back, and out stepped a naked man, or being I guess I should say. He had a harelip, face covered with severe acne scars, sallow skin, almost scaly, his body spongy and pale, his teeth broken and rotten. Darkly handsome. Very darkly handsome. A disembodied voice rang out, saying, "Elaine Miles, you have sinned, and for your sins you must pay. I condemn you to have sex with this being for all eternity." So off they went, the two of them together, and Lynnette and I were left there, shrouded in mist. Then the curtain of fog rolled back again, and an even more revolting naked being was standing there, or slouching I guess I should say. His limbs were shrunken, his spine deformed and twisted, as if he'd been born too soon. Boils were festering on his face, and lice swarming in his pubic hair. The disembodied voice rang out once more. "Lynnette Miles, you have sinned, and for your sins you must pay! I condemn you to have sex with this being for all eternity." So off they went too, leaving me there alone, shrouded in mist. I was freaking. But pretty soon the curtain of fog rolled back yet again, and out stepped Robert Redford, naked as the day he was born. He was all toned, perfect tan, handsome as hell, blue eyes sparkling, flashing that famous smile of his. A real dish. I thought, hey, this might not be so bad after all. Just then the disembodied voice rang out a third time, saying, "Robert Redford, you have sinned . . . "

We took Jimmy to court. I didn't want to go through with it myself, because I was afraid the judge would ask me questions about how I first got involved with him, whether I went to the Mansion of my own free will. Though some of the girls living there were legal minors, I was over eighteen, so there wasn't any question of making the issue into a statutory thing. The judge might ask details about our sex life, his personal habits, whether he beat me or inflicted psychological torment in some way or ways. Questions in the pursuit of trying to establish whether he was a normal guy or a pervert. Hard testimony was needed. I'm not even sure how they decide what normal is. All I wanted from the court was a peace bond, for breaking and entering, or harassment, or whatever they wanted to call it, so he wouldn't be jimmying into our place again, or idling along beside me in his car as I walked down the street, saying stuff, calling me old nicknames. "Hey, Slinky. Remember how you used to suck my cock? With your eyes closed, so you could taste it better. How come you don't like it anymore? How about another taste?" I don't know where guys get it into their heads that you think about their cocks even a tenth as much as they do.

I never wanted to lay eyes on him again. Which meant I didn't want to have to look at him face to face at the hearing. Everybody was going to be there—Dad, Stephen, Micky, not Eddie thank God—and even though they knew a lot of the details already, it's different when you have to say embarrassing stuff in public with your relatives sitting there in the courtroom. Micky kept talking about sending a couple of his bouncers over to the Mansion, settling things the quick way. I had to roll my eyes, even if Micky does mean well. I told him the situation was fucked up enough already, without his getting involved, but I could see my opinion didn't count for much with him just then. He reminded me that he'd tried to talk me out of marrying that first jerk whatsisname, I said his name is Guy, and he said, yeah, whoever, the one I'd ended up divorcing anyway. It was finally my father who talked him out of doing anything that might be prejudicial to the case and make a conviction less likely.

Dad was definitely pushing for a conviction. He'd told us not to touch anything; had the police come over and take pictures of the panties, the lipstick drawings on the bedsheets, the way they do in those detective magazines that Eddie reads. He suggested we write down as accurately as we could when the different phone calls took place, what exactly was said. Write an account of the parties at the Mansion, the thefts, the head trips. I've still got all those notes stuck in a drawer somewhere. I don't know, maybe Dad had read *Helter Skelter* too, and thought our lawyer would put on a performance like Vincent Bugliosi, passing those photos around so the jurors could get a closer look at the gory details. So he thought we needed to have reams of info, exhibit A and B and so on. He believed the guy would be sent away for years without parole, have to be put in a separate cell to keep the other prisoners from knifing him. In his heart, Dad wanted to believe I'd been kidnapped by some sort of Reverend Moon cult and indoctrinated against my will, even though I'd visited him and Mom in Louisville several times while I was staying at the Mansion. It wasn't like I didn't come and go whenever I pleased. For the most part. But Dad might have felt a little more at ease about the whole ordeal if he and Mom had had to hire a specialist in deprogramming to kidnap me back, instead of me just walking out of the Mansion one afternoon and leaving my belongings. To this day, I've seen him give those poor Moonies hell up one side and down the other when one of them is unlucky enough to lean in the car window to try to sell him a plastic flower at a traffic island. I think he holds them personally responsible for my fuck-ups.

I wanted the whole shebang to be as quick and painless as possible. Get it over with and forget that I ever met the demented bastard. I felt sorry for some of those other girls, who were always saying they were going to move out, but I didn't want to prosecute the whole thing myself. I had a feeling one or two of those girls had probably helped him break into the duplex. The woman who'd moved out when I did, and rented the duplex with me, wasn't even willing to press charges. Too freaked. She only came to the hearing because she was called in. Dad didn't sit with me during the first part of the hearing, saying he needed to sit back with Micky and keep him calm. I figured he just wanted to scope out the proceedings, kind of look at it from a distance and analyze the whole thing, finally get to see the guy in the actual flesh. See and not be seen.

The hearing went pretty quickly. It was clear that the judge wasn't that interested in the case, and was inclined to treat it more as an isolated case of offbeat vandalism and harassment, without getting into anything to do specifically with the larger scene of the Mansion itself. I guess the court docket was fairly full, and we didn't really have any people lined up to testify besides me and maybe my girlfriend if she was subpoenaed. Both lawyers seemed eager to settle the matter too. Cut and dried, ours kept saying to us, though I'm not really sure what he meant by that, because the other lawyer kept saying the same thing. Cut and dried. Like they were comparing different brands of beef jerky. The judge didn't ask me many questions, and most of them had to do with the actual break-in itself. I was afraid to look over at my dad to see how he was reacting.

A recess was called so the judge could talk to just the two attorneys, and the rest of us went out to smoke, take a powder, and hang out until they called us back in for the decision of whether the case would go to trial. Us in the hall, and the guy and a couple of his friends outside on the courthouse steps. My dad was extra quiet, but at least he was keeping his shit basically together. I kissed him on the cheek and told him I was happy he'd come with me. I just didn't want any hassles.

I went to get a peanut-butter log from one of the vending machines. While I was gone, he moseyed out to where the guy was sitting on the steps, and sat down next to him, like he was out there for a smoke. Jimmy, of course, had never seen my dad before, so he didn't know who he was. Hadn't really noticed him in the hearing, I guess. He's not the type who pays much attention to women's dads, unless they have a power mower in the garage or some stereo equipment near an unlocked window. When my father is freshly shaven and has one of his blue suits on, he looks like Joe Citizen. Member of the Kiwanis or the Optimists, honorary chairman of the community drive for the new children's hospital. You'd expect to find him manning the phones at the telethon. You'd never take him for someone who's been involved in fistfights or disturbing the peace. As he always used to say when he was about to step out for a sales appointment, he cleans up real good. If he was the one on trial, a jury would probably have trouble believing he did it. They'd be more inclined to say, "Come up here, and sit with us."

He offered the guy a Pall Mall, and the guy said, "Thanks," and took it.

"I hope you get off," said my dad.

"Beg pardon?"

"I hope you're not prosecuted. I hope your case doesn't go to trial."

"Thanks," the guy said again. He looked a little bewildered, since he didn't know this man from Mr. Smith. He wasn't expecting an endorsement from Jimmy Stewart. But he told him he was much obliged.

"Yeah," my dad said quietly, "I really do hope it's dismissed. Because if it is, and you don't go to jail, I'm going to kill you, motherfucker. You may think you're some kind of redneck hoodoo devil, and that you scare the living shit out of everybody. But I ain't scared of you. I'm Judy's father. You better hope you go to jail, 'cause if you don't, I'm going to come visit you and rip your fucking head off. So you keep thinking about that. You've been making a career out of scaring little girls, and now it's time for you to be scared." He said the guy's eyes got big as Frisbees, and he was kind of sizing Dad up, realizing that underneath the suit this man could probably deliver on what he was promising if given the opportunity.

Right before we reconvened, the guy's attorney came over to Dad and said, "My client informs me that you've been verbally harassing him. I'd like you to know that if this sort of threatening behavior continues, we'll be forced to take legal action."

"I'm not threatening him," said my father. "I was just issuing him a warning about the potential status of his flesh. Cut and dried, to use the legal phrase."

The judge issued a peace bond on the guy, that if he ever came near me again, or spoke to me or made contact in any way, shape, form, or fashion, under any arrangement, circumstance, or condition, he would be automatically arrested. There would be no trial. The decision was fine with me. It was one more monkey off my back. Not that I was overjoyed or anything. We all went back to the house and moped around, or rather I was moping and Dad and Micky were seething. Eddie had bought a big sack of fast-food hamburgers, and was trying to get us to eat them. He kept saying, "You need your strength, little sweets. You need your strength, Micky. You need your strength, Jean."

Finally he gave up and went back to reading his magazines. Eddie just wants everybody to get along and be happy. He adores his son Micky, and doesn't like to see him upset, grinding holes in the carpet.

The only thing that kept Micky from running out and doing some kind of Godfather number on my ex-housemates is that he was being investigated himself at the time for supposedly having hired somebody to kill a former friend of his. I don't remember exactly what the situation was, but the investigation against him was eventually dropped. My dad, for his part, restrained himself because I'd asked him to. I told him I knew he just wanted to protect his womenfolk, but that if he stirred things up anymore, I might end up paying for it.

He tried to keep his word. But about a month later, he was driving out Leestown Pike and happened to pass the Mansion late one night during a party. He parked his car, took a tire iron out of his trunk, and smashed the windows and headlights out of all the vehicles parked in the front yard and the driveway. I don't know what he planned to do after that, but I'm afraid it had something to do with keeping his promise to the guy rather than his promise to me. As he was heading up the front steps, two or three people started shooting at him from the windows of the house. They'd always kept guns around when I lived there. A few days later, Dad was back in court. A peace bond was issued on him, even though he was wearing his blue suit, and the guy and a couple of his friends got six-month suspended sentences. Dad drove around for months selling insurance with bullet holes in his car trunk and back windshield.

I never have run into Jimmy since. Sometimes I wonder whether the restraining order kept him away, or my father's threats, or whether he'd gotten tired of harassing me anyway and the thing with the panties was a last fling before he moved on to some new hobby. His attention span never was that long. For a while I believed that Micky had actually sent somebody over to waylay him, mess him up for good. But a year or so later, when my dad was moonlighting part time at a convenience store, the guy came in with some teenybopper hanging onto him, kissing on his undershirt and neck. My father watched them in the convex mirror as they wandered up and down the aisles getting corn chips and dishwashing liquid and ice cream and paper towels and rolling papers. Doing their late-night shopping. When they reached the checkout, the guy recognized my dad, and looked for a second like he might just leave the stuff on the counter and hightail it. But he dug some bills out of his jeans and paid for his purchases. And my father gave him his correct change.

In my first year of college, long before I ever managed to travel to Europe for a look around, acquaintances who had preceded me abroad were forever trying to impress on me the fact that I, as an American who'd never left the borders of his country, couldn't possess a true sense of history until I'd witnessed the sheer awesome physicality of massive structures like Stonehenge and the Acropolis. Anything I could point to, including the old universities and churches in New England (where I'd never been either), would be dwarfed in both age and scope by the most ancient European monuments. Or so they insisted, mysteriously producing potsherds out of their trouser pockets, as if they were real estate agents trying to convince me of the magnificence of their development sites by the reverse psychology of offering me the most modest gift, a styrofoam cooler or the like.

I might easily have countered by putting them into the framework of geologic or astronomical time, but I knew they would regard this as mere sophistry, the pettiest scholasticism, for there is no ideologue as inflexible and empiricist in orientation as a freshman recently returned from Europe, who has seen the splendors of the Continent with his or her own eyes. These are the same people who a few years later would swear to me that every person in France, from hairdresser to stock-exchange analyst, reads philosophical and theoretical tracts the way Americans read newspapers, and that the entire populations of capital cities in South America turn out en masse to poetry readings. I could no more mount a defense in the latter cases than in the former. I secretly cursed the Pueblo Indians for leaving no monuments more visually impressive than their modest rows of cliff dwellings, and for not doing at least that sooner.

To tell the truth, I probably would have conceded my friends' point eventually in any case, for I'm easily impressed by old buildings, especially since they're not a particular interest of mine. When I did pay my first visit to a major archaeological site—the (recent, by European standards) New World fortress of Machu Picchu—I was wowed as only a tourist who hasn't boned up beforehand can be. "This place is huge!" I exclaimed, immediately taking dozens of redundant snapshots before I'd proceeded past the first group of buildings, shaking my head in awe when I heard one traveler explaining to another that the gigantic stones were so expertly fitted together, without any mortar, that even a knife blade couldn't be stuck between them. I even allowed myself to be cajoled into paying for the services of a guide with questionable credentials, who casually fell in step beside me as I gawked my way along. He spent much of his time explaining how certain cool, shady slabs of stone had been used by the Inca doctors as surgical tables before the days of anesthesia, and telling me in strict confidence that a system of secret passageways ran underneath Machu Picchu for thousands of kilometers to the furthest outposts of the Inca empire at its height.

As implausible as such claims may sound, I've learned not to challenge any of them until I develop a more subtle appreciation of the material aspect of cultures more ancient than my own. I feel compelled to own up that, for me, driving past the old house on Palms Drive where I spent eight years with my family gives me a deeper sense of the endurance and disappearance of civilizations than a climb up the jungle-enshrouded pyramids at Palenque. I borrow my parents' car and make this trek to Palms Drive every time I pay a visit to Lexington. Sometimes I take a friend or girlfriend along, slowing down at the curve where the house sits in order to point out repairs that have been made to keep the site from deteriorating, or I give some historical information. Other times, when I'm feeling melancholy about certain happenings in my present life, or just wistful about my mortality, I make the drive alone. On occasion, when I see no cars in the drive, I have a strong desire to root around in the shed by the back porch, maybe find those two balls from the croquet set that got left behind when we moved.

But I would no more dare to do so than present-day Quechua Indians would pilfer the burial sites of their Inca ancestors. To be a *huaquero* is to invite one's own death, or at the least a swift, reverie-ending kick in the pants from the current owners.

Someday, though, I'm going to knock on the door and thank them for keeping the place up so well; much better, in fact, than we ever did when we lived there. The window screens we perpetually poked through and doctored with cellophane tape wouldn't let a fly in now. Someone replaced the plywood shed door my sisters and I were peeling away layer by layer. That terrible, untended tree with the bagworms has been cut down altogether, and a lawn service seems to keep the dandelions in check and the borders of the side yard edged. If we had stayed on as renters, the house and yard—and perhaps us along with it—would have perished just as surely, and inexplicably to future generations, as the early inhabitants of Chichen Itzá.

There's no question that my laissez-faire attitude toward civilizations past in no way diminishes my clannish concern for the continued existence of the remnants of me and mine. I'd be the first to try to get the jump on the ravages of nature and gentrification by declaring our former rental house an historic shrine, and converting the shed into a ticket booth, if it would ensure against the room-addition whims of future owners driven by concerns of equity and resale potential. I want there to be a record, however modest, of my family's sojourn on earth.

I'm not sure I could say the same for my sister Judy, who used to tell me that she didn't mind making plans as long as it didn't require having to write anything down. She is firmly rooted in the here and now; her normal conception of the future doesn't extend beyond the impending week. She will barely suffer such mnemonic devices as paychecks, since they require her to remember to go to the bank and cash them. Her distrust of direct deposit runs even deeper, since she would have to delay gratification long enough to make a withdrawal, and any number of apocalyptic happenings might occur in the time it takes to reach the drive-thru.

Judy fully expects a power surge to come along any day and erase all the electronic blips bearing witness to her existence. In fact, she wouldn't mind this happening in the least, since it would keep collection agencies and former boyfriends from tracking her down. Her initial impulse in moving to the Southwest was, in certain respects, an attempt to blot out the first twenty or so years of her life. This distancing act included the members of her immediate family; she half-wished—a wish she never quite defined for herself or for us during her annual visits home—that we would sort of go away forever.

One fierce winter when I was more adrift than the snow in Kentucky, I made my way out to New Mexico, lured there by its milder climate and easygoing ways, and spent a season in the little adobe house where Judy then lived. When she came home from her lunch shift as a waitress, she'd take great pleasure in emptying her pockets of crumpled bills, ones and fives and occasional tens and twenties, and tossing that day's wages carelessly on the dresser. When it was time to pay rent, go to the grocery, have a meal out, put gas in the car, Judy plucked the appropriate number of bills from the pile; otherwise they remained there uncounted and unheeded. If she got a hankering for tequila, fixings for chile con queso, a new houseplant, a nickel bag of Oaxacan grass, a pair of oversized sunglasses, she simply bought them, and her wants never seemed to exceed her means. The house had a fireplace just big enough to take the chill off the January nights, and every couple of days Judy would buy a pressed sawdust log (called Duraflame because it lasted up to three hours), which gave off a multicolored glow as it burned. I tried to persuade my sister that at the rate she was using up pressed logs she could buy half a cord of real oak at a fraction of the price and actually have a hotter fire for less, but my comparative statistical analysis was made in vain. I might as well have tried to convince her to invest in shares of Oregon timber.

Even though Judy's life has been less regimented than most, she believes that her years in Lexington were mostly spent mothering us, her younger siblings, plotting for our survival, and that as a result she never had a childhood of her own. She thinks of her youth there as similar to that of one of the coolies who helped build the Great Wall of China, and is determined to set her own agenda in adulthood. Her brief afternoon stints at the restaurant in Albuquerque didn't require her to show up until 11 A.M., so getting up at ten still left her plenty of time to, in her words, "put on my face, powder my wee-wee, and roll myself a joint." But she invariably set the snooze alarm to nine, to give herself a stolen extra hour of sleep, and her bliss was enhanced by ignoring the electronic urgings of the alarm at ten-minute intervals.

Supper took place whenever we got around to making it, usually not before ten at night, and Judy would insist on not putting the leftover chicken or pot roast into the refrigerator until morning, as if she meant for fire ants to descend on it while we slept and strip it to its bones. When she got up the next day and saw the remains of dinner still on the table, she usually chucked them into the garbage can, allowing as how she didn't like eating leftovers anyway.

When I came to Albuquerque, I was pretty much at loose ends, transient, between loves and between schools, so I provided suitable company for Judy. The local economy was as fitful and depressed as myself, and illegal aliens wandered from one neighborhood to the next, looking for stables to clean and rock gardens to landscape. I, overeducated for some forms of work and underpedigreed for others, had trouble finding a job as well. Each afternoon, after yet another vain morning of applications at research labs and Taco Bells, I'd spend an hour or two sitting at the bar of the restaurant, drinking free margaritas and eating free chips and salsa, while Judy charmed the noontime businessmen, made inside jokes with them, twitched her tiny nose, and showed some leg.

The main reason she made so much in tips (and thus could afford to work so little) was that she gave the impression, leaning on chair backs and sometimes sitting right down at the tables, that the lunch hour existed in a timeless, untroubled realm. Even when the place was packed, she appeared to have unlimited leisure to devote to the psychological and gastronomical whims of each and every customer. Though the food sometimes came late from the kitchen, she always made sure her customers got their cocktails right away, for she knew from firsthand experience that drinking early in the day on an empty stomach helped foster a temporarily pleasant sense of time and presentness. For the regulars at her two-tops and four-tops, it was a luxurious respite to idle for forty-five minutes every weekday in the Naugahyde seats of a dark lounge, suffused with gin and tonic, and with a comfortably vague sense of their importance as architects of Albuquerque's illustrious future. They were able to forget that many of its mirrored, monumental office buildings were empty due to overbuilding in a time of stagnation, and to remember only that semipermanent structures had been put solidly into place for the benefit of a fuzzy entity called "generations to come."

Though Judy, like me and like her regulars, possessed a keen sense of mortality, hers manifested itself as an eschewal of posterity rather than an enslavement to it. She had already made the decision, at twenty-five, to have her tubes tied, professing that since so many women seemed keen on propagating themselves, she didn't think her contribution would be missed. Once in a while, we drove up into the pinkish slopes of the Sandia Mountains to watch the sun set behind the distant mesas over in Arizona. As we slouched in the deep bucket seats of the gas-guzzler, in the parking lot at the base of the tram, and passed a tequila bottle back and forth, she sometimes intimated to me, in a matter-of-fact tone, her premonition that she would die young, would be the first of us siblings to go.

At the time, I was inclined to agree with her, though for reasons somewhat different from hers. In her mind, this mortal prescience was merely one aspect of an inborn pessimism springing from zodiac imbalances. I had a more direct explanation for it—namely, the fact that our other housemate, her second husband, Doug, was (heaven forgive both him and me for reinforcing the stereotype) a psychotic and a war veteran, given to beating her up and smashing her headlights in fits of rage. Ever since the night he pulled a shotgun on both of us, promising to blow our heads off, I had begun to develop premonitions about my own imminent demise. So I could appreciate the synchrony of past and future malaise in my sister's head as she lay beside Doug in bed, shielding herself with a pillow from his thrashing body and pummeling fists, as he relived, in sleep, the repetitive, never-ending onslaughts of jungle combat.

It took me a while to become familiar with these states of Doug, who, on account of his degree in archaeology and extensive backpacking through the world after the war, could be quite pleasant to listen to as he conversed with elegance about the ancient ashrams of Tibet, or remote, overgrown, dilapidated pagodas from the T'ang dynasty unknown to the common traveler. He'd smuggled various small stone deities out of Southeast Asia and perched them in niches around the house, ones originally made for figurines of Catholic saints. After he'd taken a shower, he'd light up several pieces of sandalwood incense and lounge about in a sarong or a flowing batik housecoat, and I had to admit that with the addition of his Fu Manchu mustache and swarthy complexion, he was a compelling presence to contemplate.

Judy and Doug had been separated before I arrived in Albuquerque; when she consented to his return in March, a period of relative honeymoon followed. The two of them would sometimes spend a night or two in a local hotel so they could sit in a jacuzzi, watch blue movies on cable, and have sex in the protracted manner they were accustomed to, without interruptions. I imagine that Doug enjoyed recreating the feeling that he was once again in Bangkok on a three-day pleasure pass. The fact that they had playfully named their Doberman puppy Ben-Wa gave me some insight into the probably Asiatic flavor of their erotic encounters.

One winter weekday, when Doug's construction crew didn't have work, the three of us drove up to Bandelier National Monument to see the Pueblo cliff dwellings. Like my mother, Judy was deathly afraid of heights, so while she strolled about the underbrush-lined paths on her own, Doug and I climbed a tattered rope ladder and sneaked into one of the caves to smoke some of the good hashish that he always seemed to have on hand. As we lounged against the walls smoking, like Indians in a kiva, he took from the pockets of his army jacket shells and stones which had once been used in Pueblo jewelry, and which he'd found in some of their graves when he did fieldwork as an archaeology student. Gazing on them, as he went on to explain how the cliff dwellers had perished altogether due to a lengthy drought, gave me the same eerie sensation I would have felt if he'd produced from his coat pocket the skull of one of the many Vietnamese he'd killed as a foot soldier in the war.

By the time the violent episodes between him and Judy began, I had found employment as a substitute teacher of math. Working as a substitute teacher meant that I received a phone call at 5:30 every morning informing me of my assignment and school for the day. Often I had to leave quite early in a clunker of a Korean War jeep to cover endless miles of desert freeway, since the schools in a western town like Albuquerque were spread out over such a large area. I welcomed having a certain orthodox structure to my days again, even though it meant cutting back on the late nights I spent with Judy and her restaurant friends at a cowboy discotheque, executing spins, holding Judy close for the first time in our adult lives, while she, in one of her disco skirts slit up the thigh, taught me the two-step and we rediscovered that we were brother and sister.

Though I cherished living on Judy's terms, and by her ephemeral moondial, and though I've never been an early riser by nature, I wouldn't have minded at all the predawn calls to substitute teach, except for the fact that after Doug's reappearance on the domestic scene I seldom was able to sleep more than two or three hours in succession. After a time, I tried to ignore their arguments by tightly pressing a pillow over my head, since I wasn't anxious to relive the black comedy of early youth with Doug as a more berserk and exotic version of my father, and Judy typecast in the role of my mother. But Judy got into the habit of bursting into my room at two or three in the morning, after taunting drunken, coked-up Doug into a frenzy by hurling deserved but imprudent epithets at him. While my sister danced about in the middle of my bed, crying out for me to protect her, Doug would enter the room with the speed and ferocity of an enraged water buffalo, moaning for her blood. All three of us were well aware that although I had defeated all expectations by growing into a normal-sized adult male, I was far and away no match, either physically or psychically, for a muscular, 190-pound war veteran hopped up on cocaine and adrenaline, possessed of all the subtlety of a pissed-off linebacker.

The net result of these encounters was usually that I would say diplomatic, unthreatening things to Doug, and in an intricate sonata of self-effacement, give quiet and almost invisible assent to his shouted, redundant characterizations of my sister as a fucking bitch, a fucking whore, a fucking slut, a fucking tramp, etc., until he wore himself out. Peace, more often than not, was restored, but at the cost of routinely reviving the ghosts of my puny childhood, with all its sense of inadequacy about not being able to overpower my father, to protect my sister/mother from his physical aggression. It wouldn't have been so bad humiliating myself in this way if I'd felt Judy achieved something by it. After a fight, Doug would often either conk out cold in one of the dining-room chairs, or, if he managed to stay conscious long enough, leave the house for the remainder of the night to go stay at his brother's.

In the ensuing lull, I would make all the predictable moves of trying to get Judy to go for counseling, of offering to accompany her, or to move into an apartment with her, just the two of us, since I now had some earning power, if she'd only leave Doug once and for all. She, in a predictable countermove, would flat-out refuse, or more often, promise anything but fail to make good on those promises later. These days, since the advent to Albuquerque of Art Deco juice bars, personal fitness counselors (of which Judy is one of the most popular), psychic mediums with college degrees, and all the other manifestations of the personal-growth renaissance, Judy has no qualms about speaking to total strangers at intimate length about "my therapist," tossing out the phrase as freely and possessively as when she says "my hairdresser," or "my gynecologist." But in the bad old days I'm speaking of, to suggest therapy to Judy was to set her fragile sense of normalcy aquiver to its very foundation. "Do you think I'm crazy?" my sister would accuse me—my sister who minutes before had performed a moonlit dance of hysteria on my mattress, while her second husband, a hairy arm's length away, prepared to reenact the Tet offensive on her minute, prancing body.

"No," I would answer, "I don't think you're crazy. But I do wonder how you can continue to get back in bed and be intimate with Doug after he's smashed every breakable possession you own, threatened to shoot you, blackened your eyes, cracked one of your ribs, and put bruises and welts all over your body."

"I don't know," she'd answer, beginning to weep. "It's hard. I just love him." However dubious a light Judy's succession of husbands and live-ins may cast on her seriousness about the ideal of marriage, I learned during those months that my sister takes almost too much to heart the phrase "till death do us part." Though many women and men take that identical nuptial vow, for Judy the death referred to was ever-present. It didn't require even a rudimentary sense of futurity on her part.

For many years I've nursed a persistent concern, amounting to an obsession, with there being a record of my family's existence and survival, a proof that we didn't perish due to famine, plague, meteor showers, glacial advances, wars, natural selection, or our own collective stupidity. This wish has nothing to do with a desire for greatness, for my sisters, parents, and I have done nothing that will be of significant interest a thousand years hence to anyone except perhaps our immediate descendants, or those who, like myself, have a keen appetite for trivia. I don't share the megalomania common to Cheops and Tutankhamen. I want nothing more than a notch for us on the genealogical tree of humanity, even if it's the kind thoughtlessly carved by a passing, lovestruck adolescent, an inscription that with time and the growth of the tree becomes distorted and unreadable, yet is always there. Or I'd be perfectly content with the sort of banal yet scrupulous scribblings one finds in the musty, seldom-read records of a county courthouse: we were born, we married, we transferred the title on a used car, we divorced, we changed our name back, we bought another car, we had our license suspended, we had children, we married again, we had no livestock but a lot of dogs, we died, we lived. Perhaps that's why, after many years of procrastination and unkept promises to myself to write a book, I began to keep notes toward an almanac—a modest endeavor at best and the work of a dilettante, but one that at least puts us Mileses on the books.

I could understand Judy's rejection of her prolific, smothering, self-perpetuating, self-important clan, and her conviction at that time that there wasn't a damn thing about us worth the bother of commemorating, certainly not worth writing a book about. I didn't expect the two of us, whatever genetic features we shared, to ride all the same existential hobbyhorses. During the months I lived with her, I in fact learned to love her as a grown-up sister by seconding her rejection, by living in her perpetual present, one without any need for record-happy scribes like myself. We Mileses, taken as a group, do have an irritating penchant for aggrandizing our petty domestic concerns to the status of great and enduring historical conflicts (Judy, despite her objections to this penchant, being no exception). But it distressed me to no end that for my sister, the price of trying to eradicate her memories of our clan should be destroying her own self. Judy seemed to want to cut the line short by the paradoxical means of replicating in her relationship with Doug all of our family's wickedest emotional progeny, by parodying and magnifying our worst insanities to the point where they posed a constant threat to her physical life. I didn't want her to die to make an unconscious point about our family's excesses. That willingness to die in order to get the moral upper hand is itself one of our family's most excessive traits.

I'm only able to write about these episodes because I know that Judy did in fact live through them, in spite of her strenuous efforts not to. I more than toyed with the idea of falsifying my data, of omitting Doug from this recollection altogether, on account of his being an intruder who threatened our survival. Like any good scribe, I can be a bit of a curmudgeon when it comes to my pet subject matter, and I don't mind doctoring it up to suit my crusty notions of accuracy.

One of the things that baffled me about Doug is how, with all his genuine love of archaeology, he could in his sessions of fury retain enough presence of mind to leave his smuggled stone deities intact, yet have no qualms about smashing to pieces all the secondhand lamps and dishes, the gas-station jelly glasses and scuffed end tables my parents had bequeathed to Judy when she moved out to Albuquerque without any furnishings of her own. The only reason I can forgive Doug now is that I imagine the potsherds of those possessions must still exist in a landfill somewhere on the outskirts of Albuquerque, and that they will be unearthed someday, hundreds of years from now, in all their crunched-up and unrecognizable glory.

Right after Bart passed on, I got to cussing him late one winter afternoon for never having gone in with me to buy that little farm out on Clear Creek that went dirt cheap, when I was just out of the service and could have used a VA loan for the down payment. I'd been cootering with the Mustang transmission all afternoon, because I needed to go make some sales demonstrations in Nicholasville, seeing as how I was working on commission and I'd had to take time off to run errands connected with the funeral, two or three times a day between Berea where my mother and the funeral home were, and Lexington where I was, and Richmond where this new memorial garden was. And there I was laying on my back in the parking lot underneath the car, missing another half-day's worth of commissions because the transmission had screwed up. It was raining sleet over my shins and shoes, and I'd busted my knuckles on the cold metal chassis, so I felt like somebody had the fingers of my right hand in a vise grip.

If me and him had bought that farm we all would've lived half a mile from the Chasteen community cemetery, where anybody who's ever lived in Disputanta can be buried for free, and me and a couple of buddies from around there could have built the coffin ourselves, custom made with plenty of elbow room, and hauled it up the hill to the cemetery. A coffin is a simple design, a few hours work at most, leaving us plenty of time to wash the body, shave it, dress it, put fresh clothes on it. That's the way they used to do it. No funeral homes and no embalming. I could've taken off all the time I needed without asking anybody's permission, because I would've been my own boss. That's the reason I never became an auto mechanic. I don't mind the aggravation of tinkering with my own cars—in fact, I usually enjoy it—but I don't want to be somebody else's grease monkey. Anyway, Bart wouldn't have died when he did to begin with, because there would've been too much planting to do, and topping tobacco, hanging it in the rafters, repairing fences along the creek that had gotten weatherbeaten during the winter months and been run up against by cattle, cribbed on by horses. So he never would've had the luxury of sitting for twenty years in his easy chair in the living room after that first mild stroke, watching television and waiting to die. Twenty years he waited. I'd like to know what the hell he was thinking about. Too big of a risk, he said. At 3 percent interest! They were giving the damn place away.

By the time I got the transmission working right, I was so aggravated with it, and my wet feet, my right hand throbbing and numb, my toes hurting almost as bad, and thinking about how I never did use that VA loan, that I decided to drive over to Richmond to the cemetery and have a little conversation with Bart about this matter of the farm and a few other things we never did quite get worked out between us. I'd have the upper hand, since he couldn't hardly give me any backtalk. I stopped at Doodle's first to have a few whiskeys, take the chill off, and the bartender sold me a bottle on credit. He doesn't normally sell bottles to customers even for cash, but I've spent enough afternoons there over the years, and so has he, that he never begrudged me the occasional pint when I asked for it.

When I got to Richmond it was after dark, and the gates of the memorial garden were locked. I can't understand why a cemetery should ever close. Don't they know that the next of kin need to pay their relatives an after-hours visit sometimes? Maybe it's locked because it's built in a bad section of Richmond, and the city is afraid vandals will wander around inside. But whoever put it there didn't mind building it next to an industrial park, where pollutants are illegally dumped into the ground and seep down into the graves. I guess they figured the inhabitants wouldn't know the difference. I parked my car along the road and climbed over the fence to get into the memorial garden.

All the tombstones are flat, embedded in the ground, and no kind of statuary or headstones or even baskets are allowed. The zoning laws may be lax, but the building code is strict. Anyway, everything inside is flat, and so my father's grave was hard to locate, kind of like finding a particular white cross in a soldier's cemetery. Also, nobody in the Miles family had ever been buried in this memorial garden before, not until Bart, so I didn't know my way around. If he'd been buried in the Chasteen cemetery, or in the Miles section in the churchyard at the Macedonia Church out on Holt Hill, I wouldn't have had any trouble tracking it down, even on a night as black and drizzly as this one, even though I was tanked up with a warm pint.

The place goes on for acres and acres, and I staggered from one marker to the next, squinting down at each one in the weak flame of my butane lighter, the rain dripping into my eyes. I'd forgotten to bring a flashlight or an umbrella, either one. I wasn't having much luck, but finally I came across a grave site with a canvas tent canopy set up over top of it. I wondered if maybe the funeral home hadn't left the one from Bart's service up over the weekend on account of the rain, so I headed over there to check it out. Just as I was getting close enough to see that it was a freshly dug grave, I stumbled over a section of taut rope bolstering the aluminum poles of the canopy, and slid belly first straight into the open grave. When I belly flopped on the bottom, it knocked the wind right out of me. I lay there for a while, trying to get my breath back, spattered with mud and muddy water.

Once I could sit up and breathe, the first thing I did was start to sob. I hadn't cried in probably ten or fifteen years, not even when I tried to force myself. It felt pretty odd. I hardly could remember how I was supposed to hold my face. Next thing I knew I was shouting. I figured since I was down there where nobody could hear me, I might as well use the opportunity to get some other things off my chest. I shouted, "Dad, why did you have to die? Why did you never once tell me you loved me, not even in a roundabout way? Why did it take me all afternoon to fix the goddamned transmission? I'm a good mechanic. My knuckles are raw and now I've bitten the inside of my cheek from falling down in here. Why did you buy a plot in this cheap, polluted memorial garden next to an industrial park? I can smell the faint reek of chemical by-products in the raw earth. It doesn't smell like the kind of mud to find nightcrawlers in. Why did you talk to Mom so much about financial hardship, about Social Security and the inadequate pension plan? I don't even have a pension plan myself, but we'll take care of her one way or another. What happens after death? Are there mandolins in heaven, or just harps? Are you still on the booze?"

I got no answer to any of these questions and comments, but I felt slightly better just for having the chance to jaw. I sat back down in the corner of the grave and tried to make myself comfortable. True, I was soaking wet, but at least the canopy would keep any more rain from falling on me during the night. I'd slept in worse circumstances than this. I'd once slept in the bed of a woman so sleazy that when I woke up in the morning the only clean place on her was the nipple I'd been sucking on the night before. I'd slept in sawdust shavings on top of a Skee-Ball machine in a bar in Winchester. But Constance would be wondering where I'd got to by now. I remembered that I'd promised to take Lynnette to a theater rehearsal. Besides, it was colder than a gravedigger's ass down here. I tried clawing my way up the sides, but they were too slick and muddy, and I was too drunk to get a very good grip. I cried out for help like a pig in a roasting pit, even though the chances were a thousand to one of anyone coming within earshot before the next morning.

Within a few minutes, about the time my voice started to hoarsen up, I noticed somebody looking down at me over the side, holding a butane lighter of his own, or possibly the one I'd lost when I tripped. "Hey there, feller," he said. By his thick speech and the way he teetered on the edge, I could tell that he was a drunk, like me. Maybe he was out searching for his father's grave in the rain too. I asked him if he was searching for his father's grave. "Naw," he said. "I'm just taking a shortcut home. My pap's buried in the Chasteen cemetery. It don't cost nothing, and the accommodations are a lot nicer. You can set the headstones up aright, too, the way they're supposed to be, and put your flowers in a basket. Fix it up real nice. But what you been hollering about, anyhow? What's the matter?"

"Shoot, friend," I said, "I'd be much obliged if you'd give me a hand. I'm well nigh about to freeze down here."

"Why no wonder," he said, looking down into the pit with eyes as big and round as full moons. "I ain't surprised a-tall. You done throwed all the dirt off you!"

When I was in the service in Texas, I limited my drinking to weekends. I'm the first to say that I drank steady and heavy for more than thirty years, but anybody who says I was an alcoholic back then, even beginning to be one, is telling you a tale. Sure, we'd go across the border on Saturdays to a little pueblito in Mexico, tie one on in the strip joints. I was a staff sergeant at that time. There was a place we loved to go to called the Kentucky Club. The shingle hung out front was a perfectly outlined map of the state of Tennessee, with the words Kentucky Club written across it, and we figured that was close enough. The strippers were pudgy and wore high heels they couldn't hardly walk in, ones that made the cheeks of their butts quiver. They had names like Conchita Calientita. The emcee would stand off to one side with a hand-held microphone and announce them. Conchita Calientita and her hairy taco! On the way back, we liked to have jeep races in the dark along the dry riverbed.

As soon as I finished my stint in the army, I used some of the money I'd saved up to buy a Harley with a rocking clutch, 1154 cc's, and a fairing, one that had been used as a police motorcycle, and drove back home cross-country on it to marry Constance and adopt Judy. That was quite a machine. I thought I was one badass son of a bitch. I drove all one day and all the next on state roads, in the dog days of summer, without sleeping, without a helmet, and without any sunglasses. By the time I pulled into Boone Street my eyeballs were sunburned blood-red. You've heard of keeping your eyeballs peeled; well, mine peeled the very next day.

Then I had to turn around and drive three hundred and fifty miles round-trip across the state line to Jellico, Tennessee, because it was illegal for somebody as young as Constance to marry in Kentucky without her father's permission. God, she was gorgeous then. Men used to go down to the hardware store and buy L-brackets, wire clippers, caulking, anything, even if they didn't need it, just to stand there and watch her ring it up. Hardware on the counter and easy wear on the eyes. Of course, Mamie didn't have much use for me as a son-in-law, and even Edward was as you might say kind of lukewarm about the idea, so Constance told them she was going uptown to the Porter-Moore to meet some girlfriends for a Coke float. There's a long steep hill, must be five miles at least, right before you hit Jellico. You can see the town roofs below you there as you're coming up on it. Like buzzing it in a plane. I put the gearshift in neutral and we coasted right on across the state line and into Jellico.

We moved to Lexington, and I drove a truck for the Maclean Trucking Company. I had to back forty-foot tractor-trailers into loading docks so narrow you couldn't slip a jack of spades between the truck and the concrete on either side. A tight turning space too, and you couldn't see out both sideviews as you backed up, so you had to stay sober and know what the hell you were about. I remember that rig well. Double clutch, with a bulldog gear so low that if you were driving through steep mountains, you could practically get out and walk to the next town for a cup of coffee while you waited for the truck to catch up.

I never drank on the job, or away from home. Maybe a beer at night, sitting with Constance out on the stoop, after she put Judy down. It was cooler outdoors. We couldn't sit inside anyway, not with the baby trying to sleep. The apartment was so small the mosquitoes had to take turns coming in to bite us. Constance's brother lived with us there for a while. He'd gotten a summer job at a dry cleaner's. The three of us would turn the hose on, Saturday afternoons in our bathing suits, and spray each other to stay cool, chase each other around the yard with the hose, sliding in the wet grass. We called it the Riviera. The summer on the Riviera. We ate a lot of macaroni and cheese and a lot of salmon croquettes. A lot of pancakes. I was going to a special night school, learning how to work on adding machines a night or two a week when I wasn't away on the road.

I've always had a lot of ambition. I don't mind saying that. People who know me say, "Jean, you take off like a rocket." Then something happens. It's like I fizzle out, or get sabotaged, or shoot myself in the foot somehow. I'll be sales leader for the first few months, absolutely setting records, winning plaques, then all of a sudden I'm in a slump and can't even make my minimum quota. It's happened to me a hundred times. My first big mistake was letting myself be talked into giving up Judy for a spell. Constance's brother went back to Berea College and moved out, so we didn't have his share of the rent anymore. Constance was pregnant with Elaine, and she suggested that we leave Judy at her parents for a while, just until I started making a little more money. She thought it would be good for her mother pyschological-wise, too.

The thing is, I can see clearly now that we would've done all right. I wasn't making great money, the situation was tight, but I was doing okay. I suppose I must have felt we'd kind of tricked her parents by going across to Jellico. I wanted to set things to rights with them, so they'd see that I wasn't the redneck peckerwood they'd made me out to be, that I didn't come to the table hitching up my blue jeans and saying, "Ah shore rekkin ah'll have me summer them mustard grains." I was kind of countrified, and maybe I still am, but that didn't mean I was a clodhopper, didn't have smarts. But I hadn't been around for Constance when Judy was born, and her parents had, and I guess a lot of things like that were going through my mind, so I said okay. It was my own fault, really, for ever consenting to that arrangement in the first place.

Biggest mistake we ever made. After Judy was gone, we fought about her all the time. That and money. It wouldn't always start out that way. My folks would be wanting to have us over for dinner, and Constance would say, "I don't like to go over there because I feel like your father is always undressing me with his eyes, he hugs me longer than a father-in-law should," and I'd say, "The real reason you don't want to go over there is because your mother's been feeding you a lot of crap about my family not being good enough, just because Bart doesn't wear a necktie to dinner every night like Edward, and Mom doesn't spend all her time sewing new outfits for herself, and I suppose that's why your folks never go pay my folks a visit when they're invited, or invite my folks over when they practically live in the same town," and she'd say, "If my family had something against you and your family, do you think they would have agreed to care for our baby daughter until we can get on our feet," and I'd say, "Yes, because they want to steal Judy away from us, when I'm making a decent enough living for us to have her right here if we could stick to our budget." And off we'd go. It was crazy. We really didn't have that much to fight about, especially when I think we only had one baby at the time instead of five.

And of course we couldn't just go over and get Judy. It was more complicated than that. Kind of as if we'd signed a contract and couldn't redeem it until at least three months were up. We'd go over there to visit once a week when I had a day off, like we were on a weekend pass, but that would be it. I must have thought I was back in boot camp. I remember there was a guy who'd enlisted, and then decided he didn't like the climate and the hours so well, all the crawling around on the prickly baked earth, so he got his mother to call the CO to try to get him discharged. Every time she called, the drill sergeant would march every single one of us grunts over to the phone to take the call together as a unit, and then make us run laps in the blistering

Texas sun for a couple of hours. Boy, we made that enlisted guy's life a living hell. We gave him some shit over that. Anyway, sometimes when Constance and me would talk about bringing Judy back, she'd say, "It's not fair to Mom," and I'd get a sort of hangdog look and think, "Well, maybe she's right, we're still kind of inexperienced." I still must have been pretty naive in a lot of ways. I'd try to go back to studying the manuals for adding machines, but I couldn't seem to concentrate.

Judy was only gone for a little over three months, but I swear to God it seemed more like three years. Legally, of course, I could have taken Judy back anytime I wanted. We'd gone through the adoption process and everything, since my name hadn't been on the original birth certificate. I even drove over to Mamie's a couple of times and sat at the end of the street like a criminal, a kidnapper, trying to work up the conviction to walk in there and scoop Judy up. I started hitting the booze more regular when I was out driving the rig, moping. I can't shoulder that off on anybody else. Nobody was forcing me to drink.

During the summer on the Riviera, I had always tried to make it back home of a night if I was any way half close enough to drive it. I'd drive half the night just to be able to spend two or three hours with Constance and the baby. I loved seeing that cleft in Judy's chin, just like mine. It sounds crazy to say it, but if I saw that cleft fifty times a day it wasn't enough. And Constance and me probably had fewer interests in common than any two people on this green earth, but she had the loveliest little butt you ever saw, she really did, and I was all full of muscles from running the 220 and the 440 hurdles for years, plus boot camp and the service and then loading and unloading my truck all the time. Constance says even today that when she first met me, my thighs were like tree trunks. She liked to put her arms around them. I guess that's what people call a shallow attraction and not much of a basis for a marriage, but I can tell anybody who cares to know that when I slipped into bed at 4 A.M. and we put our bodies together, it felt pretty damn sweet. The baby crying in the corner was just part of the atmosphere. And we certainly never gave a thought to whether or not Constance's brother heard us.

But with Judy out of the house and me and Constance bickering so much, it seemed real easy to make excuses for not driving back, for deciding I was too far away from Lexington to make the long haul worthwhile. And it was only one step from there to feeling sorry for myself on account of there not being any chance of getting back, and then feeling lonely, and buying a couple of six-packs to make the loneliness more bearable. If you're tanked enough, being sad even has a kind of sweetness to it. Not the same kind as going home; more of a sickly sweetness. The dangerous thing about something like a cleft chin on a baby is that it's so cute, it provides the perfect occasion for getting mawkish-mealymouth-drunk, and if you're not real careful, somewhere down the road you start getting into that crazy logic of telling yourself that the real reason you became a heavy drinker, lost one job after another, lost your house, had your wife divorce you and your whole life go to hell, is because your baby had a cleft chin. I was an expert in that kind of logic for a quarter of a century. I could give seminars in it.

My cousin finally made up her mind to sell Uncle Jay's place. Her brother and sister had been wanting to sell for years, and every time they'd get the deed drawn up and settle on a price with a buyer, she'd tell them she needed to mull it over in her mind some more, and back out at the last minute. She called me from Texas to say this time she was decided to go through with it for real, and would I mind going down to Clear Creek to make sure none of the pipes had burst over the winter.

So I went down. The pipes had held. After I'd replaced a spigot and a couple of washers, I drove on down the gravel road to the Hainted Holler to look at the little log and tar-paper house Bart had built and that we'd lived in for a year or so, back before he got on as timekeeper for the WPA. Everybody used to say somebody had killed the tannery paymaster back up in the Hainted Holler a long time ago. Nobody wanted to even walk by there if they could help it, so Bart took over that finger of land himself. He never did believe in haints. Laughed at people who did. I walked around the shack and inspected it. The shingles had rotted and the frame tilted to one side. The windows had long since been punched out. A lot of the floorboards were missing, and I had to mind my step walking through it. There was a dirty, dusty mattress in one of the two rooms. It looked like the kind of place me and my brother used to go to smoke cornsilk and make out with girls. There had been a pretty good cold spring a little piece up the hill. I found it, cleared away the dead leaves choking the mouth, and had a drink of water. It tasted sweet and cold as ever, and left an aftertaste of sulfur in my mouth. I sat down Indian-style on the ground to smoke and enjoy the silence of the woods. They hadn't changed that much. Plenty of poplars, chestnut oak, locust, sloping to a watershed down near the road.

I looked up the other way and here came Bart, wading down the holler, up to his waist in leaves. He had on the makeshift Confederate soldier costume he used to wear every year in the reenactment of the Battle of Richmond up at Indian Fort. I could see the flash of the black stripe in the leg of the steel-blue tuxedo pants as he shuffled along. The costume looked like it could stand to be dry-cleaned. Orange and yellow leaves clung to the brim of his hat. In his left hand, he was carrying his mandolin by the neck, letting it swing back and forth like it was maybe a bottle of corn whiskey he'd picked up on his way to a dance.

"Bart," I whispered, not daring to move, or even exhale my smoke too fast. "Is it you?"

"You know, Jean," he said, "I've been hankering after some of Francine's soup beans with that good chow-chow she makes. I think about those damn things all the time, and it like to drives me crazy. You can't get beans like that nowhere else, can you?"

"No, Dad. I love them too. But she's on vacation right now in Florida, down where Colleen and her husband are stationed with the air force. She went on a hydrofoil tour of the Everglades with them. I hear she likes to have her a piña colada in the late afternoon right before the early-bird special. For a while after you passed on, we really were afraid for her health and sanity. You know the way couples who've been married for that long oftentimes pass away within a year of each other. Mom looked like a pretty good candidate. She cried and cried. Moved into the spare room. But after the first few months she bounced right back. She's on a frequent-flyer plan. And has even made Maggie stop sleeping with your shoes under her bed. Maggie had them underneath there in a shoebox, and would get them out and kiss them. Was always wanting to go next door to Mom's and sleep on your bed. Mom wouldn't hear of it. According to her, grief for your daddy or your husband is one thing, but Maggie's downright deranged. She said, 'If anybody's going to be carrying on, it's going to be me. I was the wife.'"

Bart fiddled with the sword in his scabbard and didn't look me in the eye. He seemed to have his ear cocked to a dog barking off down toward the creek, or to some high-pitched sound from the other world that I couldn't hear. "Listen, Dad," I said. "We could drive up and get some soup beans for you at the Cracker Barrel. Berea finally has one of its own. They've built a new one right off the interstate."

"No," he answered, his voice full of longing. "It doesn't work that way. I can't take trips like that anymore. Besides, they put too much salt in theirs."

"That's not true. You always said the Cracker Barrel's soup beans were better than Mom's. Whenever you had a hankering for them, you made her drive you all the way to Richmond. In fact, after your stroke, it's about the only way she could get you to go out of the house."

"Well, maybe that's so. I guess Francine didn't put enough salt in hers, come to think of it. Said the doctor wouldn't allow it. But her chow-chow was better." He set to tuning his mandolin, and played a few chords from "Shady Grove," humming and mumbling along with it. Hmm hm hm hm love hmmm darlin mhm my true love mh mh Harlan. I'd forgotten how good his picking was.

Still, something about the song sounded off. I thought maybe the finger stiffness from his stroke had stayed with him. Then I noticed that the B-string was missing from the mandolin. He read my thoughts. "Yeah," he said, "I'd give my life for a replacement string. I can't make 'Soldier's Joy' come out sounding right neither, and I've even got the outfit for it. I'd like to know who in the hell buried me in full regalia and with my mandolin, and forgot to replace the damn B-string."

"I suppose it was me," I said. "I really only stuck the mandolin in the coffin as an afterthought. It had been shoved back in the closet for years. We never could persuade you to take it out of its case. I shined it up, but I didn't think you'd be playing it that much."

"Well, it looks like I ain't." He fished around in his coat pocket with his left hand and pulled out a flask.

"Where'd you get that?" I asked. "I know we didn't bury you with it, unless the undertaker's assistant stuck it in your pocket to keep his boss from finding out he was taking a nip on the job."

Bart chuckled and looked down at the flask. "That's for me to know and you to find out." He held it out toward me. "You want a snort?"

"No thanks," I said. "I don't drink anymore. I haven't for nigh on three years now."

Bart screwed the cap back on and cocked his eye at me. "Now, son, I know me and you never did communicate too well, but that's one piece of business you don't have to fib about. I never asked you about them things. But you always was the slipping-off kind. More like your Uncle Jay. One time he went out to a dance on a Friday night and rolled in home dead stone drunk of a Monday morning when he ought to have been up to the newspaper office. Ashen as a corpse. He didn't say a word; just climbed in under the covers and commenced to moan. His wife followed him into the room, took one look, and dropped down on her knees to pray. She prayed, 'Lord, please help this poor drunken sot.' Jay peeked out from under the quilt and whispered, 'Don't tell him I'm drunk. Just tell him I'm sick.'"

"Sounds like Jay. But Dad, I really don't drink. A lot of things are different. I'm more of a family man than I used to be."

"Jean, did I ever tell you that coat of arms I had hanging up by the front door isn't real? We don't really come from a noble family. I ordered that out of a magazine."

"I know that, Dad. I remember when it came in the mail. But you always swore it was genuine, and wouldn't let any of us tell you otherwise. You seem so much more relaxed about everything than you used to be. I mean, maybe you were always this easy alone with your friends, but not around me. Not at home. I really do like being around you. I think Mom would enjoy your company a lot more, too. Of course she adored you, lived for you, but I think the two of you could really be pals, maybe take a hydrofoil tour together, or one of those glass-bottomed boats at Cypress Gardens where the fish swim right underneath your feet. I feel like I can talk to you now like I never could before. Tell me, Dad. Do you think I've been a good father to my kids, a good husband to Constance? You've been lukewarm about Constance ever since that time right after we married, when she sat down to eat at the supper table before the men were done eating, saying she was hungry as you were and didn't believe in that custom. And when I finally had a son of my own, the only comment you made, about a year after he was born, was that you were glad to see he'd finally come out of the kinks. That made Constance hopping mad. She said, 'He never was in the kinks!' But I want you to tell me what you think, Dad, now that you have the long view. You must have a different perspective on everything. Do I seem like I've done okay, overall? I don't drink anymore, but I'm still at a kind of a crossroads."

Bart ducked his head like he was thinking about it, and tuned the mandolin down an octave, string by string except for the missing one. I thought maybe he was going to pick another song. "Jean," he said, "let me put it to you this way. Did I ever tell you about that trip your Uncle Clyde and Jay and me took to Appomattox, and the trick I played on your Cousin Angie? See, Charlie Poole retired in a little town not half a day's drive from Appomattox. Famous banjo picker for the North Carolina Ramblers. And Angie's always been a die-hard Charlie Poole fan, bought all his records and so forth. She acted about him the way other people do about Elvis Presley, wishing they could conjure back his haint and so forth. She wasted good money once to go to some kind of seance so she could try and talk to Charlie Poole. And of course she's never traveled no further away from home than down the road to Climax to have her bouffant tightened, so she's about as gullible as they come.

"Well, when me and your Uncle Clyde and Jay got back from seeing the battlegrounds and generally whooping it up, I went to visit Angie to tell her all about the trip. She served some pie, and after I showed her some of the souvenirs we'd bought, I said, 'You know, Angie, while we was at Appomattox, we decided to drive on down to Carolina and see the house where Charlie Poole lived out the end of his life. The fellow who unlocked the house to show us around saw how enthused we were, wanting to touch the bedspread and his banjo cases and all. So he said, "Boys, I'll tell you a secret that very few people know about. Charlie Poole ain't dead. No, he ain't. He lives in a nursing home about a mile from here, and I work over there as an aide. I'll take you to it, seeing as how you all are such keen appreciators of his music. He's not in too good a shape, but you could visit him for a couple of minutes or three."'

"By then, your Cousin Angie was climbing up the back of the couch with excitement. 'Did you all go on over there? Did you see him?' I said, 'Angie, this fellow took us into some kind of high-rise, must have been twenty-five stories, to the very tippy-top story. Down the hall, and in we went to a little apartment looking over some trees and a Kmart. Big Kmart with acres of parking. Lo and behold, there in the middle of the living room, in a rocking chair, sat this old man wearing a checkered bathrobe, his spine curvy and his face all caved in like a big old mushy jack-o'-lantern, and him a-shivering with the palsy. But I could tell that it was Charlie Poole all right.' Angie was a-champing at the bit by this time. 'What did he say?' she wanted to know. 'Did you get his autograph?' I told her his hand didn't look none too steady to write with, but that I went over to him and said, 'Mr. Poole, you don't know me, but my name's Bart Miles and I'm from a little bitty tiny farming town called Disputanta, Kentucky, and I've been a fan of your music all my life. I know you are infirm and feeling porely, but it would mean the world to me if you could only say a word or two, so I could hear your voice in the living flesh. Or even if you could acknowledge that you understand I'm here. It's a memory I would always cherish.'

"He didn't give any visible sign, and finally this aide fellow who'd brought us said I better take you all on out. This ain't one of his good days. Just as we was turning to leave, Charlie Poole reached out and caught hold of my arm. His voice was a-shaking so he could hardly get the words out. 'D-d-did you say you were from D-D-Disputanta?'

"'Yessir,' I answered.

"He brightened up, lifted his quivery head, looked at me hopeful-like, with tears in his eyes, and said, 'D-d-did you bring Angie?'

"Your Cousin Angie hauled off and smacked me on the arm. 'Dadgum you Bart,' she said, mad as a hornet, 'I should have known this was one of your stories. You led me right up to the edge.'"

"That's a killer, Dad. Nobody could have told it better. I did want to ask you, though, if you intended it as an answer to my question. Did you mean it as a parable?"

Bart looked confused. He took off his Confederate hat and shook the leaves from the brim. "Hell no, it ain't a parable. I just thought it was a good story. To tell you the truth, son, I've forgotten what the question was supposed to be."

"It doesn't matter. It's just really good to see you, Dad. To spend some time with you. Bobbie sent me out here to look over Jay's place. She's finally going to sell it. In another ten years I don't think too many traces of us Mileses will be left out here."

He busted out in a belly laugh. "Now, that's good. Bobbie's been testifying that she'd sell Jay's land and house ever since the week he passed on. And she'll be saying the same thing till the day she passes on herself, and even after that. Her epitaph will have to be: Draw Up the Deed and Raise Up the Dead."

"No, I think she's serious this time. She would've come out to see to it herself, but she's in the middle of doing a residency in homeopathic medicine."

"Homeopathic medicine? I don't even know what that is. Not regular medicine, I'll wager. Those girls of Jay's always did cultivate peculiar interests. Hell, they probably should have used some on me. Doctors and nurses stuck me full of more IVs and put more catheters up my peter." Bart had begun retreating up the holler, plunging his boots into the leaves with each backward step, raising his legs high the way a horse does. His movements were unhurried, yet he seemed to be moving away quickly.

"Dad," I said, "what's it like being dead?"

He raised his mandolin to me. "Oh son," he said, smiling and shaking his head from side to side, "I'm having a big time. Having a big time." He turned away and started to run, charging up the hill with his mandolin aloft like a Confederate soldier about to take the hill.

"But what's it like exactly?" I shouted. "Do you wish you were still here?"

"Yeah," he hollered back. "Yes I am. Having a big time. I bet your brother never had this much leisure when he was stationed at Okinawa." A whirl of leaves covered him, and I didn't see him anymore after that.

Constance has always brought home from the bookmobile stacks of plastic-coated books about ESP, past-life regressions, interpreting your dreams. As I've told her many a time, if she worked on building the pyramids of Cheops, she has some vacation time coming to her, but I don't think she ought to encourage that foolishness in our children. We had many a set-to when Constance took it in her head that Judy was a psychic in the making, all because there was a prank bomb scare at the junior high one day, and while the students all stood out in the schoolyard shivering without their jackets, Judy got a premonition and ran home. Constance had left the iron plugged in, which had melted a hole in the countertop and probably would have burned the house down if Judy hadn't found it.

I said fine, she has her womanly intuition, and let it go at that, but then Judy had a dream about a half-wit son of some friends of ours, whose appendix had busted a month or so before. Seems he came to her in the night saying he couldn't rest easy, and it turns out some kids for plain meanness had knocked over his headstone and broken it. Couldn't stop teasing that poor boy even after he died. I said okay, let's not begrudge Judy her hunches, but don't egg her on with all this Edgar Cayce stuff like she's the new child genius when she's bringing home straight D's on her report card and killing off the rest of her brain cells with marijuana. Me and Constance never have seen eye to eye about this child-rearing business or much else either, and a few years later, when we decided to have a trial separation, I guess we finally agreed to disagree.

Now, take me. Even after stumbling onto Bart in the woods, I don't try to give a name to it. If it happened, it happened, and that's all I need to know. I'm not going to poke around in it. The same goes for how I came to remarry Constance. As my Grandfather Armp used to say whenever he told us the story about the headless woman with the lantern in the cabbage patch, I don't believe it and I don't disbelieve it. I'm just telling how it came to pass, and people can draw their own conclusions.

After me and Constance separated, I was running the steak house down on Limestone, sixty and seventy hours a week. Nobody in the family had the time of day to give me, not Constance or her brothers or folks, and not even my own kids, because I had started running around with a slut named Yarlett, as the women in the household put it. Yarlett wasn't exactly a society woman, I admit, and my daughters especially thought it was an insult to Constance for me to be seen with her. People at the restaurant had their opinions about Yarlett too. Carline, one of the waitresses who'd started at the steak house back when the managers kept a gun behind the counter next to the fire extinguisher, told me that Yarlett used to solicit at the bar, and she had personally been called on to turn her out more than once. Carline had hair so glossy and hard you could have cracked a bag of ice against it, or a flying beer mug, and she didn't allow customers or employees, including me, to use foul language in her presence. But she'd weathered years of watching Wildcat betting pools and kissy-face over cocktails turn into knifings and brawls, and she certainly wasn't going to ruffle her feathers on account of one little hussy leftover from Limestone Street's bad old days.

No, she said, she liked the way I was running the establishment, families could actually bring their children here without putting their lives and mortal souls in jeopardy, it had finally got respectable and let her make some real money for a change. What I did on my own time away from the business was between me and God, it didn't discomfiture her none, like it did some of these gossipy employees. She was just offering me a word to the wise.

But I didn't give a damn about the gossip. Yarlett rubbed my feet with baby oil when I finally got to take my clodhoppers off at the end of those double shifts. She knew a body massage technique too, where she kind of manhandled me, like punching down bread dough, and it definitely took the kinks out of my shoulders and back. It didn't bother her, like it always had Constance, when I came over with my shirt reeking of smoke, because Yarlett always had two or three of her clove cigarettes sitting around lit and forgotten in ashtrays, like incense in a shrine. I'm surprised we never perished by fire. We smoked cigarettes together the way junkies smoke opium. And she made biscuits for me in the middle of the night that she cut out with a tea ball. I hadn't felt as much like a man since those early days with Constance.

About the only time I saw any member of my family was when Judy trotted over from that attic apartment, where she lived with nothing but a window fan to blow the scorching air around like a Texas scirocco while she lay limp in a beanbag chair waiting for the spell of hot weather to pass. Not that she was keen on my company, but she could walk to the restaurant from there, sit in the air conditioning and drink iced tea at the bar without anybody bothering her, and study her tarot cards until the heat slackened around ten. She had one of those ninety-nine-cent booklets on the occult that you can pick up at the supermarket checkout counter. That's the most I ever saw of her at once since she'd been a little baby.

Often I'd give her T-bones wrapped in foil out of the walk-in freezer to take home with her, and I could imagine her squeezed in next to that little round-shouldered icebox, sitting at her kitchen table rubbing the T-bone across her face while it thawed, the way fighters used to do for black eyes. The first night she came into the restaurant, she had two girlfriends in tow who looked like they'd been doing most of their personal hygiene in a washbasin at the Greyhound station, and getting their protein from ice-cream sandwiches out of vending machines. I could see she wasn't eating right either, so I had Smitty seat them in the corner, in the back room we'd added on by knocking out a wall, because business at that time was hopping like a one-legged bartender. I nodded to Carline, to let her know they could order whatever they wanted and I'd take care of it.

In the reddish light of the smoked-glass candleholders, Judy and her two friends, in halter tops and harem pants, skinny as praying mantises, huddled together in the booth, clicking their Dr. Scholl's wooden sandals against the floor. They talked to each other in stage whispers, trying to be inconspicuous while Judy spread out her tarot cards on a Formica tabletop spattered with dried Worcestershire stains. She kept the cards wrapped in a bandana when she wasn't using them, and wouldn't let me touch them with my hand when I went back to refill their iced teas. She said if any human hand besides hers touched them they'd start to lose their power.

"Your first card, Dad, is the King of Batons, reversed. The element of fire is the masculine principle, the phallus. There is a man of strict morality, austere, with a cruel streak in his nature. He is followed by the Queen of Cups, also reversed. Cups is the feminine principle, love and marriage, feeling and emotion, sensitivity and pleasure. An interfering woman, prey to fantasies. Capable of villainy and cunning."

"Baby," I said, "as you know, I never have put much stock in hoodoo. A girl once took me down to the banks of Clear Creek when I was school age, and I thought she meant to teach me a new way to French-kiss, but she had another kind of witchery in mind. She threw three cat's bones into the creek, and when one of them floated upstream, she yelled out the name of Jesus Christ. I told her I had Saint Peter in my pocket if she wanted to talk to him too, and that girl walloped me upside the head so hard that my skull nearly jumped out of my mouth and floated downstream with those cat's bones. My jaw still pops today when I yawn."

"Dad," said Judy, "you oughtn't make light of the cards. They have real consequences. You of all people shouldn't push your luck right now. And I don't appreciate your off-color jokes."

"You're absolutely right. If I'd been a gentleman of strict morality all along, like you say, I wouldn't have had the bad luck that's plagued me all these years. How's your mom?"

She picked shreds of potato peel off her knife with her thumbnail. "Why do you want to know?"

"I'm just trying to be polite and ask after her health. She is my wife, isn't she?"

"Ex-wife."

"Well, we're not legally separated yet. Not that I know, at least."

"Oh yeah. I forgot. A sixty-day trial period before the lawyers step in."

"So that gives us several more weeks. And we're trying hard to work things out. But don't get your hopes up, okay? Every time she and I talk we're like two leathery chickens scrabbling after the same dried-up piece of corn. It's not that we even want it anymore; sometimes I think we just do it for the sport."

Judy started throwing the tarot for employees on break or regulars at the bar, and though the idea kind of spooked them, they'd come around and have her do it again the very next week. Carline didn't like it one bit, and claimed it was lowering the tone of the place right after we finally went and acquired us some class for a change. She held up her tray like a shield whenever she passed by Judy's seat. I didn't cotton to it all that much myself, but I figured it was a harmless game, like in those restaurants where magicians go around to the tables doing card tricks for the married couples, bringing them a little whiff of excitement between the iceberg salad and the weekly rib eye. I'd hear her talking to different people. Harmony and peace. Tears and woe. Water and earth. All obstacles are surmounted. Disorder and chaos. A happy marriage. To me the sayings sounded like fortune cookies that you could make mean about whatever you wanted. But it kept the overflow business occupied, and I thought she might even pick up some tips, so I let well enough alone. When Judy gets in a phase, the best thing to do is keep quiet and usher her on through to the other end of it as quick as you can.

She never thanked me for any of the meals she ate there. I didn't expect her to; I only wanted her to see that I was doing well, making more money than I ever had, and she was welcome to whatever share of it she could bring herself to ask for. I'd give her twenty or fifty, whatever she requested, and about once a week I filled up her gas tank. I walked the floor to shoot the breeze with the diners, who were grateful for whatever breeze I could provide. The air conditioning kept breaking down, and with the flames from the grills and broilers roaring away, the kitchen stayed so blistering that the dishwasher kept saying he had a mind to put on a spacesuit on his day off and go hang tobacco in a barn loft, to cool off a little. When I made my rounds with the customers, I could see Judy in a back booth rubbing at her nose, studying the menu like a legal document, probably telling those stray friends what a son of a bitch her father was, and that they should order the most expensive item on the menu. They usually did; she mostly settled for a club sandwich.

What nobody knows about this so-called affair of mine is that me and Yarlett didn't have sex that much. She was fighting some yeast thing that flared up all summer long. She'd never had that kind of trouble before, and now it was plaguing her no end. "Women already have one curse to deal with their whole life," she said, "and now I've got two." I made the mistake of telling her about Judy's card tricks one night, kind of laughing about it, and next thing I knew, Yarlett fell prey to fantasies that the women in my family had it in for her, and would use any means at their disposal, including black magic, to take their revenge.

I told her to forget about the cards, that the only way a person could bewitch you is if they could make you think they had some power over you, then they had you for sure. That remark really ticked her off. "Jean," she said, "all I know is that this infection is about to drive me out of my mind, and my gynecologist hasn't done me a damn bit of good. He's exactly like you: thinks when a woman complains that it's all in her mind."

That was the only big row we ever had. We said terrible things to each other, things we didn't mean. I told her I wasn't her husband and she better not start treating me like one. I'd escaped all that misery and I didn't want to dive straight back into it. She shouted back that she had *never* suggested anything of the kind, she knew where I stood on that question, but that her home wasn't a flophouse either, where you came to drink a beer and relieved yourself and left a nickel on the table. She'd put those days behind her, and no man was going to treat her like a stupid whore ever again. Yarlett had been working part time as a go-go girl at the Red Lion, during the businessman's luncheon, but she fretted all the time, because from staying on her feet so much she'd started to develop tiny varicose veins in her legs, which she considered her only really good feature. Her idea was eventually to be hired as a beautician in a department store, where you could wear slacks and still gather a crowd around you while you gave makeovers, since she didn't want to get out of the entertainment line altogether.

It made her downright anxious that we couldn't go to bed very often, so she was always wanting to give me satisfaction some other way, saying there were ninety-nine ways to skin a cat. I guess she'd skinned enough of them to know. We'd get to talking dirty, and necking on the hide-a-bed like a couple of horny teenagers, but more often than not we wouldn't go any further than that, and wound up instead watching baseball on TV and eating beer cheese and crackers. She knew more about baseball than any woman I ever came across. One of the first things that caught my attention was when I overheard her at the bar getting worked up about a designated hitter she wanted Cincinnati to use against Montreal. "Take Tony out of there!" she was yelling. "He's a jinx. He's never gone good against a southpaw with men on base, and he never will. It's that crick in his neck!" Cincinnati never did put in enough designated hitters that summer, or break out of their slump.

I coasted along, week after week, waiting for Constance to file the divorce papers and send them to me in the mail. I knew we had to decide one way or another about being man and wife, that we couldn't keep on with one foot over the threshold, the way we had for so many years. Still, I might have let the arrangement stay that way for another week, or a month, or six months. A languid, tingly feeling settles over you when you work too many hours and don't get enough sleep, and the heat won't quit, and you're drinking more than you ought to, and indoors most of the day and night, and a woman talks dirty to you and keeps you aroused all the time without hardly ever finishing the job. Yarlett wasn't pushing me to marry her, and mostly seemed willing to settle for whatever I could give her right then, so there's no telling how long we could have kept on.

But I gathered a little too much wool. I drank more than my share of sour mash one night, while I was tallying up the day's receipts, and I called the wrong number. I asked if a red-hot pussy was waiting for me when I got off work. A long, thoughtful silence followed that remark, then a voice said, "Dad?" I hung up. It gave me the cottonmouth and the shakes all over, saying what I did, and having Judy speak my name aloud. She might as well have yelled out the name of Jesus Christ right then, with a cat's bone in her hand.

I couldn't sleep a wink and spent the whole night playing solitaire, and not winning a single game. I got to thinking about a neighbor of Bart's who had died a long time ago. The man had fallen sick and they called in a witch doctor, who warned him not to let anything go off his property for three days. Just as he was taking a turn for the better, a strange woman came through town, drank a dipper of water out of the man's rain barrel, and thirsty as he'd been with the fever, she persuaded him to drink some too. Then she mounted her horse and rode away. That night he took sick again, worse than before, and he died before the cock crowed.

Judy didn't come around for a few days after that, and I didn't have the nerve to lay my hand on the telephone. The only thing that messes me up more than a drinking binge is a binge of sobriety, and I went on one that week. I didn't booze and I didn't talk to Yarlett. She called, but I wouldn't return her messages. I figured if I could make it all the way through the coming weekend without speaking to either of them, I would be okay and everything would be okay. Knocking wood doesn't cost you anything, and if it happens to bring about the result you want, all the better.

Some people get the DTs when they go cold turkey, but it affects me a different way. When I got out of bed in the morning, I had to put my left foot down on the floor first. And if somebody shook my hand, it also had to be the left hand. I spent so much time rearranging the walk-in freezers that I gave myself bronchitis in August. I tightened every loose screw in the steel tables and replaced every faulty washer in every sink, and finally repaired the wiring to that beer light that flickered all the time like a strobe and had been driving me crazy for a year. The bartender said the flickering made him feel like somebody was trying to hypnotize him.

The next Saturday Judy showed up during the peak of the dinner rush. We'd fallen shorthanded that night, because even though they'd been making money hand over fist, Carline and another veteran waitress up and quit, on account of me introducing a lot of new procedures, telling them that the good times weren't going to last forever, and we had to start paying attention to costs and rendering stricter accounts. The cash register had come up short twice in a row. No free drinks from the bar to employees during work hours or after. Meals to friends or relatives at a fifty percent discount, but no more comps. I wanted to see a ticket for every food item coming out of that service window. No eating the dinners that got sent back to the kitchen, and waitresses would share a full 10 percent of their tips with the busboys, instead of just handing them a dollar or two, or whatever the spirit moved them to, at the end of the shift. That was the topper. Carline shot back that the only time she tithed was when she went to church, and furthermore, if she wanted a pimp she'd become a prostitute. She put special emphasis on that last part, and stared me down with that cold yellow eye a seasoned waitress can cast when you've been taking too long to make up your mind about what to order.

Next thing I knew, I was helping the other waitresses hustle entrees out to the tables, burning the hell out of my fingers where the plates had sat under the warming hood too long. The medium-rare filets had turned well-done by the time we got them to the customers, and when you serve overcooked meat to a dedicated carnivore, they usually look at you as if you'd turned up with John the Baptist's head on a platter. The cook put the orders out almost as fast as the tickets came up, and she wouldn't slow down no matter how much the waitresses carped; she just kept shoving the plates under the hood like somebody working on a factory speedup decreed by the boss man. I didn't want to get her riled too, so I waited tables and kept my mouth shut.

In the midst of all this, a commotion started up by the cash register, where all the customers on the wait list had to crowd with the front door propped half-open, letting the mosquitoes and potato bugs in, because we didn't have anyplace for the overflow business to sit and there was always at least a half-hour wait. Late at night, while I counted up the receipts, I could hear potato bugs banging around inside the hanging metal lampshades. Judy was hollering that if she couldn't get seated at a table in her own daddy's restaurant, she hoped the whole place burned to the ground in a grease fire.

I broke into a cold sweat and a dead run. When I made my way to the register, Smitty was trying to hand her a glass of iced tea, and she kept smacking it with the flat of her palm and showering bystanders. She had righteous aim. I grabbed her wrists and said how about if we took a walk together, and she could come back later after the dinner rush. All tendons and bracelets and a hank of hair, she tried to wrestle out of my grasp, and when she couldn't, she looked me dead in the eye, the way the waitress had, and the way God himself probably does when he comes to you in the shape of a four-foot eleven-inch pillar of fire, and said she wanted to meet Yarlett the Harlot right that minute.

I probably could have stalled her until the weekend was over, like I'd planned, if the nickname hadn't rhymed like that. Yarlett the Harlot. Bart used to tell me the best way to cure hiccups was to run around a barn nine times without thinking of a red fox. That advice never helped me any. Even Yarlett's hair color rhymed; she dyed it so red it turned almost scarlet, and she always left lipstick prints the same color on plastic cups of beer at the racetrack.

I didn't have any choice. I picked up the phone to call her, left poor Smitty, in a red vest soaked with tea stains, in charge of the restaurant, and drove Judy over. I could tell Yarlett had tried to spruce her efficiency up in the fifteen minutes it took us to arrive. Since there was just the one room, she'd put out the company bedspread, the way other people might change the tablecloth. All the ashtrays had been cleared away, and my eyes smarted from the particles of air freshener hanging heavy on top of the clove cigarette smoke. On the coffee table, which she wouldn't ever let me put my feet on because it was the only good piece of heirloom furniture she owned, she had set out a bottle of coffee liqueur and some Occupied Japan eggcups we'd picked up at a flea market. When she got tipsy, she liked to wisecrack, and would refer to those eggcups as the first purchase for her trousseau. She had even found time to change into a short-sleeved frock with a gathered waist that I'd never seen before. Yarlett always wore foundation, but she looked right then as pale as a Junior League debutante with the stomach flu. She didn't kiss me when I crossed the threshold of the door. I patted her arm as I entered, but she stiffened, so I didn't insist.

"You must be Jean's daughter," she said, and actually curtsied. She had a keening nasal accent that came from growing up on an ailing tobacco farm in Pikeville. "I didn't know you were so pretty. I used to have a wispy, willowy look a lot like yours. But that's been a while ago, long before Jean ever got to know me. It does suit you awful nice."

The introduction kind of threw Judy for a loop. I guess she was expecting the Queen of Cups, villainous and cunning, a bona fide harpy with a red kimono who would tell her, "Your daddy is my man, honey," and pull a long curved knife out from behind the kimono. And at that moment, I guess maybe I wished, too, that Yarlett had been wearing a red kimono, and not looking so heavy-set from eating the lamb fries with gravy I always brought her. The gathered waist didn't help any. She looked worn about the eyes from waiting by the phone all week for me to call, knowing that she couldn't come to the steak house to seek me out. I wanted to take her in my arms.

She asked us to have a seat, and poured the cups of liqueur. Judy had absently taken a hemostat from her blouse pocket, and started cleaning her fingernails with it. The ends of the hemostat were burned black.

"Your daddy tells me you're a nursing assistant at Saint Joseph's."

"Part time," said Judy. "I work relief."

"My line of work has always been aggravation. Anyway, I reckon I know what brings you here. I don't blame you for feeling the way you do."

That remark seemed to give Judy her wind back. "I don't know how you can be so sure, when I don't even know exactly why I'm here. So please don't put words in my mouth."

"You came to visit because you want to see whether I've been served as big a helping of sorrow as your mother and you. Or whether I'm a happy whore, which of course I have no right to be. It's only natural to wonder. I've sensed your thoughts settling over me like a lathery sweat many a night since the first time Jean told me about you. I've got you agitated, and you've got me the same way. Like it or not, there's what you might call a devil's compact between us, if that's not putting it too strong, even though we've never laid eyes each on the other. And now here we are. So let me put your mind at ease first, and then maybe you can do the same for me. I *have* been suffering, something terrible, as much as anybody could wish, with female trouble. It's been especially bad this past week, keeping me up nights. I've done about everything under the sun and the moon I can think of to get shed of it, but nothing seems to help. All I'm look-ing for in this life is a little relief myself, as you say. So maybe you wouldn't mind if I asked your professional opinion."

"I help prep people for cosmetic surgery at Saint Joseph's. I don't have any training in ob-gyn."

"I mean as woman to woman. What would you suggest?"

"I don't know. It's . . . well, I don't consider the topic suitable for mixed company. Even if my father wasn't sitting here, it's still kind of private."

"I don't mind leaving," I said, standing up.

"Sit tight, Jean," said Yarlett. "There's nothing shameful being talked about here. Somebody's womb brought us all into this sorry world, and there's no sense putting on airs about it. You're your father's daughter in more ways than one, I can see that. Jean can act about as raunchy as ary a soul I met in my life, but every time he visits the little boys' room, he turns on the bath-room fan and the floor fan both, to create a wall of noise. I don't believe he'd feel completely at his ease in there unless a cyclone happened to pass overhead at just the right moment. I'm asking a question about hygiene. Even junior-high schools have hygiene classes these days, so I hear. This ain't the Dark Ages."

Judy was squirming in her seat, no doubt ruing as much as I

was the fact that she her own self had asked for this meeting of the minds. "I suppose . . . I suppose when I have that problem, I find that, you know, vinegar and water gets rid of it pretty quick. As long as the solution isn't too concentrated."

"Oh honey, I've tried douches, believe me. I've tried it all, from antibiotics on down. My ailment is more complicated than you give me credit for. It started out in the place we're talking about, but lately I feel like my whole body is starting to give out. You devote your life to pleasing different men, and before you realize it, you've got sciatica, and varicose veins, and all other kinds of complaints, and you just can't put yourself into it body and soul like you used to. So you learn to make perfect little biscuits, flaky around the edges. These past few days, the weariness has spread all through me. My muscles ache, and my heart aches, and my eyes are so dry I can't hardly put my contact lenses in of a morning. I wonder if those cards of yours that I've been hearing so much about might give me some relief."

"I don't think so. I'm really a novice still, kind of practicing."

"Come on, darling. Don't shrink from your intuition now, after you been honing it all summer long. That's your womanly power. Don't squander it while you still got it in full force. I've seen too many girls, myself included, make that mistake."

Judy mulled that piece of advice over in her mind for a minute or two. Then she said, "The tarot doesn't really cure anything. It mostly divines the future. And even then, not in specific terms, like people always think. The cards just give broad indications of where possibilities lie."

"That's a whole lot more than I have right now. I believe it would probably cure what ails me to get a general idea of what my broad prospects are. For, oh, let's say matrimony. In the cards' opinion."

"That question doesn't concern anybody except those who it concerns," I said. "Don't egg her on, Yarlett."

But Judy had already unwrapped the bandana she had in her pocket, and she lay the pack of tarot cards on the heirloom coffee table. "You understand, though, that I have no influence over which cards come up. All I can do is give you an interpretation. Also, the cards are not something to be toyed with. You have to take them seriously." She gave me a pointed look. The window unit was going full blast, making a terrible racket, and strands of her bangs stuck to her forehead.

"I understand, honey," said Yarlett. "I've been toyed with plenty, but I'm not the toying kind myself."

"Look here," I said. "We're all on edge. Every morning when I wake up, I feel like somebody's been beating me all night in my sleep with a two-by-four. And considering how quick I've been making enemies lately, somebody probably has. Now that the three of us are finally together, what we need to do is have a serious talk. I admit I haven't done right by either of you, or Constance either. I'm batting about .200. Maybe .150. And I'm willing to make amends. But only if we first discuss the situation like rational, grown-up people."

"Hush, Jean," said Yarlett. "Deal those cards, honey."

The first card to come up had three crossed swords with a banner twined around them. A sow sat in the lower left-hand corner, and four crafty-looking pups were scrabbling to get at her teats. "Three of Swords," said Judy. "The element of air. Usually unlucky, especially for women. Tears and woe. Disruption of relationships, a broken love affair, separation, parting, divorce."

"I see. Does that mean *my* divorce and parting, or somebody else's?"

Judy shrugged. "There's no way to tell. It could be either. It could also simply indicate something lost or temporarily mislaid."

"You mean like my mind, or my false eyelashes?"

Judy allowed herself a brief smile, then returned her gaze to the Three of Swords. "I'm not sure. But if the card is pointing to loss, it's probably a token very meaningful to you. A ring maybe, or a love letter."

"I've had rings, and I've had letters, at one time and another. But I do have a way of mislaying things. Jean is always getting after me about leaving burning cigarettes in ashtrays. It's a bad habit of mine, but I've been trying hard to break it. I don't want to end up cremating myself like one of those women long ago on the husband's funeral pyre. I never did think much of that custom, did you?"

"No," said Judy. "A boyfriend of mine almost set me on fire once, with a highway flare, when his car broke down, which he would never take to get fixed, and we had a shouting match over it, standing on the roadside in the dark with trucks whooshing past and shaking the car with wind. He kept waving the flare in my face to punctuate his yelling, and a spark fell on the sleeve of a gauzy blouse I was wearing. Can you believe that? He said it was an accident."

"Yeah," said Yarlett. "I do believe it. Truth is stranger than fiction, that's a fact. I know all about them kind of accidents. I've had a few happen to me."

Next Judy turned up the Nine of Cups. She said it indicated physical health and well-being. An assured future, with the cup of satisfaction full and brimming over. She let her eyes come to rest on Yarlett. "There's no way of telling when that part will come to pass. But the energy is especially intense when it comes after swords. So I have a strong premonition about it in your case."

"So do I," said Yarlett. "I feel a little more peacable already."

Judy turned up lots more cards: a juggler, a fellow sitting up in bed with his face in his hands, more cups and swords and coins and people on horses with walking sticks. Some cards said happiness and some said disaster, and some said in between. I couldn't make head or tail of most of them. But Yarlett kept nodding her head, and seeming to get matters more and more fixed in her mind. When Judy finished, Yarlett leaned over the table and squeezed her hand. She said she was glad she finally had the chance to meet a member of Jean's family face to face, especially a pretty young girl like her with so many interests and talents and a whole life of adventures ahead of her. It had done her a world of good. She was going to try that vinegar again, and dilute it a little more like Judy said. When the heat wave passed, she and everybody else might finally get some relief.

The hot spell did break, within a week, and Yarlett's female troubles vanished with it. For the first time in our brief life together, we didn't have any obstacles, or any discomfort to speak of. The Indian summer snapped into a comfortable, frosty autumn. We could skin the cat just the one way if we wanted to, but there didn't seem to be that much of a spark left. Yarlett had more interest in knitting sweaters, a new hobby she'd picked up, and she landed a job as a cosmetician at McAlpin's department store. I can't really put my finger on what happened between us. She didn't give me any ultimatums, didn't tell me I had to leave or anything. Not a cross word passed between us. We just gradually stopped being together. When I tried to talk to her about it, she only replied, in that keening Pikeville twang, that it wasn't in the cards for us, as if she'd discovered a valuable piece of wisdom that she didn't aim to let go of no matter how hard I pulled.

Constance went ahead and signed the papers, so did I, and that made the divorce legal. Things were going better between us by then, but for some reason neither of us tried to stop the divorce from going through. It was a ritual we had to observe, as if squandering several hundred hard-earned dollars on a lawyer was supposed to bring us luck. Only after the divorce became final did I invite her to lunch at a place called the Saratoga, where we used to eat often. Even with new management, the ribs tasted as tangy as I remembered, and me and Constance talked for the first time in a long time like two rational grown-up people. Then we had to go through all the aggravation of turning around and getting legally married again. That's how the two of us are and always have been. If there's an easy way and a hard way, we'll take the hard way every time. It's our star, and we have to follow it.

've taken over Dad's businesses and franchises. He spent thirty-five years building an empire with his partners in the Chocinoe Management Group. Now he's handed his holdings over to me, saying he wants to retire and run his cigarette boat full throttle down at Land Between the Lakes. He's always had expensive toys—he owned one of the first DeLoreans—but no toy ever held for long the restless, roving eye that rolls from heaven to earth, from earth to heaven. He sold, not gave, his interests to me, because in spite of his freewheeling ways and the maudlin tenderness he gets when he's intoxicated by words, Dad is first and last a hard-nosed businessman. He's not going to let family feeling get in the way of a transaction. He always told me he doesn't believe in that gothic folderol about crumbling dynasties rich with tainted pseudo-patrician blood, and their eccentric pulses of attenuation and resurrection. For him, there's no such thing as primogeniture. There's only cash on the barrel. From a self-made man.

I never wanted to inherit the family business to begin with, much less take out loans to pay for it. And I most certainly never had any intention of becoming a storyteller. Dad told me that sooner or later he would have to retire, that he couldn't keep his responsibilities up forever, and that I would have to resign myself to taking over. What he wanted was a caretaker, someone to continue his legacy without tampering with it too much. I enrolled in a few courses at Kentucky Business College, just to keep Dad happy, squeaking through the accounting exams by the skin of my teeth, and spent most of my evenings, like many another son of the bluegrass just out of his teens at a fourth-rate institution, getting hammered at Lynaugh's Pub on bitters. What's more, I swore that I'd never read anything except pulp novels for the rest of my life. I'd had it with my father's accusing built-in shelves groaning with Fielding and Tolstoy. Dad would never put it this way, but I was trying to escape my destiny, muttering into the dregs of my pint glass that the worst-written screenplay by a team of salaried hacks was preferable to any novel I'd ever read.

I didn't want character voices in my head, especially the voices of those destructive and self-aggrandizing Mileses. Their excesses had practically destroyed my own family. Many was the night I'd seen Dad stagger home late from his corporate office in Versailles, where he was supposedly poring over ledgers and spreadsheets, his breath and clothes reeking of those people and their doings. He'd show up after midnight, manic, chattering about Talia or Constance, Elaine or Judy, Stephen or Jean or Lynnette, and then go days without sleeping. He sounded a lot like Judy on one of her speed trips, I admit, though the comparison pains me. Even the falsetto timbre of his voice resembled hers.

Hearing my mother through the bedroom wall trying to talk him down from his witty, reference-laden, polysyllabic delirium, I could begin to imagine the sting a devoted and long-suffering wife must feel when her husband returns to his conjugal bed smelling of another woman. Or what happens to a spouse when her partner goes through a midlife crisis, joins a Holiness church, renounces his family, and starts speaking in tongues. That I could have dealt with. I've known a few snake handlers in my day, and once you get them out on a fishing boat they're just regular people. And they're the first ones to spot the cottonmouths trailing across the water toward you.

To be honest, I hated the Mileses. I wanted my father to kill off every last one of them, or have them annihilate themselves, and often they seemed on the verge of doing just that, but they always survived. Dumb luck, canniness, or good genes, I don't know which. All I knew was that I would hang myself before I took up my father's enterprise. My most ardent desire was to develop into one of those insufferable, florid-faced, Lexington boys, who hang out at the tailgate parties and brunches before the Wildcats ball game, working on their already sizable beer paunches—the ones who think a sport jacket and an open-necked shirt goes great with a billed University of Kentucky cap. The ones who take a perverse pride in entering middle age by their mid-twenties.

I began to scalp tickets outside the coliseum. Even then, it was my father's surname that gave me an edge. I won't deny it. Actually, Dad's first, middle, and last names, because the only thing separating us is the Roman numeral II. If he wanted a namesake, why couldn't he just have called me Junior, like any other self-respecting arriviste? It sounds sportier, more in the know, and indeed I insisted that everyone use Junior as my nickname. Knowing that I was his son (and in Lexington, everybody knows who everybody else is and what they do, and we, with our false pedigrees, are as hierarchical and name-conscious as any Hindu caste), people just assumed I had good connections, and that if they paid top dollar, I could get them the seats they wanted, or if they had tickets, I could get them the money they wanted.

That was my pedigree. That was the solipsism I lived by. Solipsism—his word, naturally. The pinnacle of social life in Lexington is to have second-row, center-court seats when Kentucky plays Georgia Tech or Louisville. And there's a lot of money in this town vying to purchase that right—horse money, tobacco money, coal money, restaurant-franchise money. Or the money that comes from subdividing horse farms and building luxury homes with cedar closets.

In the most superficial sense, I knew everybody there was to know: the governor, state legislators, coaches, players, coal operators, builders, and when I branched out into scalping country-music concert tickets and the like, I made the acquaintance of some of the celebrities who passed through. Enough so that if I'd wanted, I could have written a meaty novel of my own about the high-life lowlifes in the bluegrass, one called *The Studs at Tattersalls*. What's more, I could secure backstage passes whenever I needed. So in spite of my drinking, and my vow to stay mediocre, through my scalping network and the six guys I had working for me, I was pulling in two or three thousand a week, sometimes more. Not in Dad's league, exactly, but in the Junior League, so to speak. That inborn talent didn't get a second-generation nouveau riche like me into Anita Madden's horsey parties, but she always called me at tournament time to ask about seating selections for out-of-town guests.

If I hadn't started doing cocaine, I could have raised my mediocrity to the most lucrative and illegal art form ever seen in a place already legendary for those traits. Instead, I squandered a pile of money during that time, buying people rounds of drinks at one of the sports bars after the game and paying through the nose for my drug habit. But don't worry. This isn't going to be one of those tedious confessions about substance debauchery, about the bank president who gets a jones and loses his loans. I didn't end up a soused son of the South. I was always so damnably lucid that even in the worst of my excesses, I could say "soused son of the South" six times fast, and it would tumble trippingly from the tongue. I could have given elocution lessons to the auctioneers at the Fasig-Tipton bloodstock sale. No, I went the opposite direction, from being hellbent on destroying myself to becoming a business triumph, and one of the fourteen richest men in Kentucky. And one of the fourteen most literate, though I'd always been that, through no fault of my own.

Anyway, it wasn't cocaine or booze, or the lack of them, that broke my resolve to squander my gifts. It was Elaine Miles. My father's creation. A character in a novel, and, I guess you could say, my half-sister. No doubt some of my distinguished, silver-haired, emeritus professorial readers will tell me, "Junior, I knew Quentin Compson, and you're no Quentin Compson." To them, I retort that I wholly agree, I'm not him, nor do I want to be. Yet in my own modest way, I can signify nothing with the best of them. Still, I ain't signifying nothing except what I'm signifying, which is myself.

Elaine managed one of Dad's restaurants, where people congregated after the game or the races, and like Jean, she had a good head for running an eatery. Of the seven in the franchise, hers turned by far the highest profit. Once in a while I would see her there, and we'd spoken in passing, but she didn't know me as anything besides my father's dissolute son, the one who ran up a bar tab with his friends after he'd hit on a couple of Exactas at Keeneland. The one scruple I had was that I never asked the bartenders or waitresses, let alone manager, to comp me drinks. Whatever I owed, I paid in cash at the end of the night. And it was always my own money.

On the contrary, I secretly hoped that Elaine would ask me sometime to cop her a couple of tickets for a sold-out Garth Brooks concert or a playoff game. Then I could sell them to her at face value, or better yet, comp them to her. But she never asked me for anything, and although she acted pleasant enough, I could tell she didn't quite approve of how I was conducting myself. Maybe she erroneously assumed I was getting an allowance from Dad. Anyway, with her being married, it wasn't like I could ask her out for a date, no matter how close to the stage the seats were. I was too shy around her to bring the matter up myself. Sometimes, though, I'd get smashed, and burst out with a stanza of "Ubi Sunt Qui Ante Nos Fuerunt?"

Eten and drounken and maden hem glad
Hoere lif was al with gamen i-lad
Men keneleden hem biforen
They beren hem wel swith heye
And in a twincling of an eye
Hoere soules weren forloren.

I have no idea where those words came from. I've never even read "Ubi Sunt Qui Ante Nos Fuerunt?" and I don't have the least idea what the title or the anonymous verses mean. When I saw my drinking buddies looking ill at ease, I'd cover my embarrassment and my intelligence by quickly tossing off some dirty limerick. Still, one or two of them took to calling me Book Boy.

After a time, I stopped going to that location, partly because of my outbursts, and partly so I wouldn't run into Elaine. Unlike my father, I couldn't summon at will that ferrous reserve, that holding oneself apart from others, that gives him the extraordinary sense of dignity everyone seems to admire. Don't get me wrong. He could mix it up with "his people," be festive, joke and glad-hand, even get a little crazy, the boss cutting loose, doing deadeye imitations, complete with the voices, yet always making it clear that respect was due, and that certain boundaries were not to be transgressed. His energetic charm and wit had the sheen of a well-rehearsed performance, planned spontaneity, and no one could ever accuse him of being more than tipsy, at most. Only Mom and I ever saw him really out of control. Me, on the other hand, I'm impulsive in public, I say things that I later have to retract, I exceed my limits and have to pay for it afterward. I didn't want Elaine to continue witnessing me at my most extreme, so I gave up my accustomed seat beside the brass cash register.

I didn't expect to see her much after that. And I didn't, until months later, when I walked into the first night of a statistics class I'd signed up for at the business college, and there she sat, in the front row. Coincidence is only fate with bad production values. When I occupied the desk next to hers, she looked as surprised as the dickens. Maybe she thought all I did was party and play golf. It was her first class since high school, she allowed, gazing straight at me with earnest, crystal-blue eyes—Jean's eyes. There, in the propinquity of my father's spawn, I experienced a blinding onrush much stronger than those accompanying any of my fits of poetry at the bar. It was more like what Dad must have lived through on those nights when Mom had to talk him down.

I was afraid I would blow my cover by spouting one of Rilke's *Duino Elegies*, involuntarily and in the original German. I didn't want her to take me either for a pedant or for someone with

Tourette's syndrome. Worse, I didn't want to do anything to make her self-conscious. I'd intuited that she had a thing about her lack of formal education beyond high school. She was clearly a brilliant manager, and by rights should have been a full-blown corporate executive by now. But she was self-taught, a learn-on-the-job kind of woman, in a mostly male environment, and even the local MBAs at some of the other locations (my father, in most cases, insisted on hiring educated people) used a mild condescension and a supercilious air to cover the jealousy they felt over the fact that her restaurant had turned into the flagship. As a matter of fact, hers was carrying some of the profit-losing ones. Dad would cagily use her example to berate the other managers at times.

I cursed Dad for not having created her instead as the executress of an estate, member of the Transylvania Board of Trustees, Wharton School graduate, proprietress of vast tracts of subterranean bituminous coal, the motherlord of all motherlodes. What would it have cost him? He could do anything he wanted ex nihilo, whereas I had to work with already existing characters. I suppose he couldn't stomach the potential competition.

As Elaine sat in the molded-plastic seat of her night-school desk, trying to avoid a paper cut while she turned the fresh pages of her statistics textbook, I felt that, as the Russian Formalists are fond of putting it, no other character function had ever existed before. She was a swirling nexus of sines, cosines, possible tangents. And a beautiful one, with a stone-washed blue-jean jacket, a soft, relaxed-looking, but impeccable perm framing her round, still girlish face, and the facets of her sapphire earrings sparkling at the ends of delicate earlobes. I knew that anything serious between us was hardly possible. All the same, looking into those crystal-blue eyes, a verse of Victor Hugo flitted through my consciousness. (No, I haven't read him either.)

Since it was given to me to hear you say
The words in which the mysterious heart pours itself forth.

Getting my head together, I finally remarked, "Wow. Small world."

"Yeah. I guess it is."

"This statistics is a killer."

"I know. I was looking at the first problem set. I've probably gotten in over my head."

But I, not she, was the one who had gotten in over my head. In the weeks that followed, Elaine and I became study buddies, and for the first time, I truly entered into her world. Both of us, as it turned out, had a natural instinct for statistical analysis, bringing us together in a manner that never could have happened otherwise. Dad, always the micro-manager, had her restaurant books audited regularly by an outside accountant, giving the impression he didn't trust her. It probably had more to do with his need for quality assurance of his own omniscience, through a number-crunching yes-man, than it did with his finances, but, nevertheless, I could see it bothered Elaine.

We would sit going over assignments and talking casually, even comfortably together at the table of her breakfast room on Saturday afternoons, glancing out between solving problems at her two teenage daughters and their friends doing antigravity somersaults on the backyard trampoline. Her husband Mike would pop in from time to time between work errands, always affable, always mottled with spackling compound, always with a friendly word or an off-color joke. He was a foreman for one of the builders developing some of Dad's subdivided pasture tracts into a spread of luxury homes with an eight-hole golf course attached.

It seemed that just about everybody was on Dad's payroll, directly or indirectly. Lexington had become a regular little company town—only more progressive, more manicured, more maddeningly prosperous than those squalid wastelands in Eastern Kentucky filled with gun thugs, scrip, and strip-mine pits. My father was a benevolent despot, a paternalistic baron with a soft spot for his underlings, the one who co-opts the union organizers by anticipating everybody's needs and supplying them with the hospital, the schools, the playgrounds, in the nick of time, before anybody gets incensed enough to form a grievance committee.

When Dad found out Elaine and I were studying together, he warned me off her. When he tried to conjure me by saying there was a strange, unnatural chemistry between our clan and theirs, he wasn't telling me anything I didn't know already. I answered that Elaine and I were just friends, and it shouldn't make any difference to him, unless he had some rule about me not fraternizing with his employees. He insisted I should never get personally mixed up with any of the Mileses. Our role was to tell about them, not to coexist with them in any substantive way, and certainly not to become characters in our own story any more than was necessary for narrative resolution. It wasn't a taboo, exactly, but something close to it.

"In other words, everybody has to know their place."

"Yes, if you want to put it that way."

"Then stop me. Put your foot down. Reduce us all to smoke and ashes. You can do it. Make a flood, or something."

"You've watched *The Ten Commandments*, with those hokey, pre-morphing special effects, one too many times. If you want spectacular, try reading *The Brothers Karamazov*."

"I'm sure I'd only get through one brother."

"You always do your best to make me sound like a ruthless, petty dictator. For instance, you refuse to take an allowance from me, then you complain around town that I've cut you off."

"Allowances are for eight-year-old boys."

"I'm not a dictator, of course. I can't stop you from seeing her. Overt character manipulation isn't one of my aesthetic laws."

"Thanks for referring to me as just another character. One of a cast of thousands. Speaking of *The Ten Commandments*."

"I meant her. But you'll find out eventually that there's a good reason for our separation."

That was the first big fight we'd ever had, in spite of our differences. Not that we actually raised our voices—repartee amid clinking crystal is more in our line. I reminded him that he had always wanted me to get involved in his story, that he had even tried to groom me as a narrator, in his controlling way, so that he had nothing to complain about if I was beginning to take an interest. "I wanted you to get involved," he agreed, shaking his still leonine but newly liver-spotted head. "But not this way." I pretended not to know what he meant, but of course I knew.

Then he gave me an ultimatum. He never would have threatened to disinherit me directly, because in order to do that he'd have to admit first that I was his heir. And he adamantly refused to conceive of our relationship in those antiquated, dime-novel terms, even when I tried to goad him into it. No, he had his own measured, exact way of putting things. If I genuinely wanted to take over his affairs, fine, but I had to put my money where my mouth was. If I didn't raise the necessary cash within six weeks, he was going to sell off all his holdings to a media conglomerate, one of those that had been buying up all the book publishing houses and newspapers and such.

This particular conglomerate had been trying unsuccessfully to engineer a hostile takeover of the Chocinoe Management Group for some time. So far, he'd always shown the ingenuity and inventiveness to fend them off. Still, he was getting on, and he couldn't keep putting that kind of energy into the struggle. The more so since I hadn't seemed that keen on the business. But I needn't worry in any case, he said. He wasn't miserly. He wasn't going to cut me out of his will, so I'd get my cash settlement when the time came, regardless, even if the holdings had been liquidated.

I was stunned, no question about it. I couldn't say anything in reply. The one thing I could stand less than the idea of Dad remaining in control of Elaine's destiny was for him to leave her in the hands of some Rupert Murdoch or the like, who would only be thinking about film-industry tie-ins and could care less about her as a character in a book. It surprised me to realize how strongly I was reacting, how bookish I suddenly felt, given how studiously I had avoided reading all my life.

The only reason Dad ever issued the dare was because he didn't really think I could raise the cash. He believed in his heart I was too soft, too lazy, too functionally illiterate (by his standards, that is), and if I didn't succeed, I'd be cut off from Elaine, his chattel, forever. His intuitions and anxieties as an omniscient narrator told him there was plenty to worry about where Elaine and I were concerned. And for all his nonchalant airs, the "unnatural chemistry" between our clan and the Mileses made him very uptight.

He had a pretty good fix on Elaine's psyche. He could more or less calculate what she was capable of, or so he reasoned. The one person he knew the least about, however, was his own true offspring. The demon seed, Edmund—the bastard child of the pud-pulling potentate, the unintended consequence of a hyperactive imagination, the margarita-swillin', beer-nut eatin', *Cigar Aficionado* readin' upstart, the yuppie gone bad, the Future Fart-knocker of America, castaway Cass Mastern from central casting who rose inelegantly from the shreds on the cutting-room floor like a Hammer Films Dracula from an ice floe, to put it all in my own tawdry, pulpy terms. I knew I'd been an "accident," an inadvertent seminal work from one of those nights when he had writer's block and turned instead to his wife for relief of the pressure inside his brain.

Still, here he'd given me the genetic equivalent of a stint at Harvard (since I disdained the real thing), endowing me with the leftovers of his creativity run amuck, and all I cared about was slumming, not even with a bottle-bleached sorority tart, who could at least give me a sentimental education possibly leading to art. He expected me to do a little whoring, then save myself for the grand task, the masterstroke, and here I was threatening to waste my prowess on one single primary character, Elaine. But while Dad was constructing an epic saga of failed filial ambitions in a global economy, I was starting to cook up a potboiler of my own, a local brew.

I began meeting with some of the wealthier clients on my scalping list, with an eye toward convincing them I wasn't just a party boy, and that we could make a real run at ownership of the Chocinoe Management Group, in which my father was the major shareholder. The knocks against me were obvious. Dad practically owned the town, and considered its bankers and major investors his intimates. They were all too aware he pointedly hadn't taken me, his only child, into the business, for seemingly sound reasons as far as they could tell, and didn't seem outwardly anxious to do so. Besides, the very idea that he might sell his interest to me was foreign to most of them. In Kentucky, you hand the family business down to your offspring after they've worked for you for years. Or, if they've disobeyed too flagrantly, you deny it to them, in a tyrannical, stertor-riddled, deathbed fit of pique. But you don't sell it to them, under any circumstances, so the idea that I might try to buy his properties would seem odd to these potential investors, to say the least. It was a delicate situation, me bringing it up at all.

The Miles family, stuck in their own doings, didn't have a clue that they teetered on the edge of extinction—by any other means than the usual ones, that is. There was the drama-of-the-moment to be contended with. Lynnette by this time was married and had a small child. And everyone else suspected her husband, Buck, of having an affair. The family had always treated Lynnette with an affectionate, indulgent attitude of non compos mentis in the practical affairs of life, as a sweet but savage fairy child found naked in the wilds, needing to be taught to speak human words, as if she couldn't marry, own a house, raise a child, staff a job, on her own recognizance.

And to tell the truth, there was something eerily innocent in the way she'd sprawl on Constance's living-room rug, unconsciously smiling to herself as she read an issue of *People* as if it were a school primer, sounding out the names of starlets with her lips, with her boy-child Toby crawling over her curved torso like a puppy, tugging at her silk blouse with his teeth.

So the others took up the slack, babysitting Toby for days at a time, taking him to his checkups at the doctor, cooking hot meals to drive way out to Lynnette's unpaid-for new house in Nicholasville (one of Dad's property developments) on the edge of a cornfield, putting stamps on her utility bills and dropping them in the post, afraid her electricity or gas would be cut off through sheer forgetfulness, and she and Toby would have to spend the night in the darkness, eating straight from a cardboard bucket of fried chicken, like squatters in a cave.

And Lynette really did have a tendency to forget, sometimes dropping Toby off at Elaine's at eleven in the morning so she could go have her hair done on her day off, and then getting lost in a CD store at the listening booth, drifting to happy hour for mai-tais at Dudley's downtown, and not showing up to collect her child until nine in the evening, holding under one arm a box of Sugar Pops she had picked up somewhere along the way. Mike and Elaine tried to get her to wear a beeper, like the rest of the sisters did, only in her case to be used as a kind of electronic bracelet, so they could keep track of her whereabouts. And she agreed without any fuss. But she kept losing the beeper, mislaying it in the magazine rack at Kmart or some such place, and they finally gave up on that idea.

One couldn't really call her neglectful. In her own dreamy style, she doted on Toby, calling him dozens of pet names, like munchkin man and snookerdoodle; she had a new one to add to the list every day. Each time one of the relatives handed Toby back to her, she sighed and acted as though he'd been brought out from the hospital nursery and laid in her arms for the first time. The pleasure and mild surprise that registered on her face about finding herself a mother never lessened with each new encounter with her son.

Constance, Jean, Elaine, and Mike began to discuss among themselves what to do about the situation of Buck's infidelity. They weren't even sure that Lynnette had figured out Buck's alleged messing around, and they couldn't calculate what effect it would have on her if she did. She might be shattered. On the other hand, it was true she'd had a way of letting events that would have traumatized any of the rest of them roll off with an artless beatitude.

In the years before she married, when she went through what Mike wryly called her Sheena phase, wearing clingy, over-the-shoulder leopard-spotted disco outfits that showed off her prodigious endowments, she'd fallen in with some pretty rough characters, her then-boyfriend and his cohort. They'd taken her to porno films, coaxed her into taking Ecstasy and crack, and frankly, it turned out she'd gotten into some weird bondage stuff with the boyfriend.

Yet none of it had ruined her. On the contrary, the boyfriend might as well have taken her to a pet show and bought her a chili dog for all the changes the hedonistic encounters brought about in her perspective on the world. If she ever referred to the events, she laughed them off as silly kid stuff, and called the ex-boyfriend a nuthead, the way you speak of someone who drove around in high school smacking metal mailboxes with a baseball bat. Unproductive, deviant, mildly amusing. But when the phrase "S&M" came up in connection with Lynnette's name, Mike was ready to kick the boyfriend's ass all over Lexington and the surrounding townships. The boyfriend, a sage scanner of classified ads, signed posthaste onto a drive-away car to Idaho, forfeited his deposit somewhere in between here and there, and never came back.

As Elaine could tell you, Mike, a devoted father and husband, was one of those classic Central Kentucky good old boys, pale and sinewy, with a wispy little mustache and the slouch of a suburban pappy, who didn't look like much to wrangle with, almost a Milquetoast in his head-bobbing way of getting along with everybody, but who was capable, without giving you a single syllable of warning, of picking up a tire iron and smashing your skull in if you happened to break one of his unwritten moral codes. Once when he was managing Micky's discotheque, John Barleycorn's, and a drunk patron (not me, I promise) started to fondle Elaine, Mike leaped over the bar and chased the fleeing offender through the parking lot on foot, then all the way around New Circle Road in his Blazer at ninety-five miles an hour, firing .44 bullets into the offender's rear window.

When the item of Buck's extramarital activity came up, though, the matter was more complicated for Mike. He and Elaine had kept up a close friendship with Buck and Lynnette, had counseled them, co-signed on their mortgage, held the shower for their baby. And even though Buck had a self-imposed rule about fishing all alone at Little Elkhorn Creek and Kentucky Lake, where he slipped away often before dawn, he'd broken that rule of solitude a few times with Mike, and they had gotten to be occasional fishing pals. As they pulled crappie out of the lake in dead silence at 5 A.M. together, the black sheen on the water and the limestone bluffs made them into thinking men, though whatever thoughts each had he kept to himself.

Buck had taught Mike how to fly cast, and they and their wives had whiled away several weekends down at the Smoky Mountains, sharing a cabin. Mike and Buck had thus spent a considerable number of Saturday afternoons in Gatlinburg sitting on hot concrete steps drinking pop, while the womenfolk shopped for souvenirs. They nodded silently at each other over Cokes, chuckling once in a while in the back of their throats, which was the equivalent of anybody else holding a gullet-parching gabfest in which you bare all your therapeutic secrets. So hand-to-hand combat with Buck wasn't an option. You just couldn't take a tire iron to your wife's sister's husband, not this one anyway.

Jean agreed. There was a time he would have flared up in the same hotheaded way, especially back when Judy hung out with those psychedelic thugs, but he was getting older, wiser, and to tell the truth, tireder. There comes a time in every man's life when he just wants to spend the night in his own bed and not in jail. He and Constance had gotten the kids raised, more or less, and out of the house, more or less, and independent, more or less, and he and Constance were semiretired, more or less, and he wanted to keep things that way, without all this constant ambiguity. He was a deacon of the church now, sang in the choir, sat on the board of the Token Club, did motivational speeches at the DUI school, and that was about all the hyperactivity he had any use for.

With Constance's bad heart, high blood pressure, and diabetes, they couldn't allow themselves to get excited. They couldn't pull the red-eye shift like they always had before. Lynnette's potential troubles with Buck were coming hard on the heels of Talia's having moved back to Kentucky from New Mexico a few months before. Talia was going through her usual paces, living in Louisville with a fellow weightlifter and probable felon, who had broken Talia's fingers by closing a car door on them. And Talia, who was pulling in seventy thousand a year flying around opening new locations for a super-gym chain, driving one of the owner's Porsches at his expense, living in one of his condos at a subsidized rate, was pissing away all seventy thousand in salary and commissions on paying for the boyfriend's divorce proceedings, and the phone bills he ran up calling his mother and soon-to-be-ex-wife in Albuquerque, and talking for two or three hours every single night on Talia's credit card. Talia made more money than any of the rest of her family, and she somehow managed to remain the most miserable and most hand-to-mouth.

She would call in the middle of the night, and Constance would take the portable phone into the pantry in the dark and shut the door, whispering amidst the potatoes and hanging baskets of onions with the dryer going, just in case. Jean never had a clear sense of what was taking place in these private conversations, because Constance always invoked the confidentiality rule, as if it were some kind of psychiatrist-client relationship, protected by the Constitution. Only then, just as Jean had gotten the pillow situated on top of his ever-whitening head, he would be instructed to jump in the car and drive to Louisville, as if he still had the witless stamina of two decades earlier, and would be provided only limited information about what was going on, like a secret agent who can't be told his real mission.

Talia was moving out or something, or the boyfriend was, or maybe Jean had to post bail. He'd see when he got there. Except when he'd endured the hammering rain and evaded police radar for an hour on the interstate, and arrived at the condo to pack Talia's belongings, or whatever it was, she and the weightlifter would be nestled deep and snug in the leather couch eating microwave popcorn out of the same bag, scarcely giving him a glance as he came through the door, and Talia with her still-bandaged hand and streaked mascara, would greet him, "Hi, Dad," in a hoarse, fragile, nonchalant voice, as if he'd been invited over to watch a delayed broadcast of a basketball game on television.

Then, when he returned home, at 4 A.M., Constance would be going into atrial fibrillation, lying breathless on the bed because she'd been stressing about Talia's latest fight. On the way to the emergency room she'd weep softly that she was afraid for her daughter, and nobody understood what it was like to be a mother, you just never stopped being one, hard as you tried. Jean had long ago given up on staking any claim to Talia as his own, all he'd ever had with her was responsibility without authority. If the child turned out bad, it was your fault, and if the child turned out great, it was an act of God. And maybe that wasn't so far from the truth.

Once the electric shock had been administered to Constance's heart, and the doctor had given Jean yet another lecture on protecting his wife's health and not letting her get in over her head with household problems—as if he had an actual say in the matter—he and Constance returned home at eight in the morning so he could catch thirty minutes sleep before he went out to mow waist-high lawns filled with ragweed, or rebuild somebody's deck, or reroof their house or sell programs at the racetrack or clean up the grounds at the Token Club or any of the other hundred tasks that had taken over his retirement to the point where he was working sixty hours or more a week, more than he was working when he was working; then, just as he drifted off into the old man's doze he was entitled to after fifty-odd years of hard labor on this wretched earth, then the phone would ring, startling him into a jangled wakefulness, and it would be Talia and the weightlifter inviting them to brunch.

And, of course, they would have to go, and eat eggs Roquefort in a state of stupefaction in some new, civilized, overpriced breakfast brasserie, while Talia and the weightlifter played kissy-face, and Jean would usually end up picking up the check in spite of neither himself nor Constance having a real salary, and the bank trying to screw Constance out of her disability and getting away with it, because the bank's lawyers wanted her to go through physical therapy but their own physical therapist said she couldn't be rehabilitated, and Jean having no retirement but lots of bronchitis from the ragweed spores, yet he would pick up the brunch check anyway, because Talia only made seventy thousand a year, that's why Jean mowed her grass for free, and they'd act nice to the weightlifter and ask when his next competition was, or were he and Talia working on a couples routine, and how was his divorce coming along, since Talia's most recent therapist said criticizing the weightlifter would only drive Talia further into his camp and away from her parents, as if she were still an adolescent, and so they'd gaze fondly at the pictures in the weightlifter's wallet of the kids he never went to see and wasn't paying any child support to since he'd skipped town on them, when all Jean really wanted to do was make a call to a couple of his friends on the police force who specialized in taking recalcitrant punks out to a remote limestone quarry for a little strenuous conversation, and afterwards laughing and saying the poor fellow must have fallen down a real long flight of steps.

Those cops would have done the favor for Jean, he knew, with no tip required and no questions asked. A lot of people in Lexington, the old-timers of his generation especially, still respected him, remembered what he'd been in his prime, and he had a few chits still that he'd never called in. And he was tempted. But he'd concluded, reasonably, like the elder male of the tribe he was now expected to be, that Talia would just take up with another man who would beat her up the same, or worse. She was well into her thirties, her waiflike beauty almost disappeared through hard living and hard drinking and too many tanning salons and too many nights crouched in fear in the corner of a bathroom, or standing on a countertop hurling appliances at a man. All that lavish athleticism of hers had given her, in the end, was a modest ability to counterpunch, enough so it looked on the police report like maybe she had been the one to pick the fight.

Jean hated to admit it, but Talia had started to get that hardbitten look he associated with the chain-smoking women with drawn skin, pancake makeup, and brittle, overdyed hair who used to hang out at the steak house in its rowdy beginnings. Talia had been the most beautiful of all his daughters, that was a fact, tender as a bud, but she had aged too fast, and looking at the defiant, terrified creases that lodged in her face, even in repose, made him feel much more like an old man than having grandchildren did.

Talia could have had it all, and had had it all—looks, money, career, smarts—but the way she went about things it was as though she was trying to coax somebody into killing her, just so she wouldn't have to do it herself. Jean was ready to close up shop on fatherhood. It had never suited him that well to begin with, but he had tried. He'd given it his best shot. If Talia had to be what she was by nature, he wasn't going to stop her. She had taught him that lesson afresh each time she'd crashed on her parents' couch for a few days, in between fights, and then the weightlifter would call, contrite, persistent, because he'd call thirty times in a night if he had to, over and over and over, pleading until Talia consented to speak with him for just a minute, just thirty seconds, please, five seconds, and before you knew it, like Constance, she'd move off into the dark pantry for a private conversation among the hanging baskets. When he showed up, parking her boss's Porsche at the end of the street to wait, with the running lights on, so she could walk out to him and not him in to her, then as she stuffed her belongings back into her overnight bag, and Jean ventured a faint word of caution about how Talia might not want to rush back into the same situation she had been in so many times before, she would explode, turning on him in fury and screaming that he'd better just stay the fuck out of her business, it was no fucking concern of his, and he ought to keep his fucking thoughts to himself. Bastard. Then she would leave, slamming the door behind her.

Jean expected that sometime, sooner or later, there would be a phone call, the final phone call, asking them to come identify her body. And as always, he would get in the car and drive. Probably alone, because he didn't think Constance, despite the pantry phone conversations in the dark, would want to witness for real, in the glare of morgue light, the reality of the image she'd created in her mind every night for the past twenty years, as she lay rigid in her accustomed state of insomnia. He would feel deeply sad, ambling into the morgue and looking on the brittle parchment body of a girl he never knew. The most significant and defining encounter he'd ever had with Talia was the night when she was eight years old and pulled a butcher knife on him, shouting that she would kill him if he didn't leave her mother alone, and she meant it.

But he would accept what had happened, as the police officers who specialized in domestic abuse—because doubtless they'd be acquaintances of his—would touch him softly on one of the knots in his arthritic, still muscular back and try to comfort him by murmuring that nobody understood the cycles or psychology of domestic abuse. There was no logic to why these women kept going back to men who beat them repeatedly. Even the experts agreed it didn't make any sense. He shouldn't feel guilty. In the end there was nothing he as a father could have done to save her, nothing he could have done differently. Signing off on her corpse, he would thank them, polite, quiet, appreciative, graciously receiving their condolences, and tell them what he believed in his heart, that he knew they were right. There was nothing he could have done differently.

Still and all, there is Lynnette's current situation to be dealt with. I didn't mean to get sidetracked with Talia's hideously wrenching affairs, or with Jean's for that matter, but I can't simply turn my feelings on and off like a tap. As I've already warned you, I'm impulsive, I exceed my limits, and say things I have to retract. Anyway, as you may have surmised by now, I'm not exactly omniscient. I have good instincts, that's about the best I can say for myself, but I never know where I might be careening next.

Don't you think it mortifies me to have Jean getting under my skin this way? Yes, I've bought several racing programs from him at the track, he's pleasant enough, and I like the charming way that he, in a coat and tie and jaunty English cap, hooks customers into buying the next day's program by calling out in a playful singsong, as they pass his booth, "Get tomorrow's form at today's prices!" He's like a street peddler from another age, almost courtly in his way of handling the passersby, making each one feel they're doing him a special personal favor by spending a measly dollar fifty on their own selfish pleasure. He's the anonymous man you remember at the end of a busy day of adrenaline-fueled stock transactions and irate fender benders, the man who brought an instant of joy into your heart for no good reason whatsoever.

Or if you're ninety-three years old, lame, in a walker, and used to people brusquely brushing past you in the delicatessen lobby as an inert, cumbersome, and irritating obstacle to their forward motion, Jean is the one who makes the time to open the door and holds it for as long as it takes for you to get there. Don't hurry yourself. He'll still be there. What's more, you know instinctually, as you scan the crowd of faces in the doorway, some hostile, some indifferent, most oblivious, that he and he alone will be the one to open that heavy door for you. You know it because of some little thing in his expresssion, in his eyes especially, those crystal-blue eyes like Elaine's beautiful eyes, and you feel sure he's going to make a tender joking remark as you laboriously cross the threshold of the restaurant, to put you at your ease so that you won't feel like what you are, a self-conscious old woman of ninety-three in a walker.

Besides, I concur with Jean's sentiment that the task of parenthood doesn't ideally suit all persons (I won't name names, but if the shoe fits . . . ). But beyond that, my main interest in him lies in the fact that he is Elaine's father. My Elaine. How I love the way she cradles the cellular phone against her full and rosy cheek as she whips in and out of traffic on Nicholasville Road in her 4x4.

I couldn't help noticing that Elaine kept unusually quiet on the subject of Buck's infidelity, and to the extent she said anything, seemed inclined to forgive his indiscretion on practical grounds. She reasoned that what was most important was for

Toby to have two parents in his life, a mother and a father. Everybody had weaknesses, and given the way Buck was raised with his mother always going around repeating she wished she'd never borne children, Buck was probably carrying a great big hole around in his heart. Mike, more of an eye-for-an-eye man in spite of misgivings on account of his friendship with Buck, just grunted when she said that, and his muttered rejoinder was that Buck was going to be carrying around another great big hole in his chest, of a different kind, if he didn't stop dipping his dick all over town.

Constance wanted revenge. There's no other way to put it. She'd never liked Buck, never wanted Lynnette to marry him, never thought it would work out for one single minute. He was arrogant and cold and aloof and conceited and narcissistic, and though she'd shown a lot of forbearance for her daughter's sake, she didn't take kindly to how Buck had snubbed the family since the beginning, pretty much refusing to show up for gatherings, always going on his precious fishing trips instead. She had discovered, through some online computer checking via an ex-coworker at her bank, that Buck had a couple of accounts at the rival bank, the Fifth Third Bank, ones he hadn't told Lynnette about. He was squirreling money away, and Constance didn't think it was so he could surprise Lynnette with a new set of living-room furniture, which they needed in the worst way.

Probably he was spending that money on one of his sluts. Does it seem cheap of me, to let Constance, the mother of my own private Beatrice, use a word like that? Would "slattern" sound better, more refined, more detached, more Dantesque, as the winds of the second circle of Hell, more ferocious than the infamous tornado that touched down and wrecked entire trailer parks at Stamping Ground, Kentucky, whirl about the fornicators' heads?

I understood that to this sad torment
The carnal slatterns are condemned, in whom
Reason by lust is sway'd.

Don't forget, I'm writing a pulp novel, not a masterpiece. I can't even quote Dante correctly, much less compose great sentiments on my own. Anyway, *slut* is the word she really used. Besides, I've had a few questionable, boozy one-night stands myself, in spite of my shyness, and so I'm not going to pretend to stand piously above that nomenclature. It's part of my "moral complexity"—as much as can be had by a cipher like me.

Constance knew that the matter was a deadlock, though, with her and Mike wanting to confront Buck, and Jean and Elaine hoping that maybe he would just grow tired of his affair and return to his wife, with her none the wiser, her childlike faith intact. (If I'd been the tie-breaker, I would be forced to vote with the compassionate moderation of Jean and Elaine—for Toby's sake.) Not that the math of the situation would ever have stopped her before. But like Jean, her awareness was growing of how the never-ending cycle of the kids' rocky lives, and especially Talia's return to Kentucky, had been putting too much of a strain on her heart. Every time she and Jean took a little weekend getaway, Constance ended up in the emergency room in New Orleans, or Abingdon, or Charlottesville, and she joked to her friends about how no matter where she went to recreate, she always seemed to end up staying in the most expensive room in town.

This is where I come into the picture. As a character, I mean. I've tried in the foregoing pages to acquit myself as a narrator first, to be "comprehensive," to withhold tendentious interpretation as much as I'm capable of doing so, and to accomplish that sneaky survey-roundup of the dramatis personae where you're supposedly just talking about one plot line and one major subplot (Lynnette's marriage woes, predicated on my pursuit of Elaine, as a function of my father-son conflict), but also giving a nod to other major characters, folding them in as you go along. It's a little like the breaks in jazz where each of the musicians gets featured in a solo, while pretending it's all part of the same "song."

But let me lay my metaphorical cards on the metafictional table. In the drama where one has to choose between the eternal life of a god and the temporal passion of human existence, there has never been any question about where my own sympathies would lie. Born to the narrator's manse, I discovered too soon the thrilling downward mobility immanent in playing in the scrubby back acreage with the poor white sharecropper's kids. Or, it's worse still. I'm Tithonus, enamored of Eos, and I can't really die. I get immortality without youth, the worst of both worlds, and end my days as a shriveled grasshopper, spitting what little Toby calls "tobacco juice" from my insect mouth inside the hedge in Elaine's backyard. Mike has developed a sudden zeal for landscaping, and is heading my way with the electric shears. Unfortunately, in my case they won't do him any good. I'd gladly give up my gift of song for the eventual steel taste of death. My fate, however, is to live on, crepitating just out of sight, a diminished but otherwise unperturbed thing.

> I asked thee, "Give me immortality."
> Then didst thou grant mine asking with a smile,
> Like wealthy men who care not how they give.

Gift of song? Steel taste of death? Christ almighty. I'm starting to sound as maudlin as Dad. And who wrote those insufferable Tennysonian verses, anyway? Some other resentful sap like me, no doubt. I might as well ask who was buried in Grant's tomb. It wasn't me, I know that much.

By this time, I'd sort of been adopted by the Mileses, beginning with the several occasions when Elaine brought me around to her parents' after study sessions and I was urged to stay for dinner. In the first few moments of acquaintance, the Mileses size you up, and you're either in or out. And once you're in, you stay in, at least if you're a neutral observer. Though, as I've tried to impress upon you, I have a hard time staying neutral for long. It would have been the simplest matter in the world to hang out and stay a fly on the wall (yes, I know I was a grasshopper in a hedge only a paragraph ago, but there you are), given how little self-consciousness the family displays in speaking of intimate matters before relative strangers. I could have compensated for my relative lack of ominiscience and learned every-thing I needed to know by just listening. Nothing more had been required of me, absolutely, by any of the parties involved.

Story material was there for a narrator's gathering, chunks of gold ore just lying around to be picked up, enough for five or six "posthumous" novels, after the Miles family had been sold off by Dad. I wouldn't have had the copyright on any of it, naturally, but that didn't preclude the Shanghai capitalism of pirated edi-tions, which could have made me an even bigger fortune over-seas, where copyright restrictions don't consistently apply. I could dwarf my father's wealth. The Mileses in all the Asian lan-guages, in bad translations, sweatshop literary hackwork hired by the hour. Best-sellers straightaway into movie melodramas, with overdubbing and soap-opera subtitles cranked out on demand, which in turn would generate further novelizations.

Or, if I wanted to keep my principles, I could have opted for the battered prestige of samizdat, without any messy mimeo-graph pages staining my thumbprints purple, like the undigi-tized digits of Lady Macbeth before the information age, whose outcries of protest are belied by the visible bad conscience blot-ted on her fingertips. No, my version would be made all too clean and easy by the miracle of desktop publishing, or the minimally regulated empire of the Internet. I could have gotten over my wounded pride, and avenged myself against my father, by putting out sequel after unauthorized electronic sequel to his narrative, muckraking accounts downloaded and praised by Net surfers the world over for their subversiveness.

But there were other agendas. I think Constance had her eye on me in an undefined way as a possible mate for Talia. She sort of liked the idea of having an unattached, stray, "rich" bachelor around, and she certainly knew how to talk to one. In any case, Constance, who has often felt closer to her daughters' mates and ex-boyfriends and close male friends than she has to the daughters themselves, took a shine to me. Precisely what she held against Buck was not his behavior per se, not even his tact-less infidelity, but the fact that Buck never confided in her, and really had no interest in her whatsoever. To him, she was an inconvenience, a mother-in-law who had opinions about his and Lynnette's domestic business. Let it be said on Buck's behalf that he was an even better housekeeper and interior decorator than Constance, a shampooer of couches and shaker of draperies, punctilious about his color schemes and choice of fabric, which also drove her to distraction. But even these things he didn't spend much time thinking about. His was simply the worst kind of scorn: the scorn of disregard.

That's probably why, one evening when Elaine had to hurry back to her house, Constance invited me to hang around a bit longer, for coffee and some of her homemade key lime pie (a dessert I can never resist). I had a lot on my mind. My negotiations with the people I wanted to make my acquisition partners weren't going too well. Those few who were willing to risk me at all first wanted to see me produce real hard cash, in sizable sums, and so far I hadn't been able to. I'd tried not to panic, but I only had a week left before Dad sold everything to the conglomerate. Elaine would end up in syndication, on Nickolodeon at four in the afternoon, the dead time, and I would be forced forever to watch her flickering on-screen, close yet far away, just as a widower leafs hopelessly through the album of black-and-white photos of his deceased wife. That's the problem with images on film. They hold out the tempting illusion that they can capture existence with some kind of permanence, but they offer only a facile, hollow eternity, one that further deepens our sense of irretrievable loss through their mocking vividness. That's why they call a channel-changer "the remote." I'd be able to see Elaine anytime I liked, sure, with a simple flick of the remote, but never to have her near.

Meanwhile, here was Constance, thinking about dessert, as if it could change our destinies. That's much too Proustian for me. Although I'll admit that the wicked tang of her pie did afford me some temporary solace. When we were alone, and once my sweet tooth had been satisfied, Constance started buttering me up in that coquettish Southern woman's way she can turn on when she wants to.

"More pie, Junior?"

"I couldn't eat another bite. I'm going to pop."

"Don't josh me. With a trim waist like yours? You must do sit-ups." (She's right.) "You need a woman to cook for you more often, instead of you eating that terrible happy-hour chow. Buffalo wings! Whoever considered that dinner? Did you know Talia used to cook in a French restaurant? And she's been learning some of my recipes. But you don't like my pie!" All said with a face of mock-hurt and a faint flutter of the lashes, long silky ones, like Elaine's.

"Honestly, it's the best. I'd eat three pieces if I could. But I sampled too much of your pot roast."

"Well, I just whipped up that key lime this afternoon. I make my friends bring back a certain brand of juice for me when they travel to Florida. Else the filling doesn't taste right." We sat in pleasant silence for a moment or two, sipping decaf.

"Junior?"

"Yes."

"I know you're having troubles."

"Troubles?"

"I want you to know that you can talk to me."

"No troubles are coming to mind right now. Not with whipped cream in my belly."

"Junior, there's a time to be charming and a time to be serious. And of course you're always charming. But you're not always serious. I see the sadness in those eyes, though. You can try to hide it behind a joke, but your eyes betray you. You need to get married."

"And who are you going to matchmake me with? Are you offering me one of your daughters? Rachel or Leah?"

"Did you have a particular one in mind?"

"Oh, any of them will do. Elaine, or any of them."

"Well, unfortunately Elaine is married. So is Judy. And Lynn-ette, well, she's still sort of married, unfortunately. But I'll keep my mind on the job and see what I come up with. Talia, by the way, is only living with—you know, that man. The hulking one. There's something else I want to talk to you about right now, though. You're trying to buy your father's businesses, and the banks are turning you down for loans, one after the other."

I was more than a little taken aback by her remark. Not that it's entirely a secret, but neither is it anything I expect to be discussed in circles that would get back to Constance Miles. Still, I didn't let my surprise show. "All right. That's true, more or less. I've pieced together a few small loans, but not enough to amount to anything grand. How did you find out?"

"You forget that I worked in banking for almost twenty years, before I had to take disability. You don't have to worry. Others may talk to me, but I don't say nothing to nobody. The only reason I bring the matter up is because I can help you. I may have found you a backer."

"You've found me a backer?"

"Don't sound so startled. Everybody has friends, Junior, in high places as well as low. Isn't your sitting here eating key lime pie with me proof of that fact?"

"Don't disparage yourself. Or did you mean that I was the friend in a low place?"

"There you go again, trying to hide behind a joke. Did you hear what I said to you? I've found you a backer."

"Constance, I don't mean any disrespect, but just to get in the financial door, where other banks will take me seriously, we're talking in millions of dollars in seed money."

"When I was manager of the certificates of deposit, hundreds of millions of dollars flowed through my department every year. Not that any of it belonged to me, but I know what serious money is. I can get my mind around it."

"Are we going to embezzle it, then? I forgot to bring a burlap sack."

"I'm going to pretend that was a witticism, and ignore it. What I have in mind is perfectly legal. And very simple. I keep house for a woman who used to be my bank customer. She's a widow, a fairly young one, who lives out Newtown Pike and raises horses for pleasure. I keep house for her once a week now. It's not what I'd ever planned to do, but until my disability comes through, it gives me some money to help maintain us so the bank's lawyers won't starve me into taking another job, and then claim that I'm really healthy and therefore not eligible for the settlement they owe me."

"I've told you before, Constance, I want to help you out. Why won't you ever let me give you money?"

"Let's not speak of such things. Do you let your father give you an allowance? Of course you don't. That's one of the reasons I respect you."

"Then let me hire you."

"To do what? Carry your pretzel tray around behind you? Or sharpen your study pencils? You don't have a job yourself. When you've raised the cash to buy your father's businesses, then you can hire me as your bookkeeper. I'm good at that. And I'm going to make you pay me five million dollars a year. But until that time, I don't want to hear this kind of talk."

"I can at least help cover your legal expenses. I know some good attorneys."

"My attorney is already working for me pro bono, until we get a settlement. He also used to be one of my customers at the bank, and I did him a lot of little considerate favors over the years. Honest favors. So you must pay close attention to me when I say I have friends in the right places. My housekeeping employer even says she knows you a little. Her name is Dodie Wentzler."

"Dodie? That doesn't sound familiar. I'm sure I'd remember that name."

"Well, she didn't elaborate. Maybe you broke her heart from afar, when you came in the sights of her opera glasses. But I told her about your situation, and she wants you to go out and talk to her."

"All right. I'll do it. Thank you."

I must admit, I had been rejected so many times by potential backers at this point that I didn't have much faith in Constance's well-intentioned lead. Still, I was so desperate that I wanted to rush outdoors and drive as fast as I could out Newtown Pike, faster than Mike in his Blazer that time he shot the bullets at the besotted groper, and fling myself at Dodie Wentzler's feet.

"That's settled, then."

"Do you have her phone number? Let's call her right now. Maybe I can stop by on my way home."

"At this hour? She's probably in her dressing gown."

"You're not."

"Don't get fresh with me. You weren't in such a big hurry until right now. You're too impulsive. One minute you don't even want to hear about Dodie, the next you want to go barging in on her. Is there some reason it can't wait until this weekend? I told Dodie that if you were interested, you'd come around on Sunday at eleven."

Of course I couldn't bring myself to say anything to Constance about Dad's deadline. Even if I saw this mystery backer in the coming weekend, that would still give me Monday, the final day, to transfer enough funds, providing I secured them, into Dad's account to keep him from foreclosing on the Mileses. I knew there was no question of asking him for an extension. The money wasn't the issue. Dad likes dramatic closure, the cliffhanger of a deadline to be met. A soft deadline takes all the drama out of the situation. As a narrator, he wouldn't abide such a thing. It isn't in his nature. Though this comparison would torment him, what he likes best of all is the situation you get in James Bond movies, where the snazzy-looking bomb device with all the tumblers is clicking down toward zero, and Bond defuses it with two ticks left to go on the digital display. I almost wondered if he, and not I, was really telling this part of the story, and whether he hadn't written me into a corner where everything was riding, do or die, a roll of the dice, on my one-shot, last-minute weekend meeting with Dodie Wentzler. I wouldn't have scripted it this way.

"You're right. There's no hurry. Sunday will be fine."

"That's more like it. There was one other thing. I'm sure you've heard about Lynnette's situation. We've certainly discussed it plenty around here lately."

"This and that. You don't need to give me details."

"Our business is your business, Junior."

"I appreciate your confidence in me."

"I mean it. Elaine is coming to consider you almost like a brother."

"Oh, you don't need to say that. I'm not really blood kin."

"And I already think of you as being like a son. Or a son-in-law."

"If you insist, I won't contradict you. I'm like a son-in-law, then."

"But certain responsibilities come with being part of this clan. It's pretty clear that Buck has been cheating on Lynnette, and I've found out where he takes his—well, forgive me for being indelicate, but—his little slut. It seems they shack up regularly in the lodge down at Natural Bridge State Park. Just far enough away so as not to chance running into somebody familiar. It's a safe bet for him in the off-season. Inexpensive, too, which I'm sure suits that penny-pincher just fine."

"You're quite the detective today."

"Yes, I am. But I can't do everything. I'm not as anonymous to Buck as you are, for instance. I know what his and that woman's usual night is for going down there. On Thursday evenings he takes off, supposedly to camp near one of the tributaries of the Red River so he can fish early Friday. I'd appreciate it if you could check into the lodge on Thursday night and see if you can spot them there together."

"Spying? Quid pro quo?"

"Call it what you like. That's too much Latin for me. I don't want to tell Lynnette until I'm completely sure. I mean, I already am sure, but not sure sure."

"Couldn't you hire a detective agency? I'll help you foot the bill, if you'll let me. They're much more competent at this film-noir stuff than I could ever be. Stalking people at lodges. I'm not half as competent as Clare Quilty."

"I have no idea who you're talking about."

"Never mind. He's a character from *Lolita*."

"Oh, you mean the one played by Peter Sellers? I loved that

Ping-Pong game that he plays with himself. He's a genius. Well, believe me, this hussy is no Lolita. I couldn't find out her name, but from what I hear, she's been divorced twice already, and getting the highlights in her hair takes longer at the salon than it used to."

A strong force was pulling me to accede to Constance's request—fate, narrative drive, call it what you want. Here was my chance, at last, to let myself be swallowed up within wrong-headedness instead of trying in vain to stay "detached" from events. I'd still be an observer, perhaps, but a very special kind of observer. I'd be spying on someone. I could get caught. Buck might become agitated and beat the living daylights out of me. Not that I was anxious for that particular turn of the screw, obviously, but as a plot complication, it certainly had its attractions.

No, I wanted to forswear that way of thinking—"plot complication." It was being, not the structure of prose, that I sought. If Buck came after me, I'd pop him one myself. I'm not his physical match, but I'm in pretty good shape. I spar with the punching bag at the gym (it's one of the new places Talia opened up, and it has a sensational rock-climbing wall). Besides, the way things are set up in this story, Buck is two-dimensional and lightweight. A decided advantage for me. Elaine could see me, for the first time, as someone whole.

"What if they drive the car of—what's her name?"

"As I said, I haven't been able to find that out."

"Well, the alleged trollop—Bubbles, let's call her, so we can stop using all these disparaging euphemisms. What if they take Bubbles's car down to the lodge instead of his, to avoid recognition? Or a rental? How will I spot it? And they're probably registered under an assumed name. Buck and Bubbles is too conspicuous."

"I don't think they do it that way anymore. Buck probably puts the room on his credit card. He pays that bill, so Lynnette never sees the statement. Bubbles? Did you pull that one out of your hat? Isn't Buck and Bubbles the name of a Negro tap-dance team from the forties? Weren't they in *Cabin in the Sky*, along with Ethel Waters as the good churchgoing woman and Lena Horne as the vixen temptress?"

"I've never seen that movie. I selected at random the name of an old girlfirend of mine, one I dated for a short time. It's no more unlikely a name than Dodie."

When Thursday afternoon came, there I was, standing in the lobby of the Natural Bridge State Park Lodge. You'd think a lodge in a modest state park in rural Kentucky would have only a few spartan rooms and a cinderblock office, with june bugs banging against the light fixtures, and a sallow man with a hard face peering out from behind a pine counter with saw marks visible at the ends of the planks. The drain in the poured concrete floor would be backed up, and as you filled out your form, you'd try to keep from stepping in the puddle at your feet, for fear of crushing one of the water roaches swimming there.

But this wasn't the case at all—except for the sallow man with the hard face. The reception area was "well-appointed," as they say, featuring tasteful tapestries made by Berea's Churchill Weavers, a carved wood fireplace, and stout oak beams running the length of the ceiling. Business seemed unusually brisk for the off-season, mostly couples, many of whom were at that moment watching the clogging and buck-dancing exhibition being given by a pair of zesty performers in the lounge to the cheerful thrum of a string band.

Hadn'a been for the Cotton-Eyed Joe
I'da been married a long time ago
I'da been married a long time ago

The narrow-faced, whiskery-cheeked, cotton-eyed, small-town, Gideon Bible-reading, Moral Majority, too-much-time-on-his-hands desk clerk eyed me expectantly. I could have sworn he was also a lay preacher, possibly one of the snake handlers I was talking about earlier. "A room, please. If you have any vacancies."

"We've got a few. Credit card?"

"I'll be paying in cash, if that's acceptable."

"As long as you cancel your bill in advance. Sign in on the sheet, please." I complied, scanning the page for Buck's scrawled signature, but in vain. The clerk took the sheet from me. "Junior. That your actual Christian name?"

"It's my business moniker. Is that name so unusual around here?"

"No, there's lots of Juniors in these parts. Junior Baker, Junior Whitestead. You just don't look like one." Each of his utterances was punctuated with a sharp report, like the splintering of a mineral substance, followed by a washed-out, reverberating echo.

"Those banjo dancers in the next room get good acoustics, don't they? I can hear them all the way in here. Are they wearing taps?"

"No, that's the firing range next door. Not really an official range. Boys just practice emptying their pistols against the granite cliffs until the county sherriff chases them away." I turned my head toward the plate-glass window and, sure enough, several perilously sunburned young men in army fatigue pants and sleeveless T-shirts were blasting bottles off the tops of upended cinder blocks, blowing them into the cliffs. "Single bed okay, or you need a queen?"

"Two beds, if you don't mind. My—wife and I are here together."

"Where is she?"

"In the car. She's not feeling well. All those hairpin curves."

"We like to see all our guests when they sign in."

"As I said, she's nauseous. If you mean to imply this is some sort of tryst, I'd like to point out that I'm requesting separate beds. That should prove we're married."

"I see you've thought the angles all out. Only reason I brought it up was we've had a few thefts in the rooms lately, and I've been asked to keep an eye out for nonguests loitering. We don't want trouble. Used to be a lot safer around here before a raft of these unemployed farm boys started taking LSD and subscribing to *Soldier of Fortune*. Just because a fellow has long hair these days, he doesn't necessarily wish you well. I liked it better back when a man's ponytail meant something. Those were the salad days. The hippies and farmers got together to keep the Army Corps of Engineers from flooding the river and making it into a recreational lake. If that had happened, we'd all be underwater now. I wouldn't care a hill of beans if there was a tryst going on or not. Some of the young folks in these counties, this is the only place they can get around the mamas and daddies trying to put the clamps on love. So they shack up here in the off-season, when it's a little less conspicuous, come in all nervous, their hands shaking so's they can hardly sign their fake names." I took another squint at the now upside-down ledger. In point of fact, all the signatures, including mine, were completely illegible. "I say, more power to them. Just use birth control. I been alive too long to get in somebody else's love business. Truth is, if it wasn't for all the one-nighters, we couldn't keep our occupancy rate going through the cold months."

"Oh. Well, thanks for clearing that up."

"Don't mention it." A sympathetic look flashed across his lean snake handler's face. "Just call me Cupid."

"Listen, Cupid, you didn't happen to see a tall, strapping fellow, about six-two, sandy hair, come in here earlier with a youngish woman?"

"Sorry sir. I don't give out information on the other guests. We try to be discreet."

"Of course. Forgive me for asking." I pocketed my key. The two dancers in the next room were whacking away at the floorboard with their heels, legs flying every which-a-way, one set in petticoats, the other in peg-leg trousers. "Say, you don't ever get tap dancers in the lounge for entertainment, do you? You ever hear of Buck and Bubbles?"

"No. We just have Bob and Betty there. Every Thursday night."

As you may have guessed by now, it was Elaine waiting in the car in the parking lot. It had been her idea to come along with me. Her stated, flimsy pretext was that she wanted to be nearby in case matters got out of hand with Buck. And she was the one to suggest, just after I paid the exit toll off the Mountain Parkway, that our checking in as a married couple would be less conspicuous than requesting two separate rooms.

Of course I agreed right away, even though it wasn't true. Maybe she considered me so innocuous it never occurred to her there could be any impropriety in our sharing digs. But Elaine is an intuitive person, and I couldn't help but think she sensed something larger, not just Lynnette's marriage, was about to come to an end. With her zippered leather day organizer, breaking appointments down into quarter-hours, penciled in weeks in advance, and her overnight garment bag ensuring a wrinkle-free excursion, I wouldn't call her a person of abandon exactly, so I wasn't expecting the many proprieties between us to suddenly be dropped, even so. She actually unpacks her belongings, using the chiffarobes and drawers, arranging toiletries on the bathroom counter, whereas I work straight out of the suitcase. All the same, she was quieter than usual, as we settled our belongings in the hotel, hers on her side of the room, mine on mine.

She suggested that I buy sandwich fixings at the country store next to the lodge, so we could take our dinner in the room, to avoid her risking being spotted by Buck and his escort, if they were around. The best I could rustle up from those spartan shelves was a roll of braunschweiger, a loaf of suspicious-looking bread that felt as stale as week-old stollen, a plastic squeeze bottle of yellow mustard, a jar of bread-and-butter pickles with red peppers floating in the juice, and a can of Vienna sausages. Not exactly the food of love. I upbraided myself for not having stopped by the gourmet grocery in Lexington earlier to have them make up a pannier of crusty French bread, pheasant paté, flaky cherry tarts, and a magnum of cold champagne. We could have picnicked on the carpet in true elegance. That's the sort of "hasty" meal that could lead to a seduction. Then again, such attention to detail might have made this impromptu sojourn more premeditated than Elaine had intended.

I had no idea what was going on in her mind. It was possible she was, at bottom, like so many of the girls and even grown women I had known, who unconsciously reason that if they don't prepare in advance for a sexual encounter, they're not really responsible for it. On the other hand, knowing Elaine as I did, I felt almost sure that if she had come with any romantic thoughts whatsoever, she'd be carrying condoms. For once, I longed for Dad's omniscience. Then again, I would have felt too much like a dirty-minded hypnotist, who betrays his gift and puts his patients into a trance just so he can cop a feel with impunity. It would have been easy enough, I suppose, to excuse myself to the bathroom and rifle through her cosmetics case. But I couldn't bring myself to do it. I was the worst of all possible detectives. If we were to consummate our relationship, and it somehow got back to Dad, even the slim hope I had of raising the necessary cash would disappear. I still didn't know for sure whether this story was mine or his, and whether or not his omniscience covered my little bailiwick.

There was an in-room bar, thank God, and I tossed back three or four mini-bottles of Cutty Sark on ice. I hadn't touched liquor in over a month. I knew I'd have to venture out later to reconnoiter, but as I've said before, lucidity has never been one of my problems, drink or no drink. If anything, getting a little buzz on would let me at least pretend to be less sharp than I actually was. The whole business of being alone together, which had seemed so tantalizingly promising when she first mentioned it, was starting to feel more and more dispiriting. She'd even brought along a magnetic backgammon set.

We were passing time, being companionable, with no clear object or schedule in mind. All I could hope to do at this point was to stroll outside and run into the adulterers. The TV in our room was on with the sound turned down, and Elaine sat on her bed with her legs sticking straight out, reading *The Seven Habits of Highly Effective People* while nibbling on a pickle spear. Once in a while she would steal a glance in my direction out of the corner of her eye.

"You haven't touched your braunschweiger."

"Not hungry."

"That scotch isn't going to sit so well on an empty stomach."

"I know, I'm drinking too much too fast."

"I didn't say that."

"No, you're too polite to say anything. A bundle of nerves the size of a bale of hay knocked me off the wagon."

"All you have to do is spot them. There's no reason for you to get involved. Nothing to be nervous about."

"Oh, you're wrong. There's everything to be nervous about."

"Because of Buck?"

"Because of you. My chaperone."

"Of me?" She sounded genuinely pained. "You mean I'm a liability here? I wanted to help. I didn't think it was fair, Mom asking you to do this chore. It's not even your family." She put her book down, and moved over to my bed without hesitation, as if we were nine-year-olds at a slumber party. "Are you sorry I asked to come along? Maybe staying in the same room was a dumb idea. I didn't think you would care one way or the other, us being such pals."

"I don't care. I mean, I do care, that is, yes, I don't care, but I'm not not caring in an uncaring way."

"There's a tongue twister." She gave me a girlish smile, the kind that goes well with flannel pajamas. "Hey, can you say 'I slit a sheet, a sheet I slit, upon the slitted sheet I sit' four times fast?"

"Is this a sobriety test?" I knocked back another mini-bottle, this time sour mash, straight up. There was no way I could describe to her what irreconcilable worlds we inhabited, or try to get her to understand what a sea change was about to happen to all of us. If I tried, she'd think I was using the threat of cosmic catastrophe to get in her pants, like some looter of appliance stores after an earthquake. "'I shit a sleet . . . ' No, it looks like I failed. I said the cussword on the first try."

"You're not fooling me. Your mind is as clear as a bell. I've seen you drink before, many times, and you can put away a lot more liquor than that without even getting fuzzy. Not that I'm encouraging you to drink. Say to me what you want, what's in your heart, for once in your life. But whatever you do say, I'm not going to have you pretend afterward that it was the liquor talking." Strictly speaking, she was correct—the first one to get behind my little secret—but she hadn't begun to understand the other, more occult pressure in my head. Seeing my growing agitation, Elaine tried to be kind and decent, and take the heat off me by leafing through a *TV Guide,* to change the subject. "We get free cable. Okay, there's . . . have you seen *Cabin in the Sky?* It's on right now. 'An angel and a lieutenant devil fight over the soul of Little Joe, a lovable rascal with a weakness for gambling and the ladies, while Louis Armstong plays the trumpet in Hades. Two and a half stars.' Should we give it a try?"

"*Denn wir, wo wir fühlen, verflüchtigen.*"

"What?"

"Nothing. A bite of braunschweiger stuck in my throat."

"No it didn't. You were speaking German. I heard you."

"Oh, *Gott in Himmel.* Why does this happen to me? *Ach wir atmen uns aus und dahin.*"

"Lie down. You look pale." Elaine put her hand against my alabaster brow and stroked it with a gossamer touch.

If I could have perished right then, devoured by the squirrely epigrams of German Romanticism, an ignoble victim of sacrifice, I would have laid back and let it happen. But all I'd get for my trouble was a bitch of a hangover, the kind that isn't cured by a hair of the dog. I sat up and brushed her hand away. "There once was a flaming young genius. Whose brain had grown inside his penis."

"Stop it. You don't have to act like a brute for my sake. You're smart. Just accept it."

"There once was . . . "

"Look me in the eye, Junior. What do you want?"

"For we, when we feel, evaporate. Oh, we breathe ourselves out and away; from ember to ember, yielding a fainter scent."

"I'm listening. Open your mind. Say what comes naturally to you."

"Christ, how I despise my ass-kicking assonance! Every angel is terrible, and that is no bullshit. Fucking deadly birds of the soul." My head was enlarging by the second. Yes, both of them— or were they really the same thing, after all, as per my poetical barroom boasting? I flung my hunk of stollen against the card on the door where the daily rates and fire marshal's code were posted for our safety and comfort. The bread shattered into a thousand pieces like a smashed atom. I rolled off the bed, hit the floor with my skull, and recited my limerick at the top of my lungs.

"There once was a flaming young genius
Whose brain had grown inside his penis
When thoughts made it erect
On smart girls the effect
Was—"

Elaine leaped on top of me in an instant, feral as a ferret, holding me down with no mean strength, grinding my elbows into the carpet, her round milkmaid's bosom squashed against mine. "You're going to quit acting like a maniac right this second. I didn't come this far to get kicked out of a hotel room and end up in the police roundup of the *Slade Signal* for checking in under false pretenses. I've never gotten thrown out of anyplace in my entire life, and I'm not about to start with you. You're in love with me, aren't you? Say it."

"Uncle! Glockenspiel! Sein und Dasein!"

"Admit it. But you're scared that your father is going to disinherit you, or that he's going to fire me. My boss doesn't own me. What's the worst he can do?"

"Pretty bad, actually."

"What? Bring on the apocalypse? Because if it's not that, I'm not going to lose any sleep over it. I'm in your blood."

"True, someone may tell us, 'You've got in my blood, the room, the spring's growing full of you' . . . What's the use?"

"I'll tell you what the use is. You make something happen. Guys like Mike and Buck may be rifle-range rednecks in the eyes of those haute-couture people from your circles, but at least those boys know what they want and go after it. Squirrel meat, trout, poontang."

"Poontang? That's not an epithet we should be bandying about between ourselves." I squirmed, trying to get out from under her, but she had a hellacious grip.

"You heard what I said. Pardon my German. Anybody who can spout bawdy limericks like yours can't be shocked by a little word like *poontang*. Isn't that what you want? Or are you going to pretend that the mere sight of my baby-blue eyes is all your sensitive soul can handle? You're waiting for our auras to mingle in the ether. Is that it?" Her breath was fiery, laced with pickle juice. "The men in my world go after the thing they desire. Can you say the same? Can you? Can you utter a thought that doesn't contain some wounded, self-pitying reference to your father? Or is he God?"

"He cannot retain us. We vanish within and around him."

"You're damn tooting he cannot retain us." She had unbuttoned my shirt and was kissing me on the neck. "My scruples have always been beyond reproach. But right now I'm not going to think about Mike, or the kids' ballet lessons, or the fact that we're supposed to be down here as moral watchdogs for Lynnette's sake. I've got my own fish to fry."

"Carpe diem?"

"That's too much Latin for me. Let's get it on."

She was undressing me, undressing herself with Olympic speed. I'd never become aroused in this intoxicating way before. My flesh actually felt warm, as if a cryonic coccoon surrounding me was breaking up. Her exquisite, kissable round shoulders called me out of my larval self. "Those that have beauty, oh, who shall hold them back?"

"Amen, brother. Now there's some poetry for a change."

I was completely attuned to Elaine's intense arousal, my skin as hot and malleable as candle wax beneath her touch. Our *petite mort* was going to be huge and irrevocable, an orgasm vaulting us across the ultimate threshold, *Tod* for the bod and straight off to God. Maybe simultaneous heart attacks. More likely we would vaporize, leaving no trace. That's what I had always craved, the death behind life, rather than the slow, tedious half-killing of myself that I had grown accustomed to, and there could be no deeper and more thrilling satisfaction than to carry Elaine off with me into that ecstatic instant of nothingness. I yearned to burst into a stanza of Wilson Pickett's "Midnight Hour," with the gospel croon and delayed Memphis backbeat I've always adored. But I couldn't call the right lyrics to mind.

"Hand on your hip. Backbone slip. Mashed potato. Do the alligator."

"Mmm."

"Like dew from the morning grass. Exhales from us that which is ours. Like heat. From a smoking dish. Hey! Good God now!"

"I love it when you talk dirty."

"Does the cosmic space we dissolve into taste of us, then? Do the angels really only catch up what is theirs, what has streamed from them, or is a little of our existence in it as well?"

"Junior."

"Elaine."

"Junior. Go ahead and come."

"Together. I want it to be together. Quick, quick. Nestling and jostling, the quick and the dead. I can feel us quickening into quicksand."

"Me too. Only I can't—quite—go under. I'm trying. I don't want to hold you back. You should enjoy yourself."

"What is it? The sound of me talking? I'm too chatty. I won't say another word."

"No. Not that. I hate to say it, after me giving you such a hard time. I'm just—thinking about Mike. He's always been loyal to me. We're suited to each other. I'm not trying to pretend this wasn't my idea. I even put in my diaphragm before we came down here. I'd made up my mind. But now I can't. I'm sorry. I should have faked it and let you finish. I was so close. I didn't want to cheat you, though. Too much honesty, I guess. Maybe if I'd closed my eyes and made the right sounds, your pleasure would have carried me over to the other side."

"Yes," I whispered. "I think it would have."

She kissed me tenderly on the earlobe. "I really do like you, Junior."

"You did the right thing. You need to stay where you are."

"You're sweet. Listen, if you want to try to get back in the rhythm, I don't mind playing along. My mind could change. I mean, we're already in this up to the hilt."

"I don't know. It's hard."

"You can say that again."

"Why don't we play backgammon instead? I noticed you brought your magnetic set."

"Okay. If that's what you decide." Her voice sounded cheerful and game for anything, but most of all, relieved. "What were you singing in my ear a minute ago? Wasn't that 'Land of a Thousand Dances'?"

Right then civil defense sirens started going off. Rain lashed the windows and roof with rhythmic force, like the opening stanza of an epic poem in the oral tradition, based on a flood myth.

I shit a sleet, a sleet I shit
Upon the blighted earth I spit.

Rushing naked to the television, Elaine turned up the sound, only to be informed by the Emergency Broadcast System that there were flash flood warnings in our immediate area. I know what you're thinking: that I've produced a deus ex machina to get Elaine and myself out of the plot complications we've created. But if you brood more carefully on it, the deus ex machina would only benefit us if it had come earlier, before our psychological coitus interruptus, right about the time Elaine said, "Junior, go ahead and come." Then the two of us could have been washed away in one another's arms, in a seminal flood, giving symbolic closure to the ancient, inexorable logic of fertility, silt, deltas, shamans, rainmakers, shaking the pumpkin, making the beast with two backs, not shaking my tree if you don't like my peaches, and the interconnected cycles of life and death. But as I've tried to point out emphatically, pulling out the stops at the last minute isn't my style. I'm more of a character man. Quiet epiphanies, regrets, lingering second thoughts, postcoital *tristesse.*

No, it turned out that the much-maligned Army Corps of Engineers may have had a point when it wanted to preemptively flood the gorge and river around the Natural Bridge, turning the area into a speedboat lake and using spillways to contain the overflow. Flash floods are a big problem in this part of the Daniel Boone National Forest, always destroying people's crops and sweeping defenseless hikers into a premature, watery grave. The kind of stuff that keeps Tiresias and meteorologists in business. Perhaps this was Dad's form of retribution against me, his impatient wrapping up of the story I had, in his opinion, bungled so badly.

He would wipe out the entire tribe with a flood, a Red River redux, and begin civilization anew. He could troll along afterward in his cigarette boat, among the church steeples and cupolas, barking out orders through a bullhorn to newly spawning schools of fish, like Werner Herzog shooting on location. He was getting on in years, and, as he said, tired, but I wouldn't have put it past him to rectify the situation with such a masterstroke. I remembered having explicitly dared him to make a flood when we had our first set-to about Elaine. There was also the outside chance that the real God, the one in the Bible, was punishing Buck and Bubbles, as well as Elaine and me, for our collective sinful behavior, not to mention my smart-alecky quip about Leah and Rachel.

Before we even had a chance to begin dressing, the phone rang. It was Cupid from the front desk, telling me, as if over a two-way police radio, that an irate husband was headed my way. "He may be armed and dangerous. I couldn't tell for sure, but around here, it's even money that a feller's got a weapon, even if he's not hacked off about anything. Listen, if I was you, I'd get that Gideon Bible out."

"To start praying?"

"No, if you hold it in front of you just as he fires, it will usually slow down the trajectory. Most types of bullets, except the armor-piercing ones from the local ammo shop, only go about an inch deep in the Gideon. Stops right about the ninth chapter of Nehemiah. God bless you, son."

"Is this place going to be under water in a few hours?"

"I'd say that's the least of your worries right now."

As Elaine and I hastened into our clothes, I briefly considered hiding in the chiffarobe, as befitted my sudden state as the cuckold-maker in a bedroom farce. Unfortunately, the theft-proof, soldered hangers in the chiffarobe couldn't be removed, making even less space available in the cramped interior. I grabbed the Gideon Bible. The door burst open and there stood Mike, panting, wearing a Bobcat hat, soaked to the skin, and bleeding from the nose. He had a nasty contusion around one eye. Seeing he bore no weapon, I tossed the Bible aside, formed a mental image of the punching bag at the gym, and casually got in my sparring stance, as if I had been clipping my fingernails and was just inspecting them for an even cut.

"Elaine! Where are you?"

I blurted out, "I want you to know that Elaine and I are sharing a hotel room." If there had to be fisticuffs, I wasn't going to back down.

He gave me his usual affable nod, almost as if I weren't really present in this little melodrama. His mind was obviously on something else. "Yeah," he answered absently, "she's a wizard for saving pennies. Gets five copies of the Sunday paper, clips coupons, and they end up owing her money at the supermarket. Never seen anything like it. We've got twenty boxes of Raisin Bran in the garage." He stepped around me. "Elaine."

"I'm right here, honey." As always, her appearance was spotless and neat. Her eyeliner wasn't smudged. She'd even managed to get back that little curl in her forelock in the short time it had taken me to throw on my clothes.

"I found them."

"Found what, Mike? My goodness. You look like you've been in a barroom brawl."

"After you all left, the more I thought about Buck, the more it riled me. So I booked down here, and started wandering trails by the river. Had no more of a plan than a hound in a field of fresh manure. It was getting toward sunset, me picking my way up a creek bed, and then I happened on them. A disgusting sight." He started sobbing so hard he couldn't continue speaking. I'd never seen him cry before.

"Okay, honey. Take your time."

He shook his head. "It's worse than you think."

"Worse? Was he with the woman or not?"

"Oh, he was with her all right."

"Well, then? Either they were going at it like animals or they weren't."

"No, they weren't getting it on. She and him was—I can hardly say it. They was fly-casting. With that beautiful glass-tipped Orvis rod. Made out of that stuff they use in jet fighters. My rod. The one I bought Buck for his birthday, the one he always loaned to me when me and him slipped away to Little Elkhorn. She had on hip waders, right out there in the middle of the river, shameless as you please. Didn't care who saw her. She was dropping plastic grasshopper flies right nice, I'll give her that, twitching them this way and that so it looked like they were alive but crippled. Yeah, she could lure many a brook trout to its doom with that tempting little twitch of hers. I had words with Buck. Told him now I knew why he'd been putting me off lately every time I suggested we go do a little fishing. He always had an excuse, he was too busy working, or too tired. He shouted back that he'd never promised me I'd be the only one. Said that the subject just never came up, and that it was easier not to mention it, or pretend he was solo, because he knew I'd kick up a ruckus. For months he's been going behind my back, pretending like he's getting nookie on the side, when what he was really doing was casting his rod with somebody else." Mike shook his head uncomprehendingly. "With a woman. That's what hurts the most. So we had a fistfight. I don't think he'll be fly-casting for a few weeks, anyway. I broke that unbreakable rod upside his head."

She put her arms around him. "It's all right. At least we know the truth now."

"I want you to come back home in my truck. With the water rising, you can't stay here. Anyways, I can't never sleep when you're away on a trip. I turn on every television set in the house and leave them blasting all night."

"I know you do. Give me a minute to gather my things."

She slid past me without so much as a glance, carrying a pair of stockings in one hand. "We'll see you back in Lexington, Junior. You've got your car. You and I need to schedule a study session for that last statistics test."

"Right. I'll be along soon. You two drive ahead."

"They'll probably be closing off the interstate in an hour or two. Don't dawdle."

"I won't."

Mike gave me a hearty pat, winking with his bruised eye. "Hey, when you going to cop me some decent tickets for the Georgia Tech game? Come on up to the house soon, buddy. We can grill scallops even when it's cold. And it cracks the girls up when you do backflips off the trampoline."

"I will. I'll come do some flips. I'll get you some decent tickets."

In five minutes, she and he were gone. Already, I could hear various assistant directors calling from distant bullhorns, telling people to clear out of the area. It was a wrap. I walked through the empty corridor of the hotel, past the clogging stage, now abandoned. Even Cupid had given up his post at the front desk. Outside, only shards of brown bottle glass at the makeshift firing range offered evidence that someone had ever lingered there. Rain coursed along the curbs of the parking lot, overflowing onto the grass, funneling through the mouseholes in wooden box-hockey frames, which were just beginning to float. A slow levitation of everything unmoored was taking place. Before long, the treetops would be full of baskets and styrofoam coolers. A Ping-Pong table sat beneath the recreational shelter's overhang. I half expected Peter Sellers to pop around the corner and reenact his single-handed routine.

Up ahead, thirty yards or so, I could see the operation booth for the skylift that led to the top of the ridge. Steel cables ran straight up the center of a steep hollow. As I approached the booth, I noticed a woman sitting alone in one of the motionless bucket seats of the lift. It was Bubbles. I recognized her at once, even though we'd only dated off and on. She had the same stacked platinum hair as always, and her waterproof makeup seemed to be holding up reasonably well. She was just smeary around the eyes, and her face beaded with continuously forming droplets of water. Now that I thought about it, my own clothes and skin were permeated. The rain had been falling in curtains so heavy and steady it had cast its lulling spell of quiet over me, muting my awareness that I, too, was getting wet.

Leaning into the booth, I threw the switch to the skylift. The hanging seats swayed, almost imperceptibly at first, then graduated into a jaunty little bounce. As her seat glided past me, I hopped in beside her and pulled down the iron safety bar. "Hello, Bubbles."

"Hi, Junior. Gosh, I haven't seen you since our last three-for-one night at Lynaugh's. Remember, after UK won that tournament game, everybody was out partying in the street? I slipped and cut my hand on a broken beer bottle. You took me to the emergency room at Central Baptist, and sat up with me in my apartment after, until I dropped off to sleep. Chivalry was always one of your good points."

"I remember. It's been a long time. I guess we're left behind."

"Yeah. Buck tore off to Lexington. When he got a butterfly bandage for that gash on his face at the Red Cross truck, I pretended I was going to stay behind to help the mobile unit dress wounds and give CPR to any half-drowned stragglers. I just got recertified. But I wanted to be alone, really. I know it's over between us."

"What are you up to these days?"

"Oh, teaching dance and creative movement at a studio. Tap, Jazzercise. You know, kabuki. Everybody tells me I look so good in whiteface. I admit when I get in whiteface, it makes me a little vain."

"I hear you and Buck were caught red-handed."

"Right. Well, I was over the limit anyway, so I guess technically I was breaking the law. I got carried away." She let go a deep, sultry sigh. "I won't have fishing like that ever again, I don't reckon. Buck taught me everything I know. I thought I was so grown up, but when I got with him, I realized I was still a girl. He made a fisherwoman out of me. He was so good. I would have done anything to keep him down here fly-casting. Anything. When you're after something bad enough, you'll give all of yourself to take possession of that one thing. You have no pride, or shame. I'm used to dealing with men, and I figure I pretty much know what they expect from somebody like me. Especially if you've agreed to share a hotel room. But all Buck wanted to do was fish. He never said as much—you know, he's not much of a talker—but if I hadn't shown such a knack for fly-casting, that first time off the dock at Jacobsen Park, he never would have given me the time of day. And you know the funny thing? Buck doesn't even like fish. The taste of it, I mean. He throws them right back, every single one. So he's never over his limit."

The sky bucket continued its slow ascent. Two thirds of the way up the mountainside, there must have been a power outage, because the bucket stopped, leaving Bubbles and me suspended somewhere between heaven and earth. The last pink streaks of the longest twilight in the history of humankind were edging down toward the horizon. I know, it's raining heavily, how could there be a sunset, but I think it slacked off for a few minutes, so the visibility was temporarily good. What can I say? I'm not a weatherman. It's like the couple of times I went to a movie with Elaine, a psychological thriller, and she kept pointing out the logical inconsistencies in the plot. I kept saying to her, "Elaine, it's just a movie. What do you expect? Try to enjoy it." She told me my standards were too low.

But I don't get hung up on that stuff. I'm going after an emotion. Elaine, for instance, if she were here, would probably right now be trying to figure out the rate of rainfall, and the other climatic factors determining how quickly the water level could plausibly rise. And I'd be saying, "That's why they call it a *flash*

flood. Because it happens more quickly than you think it will."
But she wasn't here with me in the sky bucket. She was gone,
with Mike, leaving me bereft. She hadn't meant to be callous.
That's just the way the Mileses are. They get fixated on the
motion of their own experience, and in the end you're peripher-
al, an accessory to the fact. Take your pick. Narrator or minor
character. It's what Dad had tried to warn me about.

What had been a hollow was now a flume far beneath our dan-
gling feet, carrying uprooted trees along in its muddy torrent.
Cars that had been left behind were already submerged beneath
the tide. From where we sat, though, the effect was not one of
emergency, or crisis. Not the Red Sea raining down on the heads
of the terrified Egyptian soldiers. Instead, it was the Red River
rising, becoming one big, continuous, slowly swirling recreational lake, as far as we could see in every direction.

"I've got a joke for you, Bubbles."

"I hope it's not an off-color one you heard in a bar."

"No, no. Nothing like that. More like vaudeville-metaphysical.
As if you and I were a whiteface, kabuki tap-dancing team who
told jokes. And you get to be my straight man."

"That could work. I wouldn't say you're a hoofer exactly, but
you're not a bad dancer, as I remember from that ecumenical
singles ballroom night where we first met. You did a serviceable
tango."

"So, there's a flash flood. In a place a lot like this. Nobody's
ever seen one happen faster. Do you follow me so far? Are you
with me?"

"Sure I'm with you. Happened fast. It's a joke, right? You're
just setting up the punch line, right?"

"That's right. And the water is rising over the tops of the
trees."

"So big, those trees. Humongous. And yet, the water covered
them in the twinkling of an eye."

"Cottonmouths trailing through the water. And this old mountain man is sitting on the crest of his roof, right on the apex, the
water getting closer and closer to where he sits. Couches floating past."

"I got shoes, you got shoes, all God's children got shoes, my Lord."

"A neighbor paddles by in a rubber raft, and hollers 'Zeke, get in the rubber raft. You're going to drown, you fool.' Old Zeke shouts back, 'I've been a churchgoing man all my life, and I've tithed my wages to God. I've prayed to him for rescue from the watery deeps, and I know that He'll save me.' So the neighbor shakes his head and goes on."

"When we get to heaven, gonna put on our shoes, we're gonna walk all over God's heaven."

"The water's now waist deep on Ezekiel, not even a corner of the roof showing, and a power boat of the Army Corps of Engineers is making the rounds. They shout, 'Sir, this area must be evacuated. All of your immediate neighbors are gone. Jump down into our boat.' And of course he answers, 'I've been a churchgoing man all my life, and I've tithed my wages to God. I've prayed to him for rescue from the watery deeps, and I know that He'll save me.' So they shrug their shoulders and roar off, leaving him to wait for that voice from the firmament. That whirlwind out of the north. That great cloud the color of amber."

"*And thou didst divide the sea before them, so that they went through the midst of the sea on dry land; and their persecutors thou threwest into the deeps, as a stone into the mighty waters.* That's the book of Nehemiah, chapter nine, ladies and gentlemen. About an inch from the front cover. Our thanks to all of you who wrote in postcards for this week's Scripture quiz."

"Finally, every last being without gills has fled, except for a couple of crows in the highest treetop on the highest hill, and Ezekiel is up to his neck in high muddy water, barely keeping his nostrils out. A Red Cross helicopter is swooping around with a searchlight, and they happen to spy Ezekiel, by sheer luck and happenstance. A voice calls down from the chopper, 'Old man! No one is left alive in these parts but you! All others have died or taken refuge! Grab hold of the rope ladder and we will haul you up to safety!'"

"Did he go? Or did he stay?"

"This time, when Zeke talks, all you can hear is his mouth

blowing bubbles in the water. But what he says is, 'I've been a churchgoing man all my life, and I've tithed my wages to God. I've prayed to him for rescue from the watery deeps, and I know that He'll save me.' Words to that effect. He drowns, and when his soul ascends, he's let through the pearly gates to meet his just reward. The angels usher him before God. But Ezekiel isn't awed. He's mad as a wet hen. He says to the Lord, 'I've been a churchgoing man all my life, and I've tithed my wages to you. I prayed to you to rescue me from the watery deeps, and you let me drown!'"

"Then what happened?"

"The Lord shakes his big, weary head, and says, 'Zeke, you idiot. I sent a rubber raft, a power boat, and a helicopter. What more do you want from me?'"

"The shaggy dog has scratched another flea."

Luckily for Bubbles and me, a helicopter came along shortly after I finished the joke, its searchlight penetrating the blue-black night. We offered no resistance to their aid. In keeping with my reputation for gentlemanly ways, I first helped Bubbles onto the rope ladder, and once she was safely seated in the helicopter, I followed. The deafening roar of the engine and the whirling blades made it difficult to keep up small talk on the ride back, but our rescuers had warm blankets and hot coffee aplenty. On the whole, I'd say it was one of the most pleasant evenings I've spent in a long while.

The next couple of days are a blur. I had chills and fever, and didn't go out of my apartment or answer the phone. Elaine called a couple of times. I could hear her voice on the answering machine, those concerned cadences, but I didn't pick up or listen to the message. Paradoxically, I felt more like a character than ever before. Not self-pitying; simply mired in my immediate physical misery, to the exclusion of anything else. Jilted, yes, but I wasn't really dwelling on it or sulking, and most especially, my mind didn't keep forming literary analogies for my situation. I just wasn't up to dealing with her. I wanted to be left, slouched in my beanbag chair, waiting an inordinately long amount of time for each cube of chicken bouillon to dissolve in a cup of hot water. It takes forever for those damn things to break apart, even when you chop at them with your spoon. I think they compress an entire chicken into each cube.

Two or three times, somebody came by and knocked at the door. They knocked, waited a while, knocked again, shave and a haircut, as if they sensed me inside. I left the lights off and didn't betray my presence by any sign. I heard them leave something by the door, but I didn't open to see what it was. It must have been her. She'd probably made up a big Tupperware container of that wonderful cold pasta salad vinaigrette with chopped tomatoes and cucumbers, it's really the best, but I wasn't in the mood for it. So I let it sit out there and spoil.

So it was that, when Sunday rolled around, I honestly forgot about my meeting with Dodie Wentzler. I wasn't blowing it off intentionally. I just blanked it. When it popped into my head, about mid-afternoon, I couldn't even remember what time we had agreed on. Most likely it had been brunch, because the horsey people really relish brunch on Sundays. I rooted around in my wallet and finally found the telephone number Constance had given me, wedged between some receipts from the automatic teller. I don't know why I carry those receipts around. I can never figure out what to do with them; they just collect and take up space. Constance is right; I do need an accountant in the worst way.

I called Dodie's number, and after a few rings, she answered. I apologized for not having stopped by earlier. I'd been sick, and my mind wasn't exactly the clearest. She acted decidedly cold and distant, but after not too much coaxing, agreed to meet with me. She said that the brunch could be reheated, it wasn't that big of a deal. I offered to bring cold pasta salad, though I confessed I couldn't attest to its current condition, but she said that wouldn't be necessary. I apologized again, and told her I'd be there within an hour. I pulled up the shades and showered. Once the hot water washed away some of my lethargy, I found myself actually looking forward to the meeting. I procured a nice, close shave with a fresh blade, and slapped cologne on my cheeks and throat. A good, musky, husky, masculine scent. Something Bubbles had given me as a present, in fact, and that I'd never worn because I thought it made me smell too much like a gigolo.

Outside, the air was the slightest bit nippy, but it was one of those gorgeous bluegrass days of the everlasting crystalline blue sky that makes you feel like somebody has set the dome of heaven right over your little town to protect you. And, of course, you know whose eyes that crystal-blue color brings to mind, but we won't get into that. I hopped into my loaner sports car from the insurance company (you understand, of course, that my other car was swept away in the flood at the state park, and, fortunately, I had been carrying flood insurance on my vehicle. When did I rent out the loaner, since I've been languishing at the apartment for the past two days? Let's see, I had the foresight to have the helicopter drop me right at the insurance place, and as coincidence would have it, somebody was working very late that night . . . ). The drive out Newtown Pike settled my scattered consciousness. In spite of the hint of frost in the air, I put the top down on the convertible and let the cold breeze wash over me—don't worry, I stuck a hairbrush in the glove box—as I sped past rock fences and experienced the sweet undulations in the road as they communicated themselves to my body.

Dodie's place is set far back from the road, at the end of a softly curving drive that takes you past a couple of drinking ponds and lots of pasture. She lives in a big, Victorian farmhouse, perfectly restored, with long, leaded windows in the front and, of course, a veranda. When her housekeeper (I almost said "servant") opened the front door, I handed off a thick bouquet of wildflowers choked with baby's breath and Queen Anne's lace. You didn't really think I was going to bring a rancid pasta salad, did you? Or that I would show up empty-handed? Dodie had deliberately waited at the top of the stairs, so she could descend them for effect as I stood in the rotunda. Yes, a farmhouse with a rotunda. I'm feeling a little nervous, and nerves make me self-conscious, as you know by now, so I'm making it up as I go along.

Say "foyer" if it sounds better, but all I know is, there was a lot of space between us, and it took her forever to come down those stairs.

Now I'm supposed to describe her facial features, or tell you she had auburn hair that fell loosely about her shoulders, in keeping with the conventions of the page-turner knockoffs of the nineteenth-century novel. As if summoning her face would really tell you what lay in her heart. Or jodphurs, or knee-length riding boots, or a tailored waistcoat. Those are nothing more than accessories. Was she statuesque? Buxom? A brick house? Was her mouth full and lascivious, like a split fig? Were her lips pouty and demure as those of the beekeeper's daughter? You'll have to ask somebody else. This may be a potboiler, but it's no saga. All I can attest is that she filled up the space of her own being. And that's what impressed me most.

During brunch we confined ourselves to small talk, observing the niceties that both of us had mastered in our respective finishing schools. Maybe she'd done a stint at Wellesley, or had a fling as editor of a fashion magazine. I didn't think so, though. Perhaps she had, like me, simply perfected her talk in countless dinner conversations, knowing a little about everything and a lot about nothing. Whatever the reason, I observed a remarkable similarity between us. The almost-broken brunch date, like the impending discussion of enormous sums of money, was all maintained skillfully at bay by the simple observance of etiquette. Elaine Miles kept herself together and propelled herself forward from moment to moment by sheer force of will. With Dodie Wentzler, there was very little effort expended. It was simply a habit of existence. And though I should be chagrined to admit it, there was something comforting to me about that easy way of hers, something that meshed all too well with my inner needs on that day. Many essential matters got dispensed with in the course of brunch, without either of us saying any words of particular consequence.

When we were done, and the dishes had been whisked away as in a magic trick, Dodie asked me if I wanted to go riding. It was the first time I'd ever seen a stable with cherry-wood inside. I know, I said I wasn't going to do that Sir Walter Scott aristo-saga thing where everybody's identity gets defined by long paragraphs listing their possessions like the auction sheet at an estate sale. But I do have a weakness for cherry-wood. A stable boy produced two fresh and saddled horses. I took the bridles from him and held Dodie's while she mounted her steed with a graceful leap. It had been a while since I'd ridden, but the horses fell almost at once into an easy gait. You couldn't have asked for a finer day, with feathery sedge grass tickling the cuffs of my pants and the flanks of my horse. There also couldn't have been a more perfect or more discreet moment, narratively speaking, for bringing up the matter of money, and Dodie chose that moment to do so.

"I suppose ten million ought to get you in the door."

"Dollars?"

She gave me a sly look, as if she had thought of a snappy and amusing put-down for my disingenuous question, but whatever she'd been thinking, she didn't say it. "Yes, dollars."

"That would definitely get me in a lot of doors. I suppose, then, that you're interested in becoming a partner in this venture."

"A partner? That's correct. But not necessarily in the way you mean. Not a silent one, because I like good conversation too much. And not really a business one, because I don't want to worry my head too much about helping to run the day-to-day affairs of an empire. As you'll discover, I consider myself chiefly a woman of pleasure."

"I'd guess your head is filled with hard-nosed, intelligent thoughts. Anyone who can casually offer ten million dollars is managing her endowment quite nicely."

"Well answered, Junior. You certainly are demonstrating your skill in handling a woman. You're also not a bad rider."

"I do everything passably well. I'm just not an expert at anything."

"That's not true. You do have a forte. You're an expert at love."

"Me? At love? I'm more inept at that than anything else."

"Don't be so unassuming. You've had your misfires, no doubt. Who hasn't? But your reputation for courtship is high in these parts. And I'm pleased to say you haven't disappointed me. By the way, you smell great. What's that cologne you're wearing?"

"I take it, then, that you're offering ten million dollars as a loan. What can I offer you as collateral?"

"Call it a loan, if you like. I consider it more of a gift. And the collateral I want, Junior, is you."

"I'm not as fungible as you think."

"Fungible. That sounds like a naughty word. We'll soon find out how fungible you are."

"Dodie, I'm flattered by your estimate of my attractions. But I'm noticing that the tone of this conversation is falling off a little from its courtly beginnings."

She took out an engraved silver cigarette case (you know the type) and offered me a smoke. I politely refused. She extracted a cigarette, lit it, and breathed a slow drag, never taking her eyes off me. They were green, I guess. Some killing color like that. "Don't act shocked, buster. I've heard you can spin out pretty wicked light verse. Like this, for instance.

> There once was a flaming young genius
> Whose brain had grown inside his penis
> When thoughts made it erect
> On smart girls the effect
> Was 'Let there be intercourse between us.'"

I could barely work up enough saliva to answer her. "How did—how did you know the last line of the limerick? I've never recited it to anyone. I only made it up a couple of days ago. Unless it's in the collective unconscious or something."

"Call it womanly intuition."

"Are you suggesting that we get married?"

She gave a hoarse, throaty laugh and narrowed her killing bedroom eyes. "No, it wasn't marriage I had in mind. Although I'd say ten million dollars would make a pretty tidy dowry for purchasing a husband."

"What, then? A lover?"

"Yes, that would suffice. Although gigolo has a more colorful ring to it. You're easy on the eyes, you dress handsomely, and in spite of your infamous outbursts in the tavern, for the most part you know how to move and behave in all circles of society. You'd look good on my arm and make a witty dinner partner, and for that reason I don't imagine I'd ever grow tired of you. You'd always have something clever to say, something with a kernel of philosophical depth in it. And there's that appealing unpredictability. The two of us together could rock this snotty bluegrass, blueblood world on its heels."

"I'm already in love with someone else."

"You think that makes a difference to me?"

"But I mean really in love. Love love."

"With who? Elaine Miles?"

I coughed evasively. "Constance must have told you that. I don't know where she got any such idea."

"No one told me anything. I'm a good guesser. I also know, without anyone telling me, that Elaine, however willing, is immune to your advances. You can't satisfy her. You can't find her sweet spot."

"Your line of bullying is unbelievably brazen. You must think I'm pretty hard up, to consider becoming someone's gigolo."

"You are hard up. Your deadline is tomorrow, as you and I are both aware. I knew you'd call me before the day was out. Your unconscious wasn't capable of forgetting this dinner date."

"That may be so. But I'd prefer to let the deadline expire. I'd rather go on living as a ticket scalper than cut this kind of deal."

"Aren't you forgetting something? Are you really prepared to let Elaine become a sit-com queen?"

"You're frightening me. How can you possibly know these things?"

"Let me give you a little hint. *Seht, mir geschiehts.* 'Look, it may happen at times that my hands grow aware of each other, or else that my hard-worn face seeks refuge within them.'"

"The *Duino Elegies.* What makes you quote from those? It has to be a freaky coincidence."

"Someone in this glade once said that coincidence is only fate with bad production values."

"Did you go to Wellesley, after all?"

"Wellesley? Wouldn't that have been dandy. That's hardly my pedigree. When I was doing my stint as a character in a Raymond Chandler novel, as a libidinous but unrequited petty secretary, with a brick-house body and hard-worn face, I had lots of time on my hands. Instead of filing my nails or reading movie magazines, I read Rilke. Guess I was on a self-improvement jag or something." I could hear the smart, sassy L.A. dialect emerge in her vowels for an instant.

"You understand, then. What I've been going through."

"Sure I do. Only more so. Because unlike you, I come from humble beginnings. I also did a gig in *Valley of the Dolls*. But I was patient. I lived through each spin of the karmic wheel, and it usually landed me in a little better place, a few more lines of dialogue, another scene or two. Bits, but still. Like the agents used to say out in L.A., when they wanted to get the whiny starlets off their backs, there are no small parts. Each of us lives many lives in the fulfillment of our destiny. Mine is tied to me being a bodacious gal of one stripe or another. Mostly in the hands of male authors, naturally, though you'd be surprised at how some of the women writers get off on it too. For a long time, I was nothing more than a self-abnegating sack of T&A, or a bundle of gold-digging attitude in a tight sweater, but even gold diggers can diversify if they're persistent. I finally made it into this incarnation, where I have untold millions, so I don't need any money, and I have more than a veneer of sophistication, so I don't have to overcompensate by misusing big words. I'm the aristocracy, even if I only come in toward the end of the novel. Plus, I'm a widow, so I don't have to put up with any more two-bit losers. But I do get a little lonesome. Like everybody else."

"I know that feeling."

"Then how about it? Wouldn't you rather spend the coming years with somebody you can be yourself around? I knew you were a narrator the first time I laid eyes on you. I've been narrated plenty, and you develop a knack for spotting them. With me, at least there would be no pretense about your literary nature."

"You've got a point. But why do you insist on buying my amorous services? Things were going along pretty well there. You were so discreet, so refined. Pretty much the real thing. You could have seduced me easily enough without pitching the transaction in such crass terms. I'm on the rebound, you know. I was starting to fall for you a little bit."

"Right. Well, what can I say? Maybe I'm still cheap around the edges. You carry that stuff with you, from each transformation to the next, in your soul. And it may set me back a couple of life-times, until I figure out how to purge it. But I want to be on top for once, and see what that feels like. I'm not cruel, but in this body, this time, I want a man to come when I whistle, and satis-fy my needs. Like I said, I'm a woman of pleasure."

There was nothing more to discuss. We dismounted, let our horses graze, and walked through the pasture grass for a while, our arms folded across our chests, letting the afternoon light further lengthen already long shadows. You may have expected us to rush into the nearest barn to consummate our pact, but even Dodie Wentzler is more delicate than that. She knows I'm a man of my word. Unlike my father, she's not that invested in meeting deadlines. Her sense of time is different, gradual, con-tinuous, more like mine. She trusted that I would take up resi-dence in her house. Our combined fortunes would put us regu-larly on the society page, in spite of us flouting the norms of our set. I could hire Constance as my accountant, if I wished, although aesthetic laws would keep me from paying her five million dol-lars a year, as she had joked. Though I would have gladly given that amount to her, if only I could.

I remembered what Bubbles told me in the skylift. That when you're after something bad enough, you'll give all of yourself to take possession of that one thing. You have no pride, or shame. Granting Dodie what she wanted would also let me have the one thing I needed to fulfill my destiny, which was to keep narrating the story of Elaine and her family. Dad would get his money, and the Mileses would go on living, only slightly encumbered by my ghostly presence. Mist was starting to rise from the pasture, giving the grass that bluish cast I associate with the onset of evening. Dodie and I were in no hurry now, so we could watch night come on, sedate but always gathering force. Dad had been right from the beginning. You can't stray too far outside your circle. I'm a storyteller, and that's that.

Without saying a word, Dodie reached into her pocket and brought out a cigar, a splendid, slightly imperfect cylinder of hand-rolled tobacco leaves. I don't know how she intuited that I'd be craving the taste of one just then, but it was exactly right for the occasion. She laid it between my lips with a consolatory flick of the wrist, and lit it for me. The first puff, with its pungent humidor aroma, roasted the insides of my cheeks and settled my nerves. Why singed mucous membranes would provide a person with comfort is beyond me, but it's so. I let the smoke drift from my mouth. The circumspection of human gestures amazes me. For the most fleeting moment, I could almost believe I was real.